Praise for Storm Child

"Robotham is quickly becoming the go-to author for the psychological thriller and this book is a superb example. . . . He twists the knife with skill and precision."

—*The Globe and Mail* (Toronto)

"[Robotham's] a brilliant, propulsive writer of crime/suspense stories. Pick this one up, and I guarantee you'll go on to a rich and wonderful backlist."

—Stephen King

"Well paced with a slow tension building to a gripping climax [and] very pleasing ending, *Storm Child* is a terrific addition to the series. Although this could be enjoyed as a stand-alone, the series really deserves to be enjoyed from the beginning. . . . A totally engrossing and captivating read from a master storyteller."

—*Mystery & Suspense Magazine*

"Robotham adds moving new dimensions to the dynamic between his well-developed leads, and shrewdly connects the central mystery to Evie Cormac's backstory."

—*Publishers Weekly*

"*Storm Child* proves once again Robotham is not just among the world's top thriller writers, he is without question the best when it comes to characters whose pain we feel. *Storm Child* is a great read with something important to say."

—Linwood Barclay, author of *No Time for Goodbye*

"Readers who fell for teenager Evie in Robotham's earlier novels will welcome her return. Robotham's prose gleams [and] the finale is satisfactorily bloody."

—*Booklist*

ALSO BY MICHAEL ROBOTHAM

STORM CHILD

— A Cyrus Haven Novel —

MICHAEL ROBOTHAM

SCRIBNER

New York   Amsterdam/Antwerp   London
Toronto   Sydney/Melbourne   New Delhi

Scribner
An Imprint of Simon & Schuster, LLC
1230 Avenue of the Americas
New York, NY 10020

First Scribner trade paperback edition May 2025

SCRIBNER and design are trademarks of Simon & Schuster, LLC

Simon & Schuster strongly believes in freedom of expression and stands against cen-
sorship in all its forms. For more information, visit BooksBelong.com.

For information about special discounts for bulk purchases, please contact Simon &
Schuster Special Sales at 1-866-506-1949 or business@simonandschuster.com.

The Simon & Schuster Speakers Bureau can bring authors to your live event. For
more information or to book an event, contact the Simon & Schuster Speakers Bureau
at 1-866-248-3049 or visit our website at www.simonspeakers.com.

Manufactured in the United States of America

10 9 8 7 6 5 4 3 2 1

Library of Congress Control Number: 2024003625

ISBN 978-1-6680-3099-8
ISBN 978-1-6680-3100-1 (pbk)
ISBN 978-1-6680-3101-8 (ebook)

Book One

1

Evie

I am a story to most people; a picture in a newspaper or on a TV screen of a little girl with filthy, hacked-off hair and dirty cheeks and eyes that looked enormous because I was so malnourished. Dressed in faded jeans with a hole in one knee, and a woolen sweater with a cartoon polar bear woven into the chest, I belonged to nobody but soon belonged to everyone, adopted by a nation of strangers.

In the most famous of these photographs, I am being carried into a hospital by a female police officer, hugging her like a kitten clinging to a sweater. Special Constable Sacha Hopewell had spent all night waiting for me to crawl from my hiding place within the walls of a house where a man had been tortured to death. That image was flashed around the world, and won a major press award, but only added to the mystery.

Who was this silent child? How did I come to be hiding in the walls? Why didn't I escape when I had the chance? More importantly, what was my name, and where had I come from?

They have some of the answers now. Not the whole story. *When is a story ever whole?* Many of the details are hidden, even from me. Instead of complete memories I have only bits and pieces, random thoughts that dangle in front of me like baited hooks. I know what a baited hook can do. It can drag a fish from the deep and leave it flip-flopping on a beach or the deck of a boat, poisoned by the fresh air and the sunlight.

This is what I know to be true. I entered the world upside down with my right hand tucked against my chin, one finger pressed to my cheek, as though contemplating whether to wait for another few weeks before troubling the midwife. That's why I have a single dimple on my right cheek, although later Mama told me that God had left his thumbprint because I was one of his special creations. That makes her sound religious, but Mama stopped believing in any greater power long before I was born. "Religion cannot fill your stomach or keep you warm in winter," she said.

I was snug in my mother's womb when her waters broke. She was bending to tie my sister's shoes at the gates of her primary school. Maybe I kicked too hard, or my elbows were too pointy, or Mama put too much strain on her back, because she felt the gush of fluid running down her legs, splashing onto her shoes.

Fearing that I might be born outside the school, she quickly waddled home, hunched over, trying to hold me inside her. Papa was at work and my aunt Polina was in Italy. Mama went next door to our neighbors, Mr. and Mrs. Hasani.

Mrs. Hasani had been a nurse during the Kosovo War. She boiled water and collected towels and made my mother squat against a wall. It took all of eight minutes for me to arrive. My head popped out like the stopper of a bottle, then my shoulders and the rest of me, slithering onto a handwoven Persian rug that had once belonged to Marco Polo, according to Mr. Hasani.

"He was the explorer who discovered China," Mr. Hasani told me when I was old enough to sit on a stool in his workshop and watch him repair radios and VCRs. I told him that China had probably discovered itself, but he accused me of being obtuse, whatever that means.

Mama had wanted a boy. Papa said he wanted a puppy. Instead, they got me. Headfirst. Hand on chin. Happy before then. Innocent. Untouched. Unspoiled.

Babies are odd-looking creatures. I am looking at one now—a chubby boy, sitting in a sandy hole on Cleethorpes Beach, splashing at the seawater around his thighs. He's wearing a cotton hat and a nappy that is so fat with water or piss that it hangs around his knees. He doesn't look like a mini-person, or a smaller version of a grown-up. Instead, he has an enormous forehead and wispy hair and no eyebrows. A baby Buddha with a bulging stomach.

Waving his arms, he splashes water into his eyes, blinks in surprise, and then cries. What did he think was going to happen? Idiot!

Out to sea, beyond the small waves, I can see Cyrus in silhouette, balanced on a rented paddleboard. For a long while, he was only a speck in the water, and I worried about losing him, but he's closer now, returning to shore.

He dives off the board and surfaces, shaking water from his hair. His skin is covered in tattoos of birds that seem to move as he moves. Swallows, finches, hummingbirds, and robins that ruffle and preen and hover. When Cyrus turns to pick up the paddleboard, I glimpse the enormous set of folded wings that are inked from his shoulders down the length of his back and his thighs. Droplets glisten on the wingtips and make the feathers look bejeweled.

The tattoos give Cyrus a "bad boy" vibe like he's a cage fighter or the drummer in a heavy metal band. But I think he's more like one of those handsome single dads who you see in rom-coms, who make women go squishy when they discover that his wife died of cancer, and now he's alone in the world, being a perfect father to a disabled child. Not that Cyrus has ever been married or had kids. He doesn't even have a girlfriend, but that's another story.

He reaches for a towel. "The water is lovely."

"You're lying. I can see your goose bumps."

"It's bracing."

"That's another word for cold."

I'm sitting in a deck chair, hiding under a wide-brimmed hat and the sunglasses I bought at Boots this morning. I think they make me look like a movie star. Cyrus says I look like a blowfly.

"At least put your feet in the water," he says.

"Why?"

"Because that's what people do at the beach."

"Not me."

He shakes his head, sending a spray of water over me, beading my sunglasses. I swear at him, and a nearby mother gives me the stink eye because her toddler is within earshot.

"You can swim, can't you?" asks Cyrus.

I don't answer.

"I could teach you."

"No."

"Why not?"

"People who can't swim don't go in the water, which means they'll never drown."

"What if you were on a ferry that sank or a plane that crashed in the ocean?"

"I'd cling to the wreckage."

"You make it sound so easy."

"I've been doing it all my life."

2

Cyrus

It never occurred to me that Evie might not be able to swim. It's another reminder of how little I know about her and how much she keeps hidden, either deliberately or as a defense. She is the stereotypical enigma, wrapped in a riddle, bound up in a mystery, dressed up in three-quarter jeans, a long-sleeved T-shirt, and chunky-heeled trainers.

Right now she's pretending to be bored because indifference is her default setting, being too cool to care. Evie is not a summer person. I don't think she's a winter person either, or spring or autumn. She's a nonseasonal, all-year-round nihilist.

Across the beach, pale, lumpy bodies are in various stages of undress. Men with middle-aged paunches and spindly arms, wearing pale polo shirts and flip-flops. Women coated in oil, desperate to tan in case the rain moves in tomorrow. White-skinned children dotted with insect bites and smeared in sunblock and sticky with melted ice cream. Teenage girls in skimpy bikinis are pretending to ignore, yet preening in front of, teenage boys with pigeon chests and gelled hair. The British don't do summer the way other Europeans do. To paraphrase Woody Allen, "We don't tan, we stroke." Are people allowed to misquote him these days, or has that been canceled?

Evie is observing all of this, but she won't participate. She is one of life's spectators, standing in the wings, peering at the audience through the curtains. Watching the watchers.

At the same time, I know that she'll be inventing stories, populating her imagination with outlandish fantasies about people. When reality is too boring or mundane, Evie makes up an alternative version. She once told me her English teacher Mr. Joubert had suffered a midlife crisis and bought a Porsche Boxster and hair plugs. He also had a Russian wife, who'd been a ballerina with the Bolshoi and danced for Vladimir Putin. When I finally met Mr. Joubert, he was balder than a snow globe, and his wife was Welsh and had the heft and grace of a Clydesdale.

"Why do you tell so many lies?" I asked Evie.

"Because everybody does."

"I don't lie."

"Yes, you do."

She rattled off a list of examples, like when I told our next-door neighbor Mr. Gibson that I didn't know who had run over his rubbish bin (it was Evie). And that I would definitely not encourage squirrels by putting up a bird feeder in the garden. Or when I say things like, "That's so interesting," and "I didn't get your text," and "I'm five minutes away," when the opposite is true.

These are white lies, of course, and Evie lies all the time, brazenly, but she admits it and that, in her opinion, gives her the moral high ground. I wonder how she breathes in the rarefied air at that altitude.

I am one of the few people who know who Evie really is. Not the whole story, but enough to understand why she doesn't trust people. How she was found hiding in a secret room in a house where a man had been murdered. How she spent weeks sneaking past his rotting corpse, stealing food from houses, and drinking from garden hoses. How she had been imprisoned, tortured, and sexually abused by people who could still threaten her if they discovered her new identity. That's why she stayed silent, refusing to reveal her name or her age or where she'd come from.

When nobody came forward to claim her, she was given the name Evie Cormac by a judge, who made her a ward of the court, a child of the state, her fate decided by social workers and lawyers.

Since then a few details have been added. I know her real name is Adina Osmani and she was born in a small village in the mountains of Albania. She was trafficked into the UK with her mother and sister, who died on the journey, but Evie doesn't remember the voyage or has chosen to forget.

I met Evie four years ago at Langford Hall, a secure children's home in Nottingham. By then she had fallen through every safety net that a modern, progressive, underfunded welfare system could provide. Twelve foster families had sent her back, saying she was too "weird" or "creepy" or "uncontrollable."

Evie was claiming to be eighteen but had no way of proving it. I was the forensic psychologist sent to interview her and asked to decide if she was ready to be released.

I knew immediately that Evie was different. Damaged. Mercurial. Self-destructive. Remarkable. Everything about her body language was defensive and closed off and antagonistic. I still see it now in the way she wraps her arms across her chest as though hiding her breasts; and the blowfly sunglasses and big hat. It's like she's wearing a permanent disguise.

I discovered something else about Evie at our first meeting—a defining detail that is unnerving and intriguing and heartbreaking. She can tell when someone is lying. I wrote my doctoral thesis on "truth wizards," a topic dismissed as frivolous by most of my tutors and lecturers, all except for one, Professor Joe O'Loughlin, who encouraged me to continue.

The existence of truth wizards—a term I hate—had been documented for more than forty years and speculated on for much longer. Coined by an American psychologist, Paul Ekman, it describes a very small percentage of the population, about one in five hundred, who have the ability to tell when someone is lying, emotionally, verbally, or physically. Ekman found that most of these "truth wizards" had spent decades working as detectives, parole officers, prison guards, social workers, teachers, or priests, listening to people lying day after day. Most picked up on micro-expressions or subtle changes to respiration or skin tone or intonation or behavior. Like a poker player reading tells, they had learned to recognize bluffing or deceit or anxiety or doubt or overconfidence.

I don't know where Evie learned this skill, but her ability is off the scale, and almost infallible. I could speculate on the reasons—whether her childhood abuse triggered a survival mechanism or some other trauma gave a savant-like aptitude. It is not a gift or a superpower. It is a curse. Everybody lies to the people they love. It is the glue that holds families and friendships together. The kind words and compliments; the accolades, promises, and denials. For Evie, these are like landmines that only she can see. Every peccadillo and harmless untruth and exaggeration and little white lie can wound her. That's why she'll never have a normal life. Never be ordinary. Always be sad.

Three years ago, Evie came to live with me in Nottingham in a house that once belonged to my grandparents. We share chores and look after a dog, and I encourage her to be more outgoing and to make friends, but mostly to be kinder to herself—nobody can self-loathe like Evie because she blames herself for every bad thing that has happened to her and doesn't believe she deserves happiness.

She didn't want to come to the beach today. I had to cajole and coax and hector her, promising her fish and chips and ice cream and a round of crazy golf. I sound like a parent, but that's only because Evie can act like a child.

"Are you hungry?" I ask.

"Starving."

"Let's go and eat."

3

Evie

Cyrus splashes vinegar on his fish and chips. The smell catches in my throat, making me want to gag.

"That's one way to ruin a meal," I say.

"Don't knock it until you try it."

"Pass."

We look for somewhere to sit and eat, preferably in the shade, but the pier is crowded with randoms who stink of suntan lotion and range in color from pink to parboiled. This is the hottest summer anyone can remember, and Cyrus says he's worried about climate change, but most of the people on the beach seem to welcome the planet getting warmer.

"Did you notice that woman looking at you?" I ask. "In the café—she was trying to make eye contact."

"Was she?"

"You never notice when women flirt with you."

"Maybe I notice, but I ignore them," he says.

"What was she wearing?"

"Apricot-colored shorts. A cream camisole. White sandals. Sunglasses perched on her forehead."

"You're an arsehole!"

He laughs. We finish our fish and chips and drop the bundles of waxed paper into a rubbish bin.

"What would you like to do now?" he asks.

"Ice cream," I say, licking salt off my fingers and tucking my arm into his. "And then I get to choose."

"When is it my turn?" he asks.

"Never. White male privilege is dead."

We leave the pier and cross the esplanade to a gelato parlor with a

brightly colored sign advertising twenty-four flavors. I order a double
scoop and insist Cyrus do the same so I can taste his choices.

"This way," I say, licking a creamy drip off my wrist. I lead him past
an amusement arcade and a promenade of shops selling tacky souvenirs
and blow-up beach toys. We stop outside a house I noticed earlier that
has a red-painted door and dark curtains and a sign in the window.

**Psychic Counseling—past lives, tarot, runes, palmistry,
numerology, and intuitive healing.**
*It is not by chance that you have found this place. You are
here for a REASON and I am here to help.*

"You're not serious," says Cyrus.

"What do you mean?"

"Palm reading. Fortune-telling. Psychic healing. It's bunkum."

"Don't you believe in the spirit world?"

"No."

"But you live in a haunted house."

"It's old not *possessed*." He looks back towards the beach. "These
people are scam artists. They ask leading questions, fishing for information, reading body language, and picking up on verbal clues."

"But that's what you do," I say.

"That's different. I'm a psychologist."

"Maybe you have a closed mind. My grandma was a psychic. She
started seeing ghosts when she was little, and she could remove curses.
She also saw auras. She'd look at someone and say, 'You're blue,' or
'You're red.'"

"Genius," he says.

"Don't be an arsehole."

"Please don't waste your money. The future isn't written on your hand
or floating in a crystal ball."

"It's my money," I say, holding out my hand, wanting his wallet.

"How does that work?"

"I'll pay you back."

I take a twenty-quid note and push open the door. A bell tinkles above
my head and a woman appears. I expect her to be dressed like a gypsy,
but she looks like she's been cleaning her oven.

"Hello. My name is Madame Semanov, but you can call me Cindy. What's your name?" she asks.

"Evie."

She peels off pink rubber gloves and lights a cigarette, waving it like a magician's wand. "Are you here for a life reading or a spiritual reading?"

"What's the difference?"

"A life reading focuses on your personal journey, while the spiritual reading speaks to loved ones who have passed."

"The second one," I say, not really understanding the question.

"Right you are." She fills her lungs with smoke and inclines her head to one side, screwing up one eye, as she studies me. "How old are you?"

"Twenty-two."

"You look younger."

"I get that a lot."

"Are you studying?"

"No."

Waving the smoke away with her hand, she crushes out the cigarette and leads me through a heavy curtain into a dark room with a round table covered in a black cloth. I expect to see shelves full of crystals and tarot cards and crystal balls, but this looks like someone's cluttered sitting room. I can see a flat-screen TV partially hidden under a blanket.

"Sit yourself down, petal," says Cindy. "Who is the loved one you wish to contact?"

"My mother."

"When did she pass?"

"A while ago."

Cindy closes her eyes and runs her hands over the tablecloth, as though drawing invisible symbols on the velvet. I hear a gurgling sound that could be her stomach rumbling, or something in her plumbing. She ignores the noise.

"I always see a reading as a spark of knowledge," she says, "and proof that we are more than just our physical form. We exist before we are born and after we die."

She opens one eye to see if I understand and then continues.

"When I converse with a spirit, I sometimes download the wrong message, so if I start to ramble or talk rubbish, you have to stop me."

Already, I have a bad feeling about this. I can't tell if Cindy is lying, because she believes what she's saying, but not completely.

"Do you have a photograph of your mother?" she asks.

"No."

"Anything at all that belonged to her?"

"I have a button that came from her coat, but I didn't bring it with me."

"Is that all?"

"Yes."

She frowns. "What was your mother's name?"

"Marcela."

"Does she ever visit you—in your dreams?"

"She talks to me sometimes."

"What does she say?"

"She tells me to keep going."

"Oh, that's very good advice. Your mother is very wise. What exactly would you like to ask Marcela?"

"I want to remember."

"Remember what?"

"How she died."

"You don't know?"

I shake my head.

Cindy reaches across the table and takes my hand. I want to pull it away because I don't like being touched, but she holds my hand firmly and strokes her finger over my palm.

"When you walked in here, you weren't alone."

"Pardon?"

"There was a lovely woman behind you. There is a connection to your name. Your mother or grandmother perhaps."

"I'm named after my grandmother."

She smiles. "Evelyn."

"No. Adina."

"I thought you said your name was Evie."

"It's complicated."

"Well, she's sitting behind you now."

Well, that's bullshit, I think, but I still look over my shoulder, hoping to see my gjyshe in her white headscarf and her high-waisted floral skirt.

Cindy's eyes are closed, and she's rocking back and forth. From some-where under the table, I hear a knocking sound.

"Is that you, Marcela? Don't be afraid. Come into the light. You're welcome." Cindy's eyes open. "She's here."

"You can see her?"

"I can feel her presence. Was she a loud woman?"

"No, not really."

"Well, she's loud now. She's talking my ear off." She looks past me. "Slow down, Marcela, I can't hear what you're saying."

My heart sinks. She's lying to me now. Cyrus was right.

Cindy is still talking. "Marcela wants you to know that she's happy in Heaven, but she misses you very much."

"Mama didn't believe in Heaven," I say.

"Well, she had a pleasant surprise."

"Is Agnesa with her?" I ask, disappointed rather than angry.

"Who?"

"My sister."

"Is she also dead?"

"Yes."

Cindy raises a thinly plucked eyebrow. "Oh, petal, that's so sad." She pulls her hand away, shaking her head.

"What's wrong?" I ask.

"She's gone."

"But you can get her back."

"Let's talk about something else. I think there's a man in your life. A boyfriend. Someone special."

"What? No. I want to talk to Mama. Ask her about Agnesa. Ask her what happened."

"It's too late."

"Cyrus said you were a fake."

Cindy looks wounded. "Who's Cyrus?"

"You tell me. You're the psychic."

She puffs up like a peacock. "My great-great-grandmother told the fortunes of Czar Nicholas of Russia and the Princess Alexandra."

"More bullshit!"

"And the Romanov children."

"I want my money back."

Cindy ignores me. "I see sadness in you, Evie. A wave of sadness. If you don't learn to trust people, that wave will drown you."

"More lies."

"Marcela said you could be closed-minded."

"She said no such thing."

Cindy reaches under the table. Moments later, I hear a door open and the curtains behind me are pulled apart, throwing light across the table. A man in baggy knee-length shorts and a sweat-stained wifebeater scratches his crotch.

"Aw right, love?" he asks.

"Yeah. This lass was just leaving," says Cindy.

He steps closer. "Time's up, sunshine. Any luck, you'll make it home in time for *Blue Peter*."

I want to tell him that I'm not a child. More importantly, I want to kick his arse. I want to swagger out of here with my chest out and my pride intact and twenty quid in my pocket.

As I reach the front door, his hand touches my backside. I spin around and try to slap his face, but he ducks and grins.

"Feisty," he says.

"Pervert," I reply, but inside I'm screaming, *Stupid, stupid, stupid girl. Hateful girl. Loser.*

4

Cyrus

A busker is breakdancing on a square of cardboard, spinning on his back and bouncing into a handstand. The crowd applauds, but nobody adds any money to the hat. Who carries coins these days?

The pier is busier now, as people leave the beach, forced off the sand by the incoming tide. A child gets tangled under my feet, losing hold of a balloon, which I manage to grab before it drifts out of reach.

At that moment a woman screams, and I fear I've done something wrong. I look for the source of the sound. A middle-aged lady is standing on the pier, open-mouthed, pointing out to sea.

Instinctively, I begin to run. I reach the steps and other bystanders have joined her. I follow their outstretched arms until I spy a dark shape rising on a swell about a hundred yards offshore. It disappears and reappears. A seal, maybe, or a dog. No, it's more human than that.

Another shout echoes along the pier. This time a man is pointing. Beyond the white water, farther out to sea, I glimpse another body in the water. And beyond that, another . . . and another.

I'm in the water, swimming against the tide, lifting my head between strokes. Reaching the first body, I grip heavy sodden wool in my fists. It's a man, floating facedown. I spin him over. His eyes are open. Lifeless. He's bearded and dark-haired, dressed in jeans, a heavy sweater, and a cheap orange life jacket.

I wrap my arm around his neck and across his chest, holding his head above the water, and begin kicking towards shore. The tide pushes us towards the beach. Others arrive to help me. My feet touch the bottom and we drag the body onto the sand, above the tideline. I tilt his head back. Open his mouth. Breathe into his lungs. Compress his chest. I remember my first aid training, keeping the beat to "Stayin' Alive" by the Bee Gees. More bodies are being pushed towards the beach. I swim again and reach another—a woman. I press my fingers to her neck. Dead.

Two lifeguards paddle past me on kayaks. A Jet Ski rears over a wave, spouting spray and weaving between rescuers. A lifeboat crew patrols the outer sandbank. All are dragging bodies to shore. Sirens are wailing on the beach, evacuating people from the water, but most have fled already, escaping to the safety of the esplanade and the pier.

The next body I reach is a child, a barefoot boy, no older than four. I carry him out of the water and a paramedic takes him from my arms. The dead are now dotted across the sand, some covered in beach towels and others receiving CPR. I don't want to count them. I want to save them. It's too late.

The sun has disappeared behind clouds and the temperature has dropped by ten degrees. Hundreds of people are still watching and witnessing. Some are in tears, others are taking photographs and videos, posting them online, updating their stories and their news feeds. Is it citizen journalism or reality TV?

I feel numb. Maybe it's the cold or delayed shock. Each time I close my eyes, I see the little boy I pulled from the water, his blue lips and dark eyelashes and hair plastered to his forehead, and the O shape of his mouth, as though he was surprised by what had happened. He felt weightless in my arms, so small and insignificant in the grand scheme of things. What grand scheme? I want to ask. Who plans something like this?

It makes me think of Evie. Pushing through the onlookers, I search for her on the esplanade, and retrace my steps to the house with the red door. The curtains are closed. Nobody answers. I return to the pier and the fish-and-chip shop and the ice cream parlor. I search the amusement arcades and novelty stores and the crazy-golf course.

I would call her, but I don't have my phone. It was in the beach bag, which I dropped when I went into the water. What else did it have? My car keys. My room key at the guesthouse. Towels. Flip-flops. A credit card.

A woman is taking photographs from the edge of the pier. I ask her if I can borrow her phone. She clutches it to her chest as though I'm going to snatch it from her hands. "They're *my* pictures."

"Yes, I understand, but I need to call someone. It's urgent. I've lost my phone."

She looks at my tattoos and my wet shirt, and I expect her to yell for the police.

Grudgingly, she surrenders her phone. I call Evie's number. I hear it ringing. A message triggers.

"Hey, you've reached my voicemail. You should hang up and text me because you're an idiot if you think I'm going to pick up. Bye."

I begin talking.

"Evie. It's me, Cyrus. If you get this message, meet me at the car."

The woman is waiting impatiently, tapping a nonexistent watch on her wrist.

I feel sick. This is what happens when you take responsibility for someone. I'm not Evie's father or brother or guardian. I'm her friend and I care about her more than anyone else in my life. I know that she wouldn't just wander off or lose track of time. Equally, I'm aware that Evie knows how to hide. She concealed herself for months in her secret room, sneaking out at night, fending for herself because the world didn't know she existed.

Back on the beach, white tents have been erected and police have cordoned off the area with crime scene tape and barricades. Forensic teams are at work, clad in overalls and face masks. The sea is no longer blue, but gleaming grey like a bruise.

The detective in charge is short and barrel-chested with a military-style haircut that makes his neck look like part of his head. I can picture him on a parade ground yelling orders to hapless recruits—a modern-day Napoleon, without the complex or the custard.

A police constable approaches me and asks if I helped pull bodies from the water. He asks for my name. "We'll need a statement, sir."

The detective interrupts, snapping his fingers as though searching for an answer that has eluded him. Triumphantly: "Cyrus Haven!"

"Have we met?" I ask.

"No, but I heard you speak at a seminar about PTSD in serving police officers."

"In Leeds."

"Yes."

He thrusts out his hand. "DI Stephen Carlson." His fingers crush mine. "We have a mutual friend, DS Lenny Parvel. She's your biggest fan. Must be nice to have a boss like that."

She's not my boss, I want to say, but it would take too long to explain. I work as a consultant for the Nottinghamshire Police as a criminal profiler, counselor, and expert witness. The crimes are normally violent or sadistic in nature or off the scale of normal human behavior, which is why the police want someone to explain to them why one human being would do such a thing to another. The mad-or-bad dilemma. I have spent my career answering this question, correcting people, often in the media, who want to blame mental illness for violence and antisocial behavior even when there's no evidence to support this. Sometimes killers are simply bad.

I glance past Carlson to the canvas tents above the high-tide mark. "Who are they?"

"'Refugees. Migrants. Two boats left Calais last night. The first came ashore in the early hours of this morning near Harwich. This one must have been blown off course, or become lost. It didn't make it." He mutters the word "madness," but I don't know whether he's commenting on the crossing or the tragedy.

I keep searching for Evie in the crowd.

"Everything OK?" he asks.

"I've lost my friend. She was on the North Promenade."

"A child?"

"A young woman. She doesn't know the area."

I think he's going to make some crack about me having been stood up, but he defers. "Go and find her. We'll talk later."

Evie isn't waiting at the car. I retrace my steps again, returning to the pier. The gates have been closed and padlocked. The restaurants and cafés won't be opening tonight, out of respect for the dead or a lack of customers.

A security guard is seated in a booth. "There's nobody left inside," he says. "I checked."

"She could be hiding. She gets scared."

I contemplate offering him a bribe, but I don't have any money. I'm shoeless in clothes that are stiff with salt. Why should he believe me?

For some reason, he relents and keys open the padlock. "You have five minutes."

I slip through the gate and begin searching every corner, alcove, doorway, nook, recess, and unlocked room on the deserted pier. There is a sad loneliness about the place because the kiosks are shuttered and litter blows across the boardwalk.

I come to the public toilet and go inside the ladies, announcing myself, hearing the words bounce back from the concrete and tiles. Glancing along the line of cubicles, I see the open doors, all except for one. I knock and say Evie's name. No answer. I crouch and look under the door. No feet.

In the adjoining cubicle, I stand on the rim of the toilet and peer over the top of the partition. Evie is below me, squatting on the toilet lid, hugging her knees, hair covering her eyes.

"Evie? Open the door."

She doesn't move.

"Did something happen? What's wrong?"

Again, nothing. I gently cajole her, but she doesn't react. She hasn't acknowledged me at all.

Clumsily, I climb over the top of the partition and squeeze down beside her, unlatching the door. When I put my arms around her, she doesn't respond. I take an inventory, examining her face, her arms, her hands, her legs. I look for blood or bruises. I shouldn't have left her alone. I should have stayed with her.

Evie is holding her phone, pressing it against her chest. I pry it from her fingers and call 999.

"I need an ambulance. I'm on Cleethorpes Pier."

The operator wants names, addresses, cross streets, the nature of the injuries . . . When I hang up, I lead Evie out of the toilet block and along the pier to the gates. She follows me compliantly, matching my steps, repeating my questions back to me.

The security guard is waiting. He holds open the gate.

"I need a thermal blanket," I say.

"What happened to her?"

"I don't know."

"Should I call the police?"

"Not yet."

5

Evie

This is different. My mind is still working, turning over thoughts inside my head, but I'm also outside of my body at the same time, watching myself or dreaming that I'm awake. Maybe I'm dead. No, if that were the case Cyrus wouldn't be talking to me, telling me that an ambulance is coming.

What is the last thing I remember? The phony fortune teller and her handsy husband and being angry at Cyrus because he was going to say, "I told you so." It must be so boring being right all the time.

He wasn't waiting for me. I walked towards the pier. There were crowds of people, gathered at the edge, staring at the water. I had to push my way through to reach the front, annoyed when they wouldn't get out of my way. Some of them were crying or shielding the eyes of children. Others were filming with their phones.

That's when I saw Cyrus, waist deep in water, carrying a child in his arms. I felt a surge of adrenaline and a sudden, overwhelming need to run. I couldn't make my legs move. I couldn't speak. It was as if somebody had hit the pause button and my life had stopped, frozen on that image of Cyrus holding a dead child, with dangling limbs and a lolling head and open eyes, staring at me. My bladder loosened and wetness spread down my thighs.

"Oh, you disgusting girl!" said a woman, but I didn't see her face. I was fixated on the dead child, who looked exactly like me. How old? Four, maybe five.

They say that the first thing we lose is our baby teeth, but that's not true. We lose our honest, unbiased memories. We begin to rewrite events, slowly altering the truth until we create a new, more acceptable story, one we can live with or tell others.

I have no photographs of me as a child. I have only a button that was torn from my mother's coat when I was dragged away from her. It is the size of a fifty-pence piece, tortoiseshell brown, and is kept on a windowsill in the attic, which is my safe space. Cubbyholes and hiding places are childish things, like security blankets and soft toys, but Cyrus says nobody should be forced to grow up before they're ready.

My life is divided into two parts—before Cyrus and after Cyrus. My therapist, Veejay, wants me to concentrate on the before and to talk about my childhood, but I don't want to remember everything that happened. Courage doesn't always roar. Sometimes courage is a little voice that says, "run," "hide," "pray," but mostly, "stay silent," be as quiet as a mouse within the walls. Don't let them find you.

Until I met Cyrus, Agnesa was the most important figure in my life. She was six years older than me. Blond. Pretty. Bewitching. And from the time I could walk, I would follow her around, dressed in her hand-me-down clothes, happy to be her pet, her slave, her accomplice, or someone to take the blame.

She was my hero and my role model and my orbiting moon, pulling me and pushing me away like the tides. I missed her when she went to school, and the hours of absence were unbearable until I heard the bus chugging up the steep road from the bridge. The grinding of the gears. The brakes. The doors flapping open. I'd kneel on a chair and lean on the windowsill, watching her step down from the bus and hook her satchel over one shoulder, tossing her ribboned hair and waving to her friends as the bus pulled away.

She was different from other girls her age. Her eyes were dark and bottomless, and she took the long view of the world, my gjyshe said, with a look that would inspire artists. She was also quietly rebellious, sneaking into Mama's wardrobe and trying on her clothes and using her makeup. I would keep watch when she stole cigarettes from Mama's underwear drawer or went searching for our Christmas presents, which were hidden in the cupboard beneath the stairs, already wrapped in colored paper. Agnesa could guess the contents just by feeling the packages. "Gloves," she'd say, or "a journal" or "a knitted scarf." She wanted a bikini and some new knickers that were lacy and small and prompted Mama to say, "Over my dead body."

We didn't look like sisters. She was the cygnet who grew into a swan and I was the duckling who grew into a duck. Small for my age, with Papa's tangled hair and pointy chin and panda eyes because I was born early. One day, when she was angry, Agnesa told me that I was a mistake. I asked Mama and she said I was "unexpected."

"What does that mean?"

"You turned up without telling us."

"Like Aunt Polina?"

"Not exactly," said Mama, laughing. "I didn't think I could have any more babies. I tried and it didn't work."

"What didn't work?"

"My plumbing."

I was none the wiser.

Still too young for school, I spent weekday mornings with Mr. Hasani in his electrical repair shop, which took up the ground floor of his house. He wasn't married to Mrs. Hasani. She was his sister and the two of them had grown up in the house and he had never left, but she had traveled to Greece and Turkey and to Kosovo during the war.

I played in the back room, amid the workbenches, which were covered in radios, TV sets, and video players in various states of disrepair or disassembly. The shelves had plastic trays of spare parts—valves, plugs, tuners, wires, heads, belts, pinch rollers, picture tubes, transformers, and cables.

When someone brought in a broken DVD recorder, Mr. Hasani had them carry it into his back room. He didn't ask what was wrong. He simply adjusted a bright light and magnifying glass on a metal arm, before taking a small screwdriver and unscrewing the base. Quietly, humming to himself, he looked inside and tested some wires, before rummaging through the unlabeled trays, looking for a spare part.

He normally found a way to make things work. If not, he'd buy the broken unit and sell the customer a secondhand one that he'd repaired earlier. I once asked him if there was anything that he couldn't fix and he said, "Only broken hearts."

Mr. Hasani's other business was renting bootlegged videos and DVDs, most of which he imported from Greece or purchased from tourists. Before I was born, the government wouldn't allow people to watch foreign films and Mama still treated it like a revolutionary act when she unboxed a pirated DVD.

She loved American movies and old-time musicals. I grew up watching Elvis Presley and Doris Day and Gene Kelly. My favorite was *My Fair Lady* about the flower seller in London who becomes a lady when she learns how to speak "proper." In the same way, Mama was determined to teach us English and used the films as training aids by pausing and rewinding scenes, having us sing the songs and repeat particular phrases. "The rain in Spain falls mainly on the plain." "In Hartford, Hereford, and Hampshire, hurricanes hardly ever happen." I started with a cockney accent and finished up talking like a lady.

Without those films, we had to watch normal TV—news programs and documentaries and ancient soap operas from Greece and Mexico and Australia. Albania didn't make many TV shows and my parents refused to watch what they called propagandë.

When we were outside the house, Papa told us never to speak English because some of our neighbors, the older ones, might think we were spiun i huaj, foreign spies.

"How can we be spies?" I asked.

"We're not, but people have long memories."

He was talking about the old Albania before communism collapsed in 1990, when the secret police had so many informants that nobody could trust family or friends or neighbors.

Papa had wanted to be a teacher at university, but it was considered a dangerous profession. He still had boxes of books in the attic, which he liked to read, but he never showed them to people or read them in public. Being a butcher was safer. Driving a truck for our landlord Mr. Berisha was safer. Being ignored was safer. None of it was safe enough.

6

Cyrus

The female paramedic shines a penlight into Evie's eyes. "What did she take?"

"Nothing. I mean, she's not a drug taker."

She glances at her male colleague, giving him a look that says, "Yeah, they all say that."

"Did she fall? Hit her head?"

"I don't know."

"Any history of seizures, epilepsy, fainting?"

"No."

"Is she allergic to anything—peanuts, bee stings, shellfish, eggs?"

"No. I don't think so."

I feel stupid and useless because I have no answers. We ate fish and chips and ice cream. Evie had a double scoop—chocolate and fudge sundae. I had hazelnut and vanilla bean.

The paramedic is looking for needle marks or bruises or abrasions. She claps her hands loudly in Evie's ear. She holds up Evie's arm and lets it drop.

"Is she your daughter?"

"We're friends. We share a house."

This earns me another odd look, as though I'm already guilty of kidnapping a child.

The ambulance is moving. Evie's eyes are open, but there's no spark of recognition or emotion. Her breath is warm, her skin is soft, her lips are moist. At any moment, I expect her to reach up and brush hair from her eyes or make some inappropriate comment.

Each time the ambulance slows at an intersection or for traffic, the siren becomes louder, as though the sound is catching up and chasing

us again. I'm holding Evie's hand and the paramedic continues monitoring her vital signs—her oxygen levels and blood pressure. She types the
details on a computer tablet.

At the hospital, the rear doors swing open and gurney wheels unfold
and rattle across the pavement, carrying Evie through the entrance. The
waiting area is crowded with the burned, bleeding, broken, and feverish,
as well as the clumsy, drunk, stoned, and unlucky.

Evie is taken to an annex room, where I answer the same questions
from a male doctor, who has the same penlight, which he shines into
Evie's eyes. He taps a reflex hammer against her knee.

"Does she have any next of kin we can contact?" he asks.

"No."

"Do you have any proof of her identity?"

"She has a driver's license, but I don't know where it is."

He scrapes the bottom of her bare left foot, looking for her toes to
curl. This is called the Babinski reflex—a neurological test developed
more than a century ago. He passes smelling salts beneath her nose and
jabs parts of her body with a needle, checking her pain receptors.

Scrawling a note on a chart, he turns to leave.

"Where are you going?" I ask. "What's wrong with her?"

"We have a neurologist on call. I've paged her."

Twenty minutes later, they move Evie to another room. She is lying
on her back, staring at the ceiling.

"Are you cold? Do you want a blanket?" I ask.

She doesn't reply, but I keep talking. "I'm sorry I wasn't waiting for
you. What did the psychic say? Did she tell you your future?"

Through the partially opened blinds, I see more ambulances pulling
up at a separate entrance. The bodies from the beach are being delivered to the mortuary. They are quickly taken through swing doors, out of
view from the TV cameras and photographers who are milling outside.

In the waiting room, nurses and patients have gathered around a TV.
I join them as a grey-haired announcer delivers the news.

"At least seventeen migrants, including women and children, have
drowned off the coast of Lincolnshire while trying to reach Britain in a
small boat. At Westminster this afternoon, the prime minister held an
emergency cabinet meeting to consider the government's response to
the tragedy, saying he was shocked, appalled, and deeply saddened by

the news. In Paris, the French president announced that he would not allow the channel to become a graveyard and called for a joint European response to the crisis."

The camera switches to a reporter standing on the beach in Clee-thorpes.

"A rescue-and-recovery operation has been underway for the past four hours, involving coastguard helicopters and fixed-wing aircraft, as well as RNLI boats. No wreckage has been found and the police have no idea how many migrants may still be missing. Local shipping has been contacted to assist with the search and to establish if the boat may have been struck by a container ship."

The camera switches back to the studio, where a reporter details the number of small boats that have arrived in Britain since the start of the year.

"Lord David Buchan, the former Tory life peer, who has campaigned for tougher restrictions on illegal arrivals, said today that the government had failed to control the country's borders and must take some responsi-bility for today's tragedy."

The footage switches again. This time the cameras are focused on a grey-haired, patrician-looking figure, dressed in black, standing on a footpath outside the Houses of Parliament. As he gesticulates at the camera, his bushy eyebrows lift and lower as though pulled by strings.

"Brexit was supposed to mean that we took back control of our borders. What a failure. What a joke! How many deaths at sea will be deemed enough? How many illegal arrivals?

"These aren't all asylum seekers. Most are economic refugees. They come in a flood, and we deport them in a trickle. Meanwhile, our coun-cil housing lists are well over a million. Hospitals and schools are over-crowded. Veterans are left waiting for vital services. . . ."

I hear someone mention Evie's name. A doctor appears at the door, a neurologist, blond-haired, blue-eyed, in her late forties. She's wearing a loose white coat over a knee-length floral dress and reminds me of a lecturer I had at university who was the subject of many male fantasies.

"I'm Meredith Bennett," she says, talking to Evie. "How are you feel-ing?"

Evie looks at her outstretched hand and very slowly matches the doc-tor's movements.

"Are you in any pain?"

"Pain," says Evie.

"Can you tell me what happened?"

"What happened."

Dr. Bennett conducts some of the same tests—more penlights and Babinski scrapes. Finally, she looks at me, as though I've been keeping secrets from her. I explain that we were at the beach when the bodies began washing in.

"Was Evie in the water?" she asks.

"No."

"Did she see the bodies?"

"I'm not sure."

She asks me about Evie's medical history. Again, I'm embarrassed by how little I know. It's strange talking about Evie as though she's not in the room, yet she can hear everything that's being said.

Dr. Bennett places herself directly in Evie's line of vision. She raises her hand and touches her right ear. Evie mimics the gesture, only more slowly. Then the neurologist raises her opposite hand. After several moments, Evie does the same.

Gently taking hold of Evie's right arm, she says, "Push against me."

Evie doesn't react. Her limbs can be maneuvered into place like a stop-motion puppet or a mannequin in a shopwindow.

"Die Katatonie," I say, speculating.

Dr. Bennett looks surprised. "Are you a doctor?"

"A psychologist. I studied catatonic breakdowns. Identified by Karl Ludwig Kahlbaum in 1874. He believed the illness progressed in fixed stages."

"Do you remember what triggers them?"

"Mood or psychotic disorders. Depression. Bipolar. Schizophrenia. Drug use."

"It can also be caused by trauma."

"Evie grew up in care—a secure children's home."

"Was she abused?"

"Yes."

Dr. Bennett's eyes seem to cloud. "The symptoms match—the agitation, stupor, and repeating words and movements."

"But why now?" I ask.

"A defense mechanism. Perhaps the bodies in the water triggered a memory."

"How do we bring her back?"

"There are several possible treatments. One of them being ECT."

I picture Evie being strapped onto a table with a rubber mouthguard clenched between her teeth as an electric current is passed through her brain.

"There must be another way."

"A drug—lorazepam. It's used to treat anxiety and sleep disturbances, but it can also bring patients out of a stupor."

Dr. Bennett seems to weigh up the options, mentioning possible side effects. "My preference is to wait until the morning," she says. "I'll give Evie a mild sedative and let her sleep. Hopefully, her mind can heal itself."

"Can I stay with her?"

"You're not family."

"I'm all she has."

A room is arranged in the neurology department. Paperwork has to be filled out. Evie waits, sitting in a wheelchair, staring at the wall like a dementia patient. As I wheel her towards the lift, I hear a shout from the emergency room.

"Incoming!"

Doors swing open. A gurney barges into view, being pushed by paramedics. A drip is held shoulder high, and stats are shouted—blood pressure numbers, systolic rates, body temperature. The detective from the beach is behind them. They found a survivor.

The patient is a teenage boy with an oxygen mask over his face. He raises his hand and pulls the mask aside, repeating the same word over and over again.

"Motra. Motra. Motra."

He tries to sit up. A paramedic holds him down, as a doctor prepares a sedative. The needle finds his arm and the boy's gaze goes out of focus. He slumps backwards onto the gurney, moaning, "Motra."

Was the boy's mother among the dead? Did I see her on the beach?

"Motra. Motra. Motra," says Evie, as I push her wheelchair along the corridor, following a nurse.

I touch her shoulder. She stops. When we reach the room, I help her into bed and pull the covers over her. I hold up her phone to her face, unlocking the screen, before changing her security settings to let me have access.

"I'm going to pick up some things from the guesthouse, but I won't be long," I say.

"The guesthouse," she says.

"That's right. Don't go anywhere."

"Go anywhere."

7

Cyrus

DI Carlson sucks on a vape and expels a cloud of peppermint-scented vapor that looks like a winter's breath. He has found a quiet corner in the ambulance bays, taking a moment to himself. I watch him from a distance, making judgments, reading his body language, his mannerisms, his unconscious actions.

He's young to be a detective inspector and this case is probably the biggest of his career to date. He's anxious about making a mistake and keen to earn the respect of his team. He's married (the wedding ring), nearsighted (the glasses), and a new father (the dried vomit stain on the shoulder of his jacket). He's also worried about his weight and wears a fitness device on his wrist.

Understanding human behavior isn't about intuition, or second sight or ESP. Everything is evidence based. Some people want to imagine that psychologists have Sherlock Holmes–like abilities and can determine someone's entire life story from a smudge of chalk on a coat sleeve or a cat hair on their lapel. That's not how it works, although I had a university lecturer who could pick holes in every excuse that I ever gave him for delivering an assignment late. He seemed to know instinctively when a student was hung-over, lovesick, homesick, jilted, stoned, penniless, sleep-deprived, or just plain horny, which was most of the time in my case.

Joe O'Loughlin taught me that being a psychologist does not involve hunches, gut instinct, guesswork, or premonitions. It is a science, based upon observation and a century of empirical research into human behavior.

I have chosen to work with the police because I want to understand why people commit crimes. What made a well-spoken university graduate studying urban preservation fly a passenger plane into the World

Trade Center, killing thousands of people? Why did the Yorkshire Ripper, Peter Sutcliffe, abduct and murder thirteen women, or a neonatal nurse inject air or insulin into the intravenous lines of newborn babies? Why did my brother, Elias, aged nineteen, sharpen a knife in our garden shed before murdering my parents and twin sisters?

His actions explain most of my life choices. I became a psychologist because I wanted to stop such a tragedy happening to another family—to another child like me.

Carlson slips the vape into his pocket as I approach.

"We found a survivor," he says. "Four miles offshore, clinging to an upturned RHIB. Those boats are supposed to be unsinkable, but this one looked like it had been chewed up and spat out by a kraken."

"A collision."

"Maybe. We haven't talked to him. I don't know if he can speak English."

Across the road, news crews and broadcast vans have taken up a section of the parking area. Reporters are doing live crosses with the "Emergency" sign in the background.

Carlson is still talking. "I'm hoping he can give us some names. None of the dead were carrying identity papers. The migrant camps in Calais are overcrowded and people are trying to cross before the weather turns cold."

"It was a full moon two nights ago," I say.

"Another reason. Four hundred small boats have arrived since May. More than five thousand people. It can't go on like this."

Like what? I want to ask. Does he suggest we put up a "No Vacancies" sign? We're full. Try next door, or next year, or never.

Carlson takes off his glasses and cleans them with the end of his tie, blowing on each lens and then holding them up against the fading light. "Did you find your friend?"

"She's been admitted for the night."

"What happened?"

"Not sure."

"Should the police be involved?"

"I'll let you know."

"If there's anything I can do," he says, but doesn't finish the statement because he is unsure what he's offering.

"You could lend me some money for a cab," I say. "My wallet and phone are missing."

Carlson reaches into his pocket and takes out two twenties. "Will that be enough?"

I nod and thank him, before turning away. He calls after me. "We still need that statement."

"Tomorrow. First thing."

The cab driver is an older guy with a Pakistani accent, who wants to talk to me about the bodies washed up on the beach.

"I've been here thirty years, but I came the right way, you know."

"The right way?"

"I came as a student. I studied. I worked. I applied to stay. I'm a citizen now. Married. Three children. Everybody has to wait their turn."

"Did you bring family members in?" I ask.

"My parents and my uncles and my two younger brothers."

"Did they wait their turn?"

He looks offended. "It was legal."

The landlady at the guesthouse gives me a new room key and I quickly shower and change into fresh clothes—jeans and a sweatshirt and desert boots. I call Mitch Coates, who is house-sitting for us in Nottingham, looking after Evie's dog, Poppy. Mitch is a freelance film editor and an odd-job man who keeps my house from falling down around my ears.

"How do you like the beach?" he asks, seeing Evie's name on the screen.

"We've had a few problems," I say.

His mood changes. "The migrant boat?"

"Yes."

Mitch's girlfriend Lilah is in the background, shouting questions. She is a nurse and has an inherent sense of empathy that comes with the uniform. I might never get off the phone. Both of them love Evie, who has a binary effect on people. You either embrace her strangeness and love her unconditionally or get as far away from her as possible.

"I may need a favor," I say.

"Anything," says Mitch.

"I have a spare set of car keys in the drawer under the Buddha statue in the hallway. I need you to courier them to me." I give him the address of the guesthouse.

"Anything else?" Mitch asks.

"If Evie is still catatonic tomorrow, I may ask you to bring Poppy to the hospital."

"You think Poppy might wake her up?"

"It's worth a try."

"I'll drive them," shouts Lilah.

"I can drive," says Mitch.

"Yes, but you don't have a car," says Lilah. They begin arguing, but in a nice way, like an old married couple who finish each other's sentences.

I end the call and collect my jacket and a phone charger before closing the door behind me. It is almost nine o'clock and the summer twilight lingers, giving everything a soft glow. Children are playing cricket in the cul-de-sacs before being summoned home to bed. Couples are promenading along the seafront or cuddling on bench seats, watching the sky darken.

The forensic tents and four-wheel-drive vehicles have gone, returning the beach to the crabs and gulls and clumps of seaweed. Tomorrow, the beachgoers will be back with their umbrellas and spades and surf craft. Some will be sunburned, others hungover, but most will put today's events into the past and not let it interrupt their holiday.

A cab drops me at the entrance to the hospital. News crews are still parked on the approach road. The postmortems will be done in the morning but the task of identifying bodies has already begun. Searches of their clothes and belongings, looking for clues.

A uniformed officer is sitting in the corridor farther along from Evie's room. Dozing. Vest loosened. Knees apart. As I pass, he opens his eyes and straightens. We return nods.

"How is he?" I ask.

"Sedated."

I knock gently on Evie's door. She doesn't answer. A tray of food is resting on a side table. Untouched. I show her the pajamas that I've brought her and act as though we're having a normal conversation, even though everything is one-sided except when she echoes my words.

"You should get changed," I say.

"Get changed," she mumbles.

"Can you manage?"

"Manage."

A nurse offers to help and I step outside, listening to their idiosyncratic conversation.

"I'm Sadie," says the nurse, who has a playful Irish accent. "What's your name?"

"Your name," says Evie.

"I just told you. It's Sadie," says the nurse.

"Sadie," says Evie.

I'd laugh if I wasn't so worried about her.

Once Evie is dressed and in bed, I return. The nurse adjusts her pillows and tells Evie she can close her eyes. Evie does as she's told.

"I wish all my patients were this well-behaved," she says, and then apologizes. "I didn't mean any offense."

"None taken."

"Are you staying?" she asks.

I nod.

She points to a chair. "It's not very comfortable. If you get hungry or thirsty there are vending machines in the ER."

After she's gone, I pull the chair closer to the bed and prop my feet on the mattress, where I can watch Evie sleeping. She breathes so quietly, as if frightened of disturbing the air, and once or twice I put my face close to hers to feel the warm exhalation.

I know I obsess over Evie. I monitor her moods and treat her differently, which she hates, but I can't help myself because I know enough about her past and worry about her future.

Clearly, a traumatic event has triggered her catatonic state—most likely the bodies in the water. Evie was trafficked into Britain as a child, making the journey by boat. I don't know the exact circumstances because Evie doesn't remember the details or has chosen to forget them. Some survivors of abuse block out what they endured. Others carry their trauma with them constantly, while a small number live in a state of permanent denial. Evie uses dissociation as her defense, escaping to another place and another time, somewhere comforting and safe.

At the same time, I'm certain that her memories of abuse haven't been erased. The worst of them are buried just below the surface of her subconscious like land mines. One wrong step and they will cripple or maim. My job is not to dig them up, but to mark where they are with tiny flags so that Evie can cross the minefield safely.

One of them has detonated and Evie has gone to her safe place. The question is—how do I get her back?

8

Cyrus

At some point during the night, I wake to the sound of an argument in the hospital corridor. Evie is still asleep. I go to investigate. A young black woman with dreadlocked hair is arguing with the police officer who is guarding the survivor.

"How did you get past the front desk?" he asks. "You're not supposed to be here."

"He can tell us what happened," says the woman. "He knows the truth."

She's dressed in motorcycle leathers and carrying a full-face helmet. She ducks under his arm. The constable blocks her way and talks into a shoulder radio, calling for backup.

Boots echo along the tiled floor as more officers arrive, surrounding the woman, pinning her arms to her sides, and marching her towards the main entrance.

"They weren't supposed to die," she yells. "They were murdered."

The automatic doors open and close. I follow from a distance and watch a sergeant lecture the woman beneath a neon light where a cloud of moths is circling the brightness. He lets her go and she walks towards a motorbike, parked near the access road. Zipping up her jacket, she flicks the straps from her helmet, before spinning to confront me. Eyes flashing. "What's your problem?"

"I heard what you said to the police—what did you mean?"

Cautiously, "Are you a reporter?"

"No. I was there today—on the beach—when the bodies washed ashore. You said they were murdered."

"They were. Did you see the survivor?"

"He's a boy, maybe thirteen or fourteen."

"Did you talk to him?"

"No. He's sedated."

Her dark brown eyes travel the length of me before resting on my face. "The migrant boat was deliberately rammed."

"How could you know that?"

"I've seen the messages."

She holds up her phone. I step closer and look at the screen.

A boat has stopped us. They are telling
us to turn back. We have claimed asylum,
but they will not listen.

The message is dated and time coded. Fourteen minutes later, a second one arrived.

The engine has stopped. We are drifting
but we can see the shore. The boat is
following us.

There is a much longer gap of forty minutes before the last message.

Help. They are killing us. People are in
the water. Help.

"You need to show these to the police," I say.

The woman looks towards her motorbike, unsure of what to do.

"What's your name?" I ask.

"Florence Gatsi. I'm a lawyer. I could get into trouble for having these texts."

"You'll have to explain that to me," I say. "How about I buy you a coffee."

She glances at the hospital and the police officers waiting outside. "I don't think I'm allowed in there."

"We can drink it here."

I point to a picnic table with bench seats, bathed in the glow from a streetlight. "My name is Cyrus Haven. I'm a forensic psychologist."

"You work with the police."

"Sometimes."

This doesn't reassure her. If anything, she looks more nervous. She's in her late twenties, with a slight accent, South African, maybe, or Kenyan, but softened by years of boarding schools and college debating contests. With her high cheekbones and slightly turned-down mouth, she could grace a glossy magazine cover. Many women are pretty in their teens or twenties or thirties or forties. Some grow more beautiful with age or find a particular sweet spot when they're at their most beautiful, but Florence is clearly parked there for a lifetime.

"You won't run away, will you?" I ask.

She tentatively shakes her head. Her dreadlocks are threaded with colored beads that make click-clacking sounds as they swing.

I go inside and negotiate two hot drinks from a dispensing machine that spits out sump oil claiming to be coffee. When I return, Florence is at the picnic table, studying her phone.

"I didn't ask if you wanted sugar."

"No," she says distractedly. "You live in Nottingham."

"You googled me."

"You don't make it easy. No Instagram page or Twitter account."

"I avoid social media."

"Why?"

"Privacy. Anonymity."

She is still reading. I know what's coming.

"Ah," she says, not looking up from her phone. She has discovered a news story about the event that shaped my life. At age thirteen, I came home from football practice and discovered the bodies of my parents and twin sisters. The killer was my older brother, Elias, a paranoid schizophrenic who heard voices in his head.

Florence blinks at me sadly. I hate that look. It makes me feel like a three-legged dog, or an aging polar bear rocking from side to side in a zoo.

"It happened a long time ago," I say, wanting to change the subject.

"And it doesn't define you," she adds.

"Not as much as people like to think."

"Where is your brother now?"

"In a secure psychiatric hospital."

"Do you ever visit him?"

"Twice a month."

She seems intrigued, but for the right reasons.

Florence has retrieved a notebook from the pannier of her motor-bike. The front cover artwork is Monet's *Water Lilies and Japanese Bridge*. She opens the notebook and clicks the button on a ballpoint pen.

"I write everything down," she explains. "Have done since university."

"So, it's not a legal thing."

"More a remembering thing."

"How did you get the text messages?" I ask.

"I work for an organization called Migrant Rescue. We provide information to people who are trying to cross the Channel. Tides. Weather. Currents. Shipping lanes."

"You facilitate unauthorized crossings?"

"No. It's not like that. These people are going to make the journey anyway. They're desperate. They've left their homes, families, friends, histories. They've traveled thousands of miles and now they're this close." She holds up her thumb and forefinger, as if showing me the distance. "We are making the journey safer."

"Is that what happened today?"

Florence narrows her eyes and sets her jaw defiantly.

"Migrant Rescue saves lives. People used to argue against needle exchange programs for drug addicts, claiming it encouraged junkies to inject themselves. Instead, it made drug use safer and cleaner and kept addicts alive until they could turn their lives around. We're doing the same thing. Keeping people safe."

"I pulled bodies out of the water today. Women and children. If they had stayed home . . . or in France—"

"Their boat was rammed."

"How did you get the messages?"

Florence sighs. "For the past month I've been corresponding with a young woman from Sudan, a university student studying in Nottingham. Her brother texted her from the beach in Calais two nights ago, saying he was on his way."

"He sent the messages?"

Florence nods.

"Is he the survivor?"

"I don't think so. He's older. Twenty-four."

I ask to see her phone again. This time she shows me earlier texts sent from Calais. One of them includes a photograph of three young men, arm in arm, who are sitting on stone steps above the sand.

"That's Jaden," says Florence. "It was taken ten days ago in Calais."

She pulls up another image. It shows Jaden sitting next to a young woman, his sister, Nadia. They could be twins. Both are wearing traditional Sudanese clothes, white with splashes of color around the hems and sleeves and collars.

"This was taken at a cousin's wedding in Khartoum, two years ago," says Florence. "Jaden arrived in Calais in March. He made two attempts to cross in July. The first time he was forced back by the weather and the second time by the French coastguard."

"He was paying people smugglers?"

"I have no information about that."

Florence is already covering herself legally. She can't admit to having knowledge of a crime.

"Nadia phoned me two nights ago and said he was coming. She wanted me to handle Jaden's asylum claim."

I read the messages again. Jaden sent them during the journey when the migrant boat was in range of phone towers on the coast. Clearly, someone tried to make the migrants turn back. Fifty-six minutes later, they were in the water, dying.

I look up at Florence. "Did you contact the coastguard?"

"Of course, but I had no coordinates or any way of tracking the signal."

I spend a moment considering the implications. I have heard stories of migrant boats being turned back or impounded by the coastguard or police. Others have been sabotaged before leaving France, but nothing comes close to a deliberate sinking.

"Where is Nadia now?" I ask.

"In Nottingham. She's waiting for me to call her."

"I'll talk to the detective handling the investigation. He'll want access to Nadia's phone."

"Can you keep my name out of it?" asks Florence.

"That's not possible, but you know that already."

She sighs and nods her acceptance.

"How do I contact you?" I ask.

"Give me your phone."

"I don't have one."

She looks at me like I'm from another planet. "I lost it today," I explain.

Florence tears a page from the back of her notebook and jots down her number.

"Call me."

9

Evie

My eyes feel like they're weighted down with warm stones. Slowly, I force them open, letting in light. Edges take shape. Shadows. Colors. I'm in a strange room with a bed and lockable cabinet and grey carpet squares and vertical blinds and an ugly black-and-white print on the wall.

Cyrus has gone, but his jacket is still hanging over the chair. I felt his presence earlier, when he leaned over me and placed his cheek next to mine, his lips within kissing distance. I wanted to make a sound, but I couldn't speak.

Vaguely, I remember the journey in an ambulance and a white room and bright lights and doctors who talked to me and about me. Asking questions. Issuing instructions. I didn't respond. My lips and limbs wouldn't synch with my brain.

Awake now, I need the bathroom. I contemplate ringing the buzzer on the wall near my head, but I don't want to pee into a bedpan with a nurse watching. There must be a toilet nearby.

I'm wearing my fire-engine-red pajamas. I don't remember getting changed. I hope Cyrus didn't see me undressed, naked, all pale and blotchy and scarred with cigarette burns.

Pushing back the covers, I swing my legs to the side, testing the floor and my strength. I wobble towards the door and crack it open, peering along the wide, brightly lit corridor. A cleaner's trolley is parked nearby, sprouting brooms and mops and bottles of chemicals. Beyond that I see a sign for the ladies. Cautiously, I cross the threshold, my bare feet leaving footprints that fade on the tiled floor.

Why does peeing feel so good? Maybe it's like having an orgasm. I've never had one of those, so I don't know if they're life-changing or earth-shattering or overrated. I know that men look stupid when they come, all red-faced and moaning. I've seen their faces. I wish I could forget them.

As I leave the ladies I wonder if I should look for Cyrus or tell someone that I'm awake. The cleaner has returned and is pushing a polishing machine that seems to float back and forth like a hovercraft. Another noise cuts through the dull humming of the machine. It sounds small and wet, like a kitten trapped in the air-conditioning vent. I follow the sound, reaching a room with a partially open door. An empty chair is leaning against the wall in the corridor.

I peer inside. The bed is empty. I hear the sound again. Someone is crying. A figure is huddled between the bed and the wall. A crouching boy, arms around his knees, tears shining on his cheeks. He looks at me.

"Motra?" he says.

I know that word. He is asking for his sister.

"Si e ke emrin?" I whisper, wanting to know his name.

"Arben."

"A ishe në . . ."—what is the word for boat?—"barkë."

He nods. "Vëlla. Motra."

"With your brother and sister?"

Another nod.

"Do you speak English?"

"Pak."

He means a little. I step farther into the room and let my eyes adjust to the darkness. Arben has stopped crying. He wipes his nose with his sleeve. He's in his early teens with curly brown hair and hazel eyes and a gap between his largest front teeth.

A shadow falls across the square of light on the floor. Not mine. A policeman. Uniformed. Hands on hips. He's wearing a stab vest full of gadgets.

"What the hell are you doing?"

"Nothing," I mumble, trying to duck past him. "I'll go now."

"You're not going anywhere. Who are you?"

"Nobody. I heard him crying."

"What language were you speaking?"

"Albanian. His name is Arben. He was on a boat that sank."

"Who is Motra?"

"His sister."

The officer reaches for his shoulder radio. "Tango Foxtrot Bravo to control."

"*This is control.*"

"I'm at the hospital with the survivor. He's talking. We need an Albanian interpreter. Can you inform DI Carlson?"

"*Roger that, Tango Foxtrot Bravo.*"

I think about running, while he's distracted, but he's blocking the door. I could headbutt his gut and knock him sideways. Then what? I don't have my clothes. Arben reaches out and takes my hand. His fingers interlock with mine. We're in this together now.

A nurse arrives, looking annoyed that we're out of bed. She is young and Irish and I remember her from last night.

"Evie, you're awake!" she says, like we're old friends. "What are you doing out of bed?"

"I needed to wee."

"She was sneaking in here," says the officer.

"I didn't sneak anywhere!"

"I'll take her back," says the nurse.

"She's not going anywhere," says the officer. "She can understand him."

The nurse looks at me for confirmation. "You've spoken to him?"

I nod.

"Ask him if he's a diabetic."

I don't know the word for diabetic in Albanian so use the English word, which seems to work. Arben talks quickly and I ask him to slow down.

"He lost his insulin when the boat sank," I say.

This seems to confirm what the nurse already knows. "Tell him we've stabilized his blood sugar levels."

This takes another feat of memory and guesswork to translate.

Arben speaks, whispering, "Vëlla? Motra?"

"What happened to his brother and sister?" I ask.

"We're still searching for more survivors," says the policeman.

"What should I tell him?"

"Just that."

Footsteps. Running. Cyrus pushes into the room and scoops me into his arms, squeezing me so tightly that I almost break wind.

"You need a shave," I say complaining. Blushing.

"You're back," he says, as though I've been missing, or on holiday.

I brush his arms away and straighten my pajamas, feeling my cheeks glow. "Can we go home?"

The police officer is adamant that I'm not leaving, but Cyrus has a soft-spoken way of winning people over and finding a compromise. I'm allowed to return to my room until morning. Cyrus folds back the covers and tucks them around me like I'm a child.

"You promised to wait for me," I say. "But you weren't on the pier."

"I'm sorry."

"I saw the bodies in the water. You were carrying a little boy and . . ." I don't finish. "I want to go home."

"After you've talked to the neurologist."

"The who?"

"She's a brain specialist. We need to find out what happened."

"I know what happened."

He waits for my explanation, but I don't have one.

"Sleep," he says, turning off the light and leaning back in a chair, propping his feet on the bed.

"You frightened me," he whispers.

"I frightened myself."

10

Cyrus

Meredith Bennett breezes into the room, all business, with her hair still wet from the shower. Her floral dress is summery and cool but professional when teamed with a white doctor's coat and the ubiquitous stethoscope slung casually around her neck.

"I heard the good news," she says, smiling at Evie.

"This is the neurologist I was telling you about," I say.

"Do you remember me?" she asks.

"Vaguely," says Evie. "You were prodding me like I was a science experiment."

"Sorry about that. Can I do it again?"

"Do I get to keep my clothes on?"

"I'd prefer it that way." She pulls a chair close to the bed. "What day is today?"

"Monday."

"What month?"

"August."

"What is the opposite of cold?"

"Hot."

"Up?"

"Down."

"Who is the prime minister?"

"Who cares?"

"What's the capital of Paris?"

"You mean the capital of France."

Dr. Bennett smiles. "That's known as a trick question. You passed."

"Can I go home?"

"Soon. Tell me what you remember?"

"I blacked out."

"Did you knock your head or fall over?"

"I don't think so."

"Did you see the bodies washing up on Cleethorpes Beach?"

Evie's silence answers the question.

"I'd like to take a closer look," says Dr. Bennett. "Just to be sure."

"To be sure of what?"

"That nothing is wrong neurologically—a brain bleed or a hematoma. I want to schedule a brain scan, an MRI. It's a machine that uses strong magnetic fields and radio waves to take pictures inside the body."

"Does it hurt?" asks Evie.

"No, but it's noisy and not great if you're claustrophobic. Do you mind small spaces?"

"I love them," says Evie, not joking.

I'm standing at the window. I hear a crowd chanting outside. Pulling aside the venetian blinds, I see people gathered at the hospital entrance. Some are holding placards and waving Union Jack flags. The protesters are predominantly white and male. Some are shirtless and shoeless, covered in tattoos or wrapped in flags or wearing Guy Fawkes masks or red MAGA caps. The apparent ringleader is wearing a camouflage jacket and holding a placard that reads "Stop the Invasion." Other signs have different messages—"Defend Our Borders," "Turn Back the Boats," "Take Back Britain"—while a few declare that "Jesus Saves" and "White Lives Matter." Maybe they took a wrong turn somewhere.

A dozen uniformed police officers are blocking the access road, preventing the protesters from reaching the hospital entrance. Each time an ambulance arrives, the officers force them to the footpath, clearing the road.

"They've been arriving all morning," says Dr. Bennett.

"One survivor. It hardly seems worth it," I say.

"More boats have been arriving. Another this morning."

"Where?"

"Farther south. I heard it on the radio."

A teenage boy begins beating a snare drum and the protesters start to sing. Eyes shining. Mouths open.

Rule, Britannia! Britannia, rule the waves!
Britons never, never, never will be slaves.

11

Evie

The MRI machine looks like one of those space pods where astronauts go to cryosleep when they're traveling to distant galaxies. It is a long metal tube with a narrow tray that slides inside. I can't wear my ear studs or rings or other jewelry.

"We have to strap your head down to hold it still," says the technician, a black guy with cornrows in his hair. "Otherwise, the images will be blurry."

"Nobody likes a fuzzy photograph," I say, making a joke, because I'm nervous. He doesn't crack a smile.

"These headphones will dampen the noise," he says as he slides them over my ears. "We can play you some music. Any requests?" I can't think of a single song. He opens my fingers, giving me a buzzer. "If you start to panic or feel unwell, press the button and we'll stop the scan."

Once I'm strapped down, staring at the ceiling, the technician leaves and the tray begins to move, sliding backward into the machine. The noise begins—a thumping sound that seems to pass right through me.

I wonder if an MRI scan can tell them what I'm thinking. What if I imagined the filthiest sex act? Would it light up some part of my brain? I don't like that idea so I try not to think of sex, which is exactly what I do. *Shit!* I try to concentrate on something else—anything but sex. I begin counting down from a thousand. Eventually, I grow used to the sound, which is hypnotic like an Albanian chant without the harmonies.

My thoughts wander and I'm a child again, smelling fried green sweet peppers stuffed with feta. Warm corn bread. Sage and lavender. Diesel fumes. Paraffin stoves. Melting wax. My mother's perfume.

Our village was surrounded by mountains and lakes, and streams that tumbled over rocks and created rivers that ran to the sea. The buildings clung to the hillsides and rose from the wildflowers like ancient ruins. I don't know if our cottage is still there. Another family probably lives there now, paying rent to Mr. Berisha. I carved my initials into the walnut tree outside my bedroom window. And we marked my height on a door frame in the kitchen, a new notch for every year, next to a spot on the wall where Mama threw a saucepan at a mouse. She missed.

What other evidence might remain? Perhaps, in some dusty local government building, there will be a record of my birth, my parents' names on a piece of paper. A signature. A stamp. Does that make it my country? My home?

When I was growing up, people cared about where you came from. Your family. Your history. People were either good or bad. Clean or stained. Trustworthy or suspicious. My mother was an only child. My father was one of four. He was named after his grandfather, who he never met, which means neither did I, but there were stories about him, passed down from one generation to the next.

As a child, I never had a day when I went hungry, or a night when I felt lonely. Agnesa lay next to me, or Aunt Polina. Mama and Papa were in the next room. Even the sound of water in the pipes, or ice forming on the windows, or Papa snoring made me feel safe.

I was an eavesdropper, a listener at doorways and at the top of the stairs. Sometimes, when my parents were entertaining downstairs, I would fall asleep lying on the landing listening to the murmur of the conversation and laughter. Papa would find me and carry me to bed, kissing my forehead as he set my head on the pillow.

When I was small, I loved to watch him cook. He hoisted me onto the kitchen counter beside the stove and I helped him rub pieces of meat with salt and preserved lemon, before he added spices and sealed the meat inside a clay pot, which he half-buried in glowing coals. Those same hands could carve up a carcass and saw wood and hammer nails but were also capable of the most graceful of gestures and gentlest hugs and unbearable tickles. They could toss me high in the air and catch me under my arms and toss me even higher. From way up there, above his head, I looked down at his wide, crooked smile, his cleft chin, his trimmed mustache, and his dark brown eyes, and I understood love.

Papa taught me how to fish and how to find worms and how to put them on a hook. He showed me how to make him tea and choose the best apples and propagate plants and graft one branch of a fruit tree onto another.

Memories like this catch in my throat, but at the same time, I know they're beginning to fade. I sometimes struggle to remember his smell and the feel of his unshaven cheek against mine and the silly song that he sang about a billy goat. I wish Agnesa were here. We could help each other remember and talk about the things that I can't discuss with Cyrus. Girl stuff.

Agnesa began as my orbiting moon, but became more like a comet, flashing across the sky, dashing in and out, changing her clothes, grabbing something to eat, barely pausing to say hello or good-bye. She had friends. Hobbies. Admirers. I was an afterthought; a nagging, needy little sister who wanted to be included and complained to Mama if I was left out.

The cottage only had two bedrooms, which meant that Agnesa and I shared a double bed, which annoyed her. We also took turns in the same water at bath time, although Agnesa insisted on going first, when the water was warmest, because she accused me of peeing in the tub, which is probably true, but I still thought it unfair.

I didn't realize we were poor, because everybody we knew was the same, except for our landlord, Mr. Berisha, who owned a restaurant and a timber yard and lots of houses. He had five children, but only one son, Erjon, who was three years older than Agnesa, but in the same class at school because he had an IQ just above room temperature.

Being older, he was bigger and stronger than the other boys and liked to throw his weight and money around. He always had chocolate bars and soft drinks and American sneakers and Levi's 501s, which none of us could afford. One of his favorite games was to open a bottle of Coca-Cola, take a sip, and leave it sitting in the middle of the road on a corner where the lumber trucks would release their brakes and accelerate after a long descent down the mountain. Boys would take up the challenge, dashing out from the trees and seizing their prize. Truck horns blasted, brakes screamed, and tires left trails of rubber on the bitumen. Some drivers, pale-faced and trembling, would pull over farther down the mountain, swing out of their cabs, and yell curses, shaking their fists at the boys, who vanished like water soaking into the ground.

Until the day that Fisnik Sopa, aged thirteen, hesitated as he left the trees. Maybe because of his spectacles or the scoliosis that bent his spine or his unusually red hair, Fisnik was always a step behind where he should have been or wanted to be. And as he snatched up the soft drink bottle, grinning in triumph, the lumber truck bore down on him with locked brakes and smoking tires.

Fisnik turned. Almost there. Almost safe. But the truck clipped his back heel, and he disappeared beneath the wheels. Bump. Bump. Bump. A red stain covered the road beside a shattered bottle and his crumpled body. Later, when the police came knocking, asking questions, nobody mentioned Erjon or the Coca-Cola or the dare.

12

Cyrus

DI Carlson finds me in the waiting room of the MRI suite. He's holding a calico beach bag with my mobile phone, car keys, credit card, two towels, and flip-flops.

"Someone handed this in at the station," he says.

"My faith in humanity has been restored."

"I'll need more proof." He glances through the observation window. "Your friend can speak Albanian."

"Evie was born there."

He runs his fingers over his short-cropped hair. "I need her help."

"She's not an interpreter."

"The boy keeps asking for her. He's frightened. Jumping at shadows. Evie might be able to reassure him."

"I heard there was another migrant boat this morning."

"It came ashore farther south. Sixteen on board."

"What about the bodies at Cleethorpes?"

"Afghans, Syrians, Libyans, and Iraqis. It could take us weeks to come up with names."

"I met a young lawyer last night who has text messages from someone on board the boat that sank."

Carlson is suddenly interested.

"The messages suggest it might have been deliberately sunk."

The detective doesn't hide his skepticism. "Who is this lawyer?"

"She works for Migrant Watch."

"A do-gooder."

"The texts are genuine."

"Bring them to me . . . and her."

Evie emerges, wearing the change of clothes that I brought her from the guesthouse—jeans, a cotton blouse, and red Vans. I introduce her to Carlson, who asks if she'll sit with Arben for the interviews. Evie is not a natural volunteer or joiner of things because her better angels are elusive but she agrees to help because she feels sorry for Arben.

Back in the main hospital building, we meet the official police interpreter, an elderly man with a bushy grey mustache and eyebrows that dance on his forehead when he speaks. He says something to Evie in Albanian. She nods but doesn't reply.

"Grandpa smells funny," she whispers, pinching her nose.

"Be nice. He's old," I reply.

"Try ancient. A fossil. A dinosaur. A wrinkly. A coffin dodger."

I put my finger to my lips. "Shhhh."

Carlson summons us into Arben's room. The boy is sitting up in bed, propped on pillows. His face looks bruised, and his eyes are red-rimmed, but they brighten when he spies Evie. Chairs are arranged around the bed. Cameras and recording devices have been set up and tested.

I take a seat near the window, making sure that Evie can see me. The protesters have gone quiet outside, having been moved farther away from the hospital buildings after complaints from patients and visitors.

Carlson begins slowly and addresses each question directly to Arben, who is answering in English when he can. We learn the boy's full name: Arben Pasha, aged fourteen. He grew up in a village outside of Tirana, the Albanian capital, with his two siblings, Besart, nineteen, and his sister, Jeta, seventeen. Their mother died of cancer three years ago. Their father went to the Middle East to find work and didn't return. Besart had looked after his siblings since then, working as a tour guide during the summer and training to be a mechanic at a garage owned by a family friend. Jeta had won a place at the University of Tirana but didn't have the money to study.

One day Besart borrowed a customer's car to take Arben to an endocrinologist because his blood sugar levels were spiking, causing periodic blackouts. Returning to the garage, he was arrested by police and charged with stealing the vehicle. Before the trial, Besart sold all of the family possessions and he and Arben and Jeta caught a speedboat across the Adriatic Sea to Italy. From there they traveled by bus and train to France and spent three months living in a migrant camp on the outskirts of Calais. They were twice evicted by police and slept under bridges and in abandoned warehouses.

Besart did odd jobs during the day. Picking up rubbish off the beaches, or weeding gardens, earning enough to buy them food. There were problems in the camp. Violence. Robberies. Some of the young men were harassing Jeta, trying to get her alone. Besart bought a knife to better protect her, carrying it in his sock.

As the weather grew warmer, they began visiting beaches south of Calais every night, hoping to find a boat that would take them to England. They would hide in the sand dunes, scanning the beach, watching for departures.

They had no money to pay a smuggler, so they tried to talk their way onto boats or sneak on board. One trick was to hide in the sand hills until the last moment. As the boat pushed off, they would sprint across the sand and try to scramble on board, but they were beaten back by passengers who feared the boat would sink if it carried too many people. After each failure, they returned to the camp, hungry and exhausted.

Besart barely slept, working all day, scrounging for food, and watching the beach at night. He met a Serbian called Keller as they waited in a food queue. Keller had big hands and a big laugh and had once been a fisherman. He said he could steer a boat to England if they could find one.

Together, they began collecting money from migrants, who each paid what he or she could afford. They drew lots to choose who would get a place on the boat. Besart found one for sale. He met the broker on the beach at Sangatte. He asked for the money up front, but Besart said he'd get paid when he saw the boat and checked it was seaworthy. They arranged to meet the following night, but it was a trick. Besart was jumped by three men, who stole the money and left him with two broken ribs.

"How did you get a boat?" asks Carlson.

"Besart found another one."

"He stole it."

Arben shakes his head.

"We checked," says Carlson. "The owner of the boat reported it stolen."

"He sold it to us."

"Your brother was a people smuggler."

"No."

The interpreter has a habit of copying Arben's tone and volume, as though dubbing a foreign film. He is also inclined to use more words than Arben does, which makes me wonder if he's embellishing the answers.

Eventually, the questions begin to focus on the crossing from Calais. Arben describes waiting on the beach for the boat to arrive. The tide was coming in and they had difficulty getting everybody on board.

"How many people?" asks Carlson.

Arben asks for a piece of paper and begins to draw a picture of the RHIB, with small stick figures representing the migrants. He holds the pencil in his fist like he wants to stab the page. Counting the figures, he estimates there were twenty people, including four women and two other children.

"Do you know their names?"

"Only some, like Keller."

"Tell us about the crossing."

"Another boat was leaving at the same time but did not come with us. People were shouting because some men had swum out from the beach and were trying to take over the other boat, but Keller helped fight them off."

"What time was this?" asks Carlson.

"I don't know. It was dark. I was seasick. Besart told me to sit at the front and to watch the lights on the shore and I would feel better. The stars came out and the wind dropped. Keller steered us along the coast.

"I must have fallen asleep. When I woke, we had changed direction and waves were lifting and dropping us into holes in the sea. I asked Besart how much longer and he kept telling me to be patient."

Evie interrupts and corrects the interpreter. "His brother said to him, 'You waited for the little thing. You can also wait for the big thing.'"

The interpreter nods to Evie, but I can tell he's annoyed.

Arben continues. "We stopped and swapped fuel tanks. That made people sicker because of the fumes and the movement. I slept again, but woke to a bright light, shining in my eyes. It came from the deck of a boat. The men on board were shouting at us, telling us to turn back.

"These men—they spoke English?" asks Carlson.

Arben nods.

"You have to answer for the recording."

"Yes."

"How many men did you see?"

"Two, maybe more."

"Did you see their faces?"

"Only shadows."

"What did they say?"

"'Go back! Turn around!' Besart said we were going to England. 'Not tonight,' said the man."

"Is that all?"

"They swore at Besart and told him we'd all drown. One of them pointed to Jeta and another girl and said they could come to Britain, but the rest of us had to go back. Besart refused."

"Did you notice any markings on the boat? Numbers. Letters. Flags."

The interpreter explains this to Arben, who begins another drawing. The only sounds in the room are the air-conditioning and his pencil scratching on the page. The lines form and join, rendering a squat-looking boat with a central wheelhouse.

"A fishing trawler," says Carlson. "Did you see a name?"

"No."

"What happened then?"

"They threw a rope across the water, saying they would tow us back to France. Besart threw it back. They sprayed us with hoses. Seawater. It was cold. People were yelling. We were scooping water out of the boat with our hands while Keller steered away. The boat followed. Then it went quiet. We could no longer hear the engines or see the lights. Keller wanted to slow down so that we could empty the water, but Besart said we should keep going. The stars had gone. Nobody talked. We prayed.

"The sky was beginning to grow light when the engine stopped. Keller said there was water in the fuel line. He and Besart began trying to fix it. That's when we saw the boat again."

"The same one?" asks Carlson.

"Yes."

"How can you be sure?"

"It was the same," says Arben adamantly. "It came quickly, with the sun behind, pushing white water. It didn't stop or slow down. We shouted and waved, but it did not stop or slow down."

"Could it have been an accident?" asks Carlson.

"They saw us. They heard us," says Arben. "We were thrown into the water. They turned and came back. We were yelling and crying. They wanted us to die."

"Did you have life vests?"

"Not all of us."

"Could you swim?"

"I am a good swimmer—I won medals at my school—but I cannot swim faster than a boat."

"When did you last see your brother and sister?"

"Besart found me. He pushed me onto the broken pieces and swam off to find Jeta. He didn't come back."

Arben wipes his eyes with his pajama sleeve, embarrassed by his tears. Evie hands him a tissue. He shakes his head. She insists. He takes it. Blows his nose. Bunches the tissue in his fist.

Carlson suggests they take a break. He motions me to the corridor. It's not until I'm away from the room that I realize I've been holding my breath for much of the past hour, trying not to make a sound.

"He estimated there were twenty people on board," says the detective. "We have seventeen bodies in the morgue. That means a few migrants may still be missing."

"You have to keep looking."

"That's not my call. HM Coastguard is coordinating the search."

Carlson tugs at his left ear, a nervous habit. "Arben could help us identify some of the victims."

"You want to show him dead bodies?"

"Photographs."

I consider the possible psychological impact on Arben, who has already been traumatized. Confirmation that his brother and sister are dead could make this worse.

"Can you give him more time?" I ask.

"I don't have that luxury."

Back inside the room, DI Carlson pulls his chair closer to Arben's bed and produces a computer tablet. The interpreter explains to Arben that the police and coastguard are searching for survivors but that some bodies have been recovered.

"We need your help," says Carlson, as he calls the first image to the screen. It shows a young man, whose face seems to have been sculpted out of white-grey wax. His eyes are closed, but the eyelids are bruised from lividity. Arben takes a look and turns his head away.

"Was he on the boat?"

"Yes."

"Do you know his name?"

"No."

Carlson swipes and another photograph appears.

"Keller," says Arben.

More photographs are shown. With each new one, I feel as though I'm watching a game of Russian roulette, waiting for the lone bullet to spin into the firing chamber.

Arben's breath catches in his throat.

"Who is it?" asks Carlson.

Arben runs a finger over Besart's face, his hand trembling. "My brother." He looks at Evie, wanting an explanation.

"Your brother is dead," she explains.

"No. No. No. Not true."

"I'm sorry," says Evie.

Arben is sobbing.

"I think that's enough," I say.

Carlson grudgingly agrees, sliding the tablet into a case.

"Motra?" asks Arben. "Jeta. My sister."

"Are there any young women among the dead?" I ask.

Carlson shakes his head.

13

Evie

The police are packing things away—the cameras, microphones, and extra chairs. Arben has become an afterthought, still propped up in bed, watching them leave. The interpreter has discovered a tray of sandwiches and is stuffing his pockets like he hasn't eaten for a week.

"Would you like a sandwich, Arben?" I ask loudly.

The interpreter mumbles something with his mouth full of food and crumbs clinging to his mustache. He grabs his hat and heads for the door. *Arsehole!*

I'm alone with Arben, trying to think of something to say. Cyrus would know. He's good with words and deals with stuff like this.

"Why did you want to come here?" I ask, instantly regretting the question.

Arben opens his hand and examines the soggy tissue, as if it might hold the answer.

"Why did you?" he whispers.

It's a simple enough question. I could tell him that I grew up reading Mama's old copies of *Hello!* magazine, which were full of stories about famous people who lived in manor houses; or that Agnesa dreamed of marrying Prince Harry and living in a castle, but the truth is, I had no choice. I was only nine years old.

Cyrus knocks gently on the door and signals that we're leaving.

"Are you coming back?" asks Arben.

I don't know what to say. I grab the drawing pad he was using and jot down my mobile number.

"If you need someone to talk to, you call me, OK?"

He takes the page and folds it into squares, then puts it into the pocket of his pajamas.

Outside in the corridor, I have to run to catch up to Cyrus.

"Where are we going?"

"Home."

"What about Arben—what happens to him?"

"Child services will find him somewhere to live."

"A children's home."

"Or a foster family."

I've been in children's homes. I grew up in them. I wouldn't wish that upon my worst enemy. "He can come and stay with us," I say.

"We're not foster carers and he needs support."

"You're a psychologist."

"Who has a job to do."

We take a taxi into Cleethorpes and find the car where I parked it yesterday, opposite the beach. A shimmer rises off the bonnet of the aging Fiat and the air smells of salt and seaweed and the bins from a nearby restaurant. A yellow notice is pinned beneath his wiper blade. A parking fine. Cyrus curses and tosses the balled-up ticket onto the back seat of the car.

"Was Arben telling the truth?" he asks.

"Mostly."

"Meaning?"

"He lied about his brother buying the boat."

"It was stolen?"

"Uh-huh."

We drive out of Cleethorpes, squinting into the afternoon sun, which is being chased by a bank of grey clouds intent on spoiling the day. I think of Arben. Instead of starting a new life in a new country, he has been cast adrift, stateless, homeless, an orphan. That was me once.

Cyrus has gone quiet, but I know something is bothering him. Finally, he speaks. "The two young women are missing."

"You think they were picked up."

"Or they could have drowned."

He doesn't believe that. The men on the trawler had offered to take the women with them.

"What are you going to do?" I ask, but I know the answer. "Can I help?"

"You have a dog to look after."

"I can leave Poppy with Mitch."

"Not this time."

When is there ever a time?

14

Cyrus

Lungs busting, legs burning, knee joints pleading, I sprint the last quarter mile through silent streets, racing Poppy home. I collapse on the back step, listening to the Labrador drink from her water bowl, panting between gulps.

I woke early, having dreamed of a dead child, weightless in my arms. Evie was in the dream. She was lying on the beach in wet clothes and a cheap life vest, staring into the sky with pale dead eyes.

I try not to read too much into the dream because psychologists, like doctors, make lousy patients. We either overdiagnose or self-medicate or fail to seek help. I'm guilty of that. Instead of talking to someone about my past trauma and ongoing dreams, I tell myself that I'm a healer not a patient. And I had my fill of therapists and counselors after my parents and sisters died. They fussed and fretted over me, telling me *how* I should be feeling, when I simply wanted to be left alone. That's why I don't push Evie to talk about what she's forgotten or repressed.

Florence Gatsi isn't answering her mobile. I text her again: *We have to talk*.

This time she replies: *Am I in trouble?*

Not from me.

Moments later, her name lights up my screen.

"Where are you?" I ask.

"Nottingham. Nadia just had a call from the police. They want her to identify her brother's body."

"I'm sorry."

"So am I."

We arrange to meet at a café in the Lace Market. Florence is still in her motorcycle leathers. She kisses both my cheeks like we're old friends and her dreadlocks brush against my neck. She takes a seat, one trousered leg crossed casually over the other, her arms stretched out along the armrests.

"Where did you stay last night?" I ask.

"With Nadia."

"How is she?"

"Devastated. She still hasn't told her parents in Khartoum."

I order coffee. Florence chooses an herbal concoction that smells like my grandmother's perfume. We share a chocolate brownie, but she picks out the chocolate chips.

"Where is home?" I ask.

"London. I share a house in Camden with some mates from university."

I ask her about Migrant Watch and how long she's worked for the charity.

"It was set up about five years ago by Simon Buchan."

"The philanthropist?"

"And the brother of Lord Buchan."

The statement is delivered with a raised eyebrow. The Buchan brothers are notable siblings who sit on different sides of the political aisle. Simon is younger and less visible, staying out of the headlines and the society pages. From the little I know, he made his money in the City, working as a hedge fund manager or an insurance broker.

His brother, Lord David Buchan, is a former Tory chairman; he was made a life peer back in the noughties, but famously tore up his membership of the Conservative Party during the Brexit referendum, when he campaigned for Britain to leave the European Union, which he called an economic and social failure, full of corrupt politicians and rent seekers.

"Have you met Simon Buchan?" I ask.

"Once or twice," says Florence.

"I don't think I've even seen a photograph of him."

"He's very private," says Florence. "Sometimes he listens in on our Zoom conferences. He asked me a question once. He wanted to know the demographics of the migrants being resettled in Britain—their education levels, training, that sort of thing. He wanted us to stress what a positive effect they could have on our economy—filling skills shortages and low-paid jobs, paying taxes, contributing to society."

Florence picks up a brownie crumb with her wetted forefinger.

"How long have you been a lawyer?" I ask.

"I qualified three years ago."

"I'm impressed."

"Why? Because I'm black or because I'm a woman?"

"You look so young," I say, sensing the danger.

Florence laughs. "Nice save." And grows circumspect. "I'm not supposed to have foreknowledge of any of the small boats that leave Europe."

"But you did this time?"

She nods.

"There was a second boat that left Calais at the same time," I say. "It arrived on a beach near Harwich in the early hours of Saturday morning. Twenty-seven people on board, all safe and well. It took the usual route, the shortest crossing, but this one went farther north. Why did they separate? We need to talk to someone on that other boat."

Florence taps her forefinger against her lips. "All new arrivals are being processed at a former RAF base near Peterborough. I *could* take you there, but I need something in return."

"What could you want from me?"

She raises an eyebrow, as though I'm flirting with her. "The survivor, Arben Pasha, somebody has to represent him."

"He hasn't applied for asylum."

"He will."

Outside, I direct Florence towards my car, but she has other ideas.

"It's quicker on the bike."

She points towards a gleaming black-and-chrome machine. She opens a side pannier and pulls out a spare helmet.

"You're kidding me," I say.

"I'm a very safe rider."

"I might not be a safe passenger."

"Just do what I do and hold on."

She throws her leg over the bike and folds the kickstand, then turns the key. The machine rumbles to life. Florence pats the leather seat. Clumsily, I slide behind her, gripping the sides of her jacket. She grabs my hands and pulls them tight around her waist, saying, "Don't let go."

The Kawasaki vibrates beneath me as we pull away, weaving between stationary cars at a red light and accelerating on the green. Florence shifts her weight, leaning into the first corner. I fight the urge to counter gravity, trying to match her movements. At the same time, I don't want to press my body against hers for obvious reasons. As though sensing my reluctance, she taps the front brakes and I slide closer to her.

Once we reach the countryside, she opens up the throttle. Trees and fences and farms flash past and instantly my senses are magnified. The outside world pours in, and I smell every whiff of grass and hint of cow-pat and the mossy earth of riverbanks.

An hour later we pull up at the boom gate of the migrant reception center, which has a sentry box and fences topped with coils of razor wire.

"Visiting hours are over," says the square-shouldered guard, stepping out of a sentry box.

"We couldn't get here any sooner," Florence says.

"Rules are rules."

"I'm a forensic psychologist who works with the police," I explain. "I'm looking for any of the migrants who arrived on Saturday morning."

"Without an appointment, I can't let you inside," says the guard, sticking to his script.

"If you call DI Stephen Carlson, he'll vouch for me."

"Not my job."

I'm close enough to read his name tag. I open my phone and type the details.

"What are you doing?" he asks.

"I'm informing the detective in charge of a murder investigation that I can't interview possible witnesses until tomorrow because private security guard Gary Parkinson won't give me access."

He hesitates. "Who said anything about murder?"

"I did. Just now."

Hitching up his trousers, the guard walks back to his sentry box and returns with paperwork. Minutes later, the boom gate pivots upwards on a counterweight, and Florence takes us along the gravel access road, parking near the admin building.

Across an old parade ground, dozens of migrants and asylum seekers are sheltering beneath shade-cloth and trees. A group of young children is playing with bright plastic toys and a painted pull-along wagon.

Florence approaches the nearest group and asks if any of them are recent arrivals. The women, many with headscarves, turn their faces away from me. A man approaches. He's in his thirties with a full beard and deep brown eyes.

"Can I help you?" he asks in impeccable English.

"I'm a lawyer," says Florence. "I'm looking for any of the migrants who arrived in Harwich two days ago."

"What sort of lawyer?"

"I can help you with asylum claims."

The man laughs bitterly. "They're going to send us back. No exceptions."

"They can't do that. Under the Human Rights Act, everyone has the right to seek asylum."

"Yet here we are, locked up like criminals."

"You're being processed."

He looks at me, as though I might offer him more hope.

"Where are you from?" I ask.

"Lebanon. My name is Mikhail. I'm a Christian. My uncle is a politician. He was murdered by the Hezbollah. If I go back, they will kill me too."

Florence gives him her business card. "Call my office."

Mikhail studies the cardboard square, as if memorizing the details.

"We're trying to find anyone who left Calais four days ago," I say. "Another boat left the beach at the same time."

"Yes. We left together," says Mikhail. He takes out his mobile phone and opens a video. The footage shows a young boy on the sand, with his arms wrapped around his mother's legs. Behind her, men are standing waist deep in water, holding an inflatable boat steady as waves roll past them. Beyond the broken water, a wide, black sea stretches out into the darkness. The time code on the footage is 20:42.

The camera pans to reveal a second RHIB. A lone man is bent over the outboard motor, trying to get it started. People are standing in the water, waiting to get on board. Most are not wearing life jackets. The mother is lifted on board the first boat, clutching a bag to her chest. A man wades back to the beach and picks up her child, a small boy, and lifts him over the waves. I remember the boy I carried from the water. He was about the same age. My chest hurts.

"Why didn't the boats cross together?" I ask.

"They weren't given permission to go."

"I don't understand."

"They had no money . . . no permission. We paid." He rubs his thumb and two fingers together.

"Permission from whom?"

He makes a shushing sound, wanting me to lower my voice. His own drops to a whisper. "The Ferryman."

"Who is that?"

"The man who must be paid."

"Does he have any other name?"

"Only that one."

I point to the footage. "This other boat went north along the French coast and then northwest. Why take such a long route?"

"To avoid trouble."

"What trouble? The coastguard?"

He makes a dismissive gesture and picks dirt from beneath his fingernails.

"Seventeen people are dead. Two are missing," I say.

"Someone rammed their boat," adds Florence. "They were murdered."

I look for empathy in Mikhail's eyes but can't find any. Either he's a sociopath or his reserves of sympathy are exhausted. It's like he's being told about a natural phenomenon, a great migration of animals, moving from one place to another, where many die on the journey, while others carry on with no time to grieve or question the losses. But this isn't about the great circle of life. People have died needlessly

"Did you know anyone on the other boat?" I ask.

"Perhaps some of the men. I may have met them in the camps."

"What about Besart Pasha—an Albanian?"

"Maybe."

A barking yell echoes across the parade ground, where a group of men has gathered to watch us. A change comes over Mikhail. It's like seeing a cloud pass across the sun, draining the warmth from the air.

Urgently, he whispers, "I cannot talk to you. Not everybody here can be trusted."

One of the distant men makes a gesture with his hand, twisting his wrist. I can't tell if it's a question or a threat. Then he puts his fingers together and makes another signal.

Mikhail backs away from us, shaking his head. Pale. Frightened.

"Did they know they were in danger?" asks Florence.

"We're all in danger," he mumbles.

The other men have gone, carried away like smoke on the breeze. Mikhail joins them. Even the children have disappeared, leaving the toys behind.

"What just happened?" asks Florence.

"We asked the wrong question."

"The Ferryman sounds like a crime boss or a cult leader."

We're back at her motorbike. Florence pulls her dreadlocks together and dons her helmet.

"What about Arben? When can I see him?" she asks.

"It's too late today."

"Tomorrow?"

"I'll do my best."

The motorbike rumbles. I slide onto the seat behind her.

"Where are you going to stay tonight?" I ask.

"I haven't decided."

"I can offer you my guest room."

She gives me a look, as though assessing my motives.

"The guest room?" she asks, seeking confirmation.

"Yes."

"Good. I wouldn't want you to think that I'd tumble into bed with some guy I've just met."

"You won't be tumbling anywhere."

Her right eyebrow arches. "Not unless I trip."

15

Evie

Cyrus has invited a woman home. She has dreadlocked hair and skin so dark and polished smooth that she makes me feel pale and scrawny like a plucked chicken. It's impossible not to stare at her, particularly her eyelashes, which are absurdly long. Nobody needs eyelashes like that.

"What's she doing here?" I whisper when Florence has gone upstairs to get changed.

"She's staying tonight."

"Why?"

"Because she lives in London and it's late and I offered."

"OK, but who is she?"

"A lawyer. She's going to help Arben."

We're both whispering, which isn't necessary.

It's my turn to make dinner. Cyrus does most of the cooking, but he's taught me to make spaghetti Bolognese and macaroni and cheese and chicken parmigiana as long as someone else crumbs the chicken because I don't like touching raw meat. I used to be a vegetarian but went back to eating meat because the doctor said I wasn't getting enough protein, which is why my hair was falling out.

Florence reappears. She's wearing one of Cyrus's sweatshirts and cargo pants. Of course, she's a vegan and she doesn't drink alcohol. Does that make her boring or more interesting?

"Evie can lend you a pair of pajamas," says Cyrus.

"They won't fit," I say. "She's a giant compared to me."

"Knickers and a T-shirt will be fine," says Florence, smiling with perfect white teeth, which are probably natural. Black people have nice teeth. Is that because of the color contrast, I wonder, and is that a racist thing to think?

"And you can use Evie's bathroom," says Cyrus. "I put a new tooth-brush in the vanity."

Which is supposed to be for me.

I steam some extra vegetables and set the table without being asked. I don't know who I'm trying to impress. Florence automatically sits next to Cyrus. I want to look under the table to see if they're playing footsie.

I listen to her stories, itching to catch her lying, but she tells the truth about her family and university and her work. I wonder if Cyrus fancies her. He doesn't show it. Maybe he doesn't want a girlfriend. He acts so gay sometimes.

If he were mine, I'd make sure everybody knew. I'd kiss him all the time. I'd do more than that, but Cyrus won't let it happen because there are rules about that sort of thing, something he calls a "duty of care." That doesn't stop people gossiping about us living under the same roof. I've seen the neighbors' curtains shiver and the venetian blinds bend when we leave the house together. Cyrus doesn't seem to notice. I like that about him.

"Are you seeing anyone?" I ask Florence.

"No."

"Do you fancy Cyrus?"

"Evie!" he says, glaring at me. "That's out of order."

"Why? I'm not saying she has to fuck you."

Florence doesn't seem upset at all. She finds me funny, or maybe it's Cyrus's reaction that makes her laugh.

My mobile vibrates. It's an unknown number. I refuse to answer. I don't want some heavy breather masturbating down the phone or a scam artist telling me my account has been hacked. A text arrives. I'll read it later.

Florence helps Cyrus pack the dishwasher and chats about growing up in Zimbabwe, which is in Africa. I want to ask her about elephants, which are my favorite animal. I sort of imagine they're everywhere in Africa, and I picture people riding them to school or catching them like buses, but I don't want to sound stupid, so I say nothing. Soon, she yawns and apologizes and wishes us good night before she climbs the stairs. I leave clean knickers outside her bedroom door and listen to the pipes clanking and rattling as she turns on the shower.

Cyrus is downstairs in the library. I wonder if he's going to join

Florence later, sneaking into her room in the middle of the night. They'd make lovely milk-chocolate babies. Why do I think things like that? I hate myself sometimes. All the time.

In the morning, I wake early, which is unusual for me, and get out of bed because I can't bear the thoughts that come to me when I'm lying awake, staring at the ceiling. Introspection leads to self-analysis, which leads to self-hatred. That's the circle of my life—the vicious kind.

Getting dressed, I go downstairs and let Poppy into the garden. Then I watch TV for a few minutes, flicking between channels, searching for nothing. The news: doom and gloom. Breakfast TV: sunny and chatty. Children's shows: patronizing. Cyrus and Florence are both sleeping in separate rooms. No beds or bodily fluids were swapped last night, which makes me want to gag, but also makes me happy.

It's my turn to take Poppy for a walk. Leaving the house, I turn along Parkside, heading towards Wollaton Park. Already the cool of the morning is being baked away by the sun as it appears above the trees. It's going to be another hot day. At a house on the corner, a young guy in faded jeans and a T-shirt is working on a car in the driveway, leaning over the engine. I slow down, noticing how his jeans hug his backside. Poppy tugs on her lead.

The boy is Liam and he's home from university and has spent his summer break stripping the engine of an old Ford Fiesta and rebuilding it from scratch. Cleaning, greasing, rewiring, and tightening bits and pieces. Liam has blue eyes and stubble on his cheeks and blond highlights in his hair that might be caused by sunshine or chemicals.

Wiping his hands on a grease-stained rag, he smiles. "Morning, Princess. Did you sleep well?"

"I did."

"Alone?"

"None of your business."

He grins and crouches down, calling to Poppy. I unclip her lead and she trots along his driveway. Liam scratches behind her ears and looks into her eyes as though practicing dog telepathy. "We're friends now," he says. And then to me, "When are you coming for a drink with me?"

"When hell freezes over."

"Are you old enough to drink?"

"Fuck off."

Another smile. "I'm off to the pub tonight if you fancy coming."

"The pub."

"Yeah. The Admiral Rodney."

Is he asking me on a date? I think of Cyrus and wonder if it would make him jealous. Probably not.

"What time?"

"I'll be there about six."

I nod and summon Poppy, clipping the leash to her collar and turning into the park. I wonder if Liam is still watching me. I want to look over my shoulder to check, but that might seem weird or needy.

My phone vibrates. It's the same unknown number as yesterday, but I know who it is now. A voice message comes next.

"Hello, Evie. It's Dr. Bennett from the Diana Princess of Wales Hospital. I need to talk to you about your MRI scan. Can you please call to schedule an appointment?"

I delete the message and think about what I'm going to wear tonight for my date with Liam. Not that I have much choice. I don't wear dresses and my jeans come in two colors, black and blue, and two styles, ripped and unripped. In truth, I'm more interested in telling Cyrus that I have a date than going on one. Maybe that's because I haven't been on many, or any, ever.

This could be a disaster.

16

Cyrus

My radio alarm wakes me. The newsreader has a plummy, authoritative voice.

"Police have abandoned the search for more survivors of the weekend's tragedy in the North Sea. Eleven emergency vessels, two fixed-wing aircraft, and three helicopters were involved in the operation when it was suspended last night due to worsening weather conditions.

"The small inflatable boat capsized twelve miles off the coast of Clee-thorpes in Lincolnshire. Seventeen migrants drowned, one survived, and two are believed to be missing.

"A Home Office spokesman told the BBC: 'Crossing the Channel in a small boat is a huge risk. The criminal gangs that perpetuate this ruthless trade do not care about loss of life. We thank all the agencies at home and abroad who led the search-and-rescue operation.'"

Getting out of bed, I splash water on my face, still listening to the report.

"The victims of the tragedy, which included two children, were from Iraq, Afghanistan, Syria, Albania, and Sudan. The sole survivor, a boy of fourteen, is still recovering in hospital and has been interviewed by police trying to piece together the vessel's last hours."

Evie's bedroom door is open. She must have taken Poppy for a walk. Uncompelled, which is surprising. A second thought bumps into the first one—what if she relapses? It has been only three days since her catatonia. I should have gone with her. I check my phone and contemplate calling her, but Evie doesn't like when I hover or micromanage. That was one of her rules when she moved into the house. I would not act like a parent or a therapist.

Downstairs, I make coffee and keep one ear out for the side gate, wishing Evie were home. Florence joins me. She's wearing one of my shirts. "I borrowed this. I hope that's all right."

"It looks better on you," I say. As the words leave my mouth, I wonder if I'm being too forward. I change the subject. "We have toast, instant porridge, eggs. Can you eat eggs?"

"No. What can I put on toast?" she asks.

"Strawberry jam, honey, or marmalade."

"Jam would be great." She looks around. "Where's Evie?"

"Walking Poppy."

"This is some house."

"It belonged to my grandparents. They gave it to me when they retired to Limington in Somerset."

"My grandparents gave me a herd of goats in Nyanga."

"Where?"

"In Zimbabwe."

"Is that true?"

"No, but it's a good story."

She checks the toaster and keeps talking. "My parents were lawyers who left Zimbabwe when the farm invasions began. Mugabe was president and he ordered a purge of all judges and lawyers who were arguing that the land seizures were illegal."

"How old were you?"

"Six. I go back every year to visit my grandparents."

Florence is exploring downstairs. I sometimes forget what sort of impression the house has on people. How it makes me seem like a man of means, yet it belongs to a childhood that I'd rather forget. Growing up, I explored every room, cupboard, and crawl space during sleepovers and games of hide-and-seek and Easter egg hunts. These should be happy memories, but they come tinged with sadness. The house is too big for me. It has too many rooms, with bulk oak paneling and thick dado rails and heavy plaster and dented crown moldings and floors worn smooth and creaky with use. Some of the rooms still have nipple buttons that once summoned servants from "below stairs." It is a house from a bygone era, patched up and refurbished but still creaking with age.

Excusing myself, I go to the library and phone Carlson's number. The detective is in his car on his way to the morning media conference.

"They called off the search," I say.

"Not my decision."

"Where's Arben?"

"We're transferring him to Birchin Way Custody Facility."

"Custody?"

"Border Force wants to interview him. After that we hand him over to social services."

"When?"

"Tonight, if they can find him a place."

"I want to help."

"In what way?"

"I can review the evidence and give you a different perspective . . . be a fresh set of eyes."

These arguments seem to land awkwardly. I can picture Carlson asking himself if he wants an outsider involved. I'm a layman not a police officer—not part of the "tribe" or the culture. This can have benefits but it can also be problematic because he has no control over me.

Carlson makes a decision. "I'm texting you an address. Meet me there at midday."

Florence is at the kitchen counter. She bites off a corner of toast. "What was that about?"

"I'm working on the case."

"That's good, isn't it?"

"I hope so."

I scroll through my contacts list and find a number. Derek Posniak picks up immediately. He and I were in university together and once shared a girlfriend, although we didn't know it at the time. Now he works for the National Crime Agency, but never talks about his job. I once joked he was a spy. Derek laughed, but there was nothing behind his eyes.

"Padfoot," he says cheerfully. "To what do I owe the pleasure?"

He's using an old nickname, given to me because Cyrus sounds like Sirius (as in Sirius Black), who was Harry Potter's godfather and could transform into a big black dog called Padfoot.

"I might have something for you," I say.

"Really? Most people *want* something from me."

He's tapping on a keyboard as he speaks.

"The small boat that capsized off Cleethorpes was deliberately rammed."

"On what evidence?"

"The eyewitness testimony of the survivor."

"A fourteen-year-old."

"And text messages from someone else on board."

Posniak pauses and I hear a pen tapping against his teeth. "Have you talked to the police?"

"I'm working on the case."

"Why do you need me?"

"Yesterday, I talked to an asylum seeker who left Calais on a different boat on the same night. It landed safely in Essex. He told me that the other boat didn't have permission to travel."

"Permission from whom?"

"The Ferryman."

Posniak makes a scoffing sound. "That old chestnut."

"What do you mean?"

"The Ferryman is a ghost, a figment, a bogeyman. He's like Keyser Söze or Lex Luther or Moriarty."

"You're saying he's not real."

"I can't tell you how many stories we hear about untouchable, faceless master criminals who are controlling the world order and running pedophile rings out of pizza shops. Debunk one myth and another one pops up, fed by QAnon believers or conspiracy websites or Russian bots."

"But you've heard of the Ferryman."

"I've also heard of the tooth fairy."

I wait for more.

Derek sighs. "I've been in this job for six years, Padfoot, and I've heard people talk about the Ferryman, but nobody has ever given him a real name or a nationality. A year ago, the NCA took part in a series of joint raids across Europe, in France, Germany, Belgium, the Netherlands, and here. We raided over fifty locations. Arrested forty suspects. Seized thousands of life jackets, more than two hundred boats, and fifty engines, as well as cash, firearms, and drugs. We rounded up the leaders of six different criminal networks. We offered them plea deals if they cooperated. Some of them accepted. Some kept schtum. Not one of them gave up the Ferryman."

"Why would asylum seekers invent him?"

"I don't think they did. I blame the people smugglers. What better way to keep people quiet? Create a terrifying bogeyman who will murder them in their beds or target their families or deliberately sink their boats."

"Someone *did* deliberately sink this boat."

"Are you certain?"

"Yes."

Derek grunts and keeps tapping at his keyboard. I don't know if he's ignoring me or waiting for me to ask another question.

"Who would benefit from a tragedy like this?" I ask.

"Well, the obvious suspects are the ultra-nationalists, neo-Nazi gangs, or white supremacists. Anti-immigration groups regularly target migrant camps and hostels. But it could also be the escalation of a turf war. The gangs that are trafficking migrants are becoming more ruthless—fighting for control of camps and crossings. Europol is dealing with a dozen different executions over the past eight months. Double taps, two shots to the back of the head, close range. The victims were found with a coin in their mouths."

"The Greek myth," I say.

"Charon's obol. A coin is placed in the mouth or near the body of the dead, as payment to Charon, the ferryman to the underworld."

"Could the Ferryman be Greek?" I ask.

"Like I said—I don't think he exists."

"Can you do me a favor?"

"Ah, that's what I was waiting for," he says sarcastically.

"If you hear anything—any whisper about the Ferryman—can you let me know?"

"And what do I get in return?"

"You're not supposed to take bribes."

"OK, I'll own your soul."

Afterwards, I realize that I did most of the talking. Maybe he is a spy.

17

Evie

I love dogs more than humans because they're loyal and love you unconditionally. They're not racist or transphobic or sexist or classist or ageist. They don't talk politics or religion or steal your boyfriend or take your car without asking. Yes, they're like having a small child in the house and they need exercise and attention and they poop a lot, but that's a small price to pay.

I volunteer three days a week at the Radcliffe Animal Centre. It was where I adopted Poppy when she was eighteen months old. Someone had abandoned her at a truck stop, dumping her in a rubbish bin. A driver heard her whimpering and rescued her before a waste truck emptied the bin into its compactor.

From the outside, the shelter looks like a small country motel, with silhouettes of dogs and cats painted on the front wall. Cyrus wants me to get a paid job because I should be paying board, but every time I look for a job, I get asked a bunch of questions or told to fill out a form. Where was I born? Where did I go to school? My address? My next of kin? I don't want people knowing that much about me.

Annie runs the place. She is one of those women who dresses in dungarees and Wellingtons, but also wears lipstick and eyeshadow. Some people think she's a lesbian, but she's married to Clive and has three children and six grandchildren. Clive delivers parcels for the post office and, according to Annie, he's so boring his preferred pronouns are ho/hum.

The shelter has about forty mesh cages for the dogs, with each cage big enough for a bed and somewhere for them to poop and rest. There is also a cat area with cat trees and cubbyholes, and a separate straw-covered hutch for the rabbits.

When people come to the shelter looking for a rescue pet, we take them into an area with artificial grass and bench seats and a toy box. This is where they get introduced to the animals.

Whenever I'm working, Annie gives me the job of interviewing adoptive families, asking them questions about their house and yard and their experience with pets. She calls me the "dog whisperer" because I can tell within moments if a family will be the right match for a particular shelter dog.

People often turn up with a checklist, wanting a particular breed of dog, or a certain size or temperament, even if it's entirely unsuitable for them. Some are allergic to dogs or have no garden, or ask what color they can choose, as if they're matching a pet with their curtains. Others want a fashion accessory that can fit into their handbag or a guard dog that will frighten away intruders or an exercise companion even though they spend more time walking to the fridge than in the park.

The rescues seem to know when someone is here to adopt, and they begin barking and whining and wagging tails, hoping it might be them. Some are desperate for love, while a few seem to have given up hope, curling up in their cages, ignoring the commotion. They're the ones I most want to take home.

When I'm not interviewing clients, I clean out the cages and change the water and scoop dry biscuits into bowls. Cyrus finds it hilarious that I'll go off to work and do all this stuff that I won't do at home.

"That's because I'm appreciated," I say.

"I should hope so. You're an unpaid volunteer."

He doesn't really mind that I don't get paid. And Annie says she's going to see if she can find some money in the next budget and that no matter what she paid me it wouldn't be enough because I'm "priceless."

There are two more text messages on my phone, both from Dr. Bennett. I keep ignoring her because I don't want to know if there's something wrong with me. Clearly, there is. I'm a freak. How else do you explain my history and the whole lie-detecting thing.

A class of preschool children is visiting the shelter today on an excursion. They are dressed in matching yellow bibs and holding hands, marching penguin style across the parking area, being led by a teacher.

I remember my first day of school. The colored wooden chairs, all in a circle, the cranky teacher, Mrs. Martini, whose hair made her head look like a half-painted bowling ball. One of the boys wanted to use the bathroom and she told him to wait. He wet his pants and cried. Mrs. Martini told him to stop being such a girl.

"Why does that make him a girl?" I asked.

She marched me to the back of the classroom and locked me inside a cupboard, which stank of paint and turpentine and white spirits. Soon I discovered it had a name among the students: dollap i qelbur (the stinky closet).

"How was your first day at school?" Papa asked me that afternoon.

"Good," I said. "But I didn't like the stinky closet."

The next morning, Papa didn't leave early for the butchery. Instead, he took us on the bus to school and walked me to my classroom. He made me wait outside while he talked to Mrs. Martini. It was difficult to hear everything my teacher said because she was inside the stinky closet and Papa was holding the door closed.

Later that morning I was moved to the other kindergarten class, where I met Mina, my best friend. She had a round face and frizzy black hair and crooked bottom teeth and she sat near the front because she had trouble seeing the blackboard.

When I sat down next to her, she smiled as though I'd given her a gift. Mina was a Roma and her family lived near the old railway sidings, where the trains used to sleep when they weren't running. That was before they closed the line to Prrenjas. After that, the carriages and boxcars were left to rust and become overgrown with weeds. Some of them were used as houses, and others for storage, but most were empty and a playground for kids.

Mina and I were "joined at the hip," according to Agnesa, who made it sound like it was unhealthy. I already knew what people whispered behind Mina's back—stories about gypsies stealing babies and robbing houses and putting curses on people, but I didn't believe any of that.

After school, we'd walk home through the village, pressing our faces against the window of the bakery, smearing fingerprints and foggy breath on the glass, until the owner Mr. Kabashi gave us a warm biscuit and shooed us away. We played games—drawing numbered squares on the old train platform for hopscotch, or catching lizards and skinks that lived under the rocks between the sleepers or tadpoles in the pond behind the timber yard.

Mina's favorite game was brides and babies, but I didn't understand the attraction in being married or pregnant. Neither had made Mama very happy. Her moods were like cycles of the moon. On her sad days she would take herself off to bed or spend hours staring into the mirror, asking us, "Am I pretty, girls?" "What happened to my face?" On her sad days nobody could make her smile or laugh or convince her there was any beauty or warmth in the world. She could be careless and cruel, but Papa never stopped loving her.

She always cheered up when Aunt Polina came to stay, even though she complained constantly about the extra work. Polina was Papa's younger sister and didn't have any children, but had lots of boyfriends, none of whom "wanted to marry her" according to Mama because she "gave it away for free," whatever that meant.

I thought she was glamorous and beautiful, with a suitcase full of cocktail dresses and high heels and handbags. She took a speedboat to Italy every summer and always came back with newer and nicer clothes and gifts for everyone. Swiss chocolates. Marzipan. Limoncello. CDs of the Backstreet Boys and Beyoncé.

People whispered about her being a strawberry picker, but I don't think she was picking strawberries in those dresses. And the men would look at her differently whenever she walked along the street. Aunt Polina didn't seem to care, although her hips always swayed a little more when she passed them.

Whenever she came to stay, we shared a bed, and Agnesa had a roll-up mattress in the sitting room. Even though she smoked, Polina smelled of lavender and some other scent that I could never place, but it was earthy and raw and dangerous.

"Make sure you marry a rich boy," she told me.

"I don't like boys," I said.

"That will change."

Agnesa must have been listening because she did like boys. Briefly. Sadly.

18

Cyrus

The remains of the rigid-hulled inflatable boat are lying like a deflated whale on the concrete floor of the warehouse. The red-and-black fabric is torn in places, revealing the skeletal frame beneath the rubberized skin. Nearby the engine and fuel tank have been placed on a wooden platform. The engine is clamped upright in a support frame, the upper casing removed, the workings exposed.

A technician in white overalls has climbed a ladder to take photographs of the RHIB from above. Another is measuring holes in the torn fabric, while a third is placing small evidence flags to indicate points of interest. She turns and acknowledges us, recognizing Carlson. Smiling.

"This is DC Gayle," he says, making the introductions.

"Call me Claire," she says.

No handshakes. A gloved wave instead. She's in her late thirties, with short-cropped blond hair and inquisitive eyes.

"What are you looking for?" I ask.

"Point of impact, velocity, direction, size, yaw axis, supplementary damage . . ."

"When you say 'supplementary damage'?"

"The RHIB was hit more than once."

"How many times?" asks Carlson.

"Three times from different angles."

She moves around the wreckage, pointing out tears in the fabric.

"The damage was caused by propellers with four blades."

"How can you tell?" I ask.

"The leading edge of each blade contacts the water first as the propeller spins. The trailing edge contacts the water last as it rotates. That's why trawler props tend to be rounded or half-oval shapes. The damage has parallel tracks, indicating twin propellers."

"How big was the boat?" asks Carlson.

"A twin-screw vessel, with counterrotating propellers twenty-five inches in diameter with a thirty-two-inch pitch—suggests something about twenty meters long."

"A fishing trawler."

"That would fit," she says.

DC Gayle steps away from the RHIB and pulls off her latex gloves.

She continues. "A typical four-blade propeller can spin at anywhere from twelve hundred RPMs to thirty-two hundred depending on the engine horsepower. A spinning blade will hit a body about a hundred and sixty times a second, causing horrific injuries. You also have the hydrodynamic effect. Propellers create a suction that can easily pull a full-sized person under a boat. When that happens, the impact to a body, head to toe, takes about a tenth of a second, and is normally fatal."

"That fits with some of the injuries we found," says Carlson.

Gayle has walked several paces to point out more damage. "The original impact destroyed two of the air chambers on the starboard side. The second impact destroyed another air chamber and briefly submerged the RHIB. We have found traces of boat paint on the rubberized fabric and evidence that the bigger vessel's prop shaft may have been damaged."

"How badly damaged?" asks Carlson.

"Difficult to say, sir."

Carlson's phone is buzzing. He steps away to take the call. Soon afterwards, I'm summoned to follow. He walks and talks. "HM Coastguard has plotted a possible point of collision. They're sending someone from their joint operations center to talk to us."

I ride in the police car with Carlson. He answers calls on the journey, receiving information about the postmortems and the ongoing investigation. Twelve of the dead have been identified.

When a call ends, he turns to me. "You haven't given me your opinion."

"On what?"

"You're my fresh set of eyes. What am I dealing with?"

"Not an accident."

"Clearly."

"It's either a random racist act or part of an orchestrated campaign to discourage migrants from making the crossing."

"What makes you think it's orchestrated?"

"This boat separated from the other migrant vessel that left Calais on the same evening. It went northeast, along the French coast, before turning northwest. This made the journey longer and riskier. Why?"

"I assume you're going to tell me."

"They were frightened because they didn't have permission to travel."

"Permission from who?"

"The migrants call him the Ferryman. The National Crime Agency calls him a myth. I talked to a friend at the NCA, who said rival gangs of people smugglers have been waging a turf war over the past year—trying to control the people trade. This sinking could have been a warning—telling migrants to choose the right side."

Carlson seems to chew this information over as we enter the outskirts of Grimsby. "Go back to the racist angle."

"Have you heard of the Identitarian movement?" I ask.

"No."

"It's a political ideology that opposes globalization and multiculturalism. Basically, they're a bunch of white Europeans who claim their land and their culture are being polluted by foreigners. One group, Defend Europe, has been leasing ships and leading patrols in the Mediterranean."

"What sort of patrols?"

"Publicly, they claim to be monitoring the humanitarian ships who are picking up refugees, but privately there are reports of migrant boats being deliberately swamped or made to turn back to North Africa."

"Vigilantes?"

"Not a word they use."

"You think a group like that could be operating in UK waters?"

"I think it's worth investigating."

"Surely, such a group would claim responsibility for the sinking—otherwise it won't be a deterrent."

"Maybe they have. The information only has to reach the camps. That's their audience."

"So, we should be looking at white nationalists or neo-Nazis?"

"Particularly anyone with a history of violence against migrants or minorities. Most are recruited when they're young. The unemployed and unemployable. The bullied and marginalized."

"You sound like you know them?"

"Men like that, yes."

"What about the missing women?"

"If they're alive, they were most likely taken on board the trawler because they had value."

Carlson knows the reason. Hundreds, if not thousands, of undocumented migrants are kept as sex slaves in British brothels; exploited, imprisoned, beaten, drugged, and threatened. They're told that their families back home will be killed if they refuse to obey orders.

One of them, a patient of mine, was only seventeen when she escaped. She had worked twenty-hour shifts in a Soho brothel in London, forced to have sex with up to forty men a day for as little as ten pounds a time. She was told she had to pay off a twenty-thousand-pound debt, which was the price the brothel had paid for her.

"We have to find them quickly," I say.

"I'm doing my best."

Birchin Way Custody Facility is built on the edge of an industrial estate and looks like a cross between a high-tech production facility and a business headquarters. The only clues to its use are the police cars parked out front and an automatic security gate signposted "custody entrance."

"State-of-the-art," says Carlson. "Thirty-six custody cells, charge rooms, interview suites, and round-the-clock processing. This is supposed to be the future."

"Does it work?"

"As much as anything will."

I'm photographed and given an electronic pass before being taken upstairs to the incident room—an open-plan office where detectives, civilian analysts, and data processors are collecting and collating information. Whiteboards display photographs of the dead, whose personal details are slowly being filled in—ages, nationalities, and next of kin.

The coastguard official is waiting in Carlson's office. He's in his mid-fifties with a weather-beaten face and pale circles around his eyes caused by his sunglasses.

"Commander Greg Stanford," he says, standing to attention. "I was the senior maritime operations officer who handled the search and rescue."

I don't know if I should salute or shake his hand.

Stanford has set up a laptop and a viewing screen. "This is what we've pieced together so far," he says, calling up an interactive map of the French coastline. "Two small boats left Calais shortly after twenty-one hundred hours. The seas were calm, visibility good. They separated almost immediately and one went northeast, following the French coastline as far as Rotterdam, before turning northwest."

His finger traces the route on the screen.

"How can you be sure?" I ask.

"Large ships carry professional radar, which can reach up to four miles. This can be limited by fog and rain but is reasonably accurate. A rigid-hulled inflatable boat is not a strong target because it doesn't have radar reflectors, but it can become more visible in larger swells due to refraction."

Stanford calls up a satellite map and points to an icon.

"We think this is the migrant boat. It was picked up by the radar on a container ship that was traveling from Harwich to Zeebrugge in Belgium. A different ship picked up a similar signature two hours later, about thirty-five miles farther north."

The screen changes again, this time showing a neon-green flight path. "These are radar images captured by a UR5 drone used for border surveillance. It was airborne at two hundred forty meters at oh five nineteen."

The footage speeds up but slows down when it reaches a chosen time stamp.

"What am I looking at?" I ask.

"These two blips indicate two vessels, one larger than the other. They appear to almost merge before one of them disappears."

"A collision," says Carlson.

"Unless the larger boat began towing the smaller one. We estimate the collision occurred sixteen miles northeast of Skegness at approximately oh five thirty-two hours. The bodies drifted northeast, pushed by the currents and wind, before coming ashore at Cleethorpes."

"What other vessels were in the area?" asks Carlson.

Stanford calls up another screen. "This is a maritime traffic map for that quadrant. It doesn't show either boat because neither was using an automatic identification system, which transmits location signals to satellites. A trawler should have been equipped with an AIS, but it was likely turned off."

"Can you track it using the radar of other ships in the vicinity?" I ask.

"The drone was only overhead for nine minutes but we're searching the radar signals of other ships, trying to get a fix on where the larger vessel went after the collision. To date, our best lead has come from the local harbormaster here in Grimsby. On Monday morning, a support tender for one of the wind farm operations reported a near collision with an unmarked trawler as it passed Spurn Head. The tender radioed the unidentified boat but got no response."

"Where is Spurn Head?" I ask.

"The narrowest point that boats enter the Humber Estuary," says Stanford. "The tender skipper thought the boat was making an awful racket, possibly from a damaged prop shaft."

"Where would it go?" asks Carlson.

"The Humber Estuary covers more than a hundred square miles. There are dozens of marinas and boatyards. A hundred places to hide."

Carlson isn't fazed. "Well, we'd best get started."

19

Evie

My date with Liam is messing with my head. It's all I can think about. What am I going to wear? What will we talk about? He goes to university. I work in an animal shelter. He can rebuild a car. I can't change a tire.

I'm not going to sleep with him. And if he tries to kiss me, I'll knee him in the balls. What if he asks for my permission? What if he smells nice? What if he doesn't *want* to kiss me? What if he finds me repulsive?

I can't decide what I want. Is being normal an ambition? My therapist, Veejay, says she's never met a normal person. We're all weird in our own ways.

I'm standing in front of my wardrobe, examining my range of shitty choices. I'm looking for something casual, but cool and sexy, but not trampy or desperate. I have ripped jeans, which look OK. I add a polka-dot top. Ugh! Next I try a linen popover shirt. Tuck it in. Pull it out. Roll up the sleeves. Roll them down. No.

Twenty minutes later, I've exhausted my wardrobe, and my bed is a small mound of discarded clothes. Finally, I settle on a white blouse, ripped jeans, and Cyrus's old denim jacket, which is too small for him and too big for me. The jacket is decorated with cloth patches from the cities he's visited. It makes me feel like I'm a world traveler. I hope Liam doesn't ask me questions about Berlin or Amsterdam or Prague.

I'm looking at my reflection in the bathroom mirror. The trick with makeup is to make it look like I haven't made an effort. Cyrus says I use too much eye shadow and eyeliner, and that my eyes are beautiful, but I don't believe him. I try a different combination of colors, using makeup wipes to remove the evidence then start again.

Suddenly, I notice the time. I'm late. I hurry along Parkside and turn into Bramcote Lane, but slow down because I don't want to get sweaty.

The pub is ahead of me. I'm half an hour late. What if Liam doesn't wait?

Normally, I'd pause outside and take a breath, maybe sneak a look through the window, but this time I push through the doors into a wall of noise and bodies. The place is heaving. I'm not tall enough to see over heads. I'm at armpit level. The deodorant zone.

I don't like crowded places, which is a phobia but I can't remember which one.

Something about the noise and closeness of people overstimulates my brain and makes me anxious.

"There you are," says Liam, materializing in front of me. He's carrying a tray of drinks. "Follow me. I'll introduce you to the gang."

Gang?

Suddenly, I want to escape, but he's waiting for me. I trail along, following him through the bar into a garden, which is cooler but just as crowded. There are tables and umbrellas and children and dogs.

"I thought you'd bailed on me," says Liam, shouting over his shoulder. The tray wobbles. Beer spills.

We reach a table under a tree where four people are waiting. Three boys and a girl.

"This is Evie," says Liam, who proceeds to tell me everyone's name, but I don't remember all of them. A couple of them smile. The others exchange a look that I can't read. I raise my hand in a little wave and put on my best fake smile.

Liam is distributing pints and something that might be a cocktail. There are empty glasses on the table. How long have they been here?

"What can I get you?" he asks.

"What?"

"A drink."

"Oh, water."

"You want water?"

"I mean, a Coke."

"Anything in it?"

"Ice."

He laughs. I feel my cheeks color.

"Back in a tick," he says.

I want to grab his hand and stop him leaving, but he's gone. I turn back to the others. They're staring at me. My heart hammers. I look for somewhere to sit. There's space on one of the benches.

"That's where Liam is sitting," says the girl, Georgia, who slides sideways, closing the gap. She's wearing tiny denim shorts that show the bottom of her arse cheeks and a sleeveless bodysuit cut high, exposing flesh from her hips to the bottom of her ribs. She's about my age. Pretty. Pouty.

Next to her is a bearded black guy wearing a red bandanna around his head and a line of studs in the cartilage of his ears. Opposite are two boys, who look like twins, with identical faux-hawk haircuts with blond highlights. One of them has a packet of cigarettes rolled into the sleeve of his T-shirt. The other has a tattoo of a tiger on his forearm.

"Sit here," says the smoker, sliding sideways, creating a space between himself and tiger boy. I don't want to be trapped between them, but I step over the bench and sit down, tucking my hands under my thighs.

Georgia lifts her sunglasses onto her forehead. "So, Edie, how do you know Liam?"

"It's Evie," I say.

She pouts. "How do you know Liam?"

"He lives near me."

"You're neighbors."

"Sort of."

"I haven't seen you around before," says tiger boy. "Where did you grow up?"

"All over the place."

"You at university?"

"No. I work at an animal shelter."

"Are you studying to be a vet?" asks Georgia.

"No."

"What do you do at the shelter?"

"I feed the dogs and clean their cages—"

"You pick up shit."

"I arrange the adoptions," I say, wanting to scratch her eyes out. "And I look after the puppies."

"I love puppies," says tiger boy.

Georgia wrinkles her nose as though she can smell me from across the rough wooden table.

"Where did you go to school?" asks the bandanna guy.

"Nottingham College."

"Really? Didn't you go there, Georgia?"

"I don't remember you," she says, her top lip curling.

"I only did a couple of subjects."

There is silence. It's as though we've run out of small talk.

Liam returns. He hands me a Coke and takes a seat next to Georgia, who is sitting close to him, staking out her territory like a stray dog. I take a sip and enjoy the sugar hit. Liam downs half his pint in a few gulps. I watch his Adam's apple bob as he swallows.

Thankfully, the conversation switches to something else. They're talking about university and some band that I've never heard of, which is coming to the campus. Tiger boy mentions Glastonbury and they swap stories about camping at the festival and what bands "killed." He tells a lie about hooking up with a girl the others seem to know. Georgia talks about going to the Mad Cool Festival in Spain and seeing Metallica and Imagine Dragons.

"What sort of music do you like?" asks Liam.

It takes me a moment to realize that he's talking to me. My mind goes blank. I can't think of a single band, let alone a song. Instead, I repeat the bands that Georgia just named.

"How original," she says.

"Anything indie?" asks Liam.

"Yeah."

"Have you heard of the Pigeon Detectives?"

"No."

"They're ancient," says the smoker.

"Liam is in a band," says Georgia.

"I used to be," he says.

"I thought you were getting back together," she says. "You said I could be a backing singer."

"If the others agree," says Liam.

He's lying. He doesn't think she can sing.

Georgia has pressed her thigh against his leg. I feel myself growing jealous, even though I don't want to care. My cheeks are hot. I hold my glass against my face, enjoying the cold, but I worry about sweat rings under my arms or, worse, my boobs. The others are discussing some show on Netflix I haven't seen. The dappled shade from the trees is falling across Liam's face. He's beautiful and he knows it.

"I have to go," I blurt.

"But you've only just got here," he says.

"I have something on."

"Now?"

He follows me through the pub, trying to convince me to stay. We're on the pavement outside. He asks for my phone number. I remember the first three numbers and then nothing.

"Give me your phone," he says.

He takes it from me and holds it up to my face to open the screen, before typing a message to himself, which pings on his phone. "I'll call you," he says.

Then he kisses me. I let him. His lips are soft. His hand is on my waist. He draws away and I tell myself to breathe. I touch my lips with my fingers.

"Sorry about Georgia, she can be a bitch sometimes."

"Have you slept with her?"

"No."

He's not lying.

"She wants to sleep with you."

"I'm on her list," he says. "Was that a terrible thing to say?"

"Yes, but I believe you."

I turn away and begin walking. I want to look back over my shoulder, but I'm too embarrassed. Why would Liam be interested in me? Georgia is prettier and cleverer and will sleep with him. Liam thinks I'm normal. Somebody should warn him.

I turn back. He's still there.

"I don't think you should call me," I say.

"Why not?"

"I'm not worth the trouble."

20

Cyrus

An expensive-looking car is parked beneath the trees on Parkside. The uniformed driver emerges from behind the wheel—a woman dressed in black trousers and a button-down white blouse. With her hair pulled into a tight bun and her eyes made-up, she could be moonlighting from a job as an airline stewardess.

I glance into the rear of the car. There are no passengers.

"Dr. Haven?"

"Yes."

"Mr. Simon Buchan requests your company for dinner."

"Now?" I ask, bemused.

"Your table is booked for eight thirty. You'll be dining at Restaurant Fourteen. I shall pick you up at eight."

She is standing at attention with her hands behind her as though on a parade ground. I want to ask why Mr. Simon Buchan didn't call me or send an email or slip a note through my mailbox. Instead, he sent his driver to wait for me, which might seem sinister or foreboding, but she has a disarming smile.

"Will Florence be joining us?" I ask.

"I'm afraid I can't answer that."

"Tell Mr. Buchan that I'll meet him there."

A slight frown. "If that's your decision, sir."

She doesn't move. I wonder if I'm supposed to dismiss her. She waits until I'm almost at the front door before she gets back behind the steering wheel.

Once inside, I call Florence but it goes to her voicemail. Opening my laptop, I type the name Simon Buchan into a search engine. It's a lesson I learned when I was job hunting after university—never walk into an interview or meeting unprepared. I have no idea why Simon Buchan wants to talk to me, but Florence must have mentioned my name.

The screen refreshes. The search results are dominated by his older brother, Lord David Buchan. The *Times* refers to him as a "retro-nationalist" who wants stricter quotas on immigration and tougher border controls but who refuses to demonize migrants and asylum seekers.

Since the wave of small boat arrivals began, Lord Buchan had led the attacks on the government, claiming they had lost control of Britain's borders. At the same time, he has denied any links with ultra-right nationalist groups in Britain and Europe, although he admitted to meeting with a self-confessed neo-Nazi called Arnout Bakker, who served ten years for fire-bombing a mosque in Cologne.

Another story details the almost obligatory tax scandal. Details of a family educational trust were leaked to the press, including millions held in shady offshore tax structures, none of which had been disclosed in Lord Buchan's parliamentary statement of interests. His opponents labeled him a hypocrite because he had previously denounced the use of tax havens.

Finally, I reach a story about Simon Buchan, the younger brother. Both boys went to the same school, King's in Canterbury, and then on to Cambridge, where Simon graduated with a land economics and law degree before joining a merchant bank in London. Following a stint as a commodities trader, he began his own hedge fund in 2002 and made a fortune during the global financial crisis in 2008.

Most articles refer to him as a philanthropist, or a self-made billionaire, with business interests that included hotels, employment services, and labor hire companies. Although deeply private and publicity shy, he had lobbied successive governments to do more to combat modern-day slavery and sex trafficking, as well as treat refugees and asylum seekers with greater compassion.

Christmas dinner must be interesting in the Buchan family—two brothers with diametrically opposed political views, breaking bread and pouring wine and exchanging gifts. Maybe they call a truce for the day, a temporary cease-fire, or perhaps they lock the elephant in a different room.

I look for photographs of Simon Buchan, but struggle to find any, apart from a rowing picture from his days at Cambridge and a corporate headshot from his time as a merchant banker.

Poppy's ears prick up as a key slides into the front door. She scrambles off the sofa and goes to greet Evie in the hallway.

"Hello," I say.

Evie doesn't answer. She walks past the library and up the stairs. I leave the desk and look up at her, noticing her clothes and her makeup and my denim jacket.

"Where have you been?"

"Out."

"Want to talk about it?"

"No."

Everything about her body language screams at me to leave her alone.

"I won't be in for dinner. There's some lasagna left in the fridge."

"Fine."

"Have you heard from Dr. Bennett?"

Her bedroom door has closed.

The restaurant is in a converted warehouse where the blackened brick walls and beams have become design features. The number fourteen is printed or embossed on every menu, wineglass, place setting, and item of cutlery.

A maître d' takes my coat and consults a computer tablet. "This way, sir."

I follow her through the restaurant, weaving between tables, past windows that overlook the city. We leave the dining room and enter a corridor.

"Excuse me, where are we going?" I ask.

"The private dining room."

"How many of us are there?"

"Two."

She ushers me into a darkened room with a small, well-lit single table covered in a starched white tablecloth with two place settings for dinner. A bottle of white wine is resting in an ice bucket on a stand, and a bottle of red wine has been placed on a sideboard. Open. Breathing.

It's only after she's gone that I realize I'm not alone. A figure is silhouetted against a large picture window that offers views across the square to the dome of Nottingham Council House, which slowly changes color from blue to red to green.

A man turns and steps into the light. "Dr. Haven, thank you so much for joining me." His handshake is dry and firm. His smile as white as the tablecloth. He holds on to my hand for a beat longer than I expect, trapping me in his gaze. "Florence has told me so much about you."

"I thought she might be here."

"She had an errand to run for me."

He pulls out a chair. "I hope you don't mind dining so intimately. I'm not comfortable in crowds."

"I could probably unpack that," I say.

He looks alarmed but then smiles. "Of course, you're a psychologist. I shall have to watch myself. Red or white?"

"White," I say.

He fills a glass, tilting it up against the light before handing it to me.

"How did you know I was a psychologist?" I ask.

"I always find it useful to know who I'm meeting."

"I'm the same," I say. "You're not as famous as your brother."

He laughs. "Or as newsworthy."

He takes a seat, crossing his legs, one hand in his lap and the other holding the stem of his wineglass. He has an interesting face, remarkable for its blandness. No features stand out. I wonder how a caricaturist would draw him because there is nothing obvious to exaggerate or distort. There is too much symmetry.

"I want to thank you for your bravery and the assistance you've given to Florence and the young boy who survived the crossing. How is he?"

"Traumatized but talking."

"What is going to happen to him?"

"He'll go into foster care until they establish if he has any living relatives."

"I wish to fund his asylum application."

"It might be better if he went home."

"He was looking for a new one."

There is a moment where the silence settles over us.

Simon begins speaking first. "What does he need? I can provide him with clothes, accommodation, a phone, an education?"

"He is fine for the moment," I say. "Can I ask you why you want to help him?"

"Despite appearances, Cyrus, I am not a pessimist. I have not lost all faith in the human condition. I also realize that not everybody is fortunate enough to be born into a country as rich and prosperous as this one. I am also aware that often in this nation's history we have taken advantage of other countries or peoples, taking more than we gave back."

"Albania was not part of the British Empire."

"I'm aware of that."

Suddenly, it dawns on me. "Buchan isn't your original family name."

"My grandfather, Josef Paumer, fled from Czechoslovakia in 1938 when the Nazis annexed Sudetenland and more than two hundred thousand people, Czechs and Jews and anti-fascists, escaped because they knew what was coming. My grandfather was sixteen. He hijacked cars, drugged guards, broke into houses, and walked for twenty-eight days, through Austria, into Italy, crossing the Alps in the depths of winter."

"Why isn't that a story I've read?"

"My father downplayed our history. He thought our grandfather was a traitor, who should have stayed and fought the fascists rather than running away."

"Why change your name?"

"My grandfather married into the Buchan family and took the name of his wife. Lucy was shunned by her parents for marrying a penniless foreigner, but she punished them by keeping her family name. Eventually, her parents begged for forgiveness."

"Your grandfather won them over."

"No. He bought them out." Simon laughs and takes a sip of wine, swirling it around in his mouth. "Death duties were forcing the Buchan family to sell their ancestral home in Scotland. By then their unsuitable son-in-law, my grandfather, had become a wealthy man. He bought the house and kept it in the family."

"A grand gesture."

"The ultimate 'fuck you.'"

"Is he still alive?"

"No."

"You and your brother are very different."

A wry smile. "David calls me the biggest people smuggler in Europe. He says I facilitate the crossings and put lives at risk. I disagree, of course, but he is entitled to his opinions."

"Even if they're racist?"

"My brother isn't a racist. He would have been mortified by the loss of those migrant lives."

"Have you ever heard of someone called the Ferryman?"

Puzzlement. "No, who is he?"

"That depends on who you ask."

We're interrupted by two waiters, carrying plates.

"I took the liberty of ordering the degustation menu," says Buchan. "I hope you don't mind."

The food is beautifully presented and matched with different wines. We eat and talk about the state of the world—energy prices, the war in Ukraine, global warming, and the rise of China. Simon Buchan is easy company, well-read and well-traveled.

"I've always imagined that philanthropy must be the perfect job," I say. "Giving away money. Helping the needy."

"There are ups and downs."

"Downs?"

"The more I spend, the more I realize how little I'm achieving. A soup kitchen can feed the hungry, a church hall can shelter the homeless, a nonprofit can teach adults to read, but without changes in public policy, problems like hunger, homelessness, and illiteracy will continue to exist. That's why I sometimes question whether philanthropy changes anything, or whether it perpetuates the status quo: the historic power imbalance that keeps the disadvantaged in their place."

"You're helping people."

"At what cost? Some argue that philanthropy is an exercise in power. It doesn't deserve gratitude; it deserves scrutiny."

"What sort of scrutiny?"

"Every dollar spent on a museum or a gallery or a theater or a dogs' home is a dollar that could have helped cure malaria or river blindness or cancer. Who decides what is effective altruism? You? Me?"

He looks at the table. "According to the World Food Programme, ten pounds could feed a hungry child in Africa for one month. For the price of this meal, lovely as it is, we could have fed a village."

"Now I feel guilty."

A wry smile. "I shall feed a village tomorrow."

21

Evie

I drift towards sleep with toothpaste on my breath, dreaming of being a child again. Eight years old. Desperate to grow up. Agnesa was in high school and wore a different uniform. Still rebellious. Still stealing Mama's makeup and rolling her school tunic higher, showing off her legs. She wanted to dye her hair black and get bangs like the woman in *Pulp Fiction* and to knot her blouse like Britney Spears when she sang "Baby One More Time."

Mama said Agnesa was suffering from the "Western disease"—which had something to do with boys and looking in the mirror and obsessing about how much she weighed. I think she caught that disease from Aunt Polina.

Papa said Agnesa was growing up too quickly. I asked him how that was possible and he said that sometimes our bodies grow quicker than our brains.

"Do they catch up?" I asked.

"Eventually," he said.

I wanted to be part of Agnesa's secret world of gossip and boy talk and clothes, but every time I thought I was catching up to her she would outgrow me again. I remained "the pest," a tiresome younger sister, who eavesdropped on her conversations and needed babysitting and asked her stupid questions.

Mama and Papa were constantly warning us about girls who went missing in Albania. Everybody knew somebody who had gone. Some had been lured by boyfriends, who showered them with gifts and promises. Others were snatched from outside school gates or from bus stops or from the street.

A girl called Kira, who came from a neighboring village and went to

Agnesa's school, was taken off the street by three men, one of them her uncle. "Come to Italy," they said, "or we kill your little brother."

They took Kira across the Adriatic in a speedboat and north to Milan, where she was beaten and raped, before being sold to a brothel. Two years later, she escaped and went to the police, but they didn't believe that she'd been abducted. They said that she'd chosen to come to Italy and work as a prostitute.

Kira was sent home to Albania. By then her mother had died of a broken heart and her father was a drunk. Two months later, her younger brother was found frozen to death on a mountainside. The police said he'd become lost in a snowstorm. We knew the truth.

These were stories that our parents told us. Modern-day folk tales. Instead of children getting lost in the woods or being lured into gingerbread houses or eaten by wolves, they were kidnapped by criminal gangs and taken on boat trips to hell. English folk tales begin with "once upon a time." In Albania they begin, "This will happen soon."

Mama and Papa wouldn't allow Agnesa to catch the bus by herself or to walk home alone. She pushed back, defying them. She was fifteen. Single-minded. Stubborn. She read magazines like *American Girl* and *Seventeen* and said she was "liberated," which meant she could decide her future. She would go to university and become a lawyer and get a job in London or New York. Papa called her a dreamer. Mama said she was a fantasist. I wanted to be just like her.

The first of June every year was Children's Day. We were given new clothes and new shoes and were allowed to visit the funfair that set up rides on the playing fields of the high school. The school choir sang from the back of Mr. Berisha's truck and the town's brass band played patriotic songs. Papa played the tuba, which Agnesa said sounded like a "hippo farting underwater."

I hung out with Mina until she had to go home after she ate a dozen tulumbas and vomited on the super slide. Papa told Agnesa to look after me and I was to look after Agnesa. Only one of us liked that idea.

At dusk, the lights came on, blinking like stars from the branches of the trees. There was music and dancing. Agnesa bought me bread stuffed with cheese and told me to wait for her near the drinking fountains. Boys had been flirting with her all afternoon, offering her cigarettes and soft drinks and compliments. She kept borrowing breath mints from me and telling me to keep watch in case somebody caught her.

I saw her talking to Erjon, the bully. He was a man now, eighteen, working for his father. He drove around in a BMW and had let his hair grow long, so it touched the shoulders of his dark leather jacket, and he had a thick gold bracelet on his wrist and a matching gold necklace.

Erjon told Agnesa he had something to show her. It was in one of the classrooms, which were supposed to be locked up for the public holiday. They disappeared. I waited. The air smelled of sugar and cooking meat and wood smoke. Some of the men were singing. A fight broke out. I grew cold. I wanted to go home.

I went looking for Agnesa. A fire door was propped open. The corridor was empty. The coat hooks were naked. I heard her voice, telling someone to stop and that it hurt. She was bent over a desk in a classroom with her dress rucked up above her waist and her knickers hooked around one ankle. Erjon was between her legs, moving his hips, pushing the desk across the floor, making a scraping sound that was no less wretched than the noise coming from Agnesa.

I threw myself at Erjon, punching his back, telling him to get off her. He swung his arm and knocked me backwards. I was sitting on the floor with my ears ringing and eyes watering. I launched myself at him again. Erjon raised his fist. Agnesa begged him not to hurt me.

"Tell her to leave," he said.

"Go," she said. "Please."

I ran out of the classroom and down the hall and out the fire door. I wanted to find Papa, but he had already gone home and most of the men were drunk and the women were dancing in a circle around a newly engaged couple.

I waited near the drinking fountains. When Agnesa came out of the school she was crouched over, holding her stomach. Her lipstick was smudged and clownlike. Sad not funny. Her hair was a mess. Her dress was torn. When she moved her hands to wipe her eyes, I saw blood.

We walked home in the dark. The sky was vast and empty and a red blinking light showed the path of a plane flying above the mountains. Agnesa stopped at a tap and washed her face. Then she ran her wrist along the sharp spikes of a barbed wire fence until blood appeared. She cut deeper, until it flowed freely, smearing it on her dress.

"What's wrong?" I asked.

"I'm an idiot."

"Why?"

She turned around and slapped me hard across the face.

"Ow! What was that for?"

"For being you."

"That's not fair."

"Nothing ever is."

When we arrived home the sound of the TV droned from the front room. Agnesa slipped along the hallway and into the bathroom. I heard the water running into the bath.

Later, she came and lay next to me in bed, shiny and pink and clean. "I'm sorry I hit you," she whispered, wrapping her arms around me.

"What did he do to you?"

"Nothing. You can't tell Mama or Papa."

She turned her body away from me, but I felt the bed shaking.

22

Cyrus

I knock on Evie's door. "Are you awake?"

"No."

"You have a phone call from Dr. Bennett at the hospital."

"I'll call her back," says Evie, half-asleep.

"It sounds urgent."

I open the door. Evie's room is darker than a cave. Poppy raises her head and thumps her tail against the mattress. She's supposed to be sleeping downstairs in the laundry, but that house rule didn't last long. I put the phone on speaker and hold it out of Evie's reach.

"She's listening," I say.

"Hello, Evie," says Dr. Bennett. "I've been trying to contact you. Did you get my messages?"

"No," says Evie.

"I have your MRI results. Can you come and see me?"

"I'm busy."

"No, you're not," I say. Evie tries to snatch the phone from my fingers. I keep it out of reach. "We can come today."

"I'll put you down for eleven o'clock," says Dr. Bennett.

"We'll be there. Thank you for calling."

Evie glares at me and rolls away, facing the wall.

"Have you been avoiding her?" I ask.

"No."

"Well, get dressed. We leave in half an hour."

"I can drive myself."

"I want to be there."

"Why? It's none of your business."

"I care about you."

"No. You like sticking your nose into my life. You're not my father or my guardian or my big brother. What am I to you?"

"My friend."

Her eyes narrow. She knows I'm telling the truth and that annoys her because she wants us to be more than friends and housemates and coparents to Poppy. I suspect I know the reason. Evie has survived so much abuse in her life that she could be forgiven for never trusting another human being, let alone a man. Then I came along and listened to her. I read between her lines and didn't judge or pity her or make her feel broken. The opposite happened. I made her feel normal and unsullied and stronger. But sometimes survivors mistake empathy and listening for something deeper and more romantic. In psychology we called it erotic transference. Evie argues that she's not my patient so it shouldn't matter. But it does, of course. And it's never going to happen. I can only love her as a friend.

We drive in silence through countryside that is dotted with pretty farmhouses and ugly barns and golden wheels of hay. Heat shimmers off the road, creating darker pools that look like puddles of water. Holiday traffic is backed up at roadworks and exits—tourist coaches with bug-splattered windscreens and jug-eared mirrors; caravans and camper vans and family wagons loaded with beach gear and children.

Evie opens a window and tilts her face into the rushing air. I notice her hands. She has picked off her nail polish and bitten her cuticles raw. A bad sign. She turns on the radio and flicks between stations, looking for a song that suits her mood, which is sour. Finally, she connects her phone and plays techno, loudly, because she knows it annoys me.

At the hospital, we wait in a patient lounge decorated with posters of healthy, attractive people doing active things because they've been vaccinated or taken the proper vitamins or eaten five servings of vegetables a day.

"It's probably nothing," I say.

"If it were nothing, we wouldn't be doing this," says Evie, who is playing on her phone.

She's right. I stop talking.

Evie's name is called. We're ushered inside an office with a desk, three chairs, two filing cabinets, and the bust of a small plastic brain that can be taken apart like a three-dimensional jigsaw. The desk also has a silver-framed photograph of two children, a boy and a girl in their early teens.

Dr. Bennett brushes hair behind her ears and rests her hands on her desk. "Thank you for coming, Evie," she says brightly. "And you, Dr. Haven," pronouncing my name with a degree of professional respect. Under her wrists she has a blue manila folder.

"What's wrong with me?" asks Evie, not interested in small talk.

"You have a small growth in your temporal lobe. It measures about three centimeters across and is a solid mass about the size and shape of a Brazil nut."

"In my brain?" asks Evie, as though wanting clarification.

"Yes," says the doctor.

"A nut?"

"About this big."

Dr. Bennett holds up her hand and makes a circle with her fingers.

"How did it get there?" asks Evie.

"Tumors form when a normal cell develops a mutation and changes its DNA. The mutation tells other cells to grow and divide, forming a tumor."

"And it's growing," says Evie.

"Most likely, yes, but it may be very slow, and it could be benign."

"What does that mean?"

"It could be harmless," I say.

Evie, incredulously: "A tumor can be harmless?"

"Yes," says the neurologist. "But even if it grows slowly, it may eventually press upon your brain and create neurological problems."

"What sort of problems?" I ask.

"Behavioral and emotional changes; impaired judgment, increased inhibitions. It can also cause memory loss or affect your sense of smell or vision."

"Take it out," says Evie.

Dr. Bennett looks at her as though she might have misheard.

Evie repeats the instructions. "I don't want it growing inside me. Take it out!"

"You don't have to decide that now," says Dr. Bennett. "I'd like to run a few more tests. A biopsy is the first thing. Under anesthetic, a surgeon will drill a very small hole into your skull and use a needle to take a sample of the tumor tissue for analysis. We'll learn if it's malignant or benign. You won't have to stay in hospital. You'll be home the same day."

"What's malignant?" asks Evie.

"Aggressive and life-threatening."

"Just take it out."

"You don't have to decide that now."

"I have something growing in my head," she says, as though she's explaining this to Dr. Bennett. "If you're going to drill a hole, just cut the damn thing out, or zap it with radiation."

"That's not how it works," I say. "We should think about this."

"There is no *we*," Evie snaps. "My head. My tumor. My decision."

I turn to Dr. Bennett. "What are the dangers of surgery?"

She steeples her fingers. "Well, we can't remove all risk. The temporal lobe controls personality and intellect. Some patients experience changes to their personality or their moods after surgery."

"I want it gone," says Evie.

"It could change who you are," I say.

"I don't *like* who I am."

"Yes, but I do."

We both realize that our voices are raised. I apologize to Dr. Bennett.

"It's my decision," Evie reiterates.

"Of course," says the doctor. "That's all ahead of you. We'll talk next week."

Evie studies her face, as though looking for the lie but is unable to find one.

Nobody speaks on the walk back to the car. Instead of silence, I hear a deafening static that fills my head with white noise. I have the sharpest almost visceral sense that Evie is going to die and I won't be able to save her. Not this time. She will disappear piece by piece, in a series of doctor's appointments, scans, lab reports, operations, anxieties, tiny struggles, small victories, gloomy setbacks, reprieves, and failures.

My lips unglue, peeling apart and leaving a sticky white residue. "Are you hungry?" I ask.

"No."

"Thirsty?"

She shakes her head.

"I could murder an iced coffee," I say.

We drive to a Starbucks on the outskirts of town. Evie follows me across the car park, walking slowly in the murmuring heat. A blast of frigid air washes over us as the door opens. We queue. Evie chooses a green-colored juice from the cold cabinet and takes a table in the corner. She stirs her drink with the straw and toys with her phone. A millennial silence.

"We could get a second opinion," I say.

"No."

"There might be other tests."

"They will tell us the same thing."

The gold flecks in her eyes seem to swim, or maybe they're floating in mine. I want to put my arms around her. I want to tell her I'm sorry and that I would change things if I could, but they're just words and everybody says them, and they mean fuck all. Up until now, Evie and I have had a cozy system worked out—sharing a house and a dog. There have been laughs and irritations and sometimes, just occasionally, the past has reached out to drag us back to less certain times, but fundamentally we have been good for each other.

Yes, she's damaged and self-destructive and a pathological liar, but she is also funny and feisty and intelligent and empathetic. I don't want her to change. Let someone else have a tumor. Someone cruel or abusive or ancient, or who's sick of living. Someone who deserves a shitty diagnosis. This isn't fair. Why should we just accept the world as it is? Sometimes we have to scream from a rooftop and foam at the mouth and say, "Fuck you, fuckers! You fucking fuckwits."

My phone is ringing. I ignore it. Almost immediately, it rings again. I look at the screen. Carlson's name.

I answer.

"A barge driver spotted a trawler being towed by a runabout on the east side of the Humber Bridge."

"I'm busy right now," I say, glancing at Evie.

"Yeah, so am I. No excuses."

23

Cyrus

Two dozen detectives and uniformed officers are gathered in the foyer of Birchin Way Custody Facility. Some I recognize from the incident room or on the beach at Cleethorpes.

Carlson emerges from the stairwell, shrugging on his jacket.

He spies Evie. "What's she doing here?"

"She was with me."

"Leave her here."

"No."

He thinks about arguing but changes his mind. "She's your responsibility."

I could have sent Evie home in my Fiat, but I don't want her being alone—not today, not after her diagnosis. And I'm not sure if she should be driving or if she has fully processed the news. I want to be nearby when the reality hits her.

Carlson quickly briefs the waiting officers before two vans and four unmarked police cars set off in convoy, pulling through the electric gates and heading west along the A180. Fifteen minutes later, we cross Humber Bridge and turn east along the northern bank of the permanently brown estuary, which marks the southern boundary of Yorkshire.

Evie and I are in the back seat of a car being driven by a uniformed constable, who keeps sneaking glances in the mirror, wondering what Evie is doing on a police operation. Carlson is on the phone, issuing instructions and receiving intel from the incident room. Whenever a piece of information annoys him, he drops the f-bomb, and the driver glances at Evie as though wanting to cover her ears.

The main road turns back on itself and uses an underpass to reach the historic docks, some of which have been demolished and built upon, creating retail parks and factory outlets. Other sections are abandoned and overgrown, waiting to be repurposed.

A small container ship is propped within a dry dock, which is separated from the estuary by large metal gates that are sealed. Water has been pumped out, and large wooden beams are braced against the sides of the vessel to stop it tipping over. Beyond that, past a rusting fence, railway tracks appear and disappear beneath mounds of rubble and waste.

We pass through an unmanned security gate, marked by rusting drums and a makeshift boom gate. The cars and minibuses pull up. Officers pile out and disperse across the docks. There must be more than thirty buildings, most of them abandoned or derelict. Bolt cutters and battering rams are needed to enter some of them.

Evie and I wait with the vehicles. The radio squawks as information passes between the teams. It's hot and I look around for some shade. A nearby building has an awning. As we get nearer, a security guard appears from around the corner, hitching his belt. Puffing. Overweight. Annoyed.

"You're trespassing," he says belligerently. "This place is off-limits."

"We're with the police," I say.

"I don't care. You need a warrant."

I motion to his unzipped fly. He zips it up, embarrassed but still protesting.

"We're looking for a trawler with a damaged prop shaft," I say.

"No fishing boats here. You got the wrong place."

Evie takes an interest. "You haven't seen a trawler?"

"No."

"You're lying. Is it that way?" She points.

"You're talking out of yer arse."

"What about that way?"

"Are you deaf? There is no trawler."

Evie looks at me. "It's that way."

"Never play poker with her," I tell the guard. "You'll always lose."

The police teams have disappeared, searching the different buildings. I call Carlson's number. It's busy.

"Let's take a look," says Evie.

"We should stay here."

"Come on. The cops are close by."

We set off, ignoring the complaints of the guard.

"He won't be here when we get back," she says.

"Probably not."

Railway lines crisscross the broken concrete docks and stop abruptly at an old slipway that has silted up and become a wasteland of weeds and thistles. Beyond that, there are acres of industrial decay, crumbling walls, rusting machinery, and mounds of rubble. We pass a gutted factory, five stories high, with every window shattered or boarded up. Beneath the graffiti is a faded sign for a long defunct trawler company. The brown water of Humber Estuary ripples in the wind. Dredgers and tugboats are at work, as well as a freighter floating so low on the water that it might be stuck on the bottom.

We reach the edge of the St. Andrew's Dock gate. Rusting. Defunct. I look down. A trawler is moored twenty feet below us. Inflatable buffers protect it from being smashed against the gates. A rope ladder hangs down the nearest stone wall.

Carlson answers his phone.

"It's here," I say. "Below the gates."

The message is relayed.

At that moment, a man emerges onto the deck, a phone in hand. Bearded and dressed in dark overalls, he glances up and notices me. He yells to someone below and a second man appears. Immediately, they run. The first man tosses his mobile phone into the water and jumps over the railing into a dinghy with an outboard. He presses the ignition and unhooks the tether rope, steering away from the trawler.

The second man jumps for the rope ladder and scrambles up, hand over hand, scaling it easily. He's heading for a car, a Land Rover parked beside the old engineering shop.

I begin to move. Evie grabs my arm trying to stop me. I pull loose and run across the metal gates between the water and the silted-up dock. The safety railings are rusted and the gates groan under my feet.

The man in the dinghy has reached open water, but a police launch appears at speed, dual engines churning. A voice cuts through the air, telling him to stop.

His mate gets to the Land Rover and jumps behind the wheel, searching for the ignition. I grab at his wrist. The keys slip from his fingers into the footwell. We both reach for them. He swings his elbow at my head but hits the door frame. Cursing.

I have the keys and fling them behind me. He's out of the car and we're grappling, rolling on the ground. He grabs my hair and drives his fist into my stomach. I double over and drop to my knees, sucking for air.

His hand reaches into his jacket. As if by magic, he's holding a black polished rod. A steel blade snaps from the handle. He twirls the knife over his knuckles like a juggler. He's in his late thirties with dark curly hair and a large scar running down the side of his neck and across his cheeks where the skin bubbles and puckers like melted plastic.

"Gimme the keys," he says in a Scottish accent.

I crab walk backwards, my arse dragging in the dirt.

"You can't get away," I say.

"Gimme the fookin' keys."

They're lying ten feet away. I pick them up. He motions with his free hand, wanting me to toss them. I do just that. High over his head. His eyes follow them as they arc, out of reach, and hit the water with a satisfying *plunk*, twenty feet below him.

"I'm gonnae gut you like a fish," he says, pointing the knife and crouching in an attacking pose.

I back away. He moves with me, smoothly, gracefully, and the blade sweeps through the air. Misses. He grins. I hear Evie yelling and officers shouting. I feint one way and go the other, skipping past the knife, but I feel it brush against my clothes.

"You missed," I say.

"If you say so."

I look down. My shirt is flapping open. The knife sliced it vertically along the line of the buttons but didn't cut my skin. "Next time ah'll draw blood," he says. "And the third time, I'll open an artery and watch you bleed out. You'll nae feel a thing."

To an outsider, it must look like a strange dance, full of lunges and parries and twirls. I dodge him again, but he's moving just as quickly, keeping me pinned down with the water behind me, blocking my escape. What would I break if I jumped?

Again, I feel the blade whisper over my clothes. My shirtsleeve has been opened up and a thin red line oozes blood along my forearm.

"That's the second warning," he says. "Where is yer car?"

"The other side of the gates."

"Gimme the keys."

I reach inside my trouser pocket and hold them up.

"Dinnae be a dickhead this time," he says.

I toss the keys at his feet and immediately turn, hoping to reach the gates before he does.

I hear Carlson's voice. "Put it down."

The detective is fifteen feet away, holding a Taser. The attacker twirls the knife across his knuckles and turns to face him.

Bang!

Two wires snake across the space and the metal probes cling to the trawlerman's shirt. Fifty thousand volts of electricity enter his body with a crackling sound. He goes rigid and drops to the ground, raising a puff of dust.

"Don't touch him," says Carlson.

Other officers wait until the electrical surge has dissipated before holding him down, one sitting on his legs and the other on his back. Pulling his arms behind him. Snapping on handcuffs. Reading him his rights. On the water, the second man is being pulled onto the police launch.

Evie is still standing on the far side of the dock gates. I raise my hand, letting her know that I'm OK, but she doesn't respond. She walks across the silted-up slipway and joins me.

"You're an idiot," she says, examining the cut on my right arm. She rips at the torn shirtsleeve, creating a bandage, which she wraps around my forearm, tying the knot angrily, ignoring my pain. I look for my car keys. Evie has picked them up.

The two suspects are being escorted to waiting police cars. Carlson joins me at the water's edge. "Does that need stitches?" he asks, pointing to my arm.

"No."

"Well, I'm not paying for a new shirt."

Below us, the trawler is moving up and down on the swell. The police launch has pulled alongside and is being held against the current by the engines.

Carlson tosses me a pair of latex gloves. "Let's take a look before SOCO arrives."

We're both wondering the same thing—could the missing migrant women be on board? The detective is first down the ladder. I follow. Flecks of rusting metal stick to my gloves and the boat sways under my weight as I step on board. I haven't spent much time around boats unless you count a ferry trip to Ireland to watch a rugby match at Lansdowne Road. I threw up most of the voyage to Dublin and was too drunk to remember the journey home.

The trawler is a squat-looking vessel with a square wheelhouse. Water slaps against the hull as I step around the anchor winch and edge along the starboard side. I've seen TV shows about trawlermen in the North Sea; fly-on-the-wall documentaries that describe it as "the most dangerous job in the world," being battered by huge waves, surviving the cold, and chasing fewer and fewer fish. The breathless narration makes every voyage look like a cross between *Survivor* and *Moby-Dick*.

I've reached the wheelhouse. The doors are open. The galley is down a set of five steps. I follow Carlson into a boxlike room with benches, a table, and a cooktop with swinging potholders. Dirty dishes fill a sink. Metal mugs. Cold tea bags. A saucepan with congealed baked beans.

We move forward to the cabins, which are lower again. The bunk rooms have thin mattresses and thinner blankets. Carlson nods towards the smaller of the two. A self-locking plastic cable tie is coiled beside the pillow. A second cable tie is lying on the floor between the bunks, curled up like a dead centipede. The bedding is disturbed. Damp. The missing women were here.

Carlson takes photographs with his phone. The engine room is through a bulkhead door. It smells of diesel and oil and rustproofing. The main hold is farther forward, beneath a waterproof hatch. Nylon mesh fishing nets are draped from hooks like enormous string shopping bags. A dull orange life vest is discarded on the floor. It's similar to the ones I saw on some of the bodies washed up on Cleethorpes Beach. More photographs are taken. Carlson signals and we retrace our steps.

Back on the deck, I skirt the side of the wheelhouse and cross the foredeck. At the bow, I peer over the railing, looking for evidence of a collision. The angle is wrong, and any damage is probably below the waterline.

A name is visible. *New Victory.* Some of the letters are obscured by a plastic bin bag that has been crudely taped over that section of the hull.

Carlson has joined me. "Sixty feet. Twin rig. Steel hull. Built in 2005 in Macduff, Scotland. She was christened the *Catelina*, but had her name changed four years ago."

"*Victory* was Lord Nelson's flagship at the Battle of Trafalgar," I say. "It established British naval supremacy for more than a hundred years."

"Is that important?"

"Far-right groups like banging on about past glories of the British Empire."

"We don't know if this is a racist attack," he says, sounding hopeful rather than confident.

Evie has been waiting for me on the far side of the dock gates. She is sitting on a broken block of concrete, arms wrapped around her chest, rocking slightly, scuffing her shoes in the dirt. To reach the cars, we have to pass near the arrested men. She suddenly stops and stares at one of them. The man with the scarred neck is sitting in the back seat of an unmarked police car.

"What's wrong?" I ask.

Evie isn't listening. Her eyes have glazed over, and she stares into the distance, at some point on the horizon, seen or unseen. Taking a step, she seems to lose her balance. I catch her before she falls. Putting my arm around her waist. She sinks against me.

"What is it?"

Her face turns to mine.

"I know him."

24

Evie

Some memories are like old photographs in dusty frames, that are fading but forever preserved, while others are like shards of broken glass. If you hold them too tightly they can cut you over and over again. This one is sudden and savage and steals my breath. I know this man. I've seen him before.

Cyrus has pulled me away from the others. He whispers, "You recognize him?"

I nod.

"From where?"

"I don't know."

"Is he one of the men who . . . one of the . . ."

"No." I answer too quickly.

Cyrus stops himself. He wants to know if this man abused me. If he's one of the many who passed me around like a birthday parcel, each unwrapping another layer, until they found their prize.

"You're sure?" he asks.

"Yes."

I would remember him if he was one of them. Most were older, richer, uglier. Maybe he worked at one of their houses—as a driver or a guard or a gardener or a tradesman. He could have been one of the men who searched for me—who ripped up carpets and floorboards and knocked holes in walls, while I hid in my secret room, as quiet as a mouse.

At Langford Hall they kept trying to place me in foster homes, but each family sent me back because I was damaged goods or was just plain "creepy." I remember the fathers; none of them had a face like his. Most of them were do-gooders or churchgoers or looking to make the world a better place for children.

Where else could I have met him? He wasn't a teacher or a therapist or a childcare worker. And it wasn't some random fleeting encounter like a charity door-knock or an Uber Eats delivery or someone in a supermarket queue. I know him.

A voice yells from across the dock. A detective waves and jogs towards us.

"Did you pick up the knife?" he asks.

Cyrus answers, "It was lying on the ground."

"It's not there—and we searched him again."

"Maybe he kicked it into the water."

The detective mutters something and turns away. I reach into the pocket of my jacket and feel the smooth black handle with my fingertips. I should tell Cyrus that I picked it up. I should apologize and plead ignorance. Better to be in trouble now than later, Papa used to say, but I have a secret now. A weapon. I am not defenseless.

"Let's go home," says Cyrus, wanting to get me away from this place.

The knife is warm from my body, but still feels cold to the touch. Papa worked with knives. He died when one of them cut his neck. Turning suddenly, I stride towards the police cars. Cyrus jogs to catch up to me.

"You can't talk to him," he says.

Moments later, I'm standing beside the open door. The man has his eyes closed and his head back, mouth open, tongue showing, pink and slug-like. His hands and feet are shackled.

"Do you know me?" I ask.

His eyes open slowly. He blinks and rolls his head from side to side. The scar on his neck moves as he swallows.

"We should go," says Cyrus, touching my shoulder.

I shrug his hand away.

"Have we met?" I ask, making it sound like a demand.

The man grins at me with crooked teeth. "Nae, lass, but I'm up for it if you are."

He nods towards the crotch of his soiled jeans. "We could do it here."

My breath catches and my fingers close tighter around the knife. I want to kill him, but I don't know why. I turn and let Cyrus lead me away.

25

Cyrus

A one-way mirror reveals the interview suite. Two detectives are seated opposite the suspect with the burns on his face and neck. He has a name now, Angus Radford, aged thirty-eight, a divorced father of two, from St. Claire in Scotland.

"When did he lawyer up?" I ask.

"First thing," says Carlson.

His solicitor is dressed in a charcoal-grey suit, with trousers that ride up his shin whenever he crosses his legs. Each time he doesn't want his client answering a question, he taps on the table with his ring finger, as though sending him a signal in Morse code.

Mostly Radford has answered "no comment" to every question. He seems to enjoy watching the frustration on the detectives' faces, but they know this game. Patience is the key. Building pressure. Brick by brick. Fact by fact.

"What do we know about him?" I ask.

Carlson rattles off the details. "No priors apart from a drunk-driving conviction and unpaid speeding tickets. He was arrested in 2018 during a right-wing protest in Trafalgar Square. He threw a traffic cone at police during the riot, which was triggered by the jailing of Tommy Robinson, the former English Defence League leader."

I remember the protest. Demonstrators took over a tourist bus and threw smoke bombs at police after Tommy Robinson was jailed for contempt of court. The English Defence League believed that Britain was under attack from Muslim extremists and that pedophiles were being allowed out of prison without supervision.

"What about the other guy?"

"Kenna Downing. Twenty-six. Says he's still living at home with his parents in Truro, Cornwall. He was interviewed over the firebombing of a migrant hostel in Bristol eight years ago. Wasn't charged."

Carlson waits for me to say something. My silence seems to irritate him.

"I don't want to automatically make this about race," he says.

"Other people will."

I understand his dilemma. Whichever way he jumps, certain groups will accuse him of being part of an institutionally racist police force that fails to investigate racially motivated attacks, or of bowing to woke pressure and scapegoating right-wing activists.

"Is Downing talking?" I ask.

"Up to a point," says Carlson. "He says they were taking the trawler from Southampton to Scotland after an engine refit. He claims to know nothing about a collision or seeing any migrant boat or picking up any survivors. We have a warrant to track their phones and retrieved one from the mud near the trawler. The boffins have it now."

"What about forensics?"

"Fingerprints and DNA. We're going to compare the sample with Arben Pasha's DNA and see if his sister was on board."

"What do you know about the trawler?" I ask.

"It operates out of St. Claire in Scotland. The owner is a company registered in the Cayman Islands, with a post office box as an address."

"I thought companies were obliged to nominate their beneficial owners?"

"Within twenty-one days, but this paperwork was never lodged."

"Someone could be trying to hide."

"Or it could be an oversight. The NCA are looking into it."

I glance through the window at Angus Radford, who leans back in his chair, knees spread, fingers idly scratching at his neck.

"What happened to his face?" I ask.

"A fire. He won't say any more."

"Can I talk to him?"

"I don't need a psych report."

"Evie thinks she knows him."

"From where?"

"She can't remember." I pause, unsure of how much I should reveal. "She was trafficked as a child."

"And you think Radford was involved?"

"I have no idea, but there is definitely some link between them. And we still have two missing migrant women."

The detective mulls this over. "His solicitor would have to give you permission."

"It wouldn't be an official interview. No cameras. No tapes. Anything Radford told me wouldn't be admissible as evidence."

On the far side of the glass, the detectives have turned off the recording equipment and left the room. Radford has a final word with his solicitor. The two men laugh and shake hands like they're arranging a card game for Saturday night.

Twenty minutes later, I surrender my belt, mobile phone, and wallet to the charge room sergeant. I follow a constable along an echoing corridor, painted in calming colors. He knocks against a metal door, calling out, "Against the wall."

"What now?" mutters Radford.

The door opens. He is standing with his legs apart and hands braced against the painted bricks. He's done this before.

"Who are you?" he asks. "You're not allowed to talk to me—not without mah advocate."

"I'm not a police officer. I'm a psychologist."

"Ah dinnae need a shrink."

"I'm not interested in what happened last weekend."

Radford sneers and returns to his bunk, where he lies on his back with a forearm covering his eyes. The skin on his neck is discolored and puckered and the dark stubble on his cheeks doesn't grow where his skin has been burned and lost pigmentation.

"How did it happen?" I ask, motioning to his face.

"A fire."

"How old were you?"

"Auld enough to know better."

"You're a fisherman."

"Fourth generation. My father. His father. His father before him."

"Tough work."

He raises his calloused hands, sitting up to face me. Greasy curls have left a dusting of dandruff on his shoulders and his eyes are a washed-out blue, set too far apart on his face.

"Have you always been a fisherman?" I ask.

"Since I was fifteen."

"No other jobs."

"Why?"

"No reason."

He screws up his face. "You were with that wee girl."

"Did you recognize her?"

"What is this?" he asks, growing annoyed. "Did she say I touched her? She's lying."

"Nobody said you touched her. What happened to the two young women? They were in the water. You picked them up."

"No comment."

"If you helped us find them, it could make things easier for you."

He laughs. "Are you offering me a deal?"

"I'm not in a position to do that."

"Thought so. Piss off!"

I notice a book lying open on the bed. The title visible. *Wealth of Nations* by Adam Smith. "Heavy reading."

Radford sneers. "You think I'm some dumb jock who reeks of fish."

"Not at all. I had you pegged as a socialist. Adam Smith is the poster boy of the free market."

"Ah'm a pragmatist."

"But are you a racist?"

His eyes narrow. "You have no idea what I believe."

"That's true. Can I call you Angus?"

"Do what yer like."

"Adam Smith drew a contrast between savage nations and civilized nations. He said that some countries were so miserably poor that they abandoned babies and old people and sick people. He said civilized nations were industrious and frugal and deserved their wealth, while savage nations would never enjoy the conveniences of life."

"People aren't born equal," says Radford. "We should look after our own."

"Is that why you sank the migrant boat?"

He glances at the camera above our heads. "Nice try. You can leave now."

"I'm trying to work out if you hate migrants or you hate yourself or if you were just going about your business," I say. "Whatever the reason, it's a low act, running down defenseless people who were seeking refuge. Some would say cowardly."

Anger lights up his face. He leaps to his feet with clenched fists. I'm ready for the punch, but he stops himself and flexes his hand, open and closed, before returning to the bunk and opening his book at a dog-eared page.

I bang on the door, summoning the guard. The lock echoes as it disengages.

Radford clears his throat.

"Tell yer friend I'm sorry. I was rude to her. She dinnae deserve that."

26

Evie

It rained for a week after Children's Day. It was like a fine mist that hung like smoke over the mountains, making everything feel damp and smell musty. The sun didn't emerge until late in the day or made no appearance at all.

I told Mama and Papa what had happened to Agnesa. I couldn't keep a secret—not back then—and I wanted to punish the person who had hurt her. I was wrong. I should have kept my promise.

Our lives changed. Mama and Papa spoke in whispers and argued in shouts. Erjon was eighteen. Agnesa underage. That made it illegal, Papa said. He wanted to involve the police, but Mama said, "It will be her word against his. And everybody will believe him because of his father."

Papa's voice rose. "I saw the blood on her dress. I saw the bruises. She was raped."

"She shouldn't have been alone with him."

"It was *not* her fault."

There were complications. Erjon's father was our landlord and he owned the meatworks where Papa worked and the truck that Papa drove. He had our livelihood in his hands. Mama said they should wait and see. That was her solution to most things—waiting and seeing. Whenever I asked for new clothes or a puppy or to be allowed to visit Aunt Polina in Tirana, she told me to "wait and see."

I went to school. I came home again. Agnesa stayed away. She helped Mama around the house and occasionally went to the supermarket, but she didn't make eye contact with people. I remember feeling jealous that she could stay at home, but I was too young to understand.

The summer holidays began. The ordinary sights and sounds of the village returned. Nobody mentioned what happened, but it hummed in the background like an old refrigerator, keeping everything cold and preserved.

It was Mama's birthday. I made her breakfast in bed and went into the garden to pick flowers for the tray. We had an old outside toilet near the vegetable garden, which nobody used anymore because Papa had built a bathroom inside the cottage. It was at the end of a stone path, beside a trellis with grapevines. The door was open and I saw Agnesa kneeling over the bowl, holding back her hair as she vomited. She shouted at me to leave, and I went to get Mama. Later, I heard them talking about Agnesa being late. Late for what? I wondered.

Mama told me to go to Mr. Hasani's workshop because she was taking Agnesa to the doctor in Prrenjas. The following day, Aunt Polina arrived on the bus from Tirana. She had dyed her hair blond and was wearing an off-white dress that made her look like an avenging angel without a flaming sword. Again, I was sent away, this time with an overnight bag and instructions to stay at Mina's house. I walked out the front gate but stopped at the next house and doubled back, climbing on top of the wall beside the cottage. I shimmied along the narrow bricks until I reached the walnut tree outside the kitchen. Papa, Mama, Agnesa, and Aunt Polina were sitting around the table. Polina said she knew someone who could make the baby go away. I wondered how a baby could go anywhere without a mother. Did that mean that Agnesa was pregnant? Would she be going too?

I didn't hear everything that was said because Mama had her back to me and Papa kept pacing the kitchen, refusing to sit down. He said that Agnesa shouldn't have to shoulder the responsibility on her own and that Erjon would "do the right thing."

"I'm not going to marry him," she replied.

"You'll do as you're told," said Mama, threatening to lock her in her room until she learned to be sensible. I couldn't imagine anything worse than having to marry Erjon Berisha. Yes, he had money, but he was cruel and he bullied people. He had hurt Agnesa, and killed Fisnik Sopa, and he once threw a dog off a cliff into a dam. The dog survived, but that's not the point.

Papa went into the bedroom and put on his coat and tie, which he wore only on special occasions. Mama followed. I couldn't hear what they were saying but I saw their shadows behind the curtains. I watched

Papa leave and then tried to climb down from the tree, but it had grown dark, and I'd climbed too high, and I couldn't see the branches below my feet. I was wedged against the trunk, clinging on, as the night pressed around me, chill and damp, full of familiar sounds that became unfamiliar in the darkness.

Finally, I summoned the courage and uncurled my fingers and reached down with my toes, scrabbling for a lower branch. Once I began falling, I couldn't stop. I landed on the edge of the trellis, slicing open my leg just above my right knee. You can still see the scar, but only when I wear short skirts, which I never do. Mr. Hasani drove me to the hospital and Mama let me sit in her lap as the doctor put eight stitches in the wound.

Papa still wasn't at home when we returned from the hospital. He was gone for hours. Much later, lying in bed, I heard him come through the front door and take off his shoes, knocking over a lamp and cursing. He fell asleep on the sofa. In the morning, I heard him climb the stairs to the bathroom and stand over the toilet bowl. Later, I noticed his faint pink handprint on the tiled wall where he'd leaned against it. It looked like blood.

In the kitchen Papa was boiling two eggs for his lunch and putting butter and jam on a slab of bread with a bandaged hand. Normally, he would have swept me into his arms and danced me around the table, one-two-three, one-two-three. A dip. A twirl. An explosion of giggles. Today was different. It felt as though someone had robbed us during the night, but we didn't know what had been stolen. Papa put his lunch in a paper bag and wheeled his bike into the cool of the morning, cycling to work.

This is how I wake now, slipping quietly out of sleep, as though I've spent the night in hiding. Poppy is nudging her head against a bell that hangs from my doorknob, letting me know that she wants to go outside for her "morning constitutional." That's what Cyrus calls it. Why don't people say what they mean?

I go downstairs and unlock the laundry door. Poppy heads outside, sniffing every corner of the garden, seeing if anyone has invaded her territory overnight. Foxes or squirrels or neighborhood cats.

There is an old tabby that lives two doors down, a moth-eaten-looking creature, who torments Poppy by sitting on the fence grooming herself, knowing that she's out of reach. This happens at least ten times a day, working the Labrador into a frenzy of barking that has caused the neighbors to complain. Just once, I want Poppy to learn how to climb and to snap her jaws around the cat's neck. Not to kill her—I'm not a monster—but to scare one of her lives away.

Upstairs, as I'm getting dressed, I catch a glimpse of myself in the mirror. Hair messy. Dark rings around my eyes. I touch my forehead, trying to picture the tumor growing inside, the parasite feeding off me, filling *my* space, pressing on *my* brain. The size of a Brazil nut, Dr. Bennett said. Why do they always compare things to fruit or nuts?

If I leave it alone, it could change me. If I cut it out, it could change me. Would that be such a bad thing? I don't want to know when people are lying. I want to be normal—but not in a boring, beige, color-between-the-lines sort of way. I want to be me without the freaky bits.

Maybe the MRI scan was wrong and the tumor was a shadow or a blob of nothing. I mean, I haven't had headaches, numbness, or dropsy or begun forgetting things. Yes, I had a meltdown on Cleethorpes Pier, but that might have been a one-off.

Dr. Bennett told me to avoid googling, but that was never going to happen. I've been researching brain tumors and how they can affect behavior and emotions. The articles use words like "deficits" and "side effects" and "cognitive changes." If the tumor keeps growing, I might not recognize facial expressions. It could reduce my reliability and foresight and emotional control, or blunt my emotions, or make me more childish or disinhibited.

Then again, if I get the tumor cut out, it could cause deficits and side effects. And if it all goes completely wrong, I could finish up with the IQ of a ramen noodle, drooling into my lap. Will Cyrus look after me? More importantly, will he smother me with a pillow if I make him promise to?

I join him downstairs. He's been for a run and his T-shirt clings to his chest and I can see the outline of his tattoos beneath the white cotton.

"Did you sleep well?" he asks.

"Meh." I put a pod in the coffee machine. It belches and coughs and spits out a brown, creamy liquid. I like the smell of coffee more than the taste.

"Can I get you something for breakfast?" he asks.

"I'm not hungry."

I think about telling Cyrus what happened on my non-date with Liam, but it's too embarrassing. Instead, I ask him about the man with the scar.

"His name is Angus Radford. He comes from Scotland."

"How did he get the scar?"

"Some sort of fire. Have you remembered any more?"

"No."

"I could help you."

"By hypnotizing me?"

"It's called a cognitive interview. You would always have control—and could stop at any time." He pulls his chair closer. "Time perception is difficult for people who suffer abuse, particularly when they're young. The sensory systems that regulate our sense of time get altered and sometimes past events can feel like the present, or the details become blurred, making it hard to pinpoint a year or a month."

"Someone like me?"

"Yes. But if we can access a single event or moment in time, we can work backwards or forwards. It's like painting by numbers, starting at the edges, and filling in the rest."

"What moment?" I ask. "I don't remember where I met him."

"It will come to you."

We sit at the table, saying nothing, until the silence seems to be taking root and sprouting leaves and bearing fruit.

"And I want the surgery," I say, challenging him, spoiling for a fight.

"OK," he says.

"I'm not going to change my mind."

"I know."

Why is he being so agreeable? Is this some form of reverse psychology? God, he can be an arsehole!

"Scrambled eggs," I say.

"Pardon?"

"That's what I want for breakfast."

Without complaint, he takes a pan from the drawer and eggs from the fridge. He talks as he cooks, asking about my plans for the day.

"The dog shelter has a team that rescues strays. I thought I might tag along with them. Help out."

"And you won't bring any animals home?"

I look at Poppy, who is hovering near the stove, begging as usual. "One is enough."

27

Cyrus

In 1954, a psychologist called Julian B. Rotter came up with a concept he described as the "locus of control." He based it upon how much each of us believes we control events in our lives. Someone with a strong internal locus believes they are pretty much masters of their own destiny and that their actions determine outcomes. But a person with a strong external locus of control will look at their success and failure, happiness and sadness, and attribute much of this to luck or chance or a higher power.

I used to think that I fell somewhere in between these two poles, perhaps leaning towards the latter, because every time I felt like I was in control of my destiny, I had the shit kicked out of me. Losing my parents and twin sisters. Elias's schizophrenia. Evie's abusive past. Even the bodies washing up on Cleethorpes Beach were beyond my control.

Now Evie has a brain tumor. I keep saying that I'll support whatever decision she makes, and that's true, but I want to make it for her. I know that's wrong. I have argued with her, but only in my head. I've presented evidence, cross-examined witnesses, and made final submissions, but the jury of one keeps voting for Evie, which isn't surprising, given that she's the sole judge and juror. Her verdict is always the same: "stay out of my life."

When I can't sleep and I'm too tired to run, I go to work. I have rooms at the University of Nottingham, where I lecture part-time and oversee several PhD students, who think they're cleverer than I am. They may be right.

Forensic psychology has become a sexy subject these days because of TV shows about FBI profilers who hunt serial killers and high-functioning psychopaths. The reality of my job is far more mundane.

I assess offenders, prepare psych reports, analyze crime statistics, and counsel the survivors of violent crimes.

My rooms are on the fourth floor, overlooking a boating lake, which is dotted with brightly colored pedalos. By "rooms" I mean a reception area with a sofa and an office with a desk, filing cabinet, shelves, and a coffee machine that doesn't work. Autumn term doesn't begin for another three weeks, but I have future lectures to prepare and submissions to read.

Florence is sitting on the windowsill. I promised her access to Arben Pasha, something I haven't managed to arrange despite my links to the investigation. She has been patient until now, having gone back to London and returned to Nottingham at my request.

"So, why have you brought me here?" she asks.

"I've been thinking about the missing women. Neither has contacted the police or the Home Office or applied for asylum."

"If they survived, they're likely to be sold off," says Florence. "They won't surface unless they manage to escape and seek help."

"From the police?"

"Or a charity or migrant group."

Florence reaches into her shoulder bag and pulls out her notebook with Monet's water lilies on the cover. Unhooking the elastic fastening, she retrieves a newspaper clipping, folded between the pages.

"This was published three days ago."

The headline reads: "UK Minister Admits 200 Asylum-Seeker Children Have Gone Missing."

Florence paraphrases the article. "The children had been placed in hotels and hostels run by the Home Office. Some were abducted off the street and bundled into cars. Others were wooed away by bribes or promises of work, or by lover boys who played Romeo and convinced them to run away. The girls are often forced into prostitution. The boys work illegally in car washes and sweatshop factories or become pickpockets or burglars. Simon Buchan has been lobbying the Home Office to set up a special task force to tackle the problem." She glances at me. "You met him, didn't you?"

"Yes."

"What did you think?"

"He's very impressive. Thoughtful."

"He's putting his wealth to good use."

I look at the article again. "If Arben's sister manages to escape, where would she go?"

"I know someone who works with the survivors of sexual slavery. We could ask her."

The address is in an older part of Nottingham, a once grand old house converted into offices, most leased to law firms and accountants. A disembodied voice answers the intercom. We give our names and hold up ID to the camera. The door unlocks automatically, and we enter a brightly lit foyer with a high ceiling. A woman is sitting behind a desk with a Perspex screen.

"Mrs. Hartley will be with you soon," she says, nodding towards a small waiting room that had once been a hat check or cloakroom. There are brochures on a table and posters on the wall. One of them shows a haunted-looking young woman in a short skirt and high heels, standing on a street corner. *MODERN SLAVERY IS CLOSER THAN YOU THINK*, reads the headline. A second poster features the image of a man huddled in a blanket on a camp stretcher. Two other men are sleeping nearby. It is captioned, *They promised me a good job. They lied. Now I'm trapped.*

A woman reverses into the room, saying good-bye to someone. She's dressed in faded jeans and a short T-shirt that slides up when she hugs Florence, revealing the bulge of her pregnancy.

"Florence, darling, my token black friend," she says, grinning broadly.

"I can't get my arms around you," says Florence.

"Rub it in, why don't you. I feel like a broodmare." She notices me and releases Florence, before shamelessly looking me up and down. "And who do we have here?"

"This is Cyrus Haven," says Florence.

"You're very good-looking. Are you gay?"

"No."

She winks at Florence and offers me a fist bump. "Call me Natalie."

We adjourn to her cluttered office, where files are moved to find enough chairs.

"Sorry about the mess. I've had meetings all morning," says Natalie.

"With clients?" asks Florence.

"No. Donors. Most of this job is fundraising. If it weren't for Simon Buchan, that darling man, we'd have closed down years ago. Give him a hug from me."

"We're not really on hugging terms," says Florence.

"Do it anyway."

Natalie has a notepad beside her elbow that is almost identical to the one Florence carries but has a different cover design: Van Gogh's *Starry Night*.

"Snap," says Florence, holding up her notebook.

"Simon again," says Natalie. "Our office furniture, stationery, computers, printers, even our loo paper—all down to him. I thank him every time I have to pee, which is a lot, I can tell you." She cradles her pregnancy.

The two women swap small talk about due dates and motherhood and someone called Benjamin, who Natalie refers to as "my sperm donor husband."

"He's treating me like the Virgin Mary about to give birth to the baby Jesus or a future England football captain."

"Which would he prefer?" asks Florence.

"Oh, the latter, of course. What man wouldn't?" Natalie winks at me. "So why are you here?"

"We believe two young migrant women crossing from Calais to England in a small boat were picked up by a fishing trawler. Now they're missing," I say.

"How young?"

"Late teens. Early twenties."

"Nationalities?"

"Albanian and Syrian."

"Photographs?"

"No."

"We don't actively investigate missing-person cases," says Natalie. "We wait for the survivors to find us and then try to pick up the pieces."

"Where might they have been taken?" I ask.

"That depends on what the gangs are looking for. Forced labor, domestic servitude, marriage, prostitution, petty crime. Every time you get your car washed for a fiver, or a pedicure for a tenner, you should be asking, why is it so cheap? And why is it cash only? And why do none of the workers seem to speak English? It's not rocket science. People must realize that these migrants are being exploited, but they don't complain because it's cheap and convenient and easier to look the other way."

The frustration breaks in her voice.

"You mentioned gangs," I say.

"Geographically, they have areas. Turf wars break out occasionally, but most of them cooperate, swapping intelligence, keeping the police at bay."

"Are they being prosecuted?" asks Florence.

"Not often enough. The Home Office has a habit of sending the victims home before the police can get enough evidence to charge anyone."

"Deliberately?" I ask.

A pained smile. "I like to give them the benefit of the doubt."

"How do we find these women?" asks Florence.

"Do you have names?"

"Yes."

"You said they were picked up by a trawler."

"Two men have been arrested."

"I know it's an age-old piece of advice, but I would be following the money. The National Crime Agency has just set up a new task force to tackle grooming gangs, particularly in the north of England. You could try to find out if your suspects are linked to any of them."

She calls up a website on her computer.

"Another option is the online bulletin boards and chat forums where survivors swap details, warning each other about particular workplaces and bosses."

"Have you ever heard anyone mention someone called the Ferryman?" I ask.

"All the time," says Natalie. "He frightens people more than Border Force or the police or the Home Office."

"You think he's real?"

"I don't think that matters."

"Would any of your clients talk to us?"

"I can ask around, but like I said, they're frightened."

28

Evie

Annie has two of her grandchildren at the shelter today who are chasing the puppies around the garden. Although deep in paperwork, Annie is keeping watch from her office. She's one of those no-nonsense, jolly women, with a booming voice and huge, pillow-like breasts that smother people when she hugs them. If one of her grandchildren ever goes missing, I know where I'd look first.

"Your phone is ringing," she calls. I retrieve the handset from my jacket. I don't recognize the number. It could be Dr. Bennett.

"Hello?"

The silence is filled with soft breathing.

I try again. "Hello?"

"Ç'kemi," says Arben, speaking in Albanian.

"Are you OK?"

"Po."

"Where are you?"

"At the police station. I leave today."

"Where are you going?"

"To a children's home."

I've been to a few of those, I want to say, but I try to be positive. "They're not so bad. The food is awful, but you get a room to yourself."

Another long pause.

"I saw Besart's body," he says. "I know they showed me a photo, but I didn't believe he was dead, not until . . ."

"I'm sorry."

He goes quiet as though expecting more.

"I know what it's like to lose someone," I say. "My parents died when I was young."

"You're an orphan?"

"Yes."

"I wish I had drowned with the others."

"Don't say that. You're safe now and the police are looking for Jeta."

"How will she find me?"

"That'll be the easy part. You're famous."

"What does 'famous' mean?" he asks.

I struggle to explain and it's probably not the right word. Cyrus would know what to say.

I try again. "You're the boy who survived. She'll find you."

The words sound convincing, but being famous didn't help me. I was the girl in the secret room. Angel Face. Nobody came to claim me.

"Will you visit me?" asks Arben, who has to go.

"Yes. Call me when you get there. Good luck." I don't know if he hears the last two words.

Out in the yard, the children are still playing with the puppies. I know all of the dogs' names because most of them were dumped on our doorstep or delivered by members of the public. I bottle-fed some of those puppies—the ones that hadn't been weaned—and I kept them warm with electric blankets or with my own body. I wanted to save every one of them because they were orphans like me.

I was sitting next to Mina, reciting our six times tables, when the message came to the classroom. My teacher took me to the administration office, where a young policeman was waiting. He stood with his cap in his hands, looking at his shoes, saying that I was needed at home.

I thought he had the wrong child until I saw Agnesa in the back seat of the police car.

"What is it? What's happened?" I whispered.

She took my hand, squeezing my fingers until they hurt.

Mama came to the door of the cottage when she heard the car pull up. Her hand went to her mouth, and she screamed so quietly that I thought only dogs could hear it because all across the village they began barking.

An older police officer waited until we were all seated on a sofa, side by side, Mama in the middle. He did not have a cruel face. He did not have a kind face either.

"Mrs. Osmani. I regret to inform you that your husband, Daniel Osmani, has been injured in an accident at the Kabazi slaughterhouse."

"What sort of accident?" asked Agnesa.

"A knife wound. Inadvertent. It is a dangerous job working with knives."

"Where is he?" asked Mama.

"Can we see him?" I asked.

The policeman looked at us with no expression. "He was taken to hospital, but he passed away. His body can be picked up from Adjensi Funeral Home."

With that, the police officer seemed to run out of things to tell us. English people would say he was "lost for words." In Albania we said his mouth was as empty as his head.

He stood up. The young officer followed suit.

"I am sorry for your loss," said the older one, clicking his heels together.

"I am also sorry," said his colleague.

After they had gone, Mama stayed sitting on the sofa. Agnesa made her a cup of tea. Nobody spoke. I went to the bedroom and looked at Papa's things—his pipe and pajamas and the book he had been reading, which had a bookmark between the pages that I had made him at school and that left tinsel on his pillow.

I crawled into his closet, among his winter clothes, and put my hands in the pockets, pressing my cheek against the wool, smelling his smell.

Later that evening, they brought Papa's body home and put it in the kitchen on the table. Mama, Mrs. Hasani, Mrs. Dushka, and Aunt Polina used warm water to wash him down, rubbing a sponge along his arms and over his hands and between his fingers. They dressed him in his best shirt and his brown suit and his polished shoes. They combed his hair and put rouge on his lips.

Later, I lay in bed beside Agnesa.

"It is my fault," she said.

"It was an accident."

"No. They killed him."

"Who?"

"Who do you think?"

I put my arms around her. I pictured the baby growing inside her and wondered if it could hear my voice or feel my hand against her stomach.

29

Cyrus

The incident room reeks of coffee, fried food, and something intangible that comes from late nights, poor pay, and relationships under pressure. It is a different atmosphere than yesterday. More focused and urgent. Carlson and his team have twenty-four hours to either charge Angus Radford and Kenna Downing or release them.

Meanwhile, local police across the north of England are checking pop-up brothels and talking to sex workers and migrant groups and informants, hoping that someone will lead them to the missing women. With Arben's help, a police sketch artist has drawn an image of Jeta that will be released to the media, along with a photograph of the other woman, Norsin Samaan, nineteen, from Aleppo in Syria.

Arben is seated at a desk in front of a computer screen, taking part in the modern equivalent of an identity parade. He is looking at mug shots and images of men who match a general description of the men in custody, to see if he can positively identify Radford or Downing.

"It was dark," he tells the interpreter. "I only saw their shadows."

"But you heard their voices," says Carlson. I can't tell if it's a question or a statement.

Arben nods unconvincingly, tugging at a forelock of hair. He looks exhausted, his eyes bruised, his shoulders sloping. A borrowed T-shirt has a brown sauce stain on the front.

"Play him the tape," says Carlson.

An audio file is selected. Voices emerge from the speaker. It's a recording of Angus Radford's police interview. Radford is responding to each question with the same answer, "No comment." At one point, he interrupts and asks, "How much longer do I have to put up with this shite?"

I watch Arben visibly stiffen and his eyes flit sideways as though Radford were suddenly in the room, standing behind him.

"Is that the voice you heard?" asks Carlson.

Arben rocks his head.

"Answer for the tape," says Carlson.

"It sounds like him. Yes. Maybe."

Carlson looks at me, knowing it's not enough. The inner ear is an acute organ, but a defense barrister will pick Arben's testimony apart in the witness box, making him doubt his own name.

I follow the detective to his office. He sits in a swivel chair, checking emails, typing a reply.

"Forensics are testing paint samples from the trawler and matching them against the wreckage of the migrant boat," he says. "We should have the results by tomorrow."

"Evidence of a collision doesn't prove intent," I say.

"We have Arben's statement and the text messages and DNA pulled from the life vests and cable ties. If we match that with Arben we'll have proof that his sister was on board."

"How long should that take?" I ask.

"Four days, maybe five."

"What happens to Arben?"

"We've found him a bed at a children's unit in Sleaford. We're waiting on a social worker to transport him."

I know the place. Rookery Lodge. It's a twelve-bed facility for troubled teenagers and children in need. I offer to take him because it's on my way home and I'd like the chance to talk to him.

Twenty minutes later, I find Arben waiting in the incident room, sitting on a vinyl chair, trying to stay out of the way. He is carrying a plastic bag containing his worldly possessions—a few pieces of underwear, socks, and a small zippered case with insulin pens, alcohol wipes, a glucose meter, and test strips.

When I unlock the Fiat, he opens the back door, but I tell him to "ride shotgun." He doesn't understand the term, but I point to the front passenger seat. He buckles up his seat belt.

"You speak a little English," I say, when he's finally settled.

He nods.

"Did you learn at school?"

"For three years. I also learned German."

We drive out of Grimsby, heading south along the A46 into the East Midlands. The dual-lane road intersects rolling hills that are dotted with sheep and cottages and crisscrossed by stone walls. Three huge wind turbines break the horizon, looking like giant robots stalking the landscape. Arben gazes into the distance, studying his surroundings as though passing judgment on the country he sacrificed so much to reach. Was it worth it? Reality rarely matches our expectations, but neither does it crush a dream so completely.

More silence. More miles. Arben is clutching the plastic bag on his lap.

"How long have you been a diabetic?" I ask.

"Six years."

"That must be hard."

"I test myself. Besart showed me how."

Mention of his brother gets caught in his throat. I change the subject and begin telling him about the Rookery Lodge, which has a games room and a community kitchen and a half basketball court. I don't mention the metal fences, security cameras, and locked doors.

"Are you hungry? We could stop for a burger."

His face lights up. "McDonald's?"

"Have you been to one before?"

"Once. In Calais."

"I thought McDonald's was everywhere."

"Not in Albania."

We're entering the outskirts of Lincoln, a cathedral city an hour's drive northeast of Nottingham. I pull into the parking area of the Carlton Centre, a shopping mall full of chain stores, liquor marts, and fast-food outlets. After finding a parking spot, I lead Arben through the heat to the restaurant. He takes his time ordering, scrolling through every choice on the screen before deciding. I tap my credit card to the reader. A few minutes later, we sit opposite each other at a table near the window. Arben crams fries into his mouth between sips of a thick chocolate shake. He saves his burger for last, peeling off the soggy green pickle with a look of disgust.

"Do you have pickled cucumbers in Albania?" I ask.

"Yes. They taste like shit."

I laugh and he doesn't understand why that's funny.

"Did your brother ever mention someone called the Ferryman?" I ask.

Arben's eyes widen and I catch a flare of recognition before he lowers his head, taking another bite.

"Is he French or some other nationality?" I ask.

"I don't know this man."

"But you've heard his name?"

"No."

"Concealing a crime or protecting a criminal is illegal," I say. "You have to cooperate with the authorities if you hope to stay in Britain."

Arben pushes his half-eaten burger away as if he's no longer hungry. His understanding of English seems to have deserted him and each question is met with a blank look or a shrug.

We leave soon afterwards, retracing our steps to the car. As I reach the driver's door, I notice the rear right-side tire is flat. I crouch and examine it, thinking I must have picked up a nail.

A large four-wheel drive pulls up behind me. Dark colored. Tinted windows. A window slides down. "Are you leaving?" asks the driver.

"No. Sorry. Flat tire."

He gets out. He's about my age, wearing jeans and a T-shirt. Gelled hair. Crooked teeth. A pinched face like a ferret's.

"Need a hand?" he asks. "I got a heavy-duty jack in the back. It'll lift this thing in no time."

"I'm OK," I say, unlatching the boot and checking the spare tire. I'm leaning inside, undoing the clamp, when I notice a second person at Arben's window, a man with tattooed arms and a hipster beard.

"Hey!" I say, straightening.

In that instant a blow lands on the back of my skull in an explosion of white-hot pain and searing light. I fall forwards and my legs are lifted off the ground. Tape screeches from a spool and is wrapped around my ankles and my arms. Blindly, I manage to grab at skin, scratching with my fingernails.

I hear a curse and feel a second blow. Metal on bone. More pain. Darkness.

The first thing I notice is the heat, radiating off every surface, making it difficult to breathe. A faint line of light is visible along the edge of the closed boot. My hands and feet are taped. My head is bleeding. The spare tire is wedged beneath my hip. I am trapped. Dying.

My phone is in my back pocket, but without my hands, I can't pull it out and dial a number. Pulling up my knees, I manage to turn onto my back. I kick hard with my legs and yell for help. The car rocks. I kick again and again, screaming, sweating, bleeding.

I picture the men who attacked me. They came for Arben. A boy. What sort of monsters . . . ?

I'm interrupted by a voice. Frail. Elderly.

"What are you doing in there?" he asks.

"I'm trapped."

"How on earth did that happen?"

"I was attacked."

He's with a woman, his wife, perhaps, who calls him Ian and tells him to be careful because I might be dangerous.

"I'm not," I say. "I'm baking in here. I need water . . . air."

"Where are your keys?" asks Ian.

"In my pocket."

"How am I supposed to let you out?"

"Call the police. Get a crowbar. Please."

I hear them arguing. His wife is called Hanneke and she doesn't want to get involved because I might be part of a criminal gang.

"I work for the police," I say.

"How do we know that?" she asks. "You could be lying."

"I'm not. I can prove it. I have ID."

A third person enters the conversation. Younger. Male. "Is there a problem?" he asks.

"Some chap has locked himself inside," explains Ian.

"No, I was attacked!" I yell. "My name is Cyrus Haven. I work with the police."

The younger man takes charge, telling me to sit tight, as though I might go somewhere. In the meantime, I listen to Ian and Hanneke talking about children and pets being locked in cars in the summer and dying of heatstroke.

I interrupt them. "I was with someone—a teenage boy. His name is Arben. Is he there?"

"No," they answer in unison.

"What about a large four-wheel drive? It pulled up behind me."

"We don't own a four-wheel drive," says Ian.

"I'm not talking about you," I say, growing frustrated.

"There's no need to be rude," says Hanneke.

"I'm sorry," I say, sweat stinging my eyes.

The young guy returns and tells the couple to step back. I hear metal scraping against metal as the sharp point of a jimmy is levered under the boot lid near the lock. Metal groans and the lock buckles, before giving way.

Air and sunlight wash over me. I feel like a vampire whose coffin lid has been opened in broad daylight. Blinded and weak from dehydration, I am lifted from the car. Someone holds a bottle of water to my lips. Another bottle is poured over my head. Tape is cut away from my hands and feet.

"Arben?" I whisper.

They look at me blankly.

He's gone.

The female paramedic has a baggy green uniform with epaulettes on her shoulders and multiple pockets. Her dark hair is pulled back from her face and she's wearing a smudge of red lipstick that accentuates the paleness of her skin.

She raises her hand. "How many fingers?"

"Three."

"Any headache, blurred vision, nausea?"

"No."

"You'll need an X-ray and stitches in that wound."

I'm holding an ice pack against the back of my bandaged head. My other hand is wrapped in a plastic bag, preserving the evidence.

"I scratched one of them," I explain.

"That was clever."

I don't feel clever. I feel stupid and angry, but most of all I'm desperate to find Arben. The paramedic forces me to sit still while an intravenous drip restores my electrolytes.

"You were lucky," she says. "You could have died of heatstroke. Your body temperature was dangerously high."

"Lucky and clever," I say, looking across the parking area. I think about the other car. What was it? A Range Rover. A Land Cruiser. Something big and boxy and black. The police will want to know. They should set up roadblocks and launch drones, put patrols on the roads.

Carlson has arrived. He waits as my fingernails are swabbed and scraped by a forensics officer and the resulting samples are bagged and labeled. Then he hands me a fresh bottle of water. "Can you walk?"

I follow him to the Fiat, explaining what happened. I give him a reasonable description of the man who hit me. The second one I barely glimpsed.

"What did they say to you?"

"The first one offered to help me change the tire."

"Which they sabotaged earlier?"

"I assume so, yes."

"Accent?"

"English. Northern." I glance across the parking area. "There should be CCTV."

"We're collecting it now. Did you notice them following you?" he asks.

"No."

"They must have been waiting outside of Birchin Way when you left the station."

"How did they know what car to follow?"

"The media have been reporting a teenage survivor."

Carlson crouches next to the flat tire. "Why did you stop here?"

"We were hungry."

"You weren't supposed to socialize with the boy."

"Oh, come on, don't try to blame me for this. Nobody thought Arben was in any danger, because if you had, you wouldn't have let him leave Birchin Way."

Carlson grunts in response, conceding nothing, covering his arse because he knows he'll be held responsible. If I hadn't escorted Arben it would have been a social worker. These men didn't care. They attacked in the middle of the day in a public place in front of witnesses and CCTV cameras. It was brazen and bold and ruthlessly efficient. What more evidence do they need of a larger conspiracy, yet nobody seems to be listening, not Carlson or Derek Posniak of the NCA or Simon Buchan.

They think the Ferryman is a myth and that ultra-nationalism is a European problem. Now we've lost the only witness to the sinking, a boy who could lead us to the truth.

My Fiat is being vacuumed and dusted for clues. In the footwell of the passenger seat I notice the diabetic kit bag. Arben doesn't have his insulin pens or glucose tablets. How long will he last without them? Twelve hours? Twenty-four?

Carlson is on the radio, issuing descriptions of the assailants and the vehicle. A young constable appears at my shoulder. "I'm assigned to take you to hospital," she says.

I start to protest until Carlson yells from his patrol car, "It's not negotiable."

30

Evie

The woman at the hospital reception desk has a sunburned nose and matching red hair that makes me think her head is on fire.

"Visiting hours are over. It's family only," she says.

"I'm family," I reply.

"What relationship?"

"I'm his wife."

She looks at me dubiously. "A child bride?"

"I'm twenty-two," I say, showing her my driver's license.

"You don't have his surname."

"That's patriarchal bullshit—why should a wife take her husband's name?"

Florence chooses that moment to interrupt. "I'm Cyrus Haven's lawyer."

That's a lie! I let it pass.

"And she'll sue your arse if you don't let us see him," I add.

Florence hushes me. "I've got this, Evie."

Who put you in charge? I want to say, but the receptionist seems to take Florence more seriously than she does me.

"The police brought Dr. Haven to the hospital two hours ago," she says. "We need to make sure he's OK."

The woman types our details into a computer and makes a phone call, seeking permission. Her desk is covered in knickknacks and ornaments, including a coffee cup full of novelty pens. I play with her Newton's cradle, swinging one silver ball into the others.

Click, clack, click, clack . . .

She stops them swinging. "Dr. Haven is in the emergency department."

"Thank you," says Florence. "You've been very helpful."

"That wasn't so hard," I add, swinging the silver balls.

We find Cyrus sitting up in bed eating a bowl of Jell-O. What is he—six? The bandage around his head is like a half-wrapped turban. Florence is first to his bedside and gives him a hug. I push past her and put my arms around him but suddenly feel self-conscious and go stiff like a board. Why can't I hug someone like a normal person?

I perch myself on the edge of his bed, making Florence take the chair.

"Why did they take Arben?" I ask.

"He's the only witness to the sinking of the migrant boat," says Cyrus.

"Then you know who did it—the guys on the trawler."

"Who are both in custody."

"They must have passed on a message," says Florence.

"Nobody except the police knew Arben's name or his whereabouts."

"It can't have been hard to work out. They were obviously watching the custody facility."

A doctor arrives and checks the stitches on the back of Cyrus's head, before giving him permission to go home. He issues instructions, addressing Florence. "You need to watch him closely in case of a delayed concussion. Headaches, dizziness, insomnia, ringing in the ears, loss of concentration."

"He's in good hands," she says, still acting like she's in charge. I'm the one who lives with Cyrus. The doctor should be talking to me.

A wheelchair is available, but Cyrus insists on walking. Florence automatically puts her arm around him in case he stumbles. Cyrus doesn't push her away. I follow behind, and pay for the parking, grumbling about the cost.

I drove my Mini-Minor, which is called "Mouse" for obvious reasons. Florence squeezes into the back seat with her knees almost touching her chin. Every time I look in the rear mirror, I see her face. None of us mentions Arben, but he's all I can think about. I told him he'd be safe. I was wrong. I know that I don't cause events to happen, but I feel as though I'm the trigger, the jinx, the bad luck charm. Cyrus has another term for it—solipsism. The sense that the world would cease to exist without me, not because I'm some sort of all-powerful deity or creator, but because everything around me is a product of my imagination. When I die, my world will die.

At the house, Florence makes no attempt to leave. She fills the kettle and offers to make dinner. Cyrus is pressing a packet of frozen peas against the back of his head. We won't be eating those. Silver linings.

"I should have noticed them following me," he says. "I couldn't give the police a decent description."

"You were ambushed," says Florence. "And you scratched one of them, which is better than a description."

Cyrus keeps checking his phone, hoping for a message from Carlson, but the roadblocks have been up for hours, and the car hasn't been sighted.

"Arben needs three injections of insulin a day," he says.

"What happens if he doesn't get treatment?" I ask.

"He'll slip into a diabetic coma."

"Can he recover?"

"Only if he's treated quickly enough."

After dinner, I take Poppy upstairs and I lie in bed, listening to the murmur of their conversation from the kitchen. Florence makes Cyrus laugh. It's a nice sound. Later, I hear them climb the stairs together. They say good night. I wait for their doors to close. I hear whispers, a nervous question, a muffled answer, a shushing sound.

I should be an expert when it comes to what men and women do when they're together—the sex bit—but I've never done it willingly because nobody ever gave me that choice. I know people are supposed to enjoy it and that boys brag about doing it all the time. I've been guilty of that, pretending to be experienced, but the truth is I've never wanted to do it with anyone except Cyrus and he won't touch me. It's not because I'm ugly or scarred or broken inside. He says there's an age difference, but he's only eleven years older than me and I'm an adult now.

I know he's not going to change his mind, but that doesn't stop me thinking about him in bed with Florence, their mouths in different places. Then my mind goes to Liam. I imagine him kissing me, lying next to me, moving when I move. Maybe I could do it with someone if I could forget all the others who came before and took it without asking.

We buried Papa in a plot that overlooked the village, next to an oak tree and away from the Berisha family plot. Papa was laid to rest in his best suit with his pipe and a pouch of tobacco in the pocket, and a compass to help him find the afterlife, and apples for the journey.

It rained at the funeral. A small grey cloud appeared in an otherwise empty sky and cried upon the circle of mourners. More than two hundred people showed up. Everybody seemed to be there except for Mr. Berisha, who sent a large wreath made of white carnations and ivy.

Mama kept gazing past the grave in the direction of the cemetery gates as if waiting for someone else to arrive. She wept quietly and I held her hand, feeling grown-up in my black dress. Aunt Polina reeked of perfume and kept leaning on people as she sobbed. She cried harder than Mama when the coffin was lowered into the ground.

Afterwards, we served food at the house: meatballs, stuffed peppers, roasted aubergines, olives, lambs on skewers, yogurt sauces, baklava, and Turkish delight. I carried plates and topped up drinks and eavesdropped as people told stories about Papa. Later in the evening, when the mourners had all gone, I helped wash the dishes and rearrange the furniture.

Aunt Polina was drunkenly snoring, spread-eagled across our bed. I went to Mama's room, where Papa's pajamas were laid on the bedspread, his shirt above his pants, as though waiting for him to step into them. Mama wasn't there. I went looking for her, in the kitchen and the sitting room and the bathroom. The garden was the last place she could be. Unlatching the door, I stepped onto the path and heard a sound like a dog snarling in a cage. I wanted to run back inside, but I kept going, past the clothesline and the vegetable garden and the outside toilet.

That's where I found her, silhouetted against the fairy lights. She was smashing Mr. Berisha's wreath against the edge of the stone wall, sending petals flying around her like snowflakes.

31

Cyrus

Morning light edges the curtains. My hand slides across the rumpled sheet. I'm alone. I wonder if I dreamed last night, but I can still feel the weight of Florence straddling my hips, her kisses on my eyelids, her hands on my body. I remember how she crossed her arms and lifted the T-shirt over her head, revealing herself.

We made love slowly, hesitantly, and when it was over, we lay together, her body aligned with mine, her arm across my chest.

"Why?" I asked.

"You had this look."

"What sort of look?"

"Like you needed reminding there are good things in life."

"You felt sorry for me."

"No. I'm attracted to you. And I wanted to be near you in case you had a delayed concussion."

"Three reasons."

"I could think of more."

Awake now, I swing my legs out of bed, feeling for the floor. In the bathroom, I splash water on my face. Gently, I unhook the butterfly clips and unfurl the bandage around my head. I examine the stitches, which are ugly and purple, set in a patch of my scalp that was shaved by the nurses at the hospital. You can barely see the stitches if I brush my hair the right way.

Downstairs, Florence is leaning over the counter reading a battered copy of *Psychology Today*. She's dressed in a pair of my track pants and the same T-shirt as last night.

"Any news on Arben?" she asks hopefully.

"No word."

I count the hours. Sixteen. He'll need insulin by now, unless they've killed him already. Why else would they take him, if not to silence him? Then I think of Evie and feel a twinge of fear. By recognizing Radford she has linked herself to this but can't explain the connection. If her memories return, she could become a target, but Radford showed no sign of recognizing her and doesn't know her name or where she lives.

I make a coffee and take a stool. Florence is still standing at the counter, flicking through the magazine.

"How did you and Evie meet?" she asks.

"She was at a secure children's home."

"What happened to her parents?"

"Her father died when Evie was little. She fled Albania with her mother and sister, who died on the journey to England."

"On a small boat?"

"I don't know exactly. Evie can't remember or won't talk about it."

"That's why she was triggered by the bodies in the water."

"Most likely, yes."

Florence pours hot water over the same herbal tea bag and takes a seat next to me, sitting cross-legged with elegant efficiency. "How did she get here?" she asks.

"I fostered her for a while—until she turned eighteen. Then I offered her somewhere to stay."

"I think she might be in love with you."

"We're working through that."

She smiles and it makes her look even more beautiful. I like her quick wit and easy charm and the way I feel nervous around her. I like how she becomes the center of any room she steps into and how her hands move as she talks and she tilts her head when she looks at me, as though puzzled, but also interested in what I have to say.

I hear the side gate open. Moments later, Poppy appears, drinking noisily from a bowl of water near the back steps. Evie isn't far behind her. She kicks off her shoes and hangs Poppy's lead in the laundry.

Florence goes upstairs to get changed.

Evie opens the fridge and takes out a plastic jug of orange juice, chugging straight from the bottle.

"Get a glass," I say.

She ignores me and drinks again, spilling juice down her front. "Is she still here?"

"Yes."

"I heard you last night. Making the beast with two backs." She's quoting Shakespeare, *Othello*, which she studied for her English A Level, and which made her an armchair expert on Elizabethan misogyny.

"I'm sorry if we kept you awake. It wasn't . . ." I pause.

"Wasn't what?" she asks.

"Planned."

Evie makes a scoffing sound. "You make it sound like a pregnancy."

"You told me I should find a girlfriend."

"Is that what she is—your girlfriend? I thought she was a hookup. A one-night stand. A pity fuck."

"That's not fair."

Evie goes quiet.

"You and I are always going to be friends," I say.

"How do you know? Maybe I'll do something unforgivable."

"You won't."

"Don't tell me what I will or *won't* do."

With that, she leaves. Poppy has sensed the tension and puts her head into my lap, blinking at me with her sad brown eyes.

Evie's voice, calling her name. The Labrador's ears prick up.

"Go, look after her," I say.

32

Cyrus

Evie is drinking an iced coffee beneath a café awning, not making eye contact with people, but watching from behind her sunglasses. Across the road, the Great Grimsby Combined Court Center is set back from the street, sentried by large plane trees.

Defendants and lawyers are milling outside, staying cool in the shade. Most are here for summary offenses—drunk-driving cases, disputed speeding fines, and charges for criminal damage, malicious wounding, and drug possession. A few have family members supporting them, who are dressed like they're attending a church service or a funeral.

Evie insisted on coming. She wants to see the men who have been charged with the small boat murders, particularly the one she recognized, hoping it might trigger a memory or tether him to a particular time or place or event in her life.

There has been no word on Arben, but a dark-colored Land Cruiser was found burnt out in a lay-by fifteen miles from where he was abducted. The car had been stolen two days earlier from a house in Manchester by someone who had cloned the fob using a scanning device.

We navigate the security screening and take two seats in the tiered public gallery, which overlooks the body of the court, directly behind the bar table and to the right of the press benches. Some of the reporters I recognize from TV or from earlier media briefings. I make Evie sit next to the aisle so we can slip away quickly if she feels anxious or her mind begins slipping.

Angus Radford and Kenna Downing arrive through a different door. They are handcuffed, wearing prison-issue clothes, being escorted by guards. Radford has a swagger about him, like he's walking onto a stage, but Downing seems more nervous and keeps checking to see if he's putting his feet in the right place.

The court usher announces the arrival of Judge Prior, a small, bird-like woman, with gentle eyes and bound black hair. She has a soft spot for her court staff, calling the clerk by his first name. She asks Radford and Downing to take a seat while she deals with several other matters for mention. The prosecutor, Mr. Holder, makes an application for a hearing date extension and seeks to change reporting conditions for a defendant.

Finally, Judge Prior asks Radford and Downing to stand. "Do you have legal representation?"

Before they can answer, a door swings opens and a man enters, striding into the courtroom like he's making a last-minute intervention.

"Your Honor, may it please the court, my name is Philip Welbeck, KC. I represent Mr. Radford and Mr. Downing."

A young woman trails after him, carrying a briefcase under one arm, and a stack of box files that she can barely see over. Welbeck has reached the bar table, where he nudges a chair back with his foot, as though worried it might be germ-ridden. Without pausing to wait for his colleague, he begins, "I wish to register my complaint against my clients' treatment in police custody and the denial of their rights."

"What rights have been denied?" asks the crown prosecutor.

"They were denied legal representation upon their arrest."

"A solicitor was present at every interview."

"They were in custody for four hours before I was notified."

"Because your clients refused to give their names or addresses."

"They gave the police my phone number."

"Yet couldn't remember their own names."

The sarcasm irritates Welbeck, who begins to argue but is cut off by the judge.

"Keep it in your pants, gentlemen." The comment triggers laughter. Judge Prior moves on quickly. "What are we dealing with, Mr. Holder?"

The prosecutor takes a sheet of paper from the table.

"Angus Fraser Radford and Kenna Andrew Downing are charged with seventeen counts of gross negligence manslaughter, as well as resisting arrest, assault, and destroying evidence."

"Allegations that will be strenuously denied," says Welbeck.

"You'll get your chance," says the judge, shutting him down.

Holder continues. "The prosecution will allege that in the early hours of August twenty-sixth the trawler *New Victory* deliberately rammed and sank a rigid-hulled inflatable boat with twenty people on board, sixteen miles northeast of Skegness in the North Sea. *New Victory* was sailing without lights or radar reflectors, and the automatic identification beacon had been disabled."

"Objection. Speculation," says the barrister.

"This is not the trial, Mr. Welbeck," says Judge Prior, signaling for the prosecutor to go on.

Holder gives Welbeck a smug smile. "Eyewitness testimony and satellite imagery will show the trawler earlier stopped the RHIB and tried to force it into turning back to France, using water cannons and ropes. When those on board refused the demands, the trawler rammed the RHIB, which overturned, throwing the occupants into the sea."

"Ridiculous," mutters Welbeck.

Holder ignores him. "According to forensic evidence the trawler collided with the RHIB at least three times and the crew made no attempt to rescue the people in the water. Given the serious nature of the alleged offenses, and the likelihood of further charges being laid, the Crown asks that bail be refused and the defendants be remanded in custody."

"Your turn, Mr. Welbeck," says Judge Prior.

The barrister gets to his feet and buttons his charcoal-grey suit, tugging down the sleeves and smoothing the creases on his thighs. Throat cleared, eyebrows knitted, he begins.

"My clients are fishermen. Mr. Radford was born to the sea, a fourth-generation trawlerman; and Mr. Downing has worked on boats since he was eighteen. They have no knowledge of any collision and, if one did occur, they insist it was accidental.

"Let me offer you a different, more credible, version of events. My clients were transferring the trawler to Scotland after an engine refit, which is why it had only two crew. The AIS had not been reactivated—an oversight, not a deliberate act. On the morning in question, Mr. Downing was on watch. He left the wheelhouse for several minutes to check on an oil-pressure light and to make himself a cup of tea. Mr. Radford was sleeping. The navigation lights were on. The trawler was on autopilot and nothing showed on the ship's radar.

"It was during this time that *New Victory* struck something in the water that damaged the propeller shaft. Both men came on deck and searched for what the trawler might have hit. They saw no evidence of a

RHIB or people in the water. They assumed it was most likely a sunken shipping container or some other flotsam or jetsam."

Mr. Holder hasn't bothered sitting down. "We have radar images that capture the moment of collision. They also show the trawler circling back to finish the job."

"More speculation," says Welbeck. "The *New Victory* is not a pirate ship. It is a fishing trawler. My clients are devastated by the loss of any life at sea. If there is evidence of a collision, it was accidental."

"Not according to the eyewitness," says Holder. "And we have text messages from someone else on board the sinking boat."

"Is this witness available?" asks Welbeck. "Can he or she be cross-examined in a future trial?" asks Welbeck. He doesn't wait for an answer. "These text messages came from a phone that hasn't been located and may or may not have been on the vessel that sank."

"Two life vests were found on board the trawler," says the prosecutor.

"Picked up floating in the sea," replies Welbeck.

"And the plastic ties found in the cabin?"

"Used for securing equipment during rough weather."

Judge Prior intervenes. "Gentlemen, we're not deciding this case today. This is a bail hearing."

Welbeck continues, "Your Honor. My clients are both family men. They have mortgages to pay. Loans to service. Mouths to feed. Keeping them in custody on the available evidence is unfair and unjustifiable. I ask that you free them on minimal bail, with reporting restrictions and whatever else you deem appropriate. Let them get back to their families."

Judge Prior takes a moment and begins to jot down notes. The whispering begins around us, rising in volume.

"What's happening?" asks Evie.

"She's deciding whether to release them on bail."

"But they killed those people."

"They're innocent until proven guilty."

Evie lets out an odd sharp cough of a laugh. Angus Radford glances towards the public gallery and his eyes settle on her. I look for some flash of recognition or sign of curiosity, but his face is blank.

Judge Prior clears her throat. The courtroom falls silent.

"Gross negligence manslaughter carries a maximum penalty of life imprisonment. Given the seriousness of the charges, I am going to deny bail and remand both defendants in custody."

"We will appeal," says Welbeck.

"That is your right," says the judge. "I will list the matter for mention on October the eleventh, when a date will be set for trial. The court is in recess."

Everybody stands except for Radford and Downing, who are deep in conversation. Arguing. Radford shoves Downing in the chest with his cuffed hands and the guards have to step forward to separate the men.

"Not a fucking word," says Radford as he is being led away.

The courtroom empties and reporters hurry to file stories and film reports from the steps of the courthouse. I look for DI Carlson in the foyer but can't see him. Evie holds on to my sleeve. She doesn't like crowded places because everybody is taller than she is and they "steal her air."

"Can we go?" she pleads.

I want to ask her about Radford and if she remembers where she's seen him before, but now isn't the time.

33

Evie

I have spent the past three years trying to fit in and become one of the crowd. Ordinary, in every way. Invisible, I have passed my driving test, learned how to cook, and studied for two A Levels (neither of which I passed). I have a bank account, a debit card, an NHS number, and a mobile phone plan. I own a car, I pay taxes, I microchipped my dog, and I voted in the last council elections because Cyrus said it was my "civic duty."

This should make me feel like I belong, but when I look in the mirror, I see an imposter or a crisis actor. My life feels like a performance without a script, where I am expected to improvise. I don't even know if I'm the hero or villain of my own story, or when it might be over.

This is how I feel as Cyrus leads me through the crowded foyer, out the automatic doors, and across the forecourt, past the TV cameras and makeshift barricades. A line of police officers prevents us going farther. The officers are standing side by side, separating two groups of protesters, who are trading insults. One side is chanting, "Our streets, not your streets! Our streets, not your streets!" While the other group yells, "Refugees are welcome here. Refugees are welcome here." A scuffle breaks out on the periphery. Someone shouts, "Nazi scum off our streets."

Cyrus puts his arm around my waist, pulling me closer. We squeeze past a barricade and ignore a woman wearing a Union Jack hat and a jacket decorated with buttons. She thrusts a pamphlet towards me, saying, "If you love this country, you should fight for it."

Cyrus keeps moving. The two groups surge towards each other and almost break through the line of police who have linked arms. A beer can arcs over my head and I hear someone shout in pain. There is more swearing, more shoving, more shouts. Violence brewing. A protester spits in the face of a female police officer. A baton is swung. Police charge forward.

Suddenly, a man springs athletically onto the roof of a car, raising his arms, motioning people to settle down and listen. In his sixties, he's dressed in moleskin trousers, an open-necked cotton shirt, and cowboy boots. His grey hair, once blond, has tight curls like an old-fashioned perm.

"You know who I am," he says, his accent posher than posh. "And you know how I feel about what's happened here today. I share your frustration, your feelings of helplessness. I love this country as much as you do. And I understand why foreigners are willing to risk their lives to get here. They admire and respect our history, our legal system, our hospitals, our schools . . ."

"Our welfare system more like it," yells a woman.

"That too," says the man.

Cyrus has stopped moving. "Who is he?" I whisper.

"Lord David Buchan."

"Didn't you meet him?"

"I met his brother."

Both groups of protesters have gone quiet and are listening.

"Some of the migrants reaching our shores are genuine refugees, who are escaping from tyranny and war, slavery, and starvation," says Buchan. "Others are economic migrants, who see that the grass is greener on this side of the Channel. But for many, the promised land leads to crime, poverty, and exploitation. The scenes we witnessed last week of bodies being washed up on our beaches should *never* be repeated. The time has come to end the carnage. To reclaim our borders. To be humane, but fair."

Cheers drown out the boos.

"I have talked to the two men who have been charged today. They are fishermen, who have been labeled as criminals because our legal system is in the thrall of wokeness. An accident on the high seas has been called a crime, when the real criminals are the people smugglers who are exploiting desperate people and encouraging them to make a dangerous voyage to our shores.

"I am not anti-immigration. I am not anti-refugee. I am a patriot and a pragmatist and a lover of human life. However, migrants who come here illegally should not have more rights than hardworking British citizens. This is about favoritism not fascism, pragmatism not racism. We need a new policy for a new Britain, independent of Europe. An orderly queue. Proper screening. And until such a system is in place, we should turn back the boats."

There are more cheers and the chanting begins again but is cut off when Buchan raises his arms. "You have every right to be angry and to protest, but violence is not the answer. I urge you to go home and talk to your friends and families. Sign my petition. Donate money to the cause. Write to your local member of Parliament. Together, we will create a system that welcomes genuine refugees but also keeps our borders safe."

There are more cheers as he jumps down. I tug on Cyrus's sleeve. "Which side is he on?"

"He wants to stop the boats."

"Doesn't everyone?"

"It's complicated."

Away from the crowd, we cross a canal and walk back to where I've parked Mouse. Cyrus's car is still with the police.

"Radford didn't seem bothered by the charges," I say.

"He was grandstanding," says Cyrus.

"What does that mean?"

"Playing the tough guy."

"There are no eyewitnesses without Arben."

"The police have his statement and record of interview."

"Will that be enough?"

"I don't know."

34

Cyrus

My phone is ringing. I fumble for the handset. The digital clock glows in the darkened room.

"Cyrus Haven?" asks a voice.

"Yes."

"I'm sorry to call you so early."

"That's OK."

The constable sounds young, but I can hear the tiredness in his voice. "DI Carlson is sending a car to pick you up. It will be there in fifteen minutes."

"Why?"

"A body has been found in Willingham Woods in Lincolnshire."

"Is it the boy?"

"I'm not sure, sir."

I get dressed and try to sneak past Evie's door, avoiding the squeaky step on the stairs. It doesn't work. She appears on the landing. Her hair is sleep-tousled. A long T-shirt reaches past her knees. "Where are you going?"

"Out."

"Is this about Arben?"

"It's police business."

I know that's not a lie, but Evie sees something in my face and the gold flecks float in her eyes.

The car is waiting for me, engine idling. The female driver is a young detective, about my age. Her first name is Fiona. She has more details. Two ramblers stumbled upon the body of a teenage boy, partially covered by a blackberry bush and ferns, as they crossed a water-filled ditch in a woodland area with walking and cycling trails.

"When?"

"Just after seven."

Rain is falling by the time we drive through the village of Market Rasen. Two miles east along the A631 we come to a side road that leads to a parking area and a small, dour building that has toilets and a shuttered café. Visitors, braving the weather, are being turned away by officers in high-vis coats.

Fiona offers me an umbrella as we walk along a single-lane forestry road before turning off on a walking trail. The mud has already been churned up beneath the shoes of police and forensic officers. Moving farther into the woods, I can smell the damp earth and rotting boles and the cavalcade of reeks made more pungent by the rain.

The trail curves and descends. Getting nearer, we reach duckboards that are arranged like stepping stones across the wet ground. I glimpse a flashgun firing. Forensic teams dressed in light blue overalls are moving in and out of a white canvas tent. More awnings have been strung from the trees, trying to preserve trace evidence from being washed away.

I barely recognize Carlson when he appears from the largest tent. He's wearing disposable overalls with the hood secured tightly around his face. His mere presence answers my first question. The body belongs to Arben Pasha.

"How?" I ask.

"Ness won't say without a postmortem."

He's referring to Robert Ness, a senior Home Office pathologist.

"Time of death?" I ask.

"Too soon to tell. The body was dumped overnight."

I plot the sequence of events in my head. Arben must have been held somewhere for at least twenty-four hours.

"Get him suited up," says Carlson.

Fiona takes me to a police four-wheel-drive vehicle and waits while I get changed. When I return to the main tent, the rain is heavier, running off the canvas, and being channeled into newly dug trenches. The tent flap opens. A camera flash blinds me momentarily.

Arben Pasha is lying on his back with his head tilted back. His eyes are open, as though watching people work around him. Leaves and grass cling to his hair. Mud is smeared on his left cheek. The flashgun pops again.

"Nice of you to join us," says Ness, who is crouching beside the body.

The pathologist is in his late forties, with rimless glasses and an oiled scalp. At six foot five he makes every space feel small. "I thought you'd be coming," he says.

"Why?"

"Because of this."

Ness reaches forward and touches Arben's jaw, pulling his mouth slowly open. He shines a light into the boy's mouth, revealing a flash of silver, a coin, resting on his swollen tongue.

"Charon's obol," I whisper.

Ness and Carlson turn to me, waiting for an explanation.

"In Greek and Latin cultures there are stories about a coin being placed in the mouth of the dead. It's supposed to be a payment to Charon, the ferryman. His job was to convey souls across the river that divided the world of the living from the world of the dead."

"How do you know this stuff?" asks Ness.

"I was reading about it the other night."

"Any particular reason?"

"Personal interest," I say, glancing at Carlson, who shakes his head, wanting me to be quiet. Ness knows I'm hiding something.

I leave the tent, escaping into the rain, which is colder than the air. The day is suddenly different, as if the storm has created a strange twilight, which is not this world or the next. Maybe we're trapped here, waiting for the ferryman.

Mentally, I begin putting the scene into context, looking for reference points and psychological markers. The distance from the car park. The isolation of the woods. The coin in his mouth. Was Arben alive when they brought him here, or had he lapsed into a diabetic coma? When the brain doesn't get enough glucose, or receives too much, it cannot function properly. The symptoms can appear slowly: an altered mental state, the inability to speak, drowsiness, weakness, headaches, restlessness, shaking, an irregular heartbeat, and eventually the loss of consciousness. If left untreated, it results in permanent brain damage and, ultimately, death.

I hold up my phone. No signal. That could be why they chose the location. Their phones couldn't be tracked and the canopy of the trees hid them from drones and satellite surveillance.

Most crimes involve a conflation of circumstances, pressure, and desire. A moment of rage, a wrong choice, a minute earlier, a different doorway, a few yards to the left or right, and the outcome could have been altered. Not this one. Whoever abducted Arben knew that he was the sole survivor of the small boat sinking and therefore the only witness. They traced his movements. They watched the police station. They followed him.

As a psychologist, I'm supposed to be perceptive, to recognize when something is out of place or unusual, but I didn't see this threat. I didn't recognize their intent. Neither did Carlson or the National Crime Agency or Border Force. This goes beyond two fishermen in a refurbished trawler who deliberately rammed a small boat. They are part of a criminal conspiracy to control the flow of people crossing the Channel. The sinking wasn't a racist attack or a hate crime. It was a warning—a lesson to those who follow—pay the Ferryman, or you'll never reach the other side.

I think about Evie. What am I going to say to her? She wanted me to bring Arben home with us. Would that have made a difference? Perhaps not, but I doubt whether Evie will agree. It is almost impossible to fathom how much tragedy she has experienced in her short life. And it makes me wonder if it can build up inside a person, accumulating like a trace metal, or a forever chemical, slowly poisoning them.

People could say the same about me, but I refuse to let tragedy define me or become an excuse. After my parents died, I was raised by my grandparents and returned to the same school. My classmates had mixed reactions. Some avoided me, treating grief like a virus. Others talked behind my back, speculating on whether I was like my brother. Two peas in a pod. Bad seeds.

I overheard two teachers talking. One of them mentioned the Menendez brothers. I had to look them up. Lyle and Erik murdered their parents in Beverly Hills. The father, José, was shot six times and their mother, Kitty, eleven times. When Kitty was lying on the ground, trying to crawl away, Lyle ran to his car, reloaded the 12-gauge, and returned to finish her off.

Years later, while I was studying psychology, I watched a true-crime show about the case. It wasn't my choice of viewing. I was with a girl, on our third date, and she made the suggestion. As the details of the crime were revealed on the show, I realized that she was watching me, instead of the screen. She asked me if I could introduce her to Elias.

"Why?"

"I think I can help him."

"How?"

"He needs a friend."

Instead of being shocked or saddened or even angry at the girl's infatuation with my brother, I was intrigued. I had learned about hybristophilia—the sexual interest in and attraction to those who commit crimes. It's the reason so many women fall in love with serial killers and marry men on death row. I wanted to understand this girl, just as I wanted to understand Elias, and am now intrigued by Angus Radford and Kenna Downing.

My old university professor Joseph O'Loughlin once told me that a piece of human brain the size of a grain of sand contains one hundred thousand neurons, two million axons, and one billion synapses all talking to one another. The number of permutations and combinations of activity that are theoretically possible in each of our heads exceeds the number of elementary particles in the universe. That's why we know less about the human brain than about the dark side of the moon.

Professor Joe also taught me that when one is confronted by a complex problem, it is sometimes best to solve the easiest part of it first, or the most obvious one. How does Evie know Angus Radford? If I trace his past, I can find where it intersects with hers.

Radford said he was a fourth-generation fisherman and gave an address in St. Claire, in northeast Scotland. A guesthouse called the Belhaven Inn. It's not much, but it's a start.

35

Evie

My therapist, Veejay, works from her house in Nottingham, where she has an office overlooking a garden, which is always littered with toys, including a paddling pool and a swing set. In all my sessions, I have never seen her children. I once asked her what she'd done with them: "Have you buried them in the garden?" Cocking her head, she studied me with her soft brown eyes and said, "Why do you ask?"

Her full name is Veera Jaffrey, but people call her by her initials, VJ (Veejay), and she has a wonderfully deep voice, thick dark hair, and the faintest trace of a Pakistani accent. She doesn't make me lie on a couch. Instead, she has an enormous armchair, which is so deep that my legs stick straight out.

This is an extra appointment. Veejay knows about what happened at Cleethorpes because Cyrus must have told her, which annoys me, because he promised to stay out of my life.

"What's the last thing you remember?" she asks.

"The bodies in the water."

"Did you feel anything?"

"Dizzy, I guess."

"Did you smell anything?"

"Why?"

"Sometimes people detect a strange odor like burning hair or rotting food just before they pass out. It's more a symptom than a trigger."

"I remember trying to run. Mentally, I was desperate to get away, but I couldn't move. The danger was getting closer and closer and I was frozen."

Veejay jots something down on her yellow notepad. I often wonder what she writes. Maybe she's reminding herself to pick up a loaf of bread or to let the children out of the basement.

I don't mention the MRI scan and the unwanted tumor growing in my temporal lobe. Cyrus has probably told her. I hate him sometimes. All the time. Never.

My tumor has become my "white bear." Cyrus once told me about a famous thought-suppression experiment where a psychologist asked people not to think about a specific thing—a white bear. That was their only goal, but the harder they tried, the more they thought about a white bear. It's a pretty stupid experiment, if you ask me, but I guess it explains why I'm fixated on my tumor and what lies ahead—the biopsy, the surgery, the chemotherapy or radiotherapy. I'm ugly enough without losing my hair.

Maybe they should leave it alone. They could spend their time and money on saving someone else. It's not as though I'm very important or productive. I'm not going to cure cancer or work with lepers or break any world records.

Veejay has been talking to me. I haven't been listening.

"Any dreams?" she asks.

"Not really."

"What does that mean?"

"I've been thinking a lot about when my father died."

"You haven't talked about him."

"He was killed at work. They said it was an accident."

"Who said?"

"The police."

"But you don't believe that."

"No."

I try to swallow a lump that is caught between my voice box and my upper chest. Veejay is waiting for me to go on. I want to ask if we can change the subject, but that would be like telling a moth to ignore the light or a salmon to stop swimming upstream.

Involuntary memories are the worst. They creep up on me unexpectedly and leave me gasping for breath. The happy ones are okay. I picture myself riding on Papa's bicycle, tucked between his forearms as we coast down the hill towards the village, urging him to go faster. Or when I'm sitting on his lap in Mr. Berisha's truck, changing the gears, while Papa works the pedals.

But happiness is like one side of a spinning coin. Eventually it lands on tails and the memories change.

· We marked Papa's grave with flowers and a small white cross that had an inscription giving his name, his date of birth, and the day he died. Forty-seven years. People said it was too young. I think it sounds too long.

After the funeral, Mama became an ancient figure, draped in black, staring at the walls. She spent weeks lying in their metal-framed bed in a darkened room with the door closed. I used to press my ear against the cool wood and hear her crying.

Aunt Polina cooked our meals, washed our clothes, and told us stories about her time in Italy.

"When you were strawberry picking," I said.

Polina smiled. "Who told you that?"

"Papa."

"I did lots of jobs."

"And you had a boyfriend," I added.

"Many," she said. "I was very popular."

Each mealtime, we put a tray outside Mama's door and collected it later, untouched.

"She has to eat," I said. "What if she gets sick?"

"She'll eat," said Polina. "Give her time."

I began sneaking into Mama's room, where I found her propped up in the corner of the bed, elbow wedged against the wall. The sunlight threw shapes on the floor and spent the afternoon inching towards her pillow. Mama was like a life-sized statue of herself, wasting away, with no light in her eyes, no spark, no joy. I tried hard to make her happy. I picked flowers, and made cards, and drew pictures, but whenever she looked at me I felt something stir in her, a tremor, barely detectable, that made her small brown eyes brim with rage.

Polina was right. Mama did return to us. She left her room and moved through the house as though wading in chest-deep water. She ate. She slept. She cooked. She cleaned.

Papa's funeral used up the last of our savings; what Mama called our "rainy day money," although I've never understood why the weather made a difference. My English teacher Mr. Joubert told me that I take things too literally and fail to see symbolism or hidden meanings. It's like when we studied *Othello*. He said Desdemona's handkerchief was supposed to symbolize her fidelity, but why couldn't she just want to blow her nose?

When school began, other children avoided me—all except for Mina. They whispered that Papa had died because he upset Mr. Berisha and that now my family had a blood feud and compensation had to be paid—an eye for an eye, a life for a life. "If only there was a son," people said, as though men were the solution to every problem.

When the rent became due at the end of August we had no money to pay Mr. Berisha. He came to the house. I was at the kitchen table doing my homework. Agnesa locked herself in the bedroom.

Mr. Berisha was a fat man with a second chin, which turned into three when he dropped his jaw to his chest to look over his half glasses. And he made a clicking sound in his throat whenever he disagreed with what someone was telling him.

Mama asked for more time to pay the rent.

"Are you working?" he asked.

"I'm looking for a job."

"What about your daughter Agnesa. I could find her a position."

"She's still at school."

"She could work in my office. I like having a pretty face to greet customers. She couldn't be pregnant, of course. Not when she's unmarried."

Mama's knuckles whitened as her hands closed into fists.

"Is your son going to marry Agnesa?"

Mr. Berisha chuckled. "This is not some Cinderella story."

"She was underage. He raped her."

"She tricked him into sleeping with her."

"I'll go to the police. Let's see what they say."

He stepped closer. Mama backed away. She was trapped against the sink, looking anxiously at me. Mr. Berisha ran his fingers down her cheek and neck and the front of her dress.

"You have ten days to sell your furniture and pack your things," he said. "You will pay me whatever you raise, and I will arrange your passage to England. I will organize jobs for you and somewhere to stay."

"What jobs?"

"Your English is good. You could work for one of the big hotels in London. Your daughters could do the same."

"And if I don't agree?"

He leaned closer and whispered something. I didn't catch the words, but Mama's eyes widened, and she spun her head to look at me, letting out a groan.

That night I was sent to bed early. Mama and Aunt Polina and Agnesa stayed in the kitchen talking. Later, Agnesa lay in bed next to me, her arm resting on my waist. "It will be an adventure," she said as she talked about England, and I fell asleep dreaming of flower sellers and chimney sweeps and magical nannies.

In the days that followed, Mama applied to get us passports. Normally it would have taken weeks, but she bribed a police officer. We opened the house to our neighbors, selling everything—the grandfather clock, the tall black wardrobe from the bedroom, three chests of drawers, a washing machine, a fridge, the TV, and Papa's bicycle. Some of the offers were insulting according to Mama. She said that "honor and reason cannot be bought," which I didn't understand.

She allowed me to fill a small suitcase with clothes and shoes, but I had to leave my toys behind. "You're too old for dolls," Agnesa said, but she saw my tears and promised to buy me a new doll in London from a famous toy store.

Mr. Berisha did not get his money and we didn't follow his instructions and meet "his man" in Durrës. Instead, we left the cottage before dawn and Mr. Hasani drove us to Tirana International Bus Terminal. We caught a bus to Kotor in Montenegro and another to Sarajevo in Bosnia and another to Zagreb in Croatia. At each border Mama said we were tourists or visiting friends, and she always had an address to give them, but I don't think they were real. A night bus took us across the top of Italy through Venice and Verona to Milan, where we caught a train to Turin and another bus into France.

Agnesa turned sixteen on the journey. I was nine, almost ten, and every new country was taking me farther away from the only life I'd ever known—hour after hour, mile after mile—away from Mina and Mr. and Mrs. Hasani and Aunt Polina and Papa's grave.

My mind aches from so much useless remembering. What does it matter? What can I hope to achieve? The past is not trying to speak to me. And even if it were, I don't want to hear what it has to say.

Cyrus is waiting for me outside Veejay's house.

"I thought I'd come and meet you," he says.

"He's dead, isn't he?" I ask, studying his face.

"Yes."

"How?"

"Let's take a walk."

Crossing the road, we descend a set of stone steps beside a bridge over the Nottingham and Beeston Canal. The rain has stopped, and the sun is out, throwing shadows on the wet towpath. We walk between patches of light and shade, passing an old lady feeding the ducks from a bench and a party of tourists wearing life vests who are paddling kayaks on the canal.

"It could have been a diabetic coma," says Cyrus. "We won't know until the postmortem."

"It's still murder."

"Yes."

"I told Arben he'd be safe."

"It's not your fault."

Then whose fault is it, I want to ask. Who can I blame? We are still walking but I'm so angry that I struggle to focus.

"I'm going to Scotland," says Cyrus.

"Why?"

"That's where Angus Radford comes from. I want to find out more about him and where you might have met him."

A lump expands in my throat.

"I'm not asking you to come," says Cyrus. "It's safer here."

"How will you know the truth if I'm not there?"

"It's too dangerous."

"Angus Radford didn't recognize me and he's in prison," I say. "And nobody else knows who I am."

Cyrus doesn't answer, which is a good sign. We walk on a while longer.

"Who'll look after Poppy?" he asks, but he knows the answer already. Mitch and Lilah.

We're going to Scotland.

Book Two

And once the storm is over, you won't remember how you made it through, how you managed to survive. You won't even be sure, whether the storm is really over. But one thing is certain. When you come out of the storm, you won't be the same person who walked in. That's what this storm's all about.

—Haruki Murakami,
Kafka on the Shore

36

Cyrus

My aging Fiat, once red, now pink, has been returned to me by the police. The boot latch has been repaired, but the signs of the forensic search remain—fingerprint dust on the dashboard and an evidence tag left in one of the door pockets. I am not a car person. The Fiat is not an extension of myself. Nor does it make a statement about my politics or my aspirations or compensate for something that's missing or under-sized. A car is just a car in the same way that a washing machine is just a washing machine.

It feels strange having Evie in the passenger seat because Arben was the last person to sit there. We head north along the M1, crossing the Yorkshire Dales, past Penrith and Carlisle. The windows are cracked open, letting in the road sounds and the rushing air and the smells of summer.

Evie turns on the radio and finds a song. Something familiar. "Yesterday" by the Beatles. I begin to sing. She joins in. It's a nice moment, like something out of a film, but eventually, she goes quiet.

"We're in Scotland," I say, pointing to a sign for Gretna Green. "It's a famous place for weddings."

"Why?" asks Evie.

"Back in the eighteenth century, anyone under the age of twenty-one was forbidden to marry in England and Wales without their parents' permission. The young and in love began eloping to Scotland, coming to Gretna Green to get married."

"Do they still do it?"

"There's a blacksmith's shop in town that's famous for marriages."

"I think it's romantic," says Evie, surprising me. Usually, she scoffs at love songs and rom-coms and public displays of affection, telling people to "get a room."

The landscape changes as we turn northeast toward Stirling and then onwards to Perth. The sun is trying to break through a thin layer of cloud, but a persistent wind steals the heat from the air. The farther north we've traveled, the cooler it has grown.

Evie falls asleep and jerks awake, as though trying to run, but the seat belt holds her back.

"A bad dream?" I ask.

She doesn't answer. Instead, she hugs her knees to her chest, rocking slightly. When her breathing returns to normal, she studies her phone, telling me when she has four bars, or three, or two. It's as though she expects us to lose touch with civilization at any moment.

On the outskirts of Dundee, I stop to fill up with petrol and to get a coffee. The smell of petrol fumes blends with the fried food and sugar from the doughnut shop. Evie goes to the toilet and wanders around the gift shop. I have a missed call from Florence. I call her back.

"Scotland? Why?" she asks.

"I'm looking into Angus Radford's background."

"Has Evie remembered anything else?"

"Not yet."

Through the glass doors, I notice Evie talking to a couple of older boys, who are driving a pickup truck with mud-splattered dirt bikes strapped upright. She's smiling and laughing, pointing her front foot, tossing her hair.

Florence: "I've been doing some research. There was a marine accident investigation about twelve years ago into the sinking of a trawler. Angus Radford gave a statement about an engine fire. It could explain the scars on his face."

"What was the name of the boat?"

"The *Ariana II*. It was registered to a William Radford from St. Claire, in Scotland."

"Could be a relative."

"I'm trying to get more details."

"Any news on who paid for the barrister who's representing Radford and Downing?"

"Not yet, but I doubt if Lord David Buchan would publicly bankroll their defense. He has too much to lose if they're convicted."

"OK. Let me know what you find."

Evie is still talking to the boys, who are leaning against my Fiat. The older of the two begins slow dancing in front of her, showing off. He has bumfluff on his top lip and grease-stained jeans.

"Where are yer heading?" he asks.

"Scotland," says Evie.

"Ye're in fookin' Scotland." He laughs.

"St. Claire."

He offers her a cigarette. Evie shakes her head.

"We could take you as far as Aberdeen," says the younger one.

"Yeah, come ride with us," says his mate.

I interrupt them. "Ready to go, Evie?"

"Who's this?" asks the younger one.

"My pervy old uncle," replies Evie, thinking it's funny.

"You should let Evie decide," says the older one.

"I would but she's only fourteen."

"I am not!" says Evie.

The young men have lost their boldness.

"You could go to jail for what you're thinking," I say.

"He's lying," says Evie. "I can prove it."

She's searching for her driver's license, which is locked inside the car. Already the boys are heading back to their truck.

"That was mean," she says sulkily when I open the passenger door.

"You were teasing them."

"I was teasing *you*."

"What's the point of that?"

"Absolutely nothing," she says disgustedly.

She stews for the next twenty miles. I know I'm supposed to be an expert on human behavior, but I have a blind spot when it comes to Evie. Just when I think I have a handle on her moods, she can deliver a withering glance or a curled lip or a dismissive shrug, and make me feel ancient and out of touch.

Two hours later, in growing darkness, we reach St. Claire, a fishing port in the northeast corner of Aberdeenshire. The road follows the natural curve of the coastline, dipping and rising over the headlands. Out to sea there are container ships and the distant lights of oil or gas rigs.

I pull up outside a guesthouse, the Belhaven Inn, a red granite building that sits three blocks back from the harbor district. A Scottish flag hangs limply out front along with a sign saying, "Live TV sport."

The engine is idling.

"Is this where we're staying?" asks Evie.

"It's the address Angus Radford gave to the police."

This statement seems to rattle her.

"He doesn't know we're here," I say. "We're undercover."

Evie seems to like that idea and unclips her seat belt.

The guesthouse has a side gate and a path that leads to a glass-walled conservatory with tables set out for breakfast. I ring a bell on the counter. A woman appears from the kitchen, pulling off an apron and wiping her hands. She has penciled black eyebrows and a long grey bob that brushes her shoulders. The web of wrinkles around her mouth looks like fine cracks in bone china.

She pulls out a bound ledger from a drawer. The book has a famous painting on the cover, *Girl with a Pearl Earring*. Inside there are handwritten columns giving the name and address of each guest.

"I haven't seen one of those for a while," I say.

"I'm auld-fashioned," she explains. "And I cannae use a computer."

She studies the photograph on my UK driver's license, quickly glancing at my face before jotting down the details. She turns to Evie.

"Does she need ID?" I ask.

"It's the law."

"I'm paying for both rooms."

"Makes no difference."

Evie hands over her driver's license. "You don't look twenty-two," says the woman.

"I get that a lot," says Evie.

Behind us in the lounge, two men are playing snooker on a green baize table. A young girl is watching them, picking absentmindedly at a scab on her knee. She has pink streaks in her hair and one side of her head is shaved tight to her scalp.

Our rooms are on the second floor. Narrow corridors seem to double back on each other, occasionally interrupted by fire doors that have been propped open, despite signs asking for them to be kept closed. My room smells of Febreze and bleach and broken dreams. Evie is next door. She unlocks the adjoining door and joins me, testing the mattress, flicking light switches, and opening cupboards.

"A Bible," she says, pulling a copy from a drawer. "Is that still a thing?"

"This is Scotland," I say, unpacking my bag.

"Are you going to ask about him?"

"Not here. Not yet."

She sits cross-legged on my bed, scrolling through TV channels, not tired at all, having slept on the journey.

Flick: *Love Island.*

Flick: *Beauty and the Geek.*

Flick: *The Bachelor.*

"Why do people go on these shows?" she asks.

"Because people like you watch them."

"No, I'm serious. You're a psychologist. Why?"

"They want to be famous."

"By embarrassing themselves."

"Some crave attention or validation. Others think fame will cure their self-doubt or anxiety or help them belong or make them rich."

"I don't want to be rich or famous," says Evie, before changing her mind. "Being rich would be OK. I'd buy an animal shelter and spend the rest of my life rescuing dogs."

"Very worthy. Can you go to bed, please?"

"I'm hungry."

"Of course, you are."

There is a Chinese restaurant farther along the road. It has about six tables with plastic chairs and plastic menus and plastic bottles of soy sauce and sweet chili. Two customers are picking up takeaways, but the dining tables are empty. The menu is a weird mixture of Thai, Chinese, Indian, and European, with chips included. It reminds me of an old Frankie Boyle joke about Las Vegas and Glasgow being the only two places in the world where you can pay for sex with chips.

The sole waitress has bleached-blond hair and an outsized rump encased in purple leggings. She calls out our meal order to the open kitchen, where the Asian chef, half her size, is wielding a wok like a sword. He's yelling at a kitchen hand, who is wrist deep in suds at the sink, wilting under the abuse.

"Is everything all right?" I ask the waitress.

"Yeah, why wouldn't it be?"

It's a challenge rather than a question—telling me to mind my own business.

The harbor is visible between buildings. Fishing trawlers are moored side by side along the dock, and men are still working under the lights, loading ice and fuel, or mending nets.

I pick up a local newspaper, which is full of ads for engineering companies, boatyards, fishing agents, hydraulic specialists, shipwrights, and vessel brokers.

"Are yer lookin' fer work?" asks the waitress, delivering our meals. Her right thumb has been sitting in my chicken chow mein. She licks it clean.

"No, just visiting," I say. "I'm hoping to catch up with a friend. We lost touch a while back."

"Does he owe you money?"

"No."

"Well, he shouldn't be hard to find. Not a big place, this."

"Angus Radford."

She thrusts out her hip. "Popular name around here."

"He's a fisherman."

"Plenty o' them." She moves away.

Evie whispers, "She's lying," and dips a spring roll into chili sauce.

Later, I notice the waitress talking on her mobile phone and glancing towards me. It could be nothing, but I'm annoyed because St. Claire is the sort of parochial, insular place where word can travel quickly. I purposely pay the bill in cash, not wanting to hand over my credit card. Outside, under a streetlight, I turn in the opposite direction to the guesthouse.

"It's that way," says Evie.

"Let's walk around the block."

"I thought you were tired."

"It won't take long."

At the next corner, I glance over my shoulder and notice the waitress standing on the pavement, still talking on her phone. Ahead of us, two dockside cranes reach into the sky like leafless trees. A red light is blinking from the highest point and a beam of silver sweeps over the sea from a lighthouse.

I hear music. A folk band is playing at the Waterfront Inn. Drinkers spill out onto the pavement, leaning on lampposts, holding pint glasses and glowing cigarettes.

"Do you recognize anything about this place?" I ask. "Could you have been here before?"

Evie shrugs or it could be a shiver.

Back at the guesthouse, we enter through the side door to slip quietly up the stairs. There are still guests in the lounge. They look like traveling salesmen rather than tourists.

Evie follows me into my room. "Can I stay with you tonight?"

"No."

"What if someone breaks into my room?"

"Yell."

"What if they cover my mouth and I can't scream?"

"Bite them."

"What if they're really quiet, like ninjas?"

"Go to bed, Evie."

She leaves the internal door open. I brush my teeth and collapse into an exhausted sleep where conscious thoughts mutate into fevered dreams and then wonderful, sweet, carefree oblivion.

37

Evie

Cyrus says I'm too young to have regrets, which makes it sound as though heartache and crushing disappointment are things people grow into or develop a taste for, like red wine or black coffee or dark chocolate. He also says that life is about fixing broken connections.

Why do they break in the first place? I asked. He said, accidents, carelessness, negligence, and loss. Sometimes the connection is broken at birth; sometimes it happens later. For Cyrus, it broke when he was thirteen years old and he came home from football practice to discover that his family was dead. That's why he became a psychologist—to understand what happened—but delving into other people's minds hasn't healed Cyrus or let him sleep peacefully at night or stopped him lifting weights until his veins bulge. Instead, I see someone who is more damaged than I am, only he hasn't realized it yet.

I don't know when my connection broke. Maybe when Agnesa was raped or when Papa was killed, or when we left home without saying good-bye to anyone. Perhaps the connection was stretched thinner and thinner the farther we traveled, until it finally snapped.

It was four days on buses and trains before we stopped moving and I saw the Atlantic Ocean for the first time. Grey, choppy, and cold, it didn't look any different from the sea that I'd seen in Tirana. We had reached an old city full of churches and squares and palaces, but also empty shops and abandoned factories and cheap hotels.

I didn't know much about Spain. I once asked Papa about a book he was reading called *Don Quixote*. He said it was set in Spain and was about a man who lost his mind and went on a quest to become a knight and defeat imaginary enemies like windmills and flocks of sheep. Papa said the story was about challenging life and how madness can be a healthy reaction to a mad world. I didn't understand it then. I do now.

Mama rented a room in a boardinghouse, and I slept on the floor because the roll-away cot collapsed on the first night and the landlady threatened to make us pay. During the day, we walked around the city and ate oranges and flaky pastries, and I tasted avocado for the first time.

I practiced my English with a Spanish girl who worked in a café downstairs. I couldn't understand some of what she said because her accent was so strong and she mixed up her tenses, but she taught me swear words that I had never heard before.

On the ninth day, we were woken in the middle of the night and told to pack our things. A covered truck was waiting downstairs. We loaded our suitcases and an extra bag of food into the truck, which took us to the port and into a warehouse where other migrants were waiting. We were told to line up. A man walked down the row, choosing people. Mama brushed my hair and told me to stand up straight.

The man stopped next to Agnesa. She didn't lift her head. He gripped her face in his hand and raised her chin.

"This one," he said.

"No, we are family," said Mama.

He ignored her and one of his men tried to pull Agnesa from the line. Mama held on to one of her hands and I held the other, pulling her back.

"We all go," said Mama.

A man slapped her across the face. I reacted without thinking, kicked him in the shins. He hopped on one leg and took a swing at me, but I ducked and kicked him again, which made the other men laugh.

Mama pushed Agnesa behind her. The man pointed a gun at her head. Mama didn't flinch. I saw the black hole at the end of the barrel and I wanted to put my finger inside to make the gun explode like it did in those cartoons when Elmer Fudd was hunting Bugs Bunny.

The man lowered the gun and grunted an order. We were pulled from the line, Mama, Agnesa, and me. Others were chosen, mainly young men, a few women, and another family with two children, a girl Agnesa's age and a younger boy. The rest of the migrants were told that another boat would come for them. Some complained and jostled, but the gun kept them quiet.

The man in charge looked at our three suitcases. "Too much."

"This is all we have," said Mama.

He picked up two of the cases, undid the latches, and tipped them upside down, spilling our belongings onto the filthy floor.

"One bag," he said. "Repack."

Choices had to be made. We each took a warm coat, underwear, socks, and a pair of good shoes. Much was left behind. It was almost dawn when they took us to a small boat with an outboard motor, which ferried us six at a time to a fishing trawler moored in the harbor amid a forest of masts with blinking lights and rattling cables.

The crew threw a ladder over the side. They wore black masks with holes for their eyes. We climbed up and then down again into the hold, which stank of fish and diesel fumes. Mama complained there were too many of us. She was ignored.

The engines started and the boat trembled and the hatches were locked down. In the darkness, I could hear people murmuring in languages that I couldn't understand. Praying. We all were, even Mama, who didn't believe in God. I was sitting between her legs, with her arms around my waist. Agnesa was next to her. Her job was to guard the suitcase, which had the last of our money.

Years later, at Langford Hall, I remember being told a Bible story about a man called Jonah who was saved from drowning by being swallowed by a big fish. It wasn't a whale, like most people think. Jonah spent three days and three nights in the belly of the fish. He prayed to God and the fish vomited him out.

When I heard that story, I thought about being back in the hull of that trawler, with its metal ribs and its smell of fish and sweat and fuel and feces, with an engine that throbbed like the heart of a whale.

38

Cyrus

There is a waiting stillness about the morning, as the sun emerges from the horizon, lighting up a bank of clouds that glow red like a floating fire above the dark sea. My running shoes make a soughing sound on the pavement, and the ground moves towards me and beneath me and behind me.

Evie was still asleep when I left the guesthouse. She probably won't wake until I'm back, but I slipped a note beneath our adjoining door, telling her I won't be long. That was an hour ago. Since then I have explored St. Claire, running along empty streets, past darkened terraces, shops, factories, and blocks of flats. Many are built from the same red granite and give the impression that the town sprouted directly from the rocky cliffs, taking root like the stunted trees, which lean away from the prevailing winds.

The lowest part of the town is on the shoreline, where the shingle beach is blanketed by seaweed. Farther east, protected by a breakwater and twin lighthouses, the harbor is surrounded by factories and warehouses. Pausing at the end of the southern breakwater, I watch a fishing trawler return to port, towing seagulls like white kites.

Retracing my steps, uphill this time, I pass a man in a tweed jacket and peaked cap, walking his Jack Russell. I stop on the corner, waiting for him.

"You picked a tough climb," he says, sounding more English than Scottish.

"More fool me."

The dog sniffs at my shoes.

"It's a lovely morning," I say. "Are you a local?"

"No, I'm visiting my grandchildren." He points along the lane. "My son married a Scottish lass. A Jock. Are we allowed to call them that? I'm not sure these days."

"Where is home?"

"Cornwall. My wife died last year. This is my first trip without her."

"I'm sorry to hear that."

"It is what it is."

He crouches to scratch the dog behind her ears.

"I'm looking for someone who knows about the fishing industry," I say. "In particular, an accident. A trawler sank off the Scottish coast about twelve years ago."

"Dylan might know. He volunteers at the lifeboat station, when he's not delivering the mail."

"Where would I find Dylan?"

"At home having breakfast. You're welcome to join us. Call me Patrick."

"Cyrus," I reply. He has a firm, dry handshake that feels like I'm squeezing a wad of crumpled paper.

I follow him to the end of a lane, where the terrace cottage matches all the others in the street. Patrick takes off his boots in the entrance hall. The dog runs ahead of him. The place smells of boiled milk, porridge, and brown sugar. Toys are scattered along the hallway. One of them squeaks under my feet and a young woman appears. Pretty. Careworn.

"Have you picked up another stray, Dad?" she asks.

"Found him on the road," says Patrick.

I begin to apologize, but she waves me to the table, where two small children with food-smeared faces are seated on matching high chairs. Twin boys.

"I'm Jessica," she says. "These two terrorists are Rory and Lachlan." She wipes their grimacing faces with a washcloth.

"And I'm Dylan," says a bearded man, who is built like a brick outhouse, dressed in dark cargo shorts, a red Royal Mail shirt, and heavy boots.

"Cyrus is looking for details about a fishing trawler that sank off the coast," says Patrick, who shows me where to wash my hands.

"The *Arianna II*," I say.

"Willie Radford's boat," says Dylan. "That was south of here. The lifeboat crew from Aberdeen got the callout, along with the coastguard chopper."

"What happened?" I ask.

"A fire in the engine room. One crewman lost. Two more airlifted to hospital."

"Lost?"

"Cameron Radford," says Jessica, her voice tinged with sadness.

"Jessica used to date him," says Dylan.

"In primary school." She laughs. "We didn't even hold hands."

"Everybody knew the family," says Dylan. "Three brothers. Cam was the youngest. Finn was never the same afterwards. You still see him around St. Claire, off his head on booze and talking to hisself."

"Who is Willie Radford?" I ask.

"Their father. He's a big wheel in town. A businessman. Runs a fish processing plant. Employs a lot of locals."

"And the mother?"

"They divorced after the sinking. She went back to her maiden name, Maureen Collie. She owns a guesthouse in St. Claire."

"The Belhaven Inn?"

"That's the place."

I think about the woman who signed us in last night. She'd be about the right age.

"Maureen is a force of nature," says Jessica. "One of eight—four boys and four girls. Bit of Irish Catholic in them."

"You mentioned three brothers," I say.

"Angus is the eldest. He was the skipper," says Dylan. "Why are you interested?"

"Angus Radford was arrested down south. I'm looking at his background."

"What's he done now?" asks Jessica, sounding resigned.

"He was on a trawler that collided with a migrant boat."

Dylan whistles through his teeth. "The one in the news. All those people washed ashore."

"He's been charged with murder."

"Fuck me," says Dylan.

Jessica glares at him. "Mind your language in front of the bairns."

"Sorry, hen."

"And don't call me hen."

Jessica lifts the twins from the high chairs and takes them into another room before returning.

"Are you with the police?" she asks.

"I'm a forensic psychologist. I study criminal behavior."

"Well, we're all pretty normal up here," says Dylan.

Jessica gives a derisory laugh. "Yeah, apart from the underage drinking, youth suicides, wife beating, and drug dealing."

"OK, but not here in St. Claire."

"How would you know? You're a well-known eejit." She ruffles his hair and smooths it down again.

Dylan gets to his feet and takes a high-vis jacket from a hook on the back of the door.

"I'm off. I'll be home at six."

Jessica stands on her tiptoes and pulls down his face in both her hands, kissing him on the lips. "Give Cyrus a lift."

"That's OK. It's not far," I say.

"No. He'll take you."

39

Evie

Cyrus has left me a note: *Gone for a run. Won't be long. Stay out of trouble.* He put twenty quid in the envelope, which I don't need, but I take it anyway because technically I'm helping him and he gets paid to do stuff like this.

Something topples in the next room. I think he must be back. Opening the internal door, I find a girl going through the pockets of his jacket. She has dyed pink streaks in her hair and one side of her head is shaved, revealing her left ear, which is like an island dotted with silver studs.

"What are you doing?" I ask.

She jumps as though startled, withdrawing her hand from the jacket pocket.

"H-h-ousekeeping," she stammers through the braces on her teeth. "I was just hanging this up." She hooks the jacket onto a hanger.

She's lying.

"Where's your cleaning trolley?"

"In the corridor."

"What's your name?"

"Molly."

"Your real name?"

She frowns, less certain than before. "Addie Murdoch."

"Shouldn't you be in school?"

"Ah'm on holidays." She looks at the door, as though wanting to escape. "Ah didnae take anything. I'm not a thief."

"Clearly you are."

A fake tremor enters her voice. "Don't tell Maureen. She'll murder me."

"Who's Maureen?"

"She's like my grandma." Addie presses her hands together. "Ah won't do it again. Ah promise. Please."

Another lie, but this one makes me smile because I've been there and done that—been caught red-handed and begged for forgiveness. Addie frowns, unsure of my reaction. There is a general skewness about her; her eyes not quite level, her mouth drooping on one side, even her shoulders look crooked.

"How old are you?"

"Fourteen."

"Really?"

"Almost thirteen."

"Don't come into these rooms again, OK?"

"What about making up the beds?"

"Not today."

After she's gone, I dress in jeans and a hooded sweatshirt, and I put on my sunglasses, even though it's a cloudy day. I leave through the side door, avoiding the breakfast room, which is crowded with families and at least one crying baby.

Walking towards the harbor, I pass shuttered shops and those just opening. A team of builders is putting up scaffolding in front of a house. One of them whistles at me and yells, "Cheer up, love, it probably won't happen."

Fuckwit!

Head down, hood up, hands in my pockets, I pass a solicitor's office with a window sign advertising "criminal defenses." Next comes a dog groomer, a bakery, a tobacconist, and a pharmacy. None of it looks familiar. Cyrus thinks I might have been here before, but he must be wrong.

At a café on Queen Street, the waitress tries to upsell me a "bacon butty," which sounds like a skin condition. She has to explain what it is. Why not just call it a bacon sandwich? I choose a muffin and a hot chocolate and take a seat outside. The street is slowly waking up as more shops begin to open.

On the far side of the road, I notice a signpost pointing out local services, including the public library. It gives me an idea. Brushing crumbs off my lap, I cross the street and turn the corner, arriving at a red-stone building with a blue-painted door. The foyer has mosaic tiles on the floor and a strange doorman—a life-sized polar bear wearing a kilt with a tartan beret.

"That's Paul R. Bear," says the librarian, a pretty woman in flared trousers and a white blouse. "The kids love him."

I think he looks creepy, but let it go.

"How can I help you, pet?" she asks.

"I'm researching my uncle's family tree."

"That's always fun," she says, pointing me towards a cluster of desks with computer terminals. "Most of the resources are available online. You should try National Records of Scotland and work backwards."

"How do I get started?"

"What's your uncle's name?"

"Angus Radford. He's thirty-eight. And he comes from around here."

She types the details into the computer and the screen refreshes.

"This could be him." She reads from the screen. "Angus Fraser Radford. Father William Fraser Radford. Mother Maureen Elizabeth Collie. He was born at the Community Hospital here in St. Claire." She opens a new page. "He has siblings. Two brothers, Finn and Cameron." The librarian rolls back her chair. "Now you have their names and ages, you should be able to keep going."

"What about newspaper files?" I ask.

"We don't keep hard copies or microfilm on site. For that you'll need to visit the National Library of Scotland. They have a reading room in Edinburgh."

I won't be doing that.

"Are there books about local shipwrecks and boating accidents?" I ask.

"Is your uncle a fisherman?"

"He was on a boat that sank twelve years ago. He didn't drown or anything."

She looks relieved. "You could try our local history section. St. Claire has been a fishing and whaling port for centuries."

She shows me to the right aisle but is summoned to the reception desk, where a coffin dodger in a wheelchair is stuck in the turnstile. "Let me know how you get on," she says, bustling across the library in her sensible shoes, all spit and polish and discipline.

I look along the titles: *Hidden Aberdeenshire*, *Forgotten Aberdeenshire*, *Aberdeenshire Remembered*. I pick one of them up and begin turning the pages, reading the first paragraph of each chapter, but mostly looking at the pictures. The old ones are in black and white, showing fishermen posing in front of boats or unloading boxes of fish.

My phone is buzzing. I put AirPods in my ears.

"Where are you?" asks Cyrus, sounding concerned.

"At the library doing some research," I say, wanting him to be impressed. "Angus Radford was born in St. Claire and he has two brothers, Finn and Cameron. I know the names of their parents and where they were born and their occupations."

"Cameron is dead," says Cyrus. "He was on the trawler that sank."

I'm annoyed that he knows this already. The librarian is walking towards me, carrying a book. I put Cyrus on hold.

"I found this," she says excitedly. "It was self-published by a local historian."

I look at the cover. *LIFEBOAT LEGENDS: A century of maritime rescues in Scotland.*

She opens it at a marked page. There is a photograph of a coastguard helicopter on a landing pad. The crew is posing under the stationary blades, dressed in orange overalls and yellow helmets.

The caption reads: *Three crew rescued in trawler tragedy. One deceased.*

Farther down the page is a picture of the *Arianna II*, a fat-bellied boat that looks more like a tugboat than a trawler. The librarian leaves me with the book. I take Cyrus off hold. "I found a story about the *Arianna II*," I whisper, turning the page.

Suddenly, the light dims and my gaze narrows and the only thing that exists is a single image showing a young man with tangled hair and blue-green eyes, who is grinning at the camera. My mind slips and I'm no longer aware of the library or Cyrus or his voice in my ears. Instead, I hear the throbbing of an engine and I smell the diesel and vomit. A hatch opens. Bright light blasts my senses. A figure is silhouetted against the square of brightness. A ghost. An illusion. A ripple across time.

Cyrus is saying my name, yelling it over and over, trying to get my attention.

My dry lips peel open. "It's him."

"Who?"

"One of them."

40

Cyrus

Evie is sitting on a low stone wall with her arms wrapped tightly across her chest, holding a book. A gust of wind stirs up an eddy of dust on the pavement and lifts her hair from her forehead.

"I borrowed it," she says. "I had to promise to bring it back."

"That's how libraries work," I say, taking a mental inventory of her demeanor and body language, concerned about her state of mind. She shows me the photograph. "He was on the boat that picked us up."

The caption reads: *Cameron Radford, aged 19, died in the fire*.

"Are you sure it's him?" I ask.

She nods. There's another photograph on the same page—a fishing trawler. The *Arianna II*.

"Could this boat have been the one?" I ask.

"I don't know."

"Where were you picked up?"

Evie spells the name because she doesn't know how to pronounce it properly.

"A . . . V . . . I . . . L . . . E . . . S."

"That's in northern Spain," I say, surprised. "I thought it would have been France."

"I know the difference," Evie says irritably. "There was a harbor and a square lighthouse and lots of old buildings."

"Who else was on board?"

"People like us. Migrants."

"How many?"

Evie struggles to remember. I try to help her fill in the missing pieces by asking about the small details. How many men? How many women?

Children? Where were they from? Where was the boat taking you? How long did it take?

She is shaking her head. "I don't know. I *can't* remember."

"Try harder."

"I'm trying."

"Do you remember a fire? What about the rest of the crew?"

She covers her ears, saying, "I can't, I can't, I can't."

Her eyes have lost focus and I can almost see her mind beginning to slip away from me. I say her name. She doesn't respond. I wave my hand in front of her face. She doesn't blink. I touch her arm near her elbow. She jerks it away, glaring at me accusingly.

"I lost you for a moment," I say.

"I didn't go anywhere."

She holds up the book, pointing to the author's name. *Ronald L. Edwards*.

"He's a local historian. The librarian gave me his address."

The landscape changes as we drive north. The trees become more gnarled and spindlier, and the heather looks like lichen clinging to the rocks. Black-cloaked rooks lift off fences as we pass and return to the same spot as though tethered by invisible strings.

Ronald Edwards lives in a village outside of Fraserburgh. His flat-fronted granite cottage has white-painted sash windows and an old-fashioned door knocker in the shape of a lion's head. It echoes through the interior, summoning an old man dressed in baggy shorts and a Scottish rugby shirt. He has white-grey hair, fluffy above his ears, and wrinkles that fold into more wrinkles around his eyes.

"Where are mah groceries?" he asks, stepping onto the pavement.

"Pardon?"

"Those eejits said between ten and twelve."

He looks at Evie and frowns. She holds up the book. "Did you write this?"

He grins. "So, you found the other one. Weren't many copies printed. Labor o' love, that one."

"We wanted to ask you about the sinking of the *Arianna II*," I say.

"Well, you'd best come in. Time for a brew."

He leads us along a cluttered passage, weaving between boxes of books that are resting precariously on top of each other. There are more books stacked up the stairs and on the first-floor landing.

"Ah'm not a hoarder," he says. "I just cannae throw anything away. Apart from my first wife. She got recycled. Married again." He winks at Evie.

The cluttered kitchen has more books and folders. He fills a kettle and makes a pot of tea, putting sugar, milk, and shortbread biscuits on a tray.

Finally seated, he opens a hip flask and pours a splash into his tea. He waves it towards me; I decline.

"I'll have some," says Evie, holding out her mug.

Mr. Edwards looks at me, as though seeking permission.

"It's her choice," I say.

He pours a splash into her mug. Evie takes a sip and makes a face. Lesson learned.

"You have quite a library, Mr. Edwards," I say.

"Call me Fishy. Everybody else does."

"You were a fisherman," I say.

"Christ noo! It's what yer might call an ironic nickname. Ah get seasick in the bathtub. Why are you so interested in the *Arianna II*?"

"It's a personal matter," I say, trying to protect Evie.

"Aye, well, that was Willie Radford's boat. He lost his youngest son. Only nineteen."

"What happened?" I ask.

"A fire in the engine room, triggered an explosion. The boat sank before help arrived."

Fishy gets up. "Wait here." I can hear him going through boxes in his study. He returns with a bound folder.

"The Maritime Accident Investigation Branch sent a team from Southampton to interview the crew and take statements. This is the final report."

I read the summary page, which describes the *Arianna II* as a twin-rig steel-hulled trawler built in 1970. Length: 17.44 meters. Beam: 6.49 meters. Draft: 2.24 meters.

The Arianna II *departed from St. Claire on the 14th of September 2010 with a crew of four and voyaged to its North Sea fishing* grounds. For the next eight days it fished Dogger Bank, about 130 kms off the Yorkshire coast, trawling for whitefish, processing the catch after each haul. At night the trawler drifted with a lookout in the wheelhouse while the remaining crew rested.

On 22 September, the trawler began the journey home. At 2130, approximately 100 nautical miles east of Aberdeen, a smoke detector began sounding in the engine room. The skipper, who was at the helm, sent a deckhand to investigate. When the door to the engine room was opened, the deckhand saw heavy smoke and flames. He raised the alarm and tried to extinguish the blaze using retardant, but the open bulkhead door added oxygen to the fire and likely triggered a flashover explosion. The deckhand was blown backwards against the bulkhead, suffering critical injuries. He was dragged from the engine room by the skipper, who sustained burns to his face, neck, and hands. The engineer performed CPR but could not resuscitate the deckhand, who died of his injuries.

The skipper and remaining crew fought the fire with portable chemical fire extinguishers and brought the blaze under control, but the explosion had caused a breach in the hull and water was welling up underneath the main engine. The skipper set up the port general-service pump to draw from the engine room bilge, but the inflow of water overwhelmed the pump.

By 2205 it was clear that efforts to stabilize the situation were failing and the skipper raised the alarm with the coastguard by transmitting a "Mayday" call on both very high frequency (VHF) and medium frequency radios; he also pressed the VHF digital selective calling distress button, and manually activated the emergency position indicating radio beacon.

On receiving the Mayday call, the Aberdeen Maritime Rescue Coordination Centre immediately tasked the coastguard rescue helicopter from Inverness and the RNLI Aberdeen lifeboat.

Using a VHF radio, the Arianna II skipper discussed the situation with the skipper of the nearest vessel, Neetha Dawn, a trawler that was fifteen nautical miles southeast of the Arianna II. Neetha Dawn responded, along with two other fishing boats that were more distant.

Water continued to rise in the engine room and at 2300 the electrical power failed when the auxiliary engine stopped, preventing further use of electric pumps. As the situation deteriorated, the crew donned immersion suits and life jackets.

At 2315 water had entered the main cabins and the Arianna II *was listing to starboard. The life raft was launched and the crew abandoned the trawler, carrying the body of the deceased crewman. The* Arianna II *was observed to sink at 2343, approximately 93 nautical miles (180 kilometers) east of Aberdeen (Latitude 56.94093°N, Longitude 0.867896°E) in 300 feet of water.*

The Neetha Dawn *spotted the life raft at 0016 and took the survivors on board. The coastguard rescue helicopter reached the scene fifteen minutes later. The injured skipper and engineer were winched from the deck of the trawler before being transferred to the Aberdeen Royal Infirmary.*

The RNLI lifeboat, Bon Accord, *from Aberdeen, rendezvoused with the* Neetha Dawn *at 0315. The body of the deceased deckhand was transferred to the lifeboat. The remaining crewman chose to remain on board the* Neetha Dawn *for the voyage to St. Claire.*

I pause from reading. "Why isn't anyone named?"

"Marine accident investigations aren't about apportioning blame," says Fishy. "Otherwise, witnesses might not cooperate."

"Do you know who was on board?"

"The skipper was Angus Radford, Willie's eldest boy. His two brothers were the crew, Finn and Cameron, along with their cousin, Iain Collie, who was the engineer. Angus suffered burns to his face and hands. Iain Collie had smoke-damaged pipes." Fishy taps his chest. "He died of throat cancer a few years back, which might have been unrelated, but he'd never been a smoker."

"What caused the fire?"

"No way of knowing for certain," says Fishy.

"Did they salvage her?"

"She sank too deep."

"But they found the wreckage? They sent divers?"

"Would have cost a fortune."

He points to another section of the report.

Investigators could not inspect the machinery or hull of the Arianna II *to determine an exact cause of the fire and explosion. However, observations by the crew during the accident provide some clues as to the source of the blaze. The deckhand who discovered the fire reported seeing flames in the vicinity of the generator, located on the port side aft in the engine room.*

Over time a hose could have become worn from contact or loosened through vibrations, allowing fuel to leak into the engine room. Leaking fuel or fuel vapor may have come into contact with a hot surface, igniting the fire that subsequently triggered the explosion.

I finish reading and lean back from the table, glancing at Evie, asking an unspoken question. Does she remember any of this? She shakes her head.

"What's the range on a trawler like the *Arianna*?" I ask.

Fishy does a quick calculation on a piece of paper, mumbling to himself about cruising speed, fuel capacity, and distances. He shows me the figure.

"Could it reach northern Spain?" I ask.

"It's a fishing boat, not a pleasure cruiser."

"But could it get there and back?"

"In theory."

"How long would it take?"

"Four, maybe five days, but they were fishing Dogger Bank."

"How can you be sure?"

He shows me an attached map labeled *Figure 1* in the report.

"The *Arianna II* was carrying an AIS transponder, which gave its location every few minutes via satellite. This shows the patterns it was fishin' each day. Dogger Bank is the UK's largest sandbank and one of the biggest fishing grounds."

The map is marked by a series of tight lines displayed in red, that seem to zigzag across the ocean. Each position is time coded, showing the location of the trawler when the signal was sent to the satellite.

"Can the transponder be turned off?" I ask.

"Aye, it happens. They call it going dark." Fishy makes air quotes with his fingers. "Some skippers don't want other boats knowing where they're fishing, or they might be doing something illegal. But do it too often, or for too long, and you'll trigger a coastguard search or have the authorities asking questions."

"They're worried about smuggling."

"Or illegal fishing."

Evie has been running her fingers along the edge of the table. "Eight days seems like a long time to be at sea," she says.

"Not really," says Fishy. "A trawler won't come home without a catch, unless equipment breaks, or they're running out of fuel."

I look again at the map. Evie doesn't remember a fire or explosion, which means the loss of the *Arianna II* could be unrelated to her past. Maybe she was on a different boat.

"Did Angus and Cameron ever work for other skippers?" I ask.

"Aye, maybe. Angus and Finn had been fishin' since they were wee lads, but Cam was different. Like it or not, he was heading off to university when the semester started."

"Did he have a choice?" asks Evie.

"Not the way of things. Willie Radford had three sons and only one boat. Angus was the eldest. He was always going to inherit the *Arianna*. The other boys had to make their own way."

I look at Evie, hoping she has another question, because I'm out of ideas. Nothing is any clearer. Whatever answers there are seem to be locked inside her head and she won't give me the key. I know the reason. Self-preservation. Sanity. Survival. Some memories are buried for a reason. How else do we carry the past?

41

Cyrus

"Where are you going?" asks Evie when I drop her back at the guesthouse.

"To look for someone."

"The crew?"

"Yes."

"Can I come?"

"No."

She's about to argue, but I stop her. "If you were on board that boat, Evie, I don't want anyone recognizing you."

"But I might recognize *them*," she says. "I can help."

"Not this time."

There is no point in lying to Evie. The best way to counter her questions is to give answers with more than one possible meaning. Ambiguity and doublespeak can sometimes conceal the truth from her, but I suspect she's beginning to work this out.

"If you're hungry, get something delivered," I say. "And if you do go out—don't talk to anyone or ask about the trawler."

She makes a *hmmmph* sound and turns on the TV, choosing my room instead of hers.

I have two missed calls. One from Florence and the other from DI Carlson. Florence is the first to answer. I tell her about the explosion and fire on board the *Arianna II* and how Angus Radford suffered burns to his face and hands.

"Evie has recognized someone else—Angus Radford's brother. He died in the fire."

"Were they trafficking people?" she asks.

"According to the satellite tracking system, the trawler didn't leave the fishing grounds."

"What about an earlier voyage?"

"It's possible, but Cameron Radford wasn't a regular crewman. There was another brother on board—I'm trying to find him."

Florence has been searching company records, looking for the beneficial owners of the *New Victory*, the trawler impounded by the police in Humberside.

"The shelf company is registered in the Cayman Islands. The listed address is a post office box linked to a vacant block of land. But I found another interesting connection. Do you remember the Panama Papers? A whistleblower working for a Panamanian law firm leaked millions of documents to investigative journalists."

"It was about tax evasion."

"On a huge scale. Some of the richest, most powerful people in the world were using offshore tax havens and dummy companies to hide their wealth and avoid scrutiny. Plutocrats. Dictators. Financiers. Politicians. Intelligence officers. Even royalty. One name that came up was North Star Holdings."

"Why is that important?"

"It's the family company of Lord David Buchan—set up by his father thirty years ago. Basically, it's an umbrella company with dozens of subsidiary businesses. Factories. Processing plants. Prefabricated building supplies. Hotels. Employment agencies. Freight companies.

"When the Panama Papers leaked, David Buchan denied any knowledge of the arrangements, saying that he handed over control of his business interests to a blind trust when he entered the House of Lords. Everything at arm's length."

"Do you believe that?"

"No."

"What does Simon Buchan say?"

"He negotiated to sell his stake in the family trust when his father died."

"To his brother?"

"I assume so, but I don't have more details and I'm reluctant to ask Simon because it might not be appropriate."

I can understand her misgivings. She works for Simon Buchan and he's unlikely to be happy if she investigates his family's business dealings, regardless of the fraternal friction.

"You mentioned a freight company. Does North Star Holdings have business interests in France or Spain?" I ask.

"I can check, but it could take a while to unravel."

"Tread lightly."

"You too."

I try for Carlson and leave him a nonspecific message, asking for news of Arben's kidnappers. He doesn't know I'm in Scotland and won't approve of a parallel, unofficial investigation into Angus Radford and his family.

St. Claire has six pubs and a handful of bars and clubs, most of them clustered around the harbor in the older part of the town. At each, I nurse a beer and strike up a conversation with whoever is working behind the bar. I can't hide the fact that I'm an outsider—my accent marks me down as an Englishman—but the staff are friendly enough until I mention the name Finn Radford.

"He's the friend of a friend," I say. "I promised to look him up."

The responses range from feigned ignorance to outright hostility, with one publican saying, "That fookin' drunk had better not come round here—not after the last time."

At the fourth pub, I don't mention Finn's name. I buy a drink and sit in the corner, watching the regular patrons who have bellied up to the bar, buttocks spreading on stools, elbows guarding pint glasses, opinions given for free on all subjects.

A woman chooses something from the jukebox. We make eye contact and I hold her gaze for a beat too long. Moments later, she sways between tables and approaches, leaning closer, cigarettes on her breath.

"Buy a girl a drink."

"I'm waiting for someone."

"That can be me."

She's older than I first thought, with lines around her eyes, but a nice smile. Her full hips are packed into a short grey dress. She holds out her hand. Red polish on long fingernails. "I'm Kellie."

"Cyrus," I reply.

She tickles the inside of my palm with a finger as our hands touch. "I'll have a Rusty Nail."

I go to the bar and order the drinks. Kellie takes out her phone and uses it as a mirror, checking her makeup. I wonder for a moment if she's a sex worker but reproach myself for making assumptions.

Back at the table, she pulls her stool closer to mine, parting her knees for a moment. She raises her glass. "Slàinte Mhath."

"What does that mean?"

"In good health. It's Gaelic."

I take a sip of whiskey. She swallows her cocktail in three gulps. Her eyes seem to light up.

"You're not a local, are you, Cyrus?"

"No. I'm visiting."

"Alone?"

"With a friend. I'm actually looking for someone. Finn Radford."

"Finn? Why?"

"I hear he's struggling."

"That's one word for it," she says. "This time of day, he'll be facedown in a cot at the Fisherman's Hostel. But give it a few hours and he'll be drinking again."

There is a poignancy in her tone—as though she remembers him as a different man.

"Where is the Fisherman's Hostel?"

"Opposite the lifeboat station."

I swallow my whiskey, feeling the burn.

"You're not leaving, are you?" asks Kellie. "We only just met." She runs her forefinger around the edge of her glass and licks it provocatively.

"Next time," I say. "Nice chatting to you."

"Your loss," she shouts, as I push out the door and get buffeted by a gust of wind that snaps at my trouser cuffs.

The lower floor of the hostel is an old storefront where the display windows have been sealed up and painted. The wooden building looks incongruous among the granite factories and workshops, most of them servicing the fishing industry. A brass call bell rests on the counter. I tap it twice and wait. Nobody answers. I hear a TV from somewhere along a corridor. Following the sound, I come to a lounge where two old guys are sitting in lumpy armchairs, one of them dozing and the other watching a nature documentary narrated by David Attenborough.

"Have you seen Finn?" I ask, making it sound like I'm expected.

"Top of the stairs. First door on the right," says the TV watcher, without looking away from a hummingbird hovering beside a flower.

I follow his directions. Knuckles tap on the door. No answer. I knock more loudly. A moaned "Piss off."

I turn the handle.

Finn Radford is fully clothed, sprawled on a single bed. The room reeks of sweated alcohol, flatulence, and stale cigarette smoke.

His eyes half open. "Who th'fuck are you?"

"A friend."

"I have nae fuckin' friends."

I pull a bottle of whiskey from the brown paper bag that is bulging in my jacket pocket. "Let's have a drink."

I take a glass from a sink in the corner and hold it up to the light, seeing every fingerprint. After rinsing it out, I pour him a shot. He signals for more. I top it up. He needs two hands to hold it steady.

"Tell me about your brothers," I say.

"I only got the one."

"How did Cameron die?"

"A fire. I should have saved him."

"According to the investigation, you did everything you could."

"How would you know?"

"I read the accident report."

"Reports," he scoffs, breaking into a hacking cough—the early stages of emphysema. He reaches for a packet of cigarettes on the bedspread next to him. A sign on the door says "no smoking." He lights up, cupping the flame. Inhaling. Swallowing. More coughing. More whiskey.

"Did the report get it wrong?" I ask.

"You ever been to sea on a trawler?"

"No."

"Ever seen one sink?"

"No."

A tiny vein twitches above his right eye.

"What caused the fire?" I ask.

He grunts. "A worn fuel line, a short circuit, a loose bearing, a spark . . ."

"Which one?"

"Take your pick." He drags more smoke into his lungs.

"Maybe the engine overheated," I say. "It's a long way from Dogger Bank to Northern Spain."

Finn's eyes narrow, not because of the smoke. "Who said anything about Spain?"

"You don't remember Avilés?"

He scoffs. "I cannae remember what I did yesterday."

"The *Arianna II* was smuggling people into Britain."

"Who told you that?"

"Somebody who was there."

"Get away from me," he shouts, struggling to sit up. He swings his feet to the floor and grabs for the bottle of whiskey, but I hold it out of reach. He curses and lunges again, but suddenly his eyes go wide, staring past me. I have the eerie sensation that he's looking at someone standing behind me.

"Can you see them?" he whispers, his eyes full of sadness rather than fear.

I look over my shoulder. The room is empty.

"I hear 'em too," he says.

"Who?"

"The ghosts."

"What do they say?"

"We can't breathe. We can't breathe."

A single tear rolls down his unshaven cheek, getting caught in the greying stubble.

Suddenly, a car horn sounds outside, breaking the spell. Finn fixes me with a stare, scowling and squeezing the empty glass. Lumbering to his feet, he takes two paces towards me, lunging. I duck his fist. He stumbles and crashes to the floor. The glass shatters and pieces bounce across the floorboards.

"Those voices you're hearing. I can help you silence them," I say. "I'm a psychologist."

"Get away from me."

"Who are the ghosts? Why can't they breathe?"

He gets to his feet and cries out as he steps on a shard of broken glass. Hopping on one leg, he lurches for me again. I'm at the top of the stairs. Slipping, I grab the handrail to slow myself as I clumsily bounce down the steps on my arse. I turn and see Finn swaying on the landing.

"Who are the ghosts?" I ask again.

"They belong tae me," he says. "Ah deserve 'em."

42

Evie

I used to be good at keeping my own company, but I've become spoiled or needy because of Cyrus. That's what bothers me about him finding a girlfriend. One day he will get married and I'll be surplus to requirements, the wonky spare wheel.

I'm hungry, but I want to wait for him. There must be a corner shop or a supermarket nearby where I can buy snacks and bottled water. As I leave the guesthouse, I pass the lounge. The same three men are playing snooker. One of them is leaning over the table, ready to take a shot. He pauses and straightens, watching me, which makes me self-conscious. Why do men stare at women the way they do—like they're hungry or hunting?

I walk as far as a rocky beach, which stinks of seaweed. Nobody is swimming because the wind has made it too cold. Instead, children are playing on a climbing frame and slippery slide. Two older girls are paddling on the edge of the water. Their bikes are resting on the grass. Both are wearing denim shorts and T-shirts, not feeling the cold. I recognize one of them—the would-be thief from the guesthouse. Addie. She's with another girl about her age, with frizzy hair and freckles.

Miss Frizzy pulls a packet of cigarettes from her pocket. Four hands are needed to shield the flame from the wind. White smoke surrounds their heads and vanishes just as quickly. Addie notices me watching and gives me the stink eye. I turn away and walk back the way I came.

I pass a group of people getting off a bus outside a factory gate. At first I think it might be a tour group, but they're dressed in shabby clothes and look more likely to be queuing for food than sightseeing. They wait for a security man to unlock the metal gates. I step onto the road to move past them. A different guard yells, "Hey, where are you going?"

He grabs the back of my hoodie and almost yanks me off my feet. "Get back in line."

"I'm not with them," I say.

"What?"

I say the words slowly as though I'm talking to a moron.

A woman from the same bus says something to him in a language that I don't understand.

"I wasn't talking to you," he says, and without warning, he backhands her across her face. It is so sudden and violent that she doesn't have time to protect herself. Stumbling backwards, she sits on the curb, holding her cheek.

"You can't do that," I say, protesting. "Leave her alone."

He takes a step towards me and raises his hand. "You want some too?" I move farther away. "Yeah, I thought so. Piss off!"

The woman is still sitting in the gutter. She's Asian, in her forties, with her right arm in a blue sling that is knotted around her neck. The others from the bus are being herded through the open gate into the factory. A different group is leaving, getting on the same bus. Shift workers.

The security guard is standing over the Asian woman. "What's wrong with your arm?"

"I work," she replies in broken English.

"Not with one hand."

"I work hard. One hand or two hand."

"This isn't a sheltered workshop."

"No. Please, I good worker. I show you." She reaches up for his arm, begging.

"Get back on the fuckin' bus."

Tearfully, the woman is helped to her feet, and I lose sight of her as she steps on board. A guard padlocks the metal gate. I'm on the far side of the road as the bus pulls away. I study the factory, which has cement walls and a tin roof and security cameras. A small painted sign is propped in one of the windows: "Polaris Pelagic."

I'm still thinking about the Asian woman when I reach the supermarket, which fronts a cobblestoned square. Boxes of fruit and vegetables are displayed on the footpath outside and the front window is plastered with discount banners and special offers. Inside, the aisles are barely wide enough for two people to pass and the shelves are crammed from floor to ceiling.

As I wander down the first aisle, I notice Addie and her frizzy-haired friend, near the canned goods. Their bikes are leaning against a lamp-post outside. As I round the corner, Addie glances at the CCTV camera above her head and turns her back. At the same time, she slips some-thing under her T-shirt, which she tucks into her shorts.

Later, at the checkout, Addie counts out coins to pay for a packet of chewing gum. A store guard is watching her—a young guy in a grey uni-form with front teeth that push out his top lip.

As the girls leave, he stops them. "What yer hiding beneath yer top, Addie Murdoch?"

"None of your business, Declan O'Keefe," replies her friend.

"I'm not talking to you, Shona."

He stands in front of Addie. "How about you untuck your shirt."

"You're not looking at my tits," says Addie.

He laughs. "Yer got nothing to look at."

The girls try to step around him.

"Looks like I'll be calling the cops," he says.

Shona looks anxiously along the street. I know she's going to run even before she takes off, ducking under the guard's arm and sprinting for the automatic doors. Outside, she grabs her push-bike, bounces it over the gutter, and takes several steps before swinging her leg over the seat and pedaling away.

A beat too late, Addie also tries to escape, but the guard grabs the back of her T-shirt. A can of tuna bounces across the floor and rolls to my feet. I pick it up and put it on the conveyor belt with my other items. "I almost forgot this. Thanks, Addie."

The guard blinks at me. "She stole that."

"She picked it up for me."

"It was tucked down her front."

"It was in her hand."

He points to the CCTV camera. "I have proof."

"I bet that's not turned on," I say.

He stammers, caught in his lie.

"How much do I owe you?" I ask the checkout girl, who blinks at me like she's been watching a performance that has suddenly stopped in mid-act.

She scans the can of tuna. Addie steps closer to me, pretending that we're together, but only until we get outside. She holds out her hand, wanting her spoils.

"I paid for that," I say.

"I'll owe you."

"You were pretty amateurish."

She gives me a nonchalant shrug. "He's a pervert."

"Really."

"Shona's older sister went to school with him. They called him Skidmark because he shat his pants in P4." She gives me a sideways look. "Are you going to tell my gran?"

"No."

She blows a puff of air that lifts the fringe from her eyes, before picking up her push-bike and wheeling it over the cobblestones. We're walking in the same direction. She looks older than twelve because of her ear studs and attitude.

"Who cut your hair?" I ask.

"Shona."

"What did your mother think?"

"Don't have no mother."

"Who looks after you?"

"My dad."

"Do you know someone called Angus Radford?" I ask.

"He's my uncle. Why?"

"No reason."

Three teenagers are walking towards us. Two boys and a girl. Addie clearly knows them but crosses the road to avoid them. The girl is about Addie's age, wearing nicer clothes. She yells, making a mooing sound.

"Scabby bitch," hisses Addie.

"Friend of yours?"

"Destiny? No way. She's a mouth breather."

"What's a mouth breather?"

"Someone too stupid to use her nose."

We turn into a narrow lane with stone steps leading down to the waterfront. Three stray cats appear from behind rubbish bins and Addie greets them. She opens the can of tuna, peeling back the lid and turning it upside down, tapping the contents onto the cobblestones.

"That's the mum, Flossie. And these are her children, Ziggy and Soot," says Addie. "A boy and a girl."

"Who named them?"

"I did."

The cats jostle to get the food and Addie makes sure each gets a share.

"I volunteer at an animal shelter," I say. "I look after the rescues and help feed the puppies."

Addie gets starry-eyed. "I love puppies, but mah dad says I'm not responsible enough and that he'd be doing all the work."

"Yeah, I know someone like that," I say.

Addie looks at her phone. "I have to go."

"Where?"

"I'm helping my auntie at the pub."

"Doing what?"

"Washing dishes."

"Two jobs and you're still nicking stuff."

Addie's top lip curls and she tosses the empty tuna can into one of the bins before wiping her hands on the back of her shorts.

"That guy you're with—he your sugar daddy?"

"No! And what do you know about sugar daddies?"

"I know all about sex," she says. "I know what boys want."

I find that funny, but I don't want to offend her by laughing.

"What are you doing in St. Claire?" she asks.

"I'm trying to work out if I've been here before."

"Don't you know?"

"Not really."

"You got that anesthesia thing?"

"You mean amnesia. Yeah, maybe, or perhaps I was never here."

43

Cyrus

There is an envelope waiting for me at reception. Unsealed. Unsigned. The message reads: *If you want to know about the Arianna II, you're asking the wrong people.*

It includes an address—a berth number at St. Claire Bay Marina—but there's no indication of what time I'm expected or who will be there.

"Did you see who left this?" I ask.

"No, love," says the receptionist, the same woman who signed us in last night.

"Was it a man or a woman?" I ask.

"Cannae tell you."

"What time were they here?"

She begins lifting folders and pens, searching the counter. "Ah must've made a note of it somewhere," she says sarcastically. "Wrote it all down—what he was wearing, what he was driving, his date of birth, his favorite color . . ."

"A man, then?"

She is no longer amused.

"We'll be checking out tomorrow, Mrs. Collie," I say.

"Aye. Good." She frowns. "How do yer know mah name?"

"You must have told me," I say, smiling.

"I don't think so."

"Well, somebody must have mentioned it."

Maureen Collie gives a caustic snort and watches me as I walk to the stairs. So much for keeping a low profile.

Evie is in my room, sitting cross-legged on the bed, eating crisps and watching TikTok videos on her phone. I tell her about my meeting with

Finn Radford, who admitted nothing but was clearly haunted by his brother's death.

"Is he the Ferryman?" asks Evie.

"No, he's a sad drunk, who sees ghosts."

"Maybe they're real ghosts," says Evie, stealing my thoughts.

I show her the note left at the reception desk.

Her forehead creases. "I don't want you to go. Let's go home instead."

"Tomorrow," I tell her. "Now lock the door and don't open it for anyone except me."

"You're scaring me."

"You'll be fine."

"But what about you? Keep your phone on . . . and send me photographs . . . and don't do anything stupid."

"When do I do anything stupid?"

"You want examples?"

"No."

Evie puts her arms around my waist and her head against my chest, which surprises me. Normally, she balks at physical contact and stiffens when anyone hugs her. Intimacy embarrasses her. This is a legacy of the abuse she survived as a child, which has made her less trusting and prone to bouts of negativity and low self-esteem. Her history is littered with drug-use, petty theft, self-harm, and antisocial behavior, but these are symptoms, not the disease.

In Greek mythology, Prometheus was a Titan who was sentenced to eternal torment because he defied the gods. Bound to a rock, Prometheus was visited each day by an eagle that fed on his liver. Each night the liver would grow back, only to be eaten again the following day. Evie is trapped in the same sort of vicious circle and I don't know if I can free her without breaking her in the process.

Leaving the guesthouse, I drive to a headland overlooking St. Claire Bay. Parking the Fiat at a lookout, I gaze across the stone-grey sea to where a bank of dark clouds is gathering on the horizon. Below me, a seawall juts out into the bay, providing a patch of calm water where the boats are moored at the marina. To the south are shipping warehouses and office accommodation of ASCO, the supply base that handles deck cargo, fuel, and water for the container ships that use the port.

Having studied the lay of the land, I approach along an access road, past the sailing club. Leaving the car, I continue on foot. I can hear waves breaking against the seawall and taste the salt in the breeze. Yachts and pleasure craft are moored side by side and opposite each other along the floating pontoons. Each berth has a number, but the layout is confusing. I double back before finding the right one.

The boat is a large, blue-hulled cruiser with sloping angles and a forest of antennae and radar dishes on the upper roof. The name painted on the stern is *Watergaw*. I notice a man appear at the opposite end of the dock. Another has followed me, blocking my escape. They seem small at first but get bigger as they get nearer. Both are dark-haired and heavily built, dressed in matching waterproof jackets, black and orange.

I take out my phone and photograph each of them, as well as the boat.

"I'm taking holiday snaps for a friend," I say, sending the images to Evie and Florence.

"Put tha' away," says the older of the two, who has a booze-stained nose and a single silver stud in his left ear. "Arms out." He pushes me up against a handrail and roughly pats down my pockets, before frisking my legs and arms.

"Shouldn't you buy me dinner first?" I ask.

"Unbutton your shirt."

"I'm not armed."

"It's not weapons I'm lookin' fer. Unbutton your shirt."

The younger one catches sight of my tattoos and whistles through his teeth. "Is that a hobby or an illness?"

"Both."

I tuck in my shirt and step on board, descending three steps into a luxurious cabin decorated in polished wood and marble. It has a circular lounge, a dining table, and a galley area with an oven and cooktop. An older man is sitting at the table. A newspaper is spread out in front of him and reading glasses are perched on the end of his nose. He gets up and carefully folds the paper.

"Thank you for coming, Dr. Haven."

He has thick, wavy grey hair and trousers that are notched too tightly into his waist. The air smells of scented oil and aftershave.

"I'm sorry, I don't know your name, sir."

"It's nae important."

"Maybe so, but it would help to call you something."

There is a pause. The old man is deaf in one ear and cocks his head to one side, presenting his good ear.

"Mah name is William Radford. Mah friends call me Willie. You can call me Mr. Radford."

A woman appears from an adjoining cabin. I recognize her bottle-blond hair and the tight grey dress. It's Kellie from the pub.

"Is this him?" asks Radford.

"Yeah. Can I go now?"

Radford nods and Kellie stumbles up the stairs, eager to get away.

A bottle of whiskey is produced from a mahogany drinks cabinet. Two glasses. A jug of water. I notice scars on the backs of Radford's hands and the deep lines around his eyes, created by squinting into sun and wind.

He pours a whiskey and pushes it towards me.

"Nothing for me."

"This is a fifty-year-old Macallan, single malt, worth sixty grand a bottle. The least you can do is try it."

I sniff the glass and let the whiskey pass my lips, tasting the peat and the moss and wood smoke.

Mr. Radford does the same, sipping more liberally, smacking his lips. "What do you think?"

"Very smooth."

"It's the juice of angels copulating in flight."

"Not the metaphor I had in mind."

He smiles. "Why are you so interested in the *Arianna II*?"

"Your note said you had the answers."

"Ah'm more interested in why ye're askin' the questions."

"Is that a problem?"

"Aye, because ye're making a nuisance of yerself. Bothering good people."

"Are you bothered?"

"Is nae about me."

"Yet here we are."

Anger in his eyes. White knuckles on his glass. A long silence.

"I met someone who was on board the *Arianna* when it sank," I say.

"Who might that be?"

"Your son Angus. He's been arrested down south and charged with killing seventeen asylum seekers, but I'm sure you know that."

Mr. Radford scoffs. "Gross negligence manslaughter—what sort of bullshit charge is that? And what does that have to do with the *Arianna*?"

"I'm trying to solve a mystery."

"There's no mystery. There was an engine fire. An explosion. The boat sank."

"Your youngest son died. I'm sorry."

"Did you know Cam?"

"No."

"Well, why are yer sorry?"

"For your loss."

His glass is empty. Mine barely touched. He pours himself another. The whiskey tilts and flashes gemlike in the glass.

"Have you ever lost a loved one, Dr. Haven?"

"Yes. My parents and twin sisters were killed."

He frowns in surprise, his eyebrows almost touching. "Did you see them dead?"

"I found their bodies."

"How old were your sisters?"

"Just turned eleven."

He shakes his head and seems at a loss for words, a rare occurrence. He gazes into his glass, the pain etched on his face.

"Cam was nineteen. He would have been thirty-one now. Ah have other sons, whose lives have never been the same. You've seen what it's done to Finn. He blames himself."

"How does Angus feel?"

"You'll have to ask him."

He makes a sweeping gesture with his hand. Whiskey splashes over his fingers and beads on the table. "Let's get back to the subject, Dr. Haven. I don't appreciate you coming here and opening up old wounds."

"That's not my intention."

"Ah think it is. Ye're picking on folks who have suffered enough."

I glance around the luxurious interior of the boat and wonder whether Mr. Radford has suffered as much as his sons.

"Would you tell me something if I asked you?"

"Aye, if I can."

"Would you be honest with me?"

"Ah dinnae know if you deserve that, but fire away."

"Was the *Arianna* being used to smuggle refugees?"

His eyes change color, growing darker and then lighter again while his mouth opens and closes as though he's unclenching his jaw.

"That's a dangerous accusation. I hope you have proof to back it up."

"The wreck was never salvaged."

"It went down in deep water. These things happen. An investigation was carried out. No blame was placed on the crew."

"I talked to Finn. He blames himself."

His eyes swim. "We have an old saying around these parts, Dr. Haven. The sea takes the saver of life, instead of the saved. Do you know what that means?"

"People sometimes die when they're trying to help."

"Who are you trying to help?"

"I'm just looking for the truth."

A deep chuckle, low down, shaking his diaphragm. "Oh, that's a dangerous beastie, the truth, a monster in the loch."

44

Evie

I fall asleep watching the TV and wake to the sound of shouting in the street outside. I turn off the light and peer through the curtains, looking directly down onto the side gate of the guesthouse.

Two people are arguing in the pool of light beneath a lamppost. One of them is Addie. A man is standing over her. Older. Taller. He raises his hand, ready to strike her, but stops himself. Addie doesn't flinch. If anything, she leans forward and lifts her chin, as though daring him.

I'm moving, out the door and down the stairs. When I arrive at the gate, Addie and the man have gone. He is dragging her along the footpath by her arm, away from the guesthouse. He could be her father. A kidnapper. A rapist. He could be anyone.

I follow them for several blocks, sticking to the shadows between the lampposts. I have the flick-knife in my back pocket, the bulge hidden by my untucked shirt. I don't know if I could use it, but I feel safer having a weapon. I try to call Cyrus. He doesn't answer. He promised to keep his phone on.

I lose sight of Addie near the Waterfront Inn. It's where she told me she worked in the kitchen. I pause outside, debating what to do. I don't like going into crowded places, but I steel myself and push through the heavy glass door into a cloakroom. To my left is a lounge with a low ceiling and round tables where people are finishing meals. To the right is a larger space with a curved wooden bar with beer taps and a mirrored wall lined with shelves holding bottles of spirits.

"Are you lost?" asks the barman.

"I'm looking for someone."

"A parent?"

"I'm twenty-two." I take out my driver's license. He doesn't bother to check the birth date. "I'll have a rum and Coke."

He scoops ice into a glass and pours a shot. I sit at a table, feeling self-conscious because men are looking at me like I'm a novelty or their next meal.

An old guy approaches, selling raffle tickets. He has a laminated photograph of the prize—a boat on a trailer.

"It's for the local youth club," he says, pronouncing it "youf."

"I don't need a boat," I say.

"Nobody *needs* a boat, but you could always sell it or give it away or donate it back to the club."

"I win and give it back to you?"

"Aye, if yer want."

"That's crazy."

"You don't have any cash, do yer?"

"No."

He grunts and moves on. I collect my drink from the bar and ask if the kitchen is still open. The barman looks at the clock on the wall. "I doubt it, but I can check."

He pushes through a swing door. I glimpse Addie before it closes. A woman is talking to her, using her hands, as though signing to someone who is deaf.

The barman returns. "Only cold stuff. They can do you a Scotch egg."

I have no idea what that is but decide to pass. I want to talk to Addie, but I can't just stroll into the kitchen. A shadow falls across my table.

"Where have you been all my life?" asks a nasally voice.

"For most of it I wasn't born," I reply.

The man laughs. He's twenty years older than me, with a fleshy face and gelled hair and a tattoo on his forearm of a cartoon character: Popeye the Sailor Man. I used to watch episodes after school and can remember the words to the theme song, but it didn't make me want to eat spinach.

The man next to him is younger and undersized with a blue-yellow bruise on his cheekbone and a droopy left eye.

"Let us buy you a drink," says Popeye.

"I have one."

He calls to the barman. "Fix her a cocktail, Stuey. Something she'd like."

"Don't bother, Stuey," I say.

Already, he's opening a fridge and taking out different juices.

The men tell me their names, but I don't take any notice.

"Are you visiting?" Droopy asks.

"Yes."

"How long you here for?"

"I'm leaving tomorrow."

"What do you think of the place?"

"The locals are pushy."

"You're funny." He turns to his mate. "Ain't she funny?"

They lean over me as they talk, smelling of alcohol and stale deodorant.

The barman sets a drink in front of me. It's pink and yellow in a tall straight glass, with a layer of foam on the top.

"Try it," says Droopy, popping in a straw.

"I don't want a drink."

"C'moan now. Stuey made it especially for you."

"What's in it?"

"Juice. Alcohol. Normal stuff."

I put the straw to my lips. The cocktail explodes in my mouth, cold and sweet and sour all at once.

"Good, aye? Drink up."

The men lift their pint glasses and clink them against mine.

"You here with anyone?" asks one.

"With a friend."

"A boyfriend?"

"No."

"A girlfriend?" He sniggers.

I don't bother answering.

"Plenty of nice views around here," says Popeye. "We could give yer a tour."

He extends his finger and strokes the back of my hand. I pull it away. He grins. The pub seems busier and noisier than before. The men are talking about St. Claire and places I should visit and bragging about themselves. One of them reaches into his shirt pocket and uncurls his fingers, showing me a joint with twisted paper ends.

"We're going to smoke this outside. Want to come?"

I tell myself it's not a good idea, but the cocktails were nice and maybe they can tell me something about Angus Radford.

We leave through a rear door, which leads to a council car park. The temperature has dropped and I wish I'd worn a jacket. We're standing under a lamppost where moths kamikaze against the bulb. Popeye lights the joint and passes it around. I put the soggy tip between my lips. Inhale. Swallow. Smoke bites the back of my throat. I stifle the urge to cough.

A man appears at the pub door. He's the one I saw outside the guesthouse with Addie. He's wearing black jeans, Doc Martens, and a brewery-sponsored T-shirt, acting like he owns the place. He seems to be staring at me with intense blue eyes. I look away and talk to Droopy and Popeye.

"Are you fishermen?" I ask.

"Aye," they answer in unison.

"Do you know Angus Radford?"

Popeye inhales, holds the smoke in his lungs, wheezing, "Why yer askin'?"

"No reason."

"Must be a reason."

"I met his niece," I say. "Addie Murdoch."

The men both look towards the pub, but the blue-eyed man has gone. The joint has come back to me, but I don't want any more. Dizzy but relaxed, I tell myself that I'm making friends and gathering information. We return to the bar. A good song is playing on the jukebox. I start to dance. The men are watching. One of them joins me. Popeye puts his hand on my waist and twirls me around, tipping me over his arm and up again.

Again, I notice the man from the guesthouse, who is talking to the barman. I try to meet his gaze but can't stare into his blue eyes for more than a few seconds before looking away. It's like he can see straight through me. I don't mean that he's undressing me or anything like that; it's more like X-ray vision, or that MRI scan I did at the hospital that showed my tumor.

The song changes to a ballad. Popeye wants to slow dance and pulls me closer, but I push him away and go back to the table. Another cocktail is waiting for me.

The blue-eyed man approaches and says something to the men.

"We're just having a bit of fun with her," says Popeye.

"We saw her first," says Droopy.

They seem to be arguing, but I can't make out the words because their accents are so heavy. Suddenly, the blue-eyed man swings his fist from low down and Popeye doesn't see it coming. It slams into his stomach and I hear the breath leave his lungs. He doubles over and has to be held up and lowered into a chair.

"It was just a wee dance, Sean. No harm intended," says Droopy, raising his hands.

Within moments the entire incident is over. Does one punch count as a brawl? Was it even a fight?

The blue-eyed man takes the seat next to me. His hands are large and uncalloused and one set of knuckles is red from where he landed the punch.

"I believe ye've met mah daughter, Addie."

"I saw you almost hit her."

He doesn't react. "My name is Sean. What's yours?"

"Snow White."

"You look more like Little Red Riding Hood. And ye're a long way from yer grandma's hoose. You shouldn't be here. Not by yerself."

Droopy and Popeye are watching from the far end of the bar, muttering darkly to each other.

"They don't like you," I say.

"This is mah pub. They can always drink somewhere else."

"Are you going to buy me a drink?"

"Nae, lass, yer've had enough."

He's right, but I don't want to admit that. I feel drunk and stoned and nauseous.

"Where is the bathroom?" I ask.

"Through there. Second door on the left."

Standing up, I try to walk as though I'm sober, but I feel like a puppet being controlled by strings, lifting each leg in an exaggerated step. Inside the ladies, I lean over the sink and scoop water into my mouth, splashing my face and trying to stop the room from turning. The door opens. Addie slips inside. She's holding a large glass of orange juice mixed with soda water and has two small white tablets. Tylenol.

"Auntie Isla says you should drink this," she says. "For the hangover."

"I don't have a hangover."

"You will." She smiles, one dimple showing, and leans towards the mirror, checking her pink hair where the roots are beginning to grow out.

"Does your dad hit you?" I ask.

"Nah. He's all bark and no bite."

"Why was he angry?"

"The supermarket called the police, and the police called him."

"Are you in a lot of trouble?"

"No more than usual." She looks back at the door. "I can't stay. Auntie Isla is waiting for me."

When I return to the bar, Sean is safeguarding my phone.

"I'll walk you home," he says.

"No. I'll be fine."

Before I can argue, he is steering me towards the main doors. Popeye and Droopy are smoking outside. For a moment, I think there'll be another fight, but they're scared of Sean or not drunk enough to be brave.

As we walk along the footpath, I pull loose from Sean's grasp and bend over, vomiting into the gutter. He holds me around the waist as the orange juice, cherries, and alcohol gush out of my mouth and nose, splashing my sneakers.

The flick-knife falls from my jeans and bounces on the pavement. Sean picks it up and holds it in his palm. Finds the trigger. The blade snaps out.

"Where did you get this?"

"It's mine. Give it back."

"Who gave it to you?"

"Nobody. I found it." I try to snatch it, but he holds it out of reach.

"It's an illegal weapon and it doesn't belong to you," he says, slipping it into his pocket. I'm too tired and drunk to argue. I want to curl up in a doorway and fall asleep.

"Come on, Snow White," he says. "It's not far."

How does he know where I'm staying? Addie must have told him.

The temperature has fallen and I begin to shiver. Sean makes me wait and goes to a nearby car. Lights flash. Doors unlock. He takes a leather jacket from the front seat and puts it around my shoulders. It smells of something wild and drapes down to my knees.

"Why did you come here?" he asks as we walk under the lampposts.

"I'm trying to find my memories."

"Good ones?"

"No."

"You're too young to have bad memories."

"What would you know?"

We've reached the Belhaven Inn. I use the side gate. Sean watches as I fumble with the code.

"Can I give you a piece of advice, Snow White? You should go back to Nottingham."

"How do you know where I live?"

"Good night."

45

Evie

That night I dream I'm back in the belly of the whale, filthy, frightened, and cold.

We started the voyage with such mixed feelings, caught between hope and dread. As time passed, the wind blew and the weather turned and sickness spread until the stench clung to my nostrils and the darkness filled my lungs.

During the long hours of boredom, people told stories and sang songs. A Syrian man could speak English. He told me that he had a son my age who was at home with his mother in Damascus. He said they were Christians who were being persecuted in Syria and that young boys were being turned into soldiers and made to fight in the civil war.

Two men were from Pakistan. They were brothers and one of them was deaf, but the other would sign for him. He taught me how to say hello and good-bye and to sign my name.

There was a group of men from Albania, all from the same village, which I had never heard of, but they spoke so lovingly of "home" that I wondered why they had ever left.

The men rigged up a makeshift curtain at one end of the hull to give privacy to the women when we used the bucket toilet or did womanly things. But we couldn't escape the darkness or the smell or the constant movement.

If the seas were calm, the crew would open the hatches and allow fresh air into the hold. And at night, we were allowed on deck for ten minutes at a time, but only the women and children, or the men in pairs, because the crew was afraid of being outnumbered.

I counted four of them. Mostly they wore masks or made us look away when we came on deck. Only one had kind things to say to us. He was the youngest, who was not much older than Agnesa, and he was nice to her because she was pretty or perhaps because she was sicker than the others. She had kept her pregnancy a secret and Mama had used a needle and thread to alter her dresses, hiding the bump that grew below her swollen breasts, pressing against the fabric.

We ate only one meal a day. Some of the men complained of being hungry and scuffles broke out. A speargun appeared through the hatch, aimed at a Syrian man's chest. He stood up, ripped open his shirt, and pointed to where he wanted the spear to go—straight through his heart. "I would rather die now than starve to death," he said.

A few hours later, the hatch opened and a man pointed at Agnesa.

"You speak English," he said. "You will cook."

Mama didn't want her to go but Agnesa raised her arms and they lifted her out of the hold. In the galley, she washed and peeled potatoes, boiled rice, made sauces, cooked pasta, stewed meat, and opened cans of vegetables and fish.

When the hatch opened again, she lowered a pot of stewed meat and potatoes, which we ladled into tin mugs that were almost too hot to hold with our hands, but we ate because we were hungry. Agnesa had also managed to hide small treats under her dress, chocolate bars and biscuits, which she gave to me.

"What are they like?" I asked her.

"They drink too much and they tell dirty stories."

"About what?"

"About us."

I couldn't think of what dirty stories they could tell. We were trying to stay clean.

From then on, twice a day, the front hatch would be pulled open on hinges, and Agnesa would raise her arms and the youngest crewman would pull her up, into the daylight or the darkness.

One night, when I was allowed on deck, I noticed how the men treated Agnesa, particularly the young one. He was nervous around her. Almost shy. The others didn't show their faces. I saw stars and a half-moon, but there was no horizon, and if I let myself believe, I could imagine we were sailing through space to a distant planet, a beautiful new world.

This same fantasy returned to me many times in the years that followed, as I lay in bed, listening for the creak of the floorboards or the door opening, or felt the weight of someone pressing down on the mattress. I don't remember the pain of the rapes, only the faces and the waiting. Sometimes I asked myself what was worse, the act or the dread of it. The awful wondering.

I wake sticky-eyed and stumble into the bathroom, leaning over the toilet bowl. My stomach spasms, but nothing comes up except a sour taste that I can't spit away. I drink water and wait for the nausea to pass.

My clothes are neatly folded on a chair. My canvas shoes have been washed. Did I do that? Cyrus has left a note. He's downstairs having breakfast.

By the time I shower and get dressed, they have cleared the tables and the buffet, but Cyrus has saved me a serviette full of pastries and a milky coffee. Lukewarm.

"What happened last night?" he asks.

"I tried to help someone," I say, not in the mood for lectures.

"I wanted you to stay in your room."

"I'm not a prisoner."

"I'm trying to protect you. You have a brain tumor."

"No! You don't get to throw that in my face," I snap. "My body. My choices. Remember?"

He's going to argue but stops himself. I'm not willing to let it go. "Did you undress me?"

"You had vomit on your shirt and shoes."

"You saw me naked."

"You were wearing underwear."

"That's no excuse."

Our voices are raised. No, it's only my voice. A waitress appears. Cyrus composes himself and apologizes. I'm supposed to do the same, but I don't because I don't like Cyrus seeing my scars. It's bad enough that I see them when I look in the mirror. The coin-sized lesions on my stomach and buttocks, caused by cigarettes being stubbed out against my skin.

"Can we start over again?" asks Cyrus, his voice softening. "Good morning, Evie. Did you sleep well?"

"Like shit. You?"

"I was worried about a friend who was late getting home. But I'm happy now."

How can I be angry at him?

I nibble at the end of a croissant as he tells me about meeting Angus Radford's father, who warned him to stop asking questions.

"Is Willie Radford the Ferryman?" I ask.

"I don't think he's big enough. I mean, he's clearly a big fish in St. Claire, but this is a small pond, barely a puddle. The Ferryman has international connections. He's trying to control the movement of people across borders and oceans."

I feel an ache in my chest. "They know we're here now."

"Which is why I'm taking you home."

"We haven't found out what happened to me."

"I'm not putting you in danger. This was always a long shot."

We sit quietly. Somewhere above us, a cistern empties and refills.

"Who were you trying to help last night?" he asks.

"A girl. Her name is Addie. Her grandmother owns this place."

"Addie must be related to Angus Radford?"

"Her uncle. Her father runs the Waterfront Inn. Her aunt works in the kitchen."

"How did you get back to the guesthouse?"

"Her father took me. He told me to go back to Nottingham."

"Did you tell him where you lived?"

I shake my head. "I also didn't tell him where I was staying."

Cyrus frowns in concentration. "What was his name?"

"Sean Murdoch."

His mobile interrupts us. Cyrus answers brightly. "DI Carlson. To what do I owe the pleasure?"

"What in fuck's name are you doing in Scotland?" he bellows, loud enough for me to hear every word.

"Having breakfast," says Cyrus, completely unruffled.

"Don't fuck with me," says Carlson.

"I'm investigating Angus Radford."

"You are *not* a detective."

"This is a private matter."

"You're unauthorized."

"I prefer to call it unconstrained. Free to ask the questions that you can't."

"That's bullshit," I hear, but I don't catch the rest of Carlson's complaint because Cyrus covers the phone and walks out of the conservatory into the garden, where the argument continues. Meanwhile, I finish another pastry and begin to feel vaguely human.

Minutes pass. They always do. When I next look up, Cyrus is standing next to me.

"Come on," he says.

"What's happened?"

"Radford's lawyer is applying for the charges to be dropped. He knows the police no longer have an eyewitness."

"Are they letting him go?"

"Not yet."

"Where are we going?"

"To roll the dice one final time."

46

Cyrus

Outside, the sky has turned dense blue, and sunlight glitters off glass and chrome. Days like today make you wonder if the rain and clouds actually exist. We walk towards the harbor, Evie jogging to keep up with me.

"I want you to meet Finn Radford," I say.

"Why?"

"Because if you remember him, he might remember you, and we'll know you were on board the same trawler."

Evie stops moving. "What's wrong?" I ask.

"He'll know what happened to the others."

"Yes," I say, remembering the ghosts that haunted Finn Radford.

At the Fisherman's Hostel I go upstairs to the same room as before but find it empty. This time, the two old guys are playing backgammon at a table in the lounge, ignoring the bright commentary of the morning TV hosts.

"I'm looking for Finn Radford," I say.

They answer in unison. "You're too early."

"Where would I find him?"

"Home," says one.

"Where's home?"

He finally looks up. "Rattray Head." He pronounces it "rattery." "Last place before you reach the lighthouse."

Evie googles the location on her phone and we drive north out of St. Claire, heading along the A90, which cuts through plowed fields and summer crops. The road runs ahead of us, curving and cat's-eyed, patched in places with fresh tar. We pass a makeshift shrine of flowers and a small white cross beside the road—a memorial to someone who died away from home.

Two miles past the St. Fergus Gas Terminal we turn right at a signpost for Rattray and follow a single-lane blacktop between overgrown hedges and thickets of trees, and open farmland. We pass a ruined church and whitewashed farmhouses, shadowed in places by clouds that have interrupted the solid blue, sweeping in from the sea. Silhouetted against the skyline, I see the ruins of a long grey building, now partially collapsed with the charred roof beams exposed and three remaining walls canted at different angles.

The road narrows again as we reach a cluster of buildings with a sign saying "Lighthouse Cottages." The tarmac is crumbling in places, or barely visible beneath weeds and muddy puddles. We weave along the track, avoiding the potholes, heading towards the dunes. More ancient ruins are just visible in the fields, poking up through the breeze-riffled grass. They could be gravestones or the remnants of ancient dwellings.

"I don't think there is another house," says Evie, as the dunes get nearer. "We must have missed it."

At that moment a bus rumbles over a rise, taking up the entire track. I'm so surprised to meet another vehicle that I almost steer us straight into a hedge. At the last moment, I hammer the brakes and the bus driver does the same, skidding sideways and putting one front wheel into a ditch.

Both of us get out. He examines the sunken wheel and I apologize, even though it's nobody's fault. The bus is full of people, who I assume are sightseers coming back from the lighthouse, although nobody gets off.

"It's not stuck," says the driver, who gets back behind the wheel and reverses. I do the same, pulling over at the next farm gate, allowing him room to pass.

"I've seen that bus before," says Evie. "At a factory in town."

"What factory?"

She tells me about Polaris Pelagic, sounding out the name, one syllable at a time.

"It must be a fishing company," I say. "'Pelagic' means living in the open sea."

The family I met on my first morning in St. Claire told me that Willie Radford owned a fish processing plant, one of the town's biggest employers.

"'Polaris' means North Star, doesn't it?" says Evie.

"How do you know that?"

"A friend taught me about stars. He knew all the names of the constellations. Ursa Major. Cassiopeia. Cepheus. The Big Dipper. Orion's Belt. He said that shooting stars aren't stars at all, but meteors falling through the darkness."

The bus edges past us, inches from my mirror. I catch a glimpse of the passengers, some leaning against the windows, as though trying to sleep. Others make eye contact. Unsmiling. Uninterested.

Steering back onto the track, I look for a place to turn around. At the next break in the hedge, there is an open gate and fresh tire tracks. I turn off and we splash through puddles, crossing a narrow bridge with no safety rails.

Cresting a small rise, the nose of the Fiat dips and offers a sudden view across open grassland and sand hills. Caravans and tents are clustered beside a grove of trees that mark the line of a watercourse. At first glance it could be the camping area at the fringes of a music festival, but the sound stages and food stalls are missing. These tents are crude. Some are little more than sheets of tarpaulin, strung over branches and held down at the edges by pegs and rocks. Campfires are smoldering and women are hanging washing or carrying water from a tank. Children chase after a lame dog who wags a limp tail and lopes ahead of them.

"Are they Gypsies?" asks Evie.

"I don't think you can call them that."

"What do we call them?"

"Travelers. Roma. Itinerants."

"My best friend Mina was Romani," she says. "I met her on my first day at school and we sat together. Mina's father drove a horse and cart and collected scrap metal and had a horse called Mother Theresa. That's the name of a famous nun who was born in Albania. I learned about her at school."

Evie stops talking and notices that I'm smiling.

"What?" she asks, self-consciously. "Did I say something wrong?"

"No."

"Why the stupid grin?"

"You just told me more about your childhood in one breath than you've told me in a year of living together."

"So?"

"It's good."

One of the children notices our car and raises the alarm. Suddenly, the occupants of the camp begin scattering through the hedges and towards the sand hills or into the scrubby trees. Women are picking up toddlers and babies, pulling veils over their faces, leaving their belongings behind.

"They're frightened of us," says Evie.

"They think we're the authorities."

"The police?"

"The Home Office. Border Force."

We continue driving down the track. As we near the camp, I notice that one woman has remained. She is sitting on a small wooden crate beside a fire. As the car approaches, she raises her eyes, pushing hair under the veil that is slipping off her forehead. Her right arm is supported by a blue sling knotted around her neck.

"I know her," says Evie. "She was outside the factory. They wouldn't let her work."

Leaving the car, we walk towards the woman, who turns back to the fire, using a twig to push coals beneath a blackened pot. The lame dog barks but doesn't come closer.

"Hello," says Evie. "Remember me?"

The woman looks up, waving smoke from her eyes.

"How is your arm?" asks Evie.

"I can work. They won't let me."

"Who won't let you?" I ask.

"The one in charge." Dipping a spoon into the pot, she lifts it to her lips, tasting, adding a pinch of salt, stirring.

"Where are you from?" I ask.

"Afghanistan."

"How did you get here?"

She nods towards the sea and eyes me suspiciously. "Are you here to arrest us?"

"We don't work for Border Force," I say.

"It's true," says Evie.

The woman breaks up twigs and feeds the fire.

"How long have you lived out here?" I ask.

"Me? Four months. We work to pay off our debts, but the boss man charges us for food and for these tents."

"What happens if you don't pay?"

"We taste the coin of Charon."

I think of Arben's death and the coin placed in his mouth. "Have you ever met the Ferryman?" I ask.

She shakes her head.

"How do you know he exists?"

"I have seen what happens when people don't believe in him."

Evie has stepped away, moving closer to the lame dog, which has fallen silent, flattening its ears and lying on its belly.

"Be careful. He bites," says the woman.

Evie crouches and slowly holds out her hand, palm down, fingers curled, waiting. The dog edges closer, sniffing at her. His tail begins to sway, beating out a steady rhythm. Evie whispers something and scratches the dog's chin. It rolls over, wanting a tummy rub.

"That dog has a better life than we do," says the woman. "More rights."

"Who runs this place?" I ask.

She nods towards the grove of trees. Through the thinner, lower branches, I notice the ruins of a wooden fishing hut with boarded-up windows and paint peeling from the planks. It looks abandoned apart from a newer plastic rainwater tank squatting under the eaves.

Evie follows me as I walk towards the hut along a compacted dirt track weaving through the trees. We emerge into an unmown yard where a bleached wooden dinghy is resting in a metal cradle. A goat is tethered to a post. Chickens wander through the yard. Odd objects stick up through the grass—the rim of a tire, a rusting mangle, a beer keg, an old fridge without a door . . . Wire crayfish pots are rusting in a clump of weeds near the open front door and a thin stream of smoke curls from the pipe chimney.

A figure emerges. Finn Radford is dressed in baggy track pants and a stained sweater. Unshaven. Hollow-eyed. Spying us, he croaks, "You can't be here. I can't talk to you."

"This is Evie," I say.

Finn shifts his attention, but his bloodshot eyes don't seem to focus. Alcohol is oozing from his pores, forming a sheen on his face, which is

alive with tics and twitches. Evie has stopped moving. Sunlight and recognition flare in her eyes.

"Who are your neighbors?" I ask.

"Holidaymakers," says Finn.

"That's an illegal campground."

"We give them permission to stay."

"And you give them work?"

Finn doesn't answer. Instead, he walks to the nearby wood pile and
picks up an ax. For a moment, I think he's going to threaten us, but he
takes a log and balances it upright on a sawn-off stump. The ax swings,
cleaving the wood in half.

"We want to know what happened to the *Arianna*," I say.

"It sank."

"You weren't fishing."

"On our way home."

The ax swings again and again, until his Medusa-head of tangled hair
is wet with sweat. Exhausted, he sits on the stump and lights a cigarette,
sucking so heavily the filter collapses between his lips. He squints into
the smoke.

"You were smuggling people," I say.

His eyes are slitted against the smoke. "Yeah. Who says?"

"I say," says Evie.

Finn regards her again, more closely this time. His sallow face has the
depth of a pie plate and I wonder if the alcohol has damaged his brain.
He twists his neck as though releasing a crick.

"They gave us no choice," he mutters, as though talking to himself.

"Who?"

"The government, Brussels, Marine Scotland—all the lying, duplici-
tous bastards who told us where to fish and what to fish and how many
fish we could catch and what we had to throw back. You know how soul-
destroying it is to toss dead fish back into the sea because of quotas that
no other bastard country in Europe is abiding by?"

He doesn't expect an answer. "We had families. Children. Mortgages.
Debts. The politicians didn't care. Not down south. We were Scottish
scum. They hated us as much as we hated them, but we wouldn't go
quietly. We fought back. We found a way to survive."

"By smuggling."

"I prefer to call it free trade. The open exchange of goods and services."

"You were trafficking human beings."

He looks again at Evie, cocking his head to one side. A soggy stub of cigarette hanging from his lips. "Do Ah know you?"

"She was on board the *Arianna*," I say.

He shakes his head. "They're all ghosts."

"I'm real," says Evie.

Raising his right hand, he reaches towards her, as if he can touch the past with his fingertips. Then he rocks his head from side to side, saying, "No. No."

He gets to his feet and picks up the ax, swinging it a final time, driving the blade into the stump. Turning, he shuffles slowly towards the hut. I call after him. "Why are they ghosts?"

Ignoring me, he disappears inside and I can hear him rummaging, opening drawers and cupboards.

Evie has gone quiet. "Something is wrong," she whispers.

"Was he telling the truth?"

She nods.

When he reappears, there is a dark object in his right hand. It takes me a moment to recognize the shape. He holds up a semiautomatic pistol, running his finger along the barrel, treating it like an artifact.

"The Russians smuggle these," he says. "This one cost me a case of whiskey."

He slides off the safety catch and closes one eye, checking the chamber of the pistol. A fly lands on his forehead. I expect him to brush it away, but it crawls across his nose and pauses at his left nostril. He doesn't seem bothered.

I push Evie behind me. "Put the gun down, Finn."

He looks at the weapon and back to me, running his tongue across his lips.

"We only want to talk," I say.

"Ah'm done talking."

Evie steps out, giving him a clear shot. The gun moves from pointing at my chest to Evie and back again to me.

"What happened to my mother and sister?" asks Evie. "Agnesa was the pretty one. She cooked for you."

"All ghosts," groans Finn, raising one hand and slapping his face, cursing, "Fuck! Fuck! Fuck!"

"Finn, listen to me. Put down the gun," I say.

"Leave me alone. Please?" he begs, but I don't think he's talking to us. His eyes are peering into the distance.

"What happened to the others?" asks Evie.

"They're here," he mutters. "They watch me. They talk to me."

"What do they say?"

Raising the gun, he presses the barrel under his chin.

"No!" I cry.

He pulls the trigger. Instead of an explosion, I hear a dull click. The round has jammed, or the chamber is empty. Finn moans and lowers the gun, looking at it traitorously. He bangs it against the heel of his other hand, as though trying to dislodge an impediment. Then he pulls the slide, poking his finger into the ejection port, breathing hard in frustration.

I move towards him. Just as quickly, he aims the pistol at me. I stop. Evie grabs my arm, pulling me away. We retreat past the ramshackle hut and the tethered goat and the abandoned dinghy. With each step, I expect to hear the bullet sliding into the chamber. The trigger. The explosion.

We're almost at the Fiat when the sound comes—a sharp crack that echoes off the sand dunes and the low hills. Evie throws herself to the ground. I fall with her, shielding her with my body. My face is pressed against her back. I can feel her heart beating.

"Are you hurt?" I whisper.

"Nuh. You?"

"No."

"We have to help him," she says.

I get up and begin walking slowly back towards the hut. Even the birds and insects have gone quiet.

"Finn?" I yell. "Are you OK?"

Nothing.

Crouching low, I use the dinghy and old machinery as cover. A breeze bends the grasses. The goat bleats. A chicken flies to the top of the water tank. Finn Radford is lying on his back, his legs twisted beneath him, the pistol still in his hand. The bullet had entered through the roof of his mouth and exited from the back of his head, spilling teeth and bone and brain matter across the newly chopped wood.

I take out my phone and call 999, speaking calmly to the operator, requesting the police. "A gunshot victim," I say. "His name is Finn Radford. He's dead."

"Who fired the weapon?"

"He did."

"Has the gun been secured?"

"Yes. Nobody has touched it."

I give her my name and details and tell her that I'll wait for the police on the road.

When I next look up, I see Evie standing over the body. I want to shield her and to get her away from here, but she ignores my words and continues staring at Finn. The bright day remains, the sunstruck sea, the white wispy clouds, the pecking chickens and tethered goat. The smell of wood smoke and salt. And a silence to end all silences.

47

Evie

Another body. I keep adding to the dead. Would Finn still be alive if I hadn't asked about Agnesa and Mama...about the ghosts? I keep picturing the gun pointing at his chin, his finger on the trigger, the blankness in his eyes. He wasn't scared of dying. It was like he'd stopped living a long time ago and every day was an ordeal to be endured.

I have seen bodies before. Papa laid out on the kitchen table. Fisnik Sopa crushed beneath the wheels of a truck. My friend Ruby lying dead in my bed. If this world is my creation, I can make the suffering stop if I choose death. Nothing will exist without me.

From a distance, I see the flashing lights of the police cars weaving along the track, over the humped bridge. Cyrus is waiting at the gate, showing them where to park like he's directing traffic at a garden party.

I have stayed out of the way, sitting in the passenger seat of the Fiat. Through the trees I can see the migrant camp, now deserted—the police cars made that a certainty. The cooking pot is next to the fire. The lame dog sniffs at the contents.

The police are talking to Cyrus. His hands move through the air as he explains what happened. He points to the fisherman's hut and the woodpile and the body. The detective is taking notes on a computer tablet.

Other cars arrive. A tent is erected over the body. Crime scene tape is strung across the gate. A moment ago, the sky was blue, but now the clouds are closing in and the temperature is falling.

The detective is heading towards me, stepping across the grass like it's covered in dogshit. He's wearing black trousers and a business shirt and a fluorescent vest with the word "POLICE" stitched across the chest. He leads me to a waiting police car and asks me to sit inside. He leans on the open door.

"I'm Detective Sergeant Ogilvy. I need to ask you a few questions." He calls me "Miss Cormac," which doesn't happen very often.

"Firstly, can you confirm your full name and age?"

I show him my driver's license.

"What is your relationship with Cyrus Haven?"

"We share a house."

"What are you doing in Scotland?"

"Researching my past."

"Your family tree."

"No."

He frowns and waits, but I have nothing to add.

Detective Ogilvy speaks again. "How do you know the deceased, Finn Radford?"

"We met twelve years ago on a fishing trawler."

He does a mental calculation. "You were ten?"

"Nine."

Doubtfully: "Why were you on the boat?"

"I was with my mother and sister. We were seeking asylum."

"Where are they?"

"They're dead."

"How did they die?"

"I don't know."

He sighs tiredly. "A word of warning, Miss Cormac. It's an offense to lie to the police. You could be charged with wasting my time or perverting the course of justice."

"I'm not lying."

Detective Ogilvy regards me in silence, his pale face full of freckles that must come out every summer. I bet he tried to scrub them off when he was a kid. I did. Mama caught me in the bathtub with lemon juice and a scouring pad.

"You'll need to come back to the police station to provide us with a full statement," he says.

"We were going home today."

"That won't be possible."

I don't want to tell him about Angus Radford—not if Cyrus hasn't told him already. Ogilvy moves away and signals a young female constable, who escorts me to a waiting police car.

Cyrus is in the Fiat.

"Why can't I go with him?" I ask.

"He'll be following us."

48

Cyrus

The local police headquarters in St. Claire is so new that I can smell the paint drying and see scaffolding marks on the carpet. The interview room is sparsely furnished and decorated in pastel colors because some organizational psychologist will have told them that light blue reduces anxiety.

Ogilvy has taken off his jacket and loosened his tie. His crumpled shirt is one size too small, putting pressure on the buttons across his belly. He turns on the recording equipment and announces the date and time and the names of those present.

Finally, he leans forward, elbows on the table. "OK, for the record, tell me again why you visited Finn Radford."

"First, can I ask you a general question?"

He nods.

"When offenses are committed off the coast of Scotland, who has the jurisdiction to investigate?"

"The police. The National Crime Agency. The Home Office."

"And who deals with the fishing industry?"

"Marine Scotland manages fishing vessels, licenses boats, and monitors catches."

"Theoretically, if a fishing boat was involved in human trafficking, how hard would it be to detect?"

One eyebrow is raised. "Theoretically?"

"Yes."

"Theoretically, I'd say you've been pissing on my leg and blaming the dog. What evidence do you have?"

"An eyewitness."

"Ah, your friend Miss Cormac. What boat?"

"The *Arianna II.*"

"Which belonged to Willie Radford."

"You know him?"

"He employs a lot of people in St. Claire."

"Including undocumented workers."

Ogilvy lets that comment pass.

"Mr. Radford is a pillar of this community whose roots go back centuries. He's a big employer, and he's generous. This year he bought an inshore boat for the local lifeboat station that must have cost six figures."

"Sounds like the perfect candidate for higher office."

My sarcasm fires something in the detective, who swallows and takes a moment to compose himself. "Let me get this straight, Dr. Haven. You went to see Finn Radford and you accused him of people trafficking?"

"I wanted to see if he remembered Evie."

"And did he?"

"He said they were all ghosts."

"Who?"

"The people on board—the ones who died."

"Allegedly," says Ogilvy. "You have no proof."

"Finn admitted to being involved in smuggling."

"Was that before or after he blew his head off?"

I don't respond.

"Had you met Finn Radford before today?" asks Ogilvy.

"Yes."

"We have two witnesses from the Fisherman's Hostel who recall Finn shouting at you, telling you to stay away from him."

"He was drunk."

"He's *always* drunk. And Willie Radford asked you to leave his family alone, but you ignored him. He wants you charged with harassment, stalking, trespass, and assault."

"That's ridiculous."

"Did Finn Radford ask you to stay away from him?"

"Yes, but I didn't harass him and there was no assault."

"Yet the question I find myself asking is whether Finn Radford would still be alive if you hadn't gone out there today. That young man had mental health issues. He was an alcoholic. He suffered from depression and paranoid delusions. You're supposedly a psychologist. You should have realized that."

"Instead of accusing me, you should be looking into that illegal camp next to Finn Radford's shack."

"What camp?"

"The caravans, tents, and tarpaulins strung under trees. Pit toilets. Cooking fires. A bus is delivering undocumented workers to Polaris Pelagic."

"How do you know they're undocumented?"

"They scattered when they saw us, running off in every direction. They're frightened of being caught up in an immigration sweep."

Ogilvy wants to dismiss this new information, but he stops himself and ends the recording. He gets to his feet and hitches up his trousers. One button on his shirt has surrendered and his white undershirt is visible where his shirt gapes open.

"I'm holding you both in custody until I decide what crime I can charge you with."

"I want a lawyer."

"That might be the most intelligent thing you've said today."

I'm allowed a five-minute phone call. I weigh up who to contact. Carlson will say I told you so and wash his hands of me. Lenny Parvel is my oldest friend and my longtime employer at Nottinghamshire Police, but she has no jurisdiction in Scotland, and this isn't her fight. Finally, I settle on Florence. She answers before the phone even rings.

"Where are you?"

"I'm still in Scotland. There has been a complication."

I quickly tell her about Finn Radford's suicide and how the family has accused us of harassment and trespassing.

"Where are you right now?" she asks, as though sensing trouble.

"At the police station in St. Claire."

"Have you been arrested?"

"We're in custody."

"Charged?"

"Not yet."

"Please tell me you haven't been interviewed without a lawyer being present."

"OK. I won't tell you that."

"And I thought I'd met a smart man. Where's Evie?"

"She's with me."

Another silence. I can hear my breathing in the phone. Florence makes a note of the police station and the arresting officer.

"No more interviews—not without me," she says. "If I leave now, I can be there by early tomorrow."

"From London? That's six hundred miles. Find me a local lawyer."

"Not happening."

Before my time runs out, I ask her to check on a company called Polaris Pelagic. "It's a fish processing plant in St. Claire."

"Why is that important?" she asks.

"'Polaris' means North Star."

"You think it could be linked to the Buchan Family Trust?"

"What are the chances?"

49

Cyrus

Evie is sleeping on her side on the sofa, knees together, lips parted, hair tucked behind her ear, showing her multiple piercings and jewelry. I have never had any desire to pierce my body with metal studs or rings or hoops, but I have no problem with needles. My skin is a tapestry of ink drawings created by a million tiny pricks made by hand, each forming a picture, a tapestry of pain.

Ogilvy has allowed us to stay together in a small conference room next to where the detectives are working. Periodically, someone arrives to make tea or coffee or to take drinks from the fridge, but it has been quiet since midnight.

Evie wakes and sits up, plunging her hands into her hair, lifting it from her neck, and tying it into a bundle with a hairband. I'm always amazed at how women can do that with such skill and grace.

"I was having a dream," she says.

"About what?"

"Mama and Agnesa."

"You want to talk about it?"

She hesitates.

"You recognized Finn Radford," I say.

She nods, biting her bottom lip, leaving a mark. The silence seems to add to her frustration. She's getting closer to remembering what happened yet is terrified of what it might mean. Redemption. Relief. More trauma. Greater pain.

After my parents and sisters died, I was passed between psychiatrists, therapists, and counselors who spent months asking me about my innermost thoughts, when I simply wanted to be left alone. Later, as a psychologist, I came to understand that talking about trauma can be like sunlight, a disinfectant that diminishes the power of harrowing events. But there is another, equally possible outcome, where talking turns the unspeakable into words, energizing rather than neutralizing trauma, trapping a survivor instead of freeing them.

Evie has all the hallmarks of PTSD—the flashbacks, anxiety, avoidance, anger—but she's also incredibly resilient and self-contained. I want to believe she can survive her memories. I need it to be so.

Getting up from the sofa, she stretches like a cat and walks to the window, her arms wrapped around her chest.

"Are you cold?"

"No." She lifts her eyes to mine. "You said there was some way you could help me remember."

"It's called a cognitive interview."

"Use normal words."

"OK, but first let me explain how our memories work. We gather information with all our senses, which is coded and stored in our minds. It could be a smell or a sound or a face or an object that allows us to retrieve the memory later. Very rarely does it come back all at once. We recall one piece of information, which helps us get the next piece and the next piece.

"We also have different levels of memory. Shallow and deep. I can't remember what I had for dinner two nights ago, but I can remember the first girl I kissed, her name, her strawberry-flavored lip gloss, the smell of her hair. Deep memories are bedrock, but they can still be hidden away because of trauma or illness or injury."

"How do I get them back?"

"It begins with one small detail, a moment, and we build from there. Do you want to try?"

She nods and returns to the sofa. I ask her to close her eyes and take a deep breath and to feel the air filling every corner of her lungs.

"Exhale. Inhale. Exhale. Inhale. Feel the coolness of each breath in your nostrils. Feel your heartbeat slow."

Evie has her head tilted back and her chest rises and falls.

"Now I want you to think back to the trawler. The movement. The noise. The smell. The voices . . ."

"It was cold," she whispers.

"How did you stay warm?"

"We wore all our clothes. Layers. Socks upon socks. Socks on my hands."

"What clothes? Describe them."

"I had a long dress and a sweater."

"Tell me about the dress."

"It was blue and green and had buttons down the front."

"How many buttons?"

"I can't remember."

"Picture the dress. Imagine putting it on. Doing up the buttons."

She counts. "One . . . two . . . three. Four buttons."

I notice a change in Evie. Her eyelids begin to flutter. Her hands close into fists. Her knuckles whiten. Each breath is ragged. She's back there, a child again, all at sea . . .

50

Evie

The storm arrived when we were sleeping. It came bashing on the hatches and flooding across the decks, trying to get inside. The boat moved like it wanted to break free from the sea, bucking and heaving, creaking and groaning. Trapped belowdecks, we were tossed around like marbles in a rolling jar.

People were sick. Mama was the worst, retching into the same bucket until it overflowed, and the hold reeked of vomit and sweat and human waste. Mama's skin grew cold and clammy, sunken in places and clinging to the bones of her face. I gave her a spoonful of water at a time, holding it to her lips, but it dribbled down her chin and onto her blue coat that Aunt Polina had brought back from Italy.

I prayed. Agnesa prayed. The storm raged, the wind and the waves were relentless. We hammered our fists against the hatches, trying to signal the crew, but nobody came to let us out.

"Tell me about the crew. How many of them were there?" asks Cyrus.

"Four."

"Did you see their faces?"

"Not at first, but the masks came off."

"Did you hear their names?"

"Only the youngest. Cam."

"What did he look like?"

"He had pimples and pale skin and soft hands. He was nervous around Agnesa. He said she was a good cook, like his mother, and told her he was going to university to study engineering."

"What about the others?"

"They drank a lot and swore."

"You saw them?"

"Once, before the storm."

"Why were you on deck?"

"At night, if the seas were calm, they let the women and children out of the hold. And sometimes I would help Agnesa prepare the meals."

"What did you see?"

"Four men at a table. They were playing cards for money. Poker. I knew the rules because Aunt Polina taught me. I knew when to bluff and when to fold and how to ride out a run of bad cards. We never played for money—only for matchsticks or biscuits."

"What do you remember about the men?"

"They were drunk."

"Was one of them Angus Radford?"

"He had a beard and dirty hair and hooded eyes."

"Did he have burns on his neck?"

"No, but he had a mermaid tattoo just here." I point to my biceps. "The tail curled down to his wrist and when he bent his arm, she looked like she was swimming."

"Picture the table. Where were they each sitting?"

"It was shaped like a horseshoe. Finn sat facing the stairs. He was eating baked beans from a saucepan. Spooning them into his mouth, wiping his chin. Another man was on his right, but I only saw the side of his face. Angus and Cam were next to each other."

"Go back to the storm," says Cyrus.

"I don't want to."

"It's important."

I force myself, returning to a time when everything shook and rocked and heaved. Water had begun leaking through the hatches and sloshing back and forth as the boat moved.

We were yelling for help. Cam opened one of the hatches and emptied the bucket. Agnesa begged him to let Mama out of the hold. She needed fresh air. A horizon. A sky to focus upon. He said it was too dangerous.

Time passed. Mama's pulse grew rapid and feeble, and her legs could no longer support her. More water entered the hold. First it came to our ankles and then our knees, sloshing from side to side as the boat rolled. Again, we screamed for help and hammered on the hatches. Nobody came. We thought the crew had abandoned us, left us to drown.

I was afraid of dying, but I was more afraid of living for another minute or an hour in that horrible place. Nothing before or since has matched that terror and that includes hiding in a secret room, hearing them search for me, ripping up carpets and knocking holes in walls, calling my name.

My chest heaves and I feel myself scream. I'm halfway across the room when Cyrus catches me. Holds me. Whispers, "You're safe, Evie. You're here with me. Shhhh."

"I almost remembered."

"I know, but it's too much. We can try again another time."

"No. Take me back. Please."

"I won't risk damaging you."

"I want to go back. You said I was strong."

He leads me to the sofa. Again, I lie back, listening to his voice. Cyrus tells me to breathe. Relax. Clear my mind. He has me picture things— the trawler, the hold, the rising water. My heartbeat slows and I fall back into that half world between now and then, back to the endless storm. One image swirls and floats to the surface. A body lying against me. Mama. Something is wrong. I can't wake her up. I can't breathe. There is a poison in the air, filling my lungs, squeezing my chest. I try to sit up. I topple over. The poison is stinging my eyes and choking me, making me cough and inhale and cough and inhale.

Mama's chest sighs and gurgles and a bubble of spit pops in her mouth. From somewhere nearby, I hear a muffled *whump!* sound and the boat shakes. There is a secondary sound, a buckling groan, as if something has broken or given way. In the darkness, I see a man pushing against the locked hatch. He raises his face, pressing his lips against the edge, sucking at the seal, trying to get air. Someone joins him. Another man. They are bashing on the hatches, clawing at the painted metal and at the hinges, desperate to get out…to breathe.

Mama slips sideways. I hold her head to keep her face above the water. My cheek is pressed against her chest. A button from her coat is curled inside my fingers.

I am losing touch with her. My fingers are numb. My eyes are closing. The screams are fading. I feel myself being lifted away from Mama. I cling to her. My arms and legs are pried loose. My fingers uncurl.

"Wake up, Evie! Wake up!"

And then it's gone—the darkness, the poison. Cyrus is leaning over me. He is holding my face, telling me to wake up.

"No," I groan.

"That's enough," says Cyrus.

"Did you hear?"

"Yes."

"I thought it stayed inside my head."

"No."

He pushes hair away from my eyes. "You were there when the boat caught fire."

"But how did I get off?"

"What's the last thing you remember?"

"Voices."

"What were they saying?"

"I couldn't hear them properly. I couldn't open my eyes or speak."

Memories crowd in on me, overwhelming my thoughts entirely. Worlds within worlds, bleeding into each other. Here and there. Then and now. For years I have blocked out the details, but they've come back to me in a rising wave, carrying debris and driftwood and the bodies of the dead.

51

Cyrus

"What time is it?" asks Evie, without opening her eyes.

"Almost seven."

"When can we go home?"

"Soon. Florence is coming."

Sarcastically, "You make her sound like a superhero."

"Be nice."

"What if she takes you away from me?"

"She won't."

A fresh-faced constable brings us coffee and tea. He's young and new to the job and he doesn't know whether to treat us as suspects or witnesses. Later, he escorts Evie to the ladies and waits outside. "I had to run the taps," she says afterwards, annoyed at being so closely chaperoned.

Ogilvy enters at nine, looking showered, shaved, and rested. A torn piece of toilet paper is sticking to a bloody spot on his neck.

"Your lawyer is here," he says. "I can't tell if she's modeling for Ducati or the real deal."

"She's the real deal."

"Lucky you."

Florence steps around him, ignoring his comment. Her motorcycle leathers are stained with road grime and splattered with bugs. She has ridden through the night to be here.

"I'd like to be alone with my clients," she says.

Ogilvy leaves reluctantly, his gaze lingering as the door closes.

Florence motions me to the far side of the conference room, away from Evie. Her fingers brush the back of my hand, and she pecks me on the lips. Not very professional but welcomed.

"Did Finn Radford make any admissions?" she asks.

"He admitted to smuggling. That's how he got the gun."

"That's not enough."

"Evie was there. She was on board the *Arianna II*."

"Nobody is going to trust the memories she had as a child."

"We can get more evidence," I say, but can't think of how. The *Arianna II* sank in deep water. Even if we could locate the wreckage, what would be left after twelve years?

"What have you told the police?" asks Florence.

"I told them that Angus Radford and his brothers were involved in human trafficking."

"Did you identify Evie?"

"They know."

"Well, my advice is to say nothing more. This is bigger than the local police. You should talk directly to the National Crime Agency or to Border Force."

A knock on the door. Ogilvy again. "You've had your twenty minutes," he says.

We all stand. He points at me. "Stay here. I'm interviewing you separately. Miss Cormac is first."

I begin to protest, but Florence stops me. "I'll take care of her."

52

Evie

I've decided there are two types of people in the world—the overachievers and those who want to see all the overachievers die in a flaming car crash. I fall into the second category. Florence falls into the first one.

Cyrus is always telling me I should look for the best in people instead of trying to find faults or calling them liars, even if they lie all the time. "Absolute honesty is an impossible ideal," he says. But I don't care if most people are well-meaning and have a desire to be good. They also lie and cheat and steal and rarely show remorse when they get caught.

Cyrus says I'm being a hypocrite, but I'm not being two-faced. I admit that I'm a liar. And I don't care if I'm unpopular. I'm not even sure that I want to be happy or in love. Love is for the birds and the bees and romantic comedies and soppy love songs and coming-of-age movies where the ugly duckling turns into a swan or the geek gets Invisalign braces and contact lenses and is suddenly beautiful. Voilà! Life is good. Hand me a bucket!

Ogilvy has a hard-on for Florence. I mean that literally. He keeps adjusting his crotch like he's turning a sausage on a barbecue.

Florence sits close to me.

"Don't say anything unless I give you permission," she whispers. "And if you're not sure, say, 'No comment.'"

Ogilvy leans forward, putting his palms facing up on the table like we're going to hold hands and make a prayer circle.

"Perhaps you could help me, Miss Cormac. I can't seem to find any record of your existence. No birth certificate. No medical records. No rap sheet. No social security file. I'm not even sure that Evie Cormac is your real name."

"Is there a question in there somewhere?" asks Florence.

"I'm a ward of the court," I say. "My identity is protected."

"You're no longer a child."

"The protection order is ongoing."

"Why?"

"People aren't supposed to know who I am."

"Are you someone famous?"

"No."

"A protected witness?"

"No."

"Do you have a passport?"

"No."

"Where were you born?"

"I don't see why this is relevant," says Florence. "You have Evie's name and address."

"Which could be fake."

Florence gives him a mocking laugh. Ogilvy colors slightly and moves on.

"You said that you'd met Finn Radford before."

"We didn't really meet. I was on a fishing trawler with my mother and sister and other migrants."

"How many?"

"I can't remember."

"More than ten?"

"Yes."

"Twenty?"

"Yes."

"Thirty?"

"No."

"What was the name of the boat?"

"The *Arianna II*."

"That was twelve years ago, Miss Cormac. You seem very sure."

"My mother and sister died on the voyage."

Ogilvy leans back. "That's a very serious allegation. You must have evidence—witnesses, letters, photographs—something that can corroborate what you're telling me."

"She was a child," says Florence.

"Exactly," says the detective. "And children make things up."

"Angus Radford was the skipper of the trawler," says Florence. "He's facing charges of deliberately sinking a small boat off the Lincolnshire coast. Seventeen people drowned."

"That doesn't make him sound like a people smuggler. Quite the opposite." Ogilvy hasn't taken his eyes off me. "Did Finn Radford recognize you?"

"Yes. I think so."

"Did he threaten you?"

"He told us to leave."

"But you refused."

Florence interrupts. "Excuse me, Sergeant, but you haven't offered one scrap of evidence to support any charges against my clients. A deeply troubled young man, with a history of alcoholism and depression, took his own life. Evie and Cyrus will sign statements to that effect. Unless you have something more, we're done here."

She gets to her feet. Ogilvy tries to hold her gaze or to summon some killer one-liner that might restore his self-esteem but fails miserably. Florence is at the door.

"Wait," he says, before leaving the interview room. He returns a few minutes later with a typed one-page statement, I read the words. There's no mention of people smuggling or the sinking of the *Arianna* or why we visited Finn Radford. Does my signature make it the truth?

"You were amazing," I whisper to Florence as we leave the room.

"Did you notice anything unusual about that interview?" she asks.

"How you torched him?"

"He didn't have the recording equipment switched on."

53

Cyrus

The custody sergeant returns our phones and personal belongings, including belts and shoelaces and Evie's hairclip. It has been sixteen hours since Finn Radford's suicide, but it feels like a week has passed. My Fiat is parked opposite. Florence has her Kawasaki propped nearby.

The first order of business is breakfast. We find an old-fashioned "caff" in the high street with a chalk menu, Formica tables, and enough steam in the air to fog up the front windows. A nervy waitress with a nose stud takes our orders, and nobody says anything of importance until our plates are clean and the tea leaves can be read in our empty mugs.

Florence has been on the road since yesterday afternoon but rejects any suggestion that we stop to let her rest. She takes her laptop from her satchel.

"You asked me about Polaris Pelagic. It's a private limited company, incorporated fourteen years ago. The nature of the business is processing and preserving fish, crustaceans, and mollusks."

"What's a mollusk?" asks Evie.

"Scallops, oysters, mussels, limpets."

"Snot rocks."

Florence laughs. "The directors are Maureen Collie and William Radford, but there is a third party, Temple Court Holdings—a nontrading company that was dissolved six years ago. The shareholders of that company were both lawyers from Edinburgh."

"Any link to North Star Holdings?" I ask.

"None that I've found. I asked Simon Buchan, but he had never heard of Polaris Pelagic. He suggested I talk to the trust's lawyers."

"Lawyers who work for his brother."

"Who is *nothing* like Simon," says Florence, with a sharp edge to her voice. She goes back to her laptop. "Polaris Pelagic has no debts, no overdue tax returns, and no VAT issues. I might be able to find out more details from council records and local newspapers."

"St. Claire has a library," says Evie, trying to get involved. "I can take you there."

"OK, you do that. I have a few errands to run," I say.

"Shouldn't we stick together?" asks Florence.

"We will, but first I need some answers. If the *Arianna II* went to Spain and came back with a boatload of refugees, why does satellite tracking show it never left Dogger Bank in the North Sea? And how did Evie get off the trawler? A coastguard helicopter flew from Inverness and a lifeboat was sent from Aberdeen to pick up the survivors. Surely somebody would have noticed a girl among them."

"You think it was covered up?" says Florence.

"Either that or I'm missing something obvious."

The old author is weeding his small garden when I arrive at his cottage. He is dressed in a wide-brimmed hat with his white hair poking out at the sides, making him look even more Hobbit-like than I remember.

"You're still here," says Fishy, setting down his shears and taking off his gardening gloves to shake my hand. "Cold drink? Ah'm having one."

I wait at an outside table while he fetches a jug of iced water and a bottle of concentrated lemon cordial. Ice rattles in the glasses as he pours. Sits. Drinks. Wipes his lips. "How can I help you?"

"I want to ask you about smuggling."

"The world's second oldest profession."

"Are trawlers ever involved?"

A rumbling laugh. "Does a bear shit in the woods? Does the tin man have a sheet-metal cock?"

"I'll take that as a yes."

"Back in the day, trawlers were regularly crossing the Channel or the North Sea, bringing back booze, cigarettes, cheese, caviar. The Russians, the Dutch, the Norwegians, they'd come here. We'd go there."

"What about customs patrols and the police?"

"Scotland has more'n eleven thousand miles of coastline if yer count the islands. Nobody can patrol that."

"How easy would it be to smuggle a person on board a trawler?"

"Just the one?"

"Maybe more."

"Aye, well, I could tell yer that never happens, but I'd be lying. Trawlers come and go as they please. Some skippers don't bother providing a crew list before they leave port. They might fill out the logbook once the boat has sailed, but if the trawler goes down, there's no record of who was on board."

"So, they could pick up someone and bring them back?"

"Yeah. If they wanted to break the law, but these are professional fishermen. Good men, most of 'em. Trusted." He pauses and lowers his glass. "Does this have something to do with the *Arianna*?"

"She was smuggling people from Spain when she sank."

"I showed you the satellite tracking. She was fishing Dogger Bank."

"Can two trawlers have the same AIS signature?"

"No. Each signal is unique."

"If you were trying to hide a trawler's movements, what would you do?"

Fishy pauses in contemplation. "Well, yer cannae turn off the AIS withoot raising an alarm, but yer could transfer it to another boat. It would only stop transmitting for a few minutes, while yer made the switch."

"One boat could pretend to be another," I say.

"Aye. It's possible."

The idea seems to trigger a memory in Fishy, who goes into the cottage and returns a few minutes later with a folder.

"Ever heard of pair trawling?" he asks.

"No."

"It's where two boats fish together, each towing a warp—a towing cable attached to the same net. By combining, the trawlers have more power and can pull a bigger net and move faster. It's useful in shallow waters where the noise from a single vessel can scare fish away, but two vessels, working together, can herd fish into the path of the net."

He shows me a photograph of two boats on the open sea, about two hundred yards apart.

"They're pair trawling," he says, showing me where the cables touch the water. He points to the nearer of the two boats. "That's the *Arianna II*."

"And the other boat?"

He turns over the photograph. The caption is written in smudged ink. *Neetha Dawn*.

Fishy raises his eyes to mine, as we both recognize the name. This was the nearest trawler to the *Arianna II* when Angus Radford sent the Mayday call. The *Neetha Dawn* rescued the crew from the sinking vessel before the coastguard chopper and RNLI lifeboat arrived.

"It could be a coincidence," says Fishy, scratching at his unshaven cheek.

"Who owns the *Neetha Dawn*?" I ask.

"It used to belong to Sean Murdoch, but he sold her a while back. Now he owns a pub in St. Claire."

"The Waterfront Inn?"

"Aye."

I look again at the photograph, thinking out loud. "That's how a boat can be in two places at once."

54

Cyrus

It's still too early for the Waterfront Inn to be open. The pavement outside has been hosed down and two men in soiled jeans and threadbare sweaters are washing the windows, leaving soap suds at the corners of the glass. Both are smoking roll-your-own cigarettes and talking to each other in a language that I don't recognize.

I wish them good morning and they lower their heads. I remember the illegal camp near Rattray Head Lighthouse and wonder how many businesses are hiring undocumented migrants and what they're paying them. There must be a labor hire company or a broker organizing the workers.

The rear entrance to the pub is in an alley lined with industrial bins and empty beer kegs awaiting collection. A woman appears carrying a rubbish bag in each hand. She tosses them into a wheelie bin and wipes her hands on the back of her jeans, gazing towards the harbor, where Filipino crewmen are repairing fishing nets.

The woman returns to the pub, and I manage to wedge my foot in the door before it closes. Stepping inside, I smell the cooking fat and bottled gas and soapy water of a kitchen. Copper pots hang from hooks above the counter and a meat sauce is bubbling on the stove. Chili con carne.

The woman is cutting up vegetables on a scarred wooden table that reminds me of a piece of polished bone or bleached driftwood.

"We're not open," she says, without looking up. "There's a café on the corner that does a full Scottish—haggis, tattie scones, eggs, bacon."

"Sounds like a heart attack on a plate," I say.

"Aye, that's why Scottish life expectancy is falling." She finally makes eye contact. "How can I help you?"

"My name is Cyrus Haven. I was looking for Sean Murdoch."

"He's sleeping."

"Are you Mrs. Murdoch?"

"Aye, close enough. I'm Isla Collie."

"Any relation to Maureen?"

"She's my auntie."

"Sean helped a friend of mine two nights ago. He walked her back to our guesthouse. I wanted to thank him."

"How did Evie pull up?"

"Hungover. Embarrassed. She says she's never drinking again."

Isla smiles. "Ah've heard that before. I might have said it myself once or twice."

I don't move. The silence drags out. "I'll pass on your thanks to Sean," she adds.

"I'd rather do it personally."

"Like I said—he's sleeping."

"He used to be a fisherman?"

"Aye."

"Twelve years ago, he skippered a trawler called *Neetha Dawn*. It rescued the survivors of the *Arianna II*."

"My brother was among them," says Isla. "And my cousins."

"The *Neetha Dawn* picked up another survivor—a nine-year-old girl."

A different emotion enters her eyes. She reaches for her phone, which is resting on the counter near the knives. She makes a call. Cups the mouthpiece.

"There's a guy here asking about the *Arianna*."

She nods quietly, acknowledging an unseen voice. "Yeah, that's him."

I hear footsteps on the ceiling above our heads and the creaking of weight on the stairs. Moments later, a man appears in the doorway. Half-asleep, with pillow creases on his right cheek, he's shirtless, wearing blue sweatpants that sag at the crotch. A short wooden truncheon is hanging from a strap around his right wrist.

"Who the fuck are you?" he asks.

"Cyrus Haven. I wanted to talk about the *Arianna*. You picked up the survivors."

"Ancient history. Get out of mah pub."

"How did you know that Evie came from Nottingham?"

"She told me."

"No."

Murdoch takes a step towards me. He flicks his wrist and the truncheon swings into the palm of his hand with a slap.

"Fuck off! And take the runt of the litter with you."

Moments later, I'm outside, moving away, hearing his voice call after me.

"Yeah, that's right. Don't walk. Run."

55

Evie

"How goes the family search?" asks the librarian. "Discovered anyone famous?"

"Still hopeful," I say.

We're standing at the front desk, waiting for her to finish checking out books for two pensioners with pudding-bowl haircuts and plus-sized bodies. They both gawp at Florence like she's from outer space. I've noticed that people stare at her all the time. Men. Boys. Other women. It happened the moment she walked into the library. Everyone stopped what they were doing: reading, studying, photocopying, shelving books. It's like she has this weird superpower—the ability to interrupt.

The librarian helps us log into the council website and call up the minutes of council meetings and the records of local businesses.

"What are you looking for?" I ask, pulling a chair next to Florence.

"Information about Polaris Pelagic," she says, scrolling through pages. "What we do know is that until six years ago, the third-party owner was a non-trading company, Temple Court Holdings. The shareholders were both lawyers."

"Like you?"

"Yes. Solicitors in the UK must be registered with the Law Society and are given an SRA number. Barristers have their own register."

"What's the difference?"

"Barristers defend people in court, while solicitors do most of their legal work outside court."

I still don't know why this is important, but I'm impressed with how quickly Florence can scan entire pages of text and pluck out details that lead her to a new search.

"Are you in love with Cyrus?" I ask, making it sound like we're carrying on the same conversation.

She laughs. "Where did that come from?"

I wait for a proper answer. Her expression changes. "He's easy company."

"What do you mean by 'easy'?"

"He's not always trying to impress me or say clever things or explain everything the way men often do. And he doesn't bombard me with polite questions. I tell him a story. He offers one in return."

"You make it sound like a tennis match," I say, but the truth is she just summed up Cyrus in a way that I never could.

"He cares about people," she continues. "You must see it. Look how he cares about you."

"Me?"

"He talks about you all the time. It makes me a little jealous."

I want to scoff, but she's being serious.

"I'm not going to hurt him," says Florence.

"How do you know? He might fall in love with you, and you'll leave, and he'll be heartbroken."

"He could do that to me," she says. "There are no guarantees, but I promise I'll be honest with him."

She's telling the truth.

The screen refreshes. "Here they are," she says, jotting down the names of Philip Welbeck and Charles Pembroke.

"I know him," I say, pointing to Welbeck's photograph. "He was in court when Angus Radford and Kenna Downing were charged."

"He defended them?"

"Yeah, I guess."

She keeps reading and pulls out a yellow legal pad, jotting down details. Opening her laptop, she begins comparing information and underlining some of her notes.

"What is it?" I ask.

"These are businesses that belong to North Star Holdings, the umbrella company for the Buchan Family Trust. Employment agencies, labor hire companies, warehouses, shipping brokers, manufacturing plants."

"Why so many?"

"It's a very valuable trust. But look how each company has Temple

Court Holdings listed as a third-party owner. And the only names linked to the law firm are these two solicitors. They're the common denominator."

"The common what?" I ask.

"The link."

Florence types in a different search and pulls up another photograph of Philip Welbeck, dressed in a black suit and red tie with his oiled hair slicked back in a dark wave, curling over his eyebrows.

She reads from his biography. "Welbeck went to the same school as the Buchan brothers. He could have been a friend. And look here. He's a director of Glengowrie Lodge—a private estate that has been owned by the Buchan family since 1850."

"Is that important?"

"It's a link between David Buchan, Philip Welbeck, and William Radford."

The next webpage displays aerial photographs of a grand-looking country house, surrounded by trees and streams and rolling hills.

"Is it a hotel?" I ask.

"A sporting lodge for fishermen and grouse shooters."

"What's a grouse?"

"A game bird," says Cyrus, who has found us in the library.

"What game does it play?" I ask.

"The one-sided sort," says Cyrus. "They're bred to be hunted."

He pulls up a chair and Florence shows him the screen. "William Radford and the Buchan family used the same firm of lawyers to set up a non-trading company that has partial ownership of dozens of businesses."

"Until when?" Cyrus asks.

"Six years ago."

"How far is Glengowrie?"

"Fifteen miles from here."

"We should take a look."

"I thought we were going home," I say.

"We are. Soon."

He spins the chair, facing me, knee to knee, and I get the feeling I've done something wrong. He continues gently. "When Sean Murdoch walked you home from the pub the other night, he told you to go back to Nottingham."

"Yeah."

"And you didn't tell him where you lived?"

"No."

"Did he recognize you?"

"From where?"

"The sinking of the *Arianna*."

"I don't think he was there," I say, less certain than before.

"Not on the *Arianna*," says Cyrus. "He was the skipper of a second trawler, *Neetha Dawn*, which rescued the crew. I think he took you on board."

"I don't remember being rescued."

"It's the only way you could be here."

56

Cyrus

There are no signposts pointing to Glengowrie Lodge, either in the nearest village or on the approach road or at the entrance, which is flanked by sandstone pillars weathered by age. The electronic gates are open and we follow the crushed gravel drive through a tunnel of oak trees and across a single-lane stone bridge over a salmon river, streaked with rapids.

The lodge is a large Adam-style house surrounded by manicured lawns with perfectly mown stripes running down to the river. Near the house, a walled kitchen garden includes a small maze around a central fountain. A number of four-wheel-drive cars and luxury vehicles are parked in the turning circle.

Our arrival is greeted with a volley of gunshots and my first reaction is to duck. Nerves frayed. Memories fresh. The guns fall silent but begin again moments later. On a distant hill, I see a column of men and women, moving in a straight line, some waving red and white flags, others beating the bushes with sticks or banging drums or blowing horns and whistles. Birds fly up and shotguns blast, knocking them from the sky.

"What are they doing?" asks Evie.

"Shooting grouse," I say.

"That's not a game. That's a massacre."

A woman emerges from the house. Middle-aged, pear-shaped, with hair pinned high on her head, she is all business. "Have you brought the pâté?"

We look at each other blankly.

"You're not from the butcher's," she says.

"No," I say.

She lifts the watch pinned to her apron near the breast pocket. "I knew they'd be late. I'm going to need a new entrée."

She pauses to examine Florence, who is still dressed in her leathers, and then Evie, and lastly me. What an odd trio we make.

"How can I help you?" she asks.

"We're sorry to intrude," says Florence, "but we're scouting for wedding venues and wondered if Glengowrie Lodge might be available."

"This is a private estate."

"Which can be leased."

"For grouse shooting and salmon fishing parties—small groups, not weddings." She looks from Florence to me. "Who is getting married?"

"We are acting on behalf of a prominent public figure, a famously private one, who is seeking to secure a wedding venue off-market, so to speak. Under the radar. Money being no object."

"Who is it?" she asks, intrigued.

"We can't tell you that."

"I bet it's Lewis Capaldi, isn't it? Or maybe Ed Sheeran. My daughter loves Ed Sheeran."

"I think he's already married," says Florence.

"Oh, yeah. Well, Lord Buchan would have to agree."

"Lord David Buchan?" I ask, feigning surprise.

"Do you know him?"

"Only by reputation."

The housekeeper is studying Florence. "Why are you dressed like that?"

"I normally ride my motorbike when I'm scouting for locations. I left it in St. Claire when we caught the helicopter. You might have heard us flying overhead a few hours ago. That's how we found this place."

"Oh, that was you," she says, eager to convince herself that it must be true.

Evie turns her skepticism into a cough.

"What nationality is your client?" asks the housekeeper.

"Does it matter?" asks Florence.

"Lord Buchan is quite discerning about his guests."

"Are you saying he doesn't like foreigners?"

"No, it's not that," she replies hesitantly. We wait for her to explain. Her voice drops to a whisper, "But if your client were to be . . ." She doesn't finish.

"A person of color?" asks Florence.

"Muslim. He lost a childhood friend in the World Trade Center attacks. The best man at his wedding." She stops herself, as though she's said too much. "I could ask Mr. Collie about wedding bookings, but he's with the shooting party."

That name again. "Who is Mr. Collie?" I ask.

"The gamekeeper, but he also manages the lodge."

"Is he any relation to Maureen Collie?"

"Her father. Why?"

"We've been staying at the Belhaven Inn, but Maureen didn't mention this place. Has Mr. Collie worked here long?" I ask.

"Longer than you've been born, laddie. His wife was the housekeeper before me, until she passed away." She points to a squat stone building, camouflaged by ivy. "They raised eight children in the gamekeeper's cottage. Four boys and four girls, Maureen among them."

At that moment, a group of men appears from the far side of the tree line, carrying something between them. Leading the way is a heavyset man in an oilskin jacket and a tweed deerstalker hat. From a distance, I think it might be Lord Buchan, but this man is older, with white hair and a pirate's limp.

"Call an ambulance, Diana," he bellows.

"Yes, Mr. Collie," says the housekeeper, who dashes into the main house, leaving us standing on the front steps.

The approaching group is carrying a wounded man, whose torn shirt is stained with blood and pitted with shotgun pellets.

"Put him in the shade," says Mr. Collie.

The beaters do as they're told. Dressed in shabby clothes and old shoes, they look Eastern European or Polish or Balkan. Migrant workers.

"You can bring him inside," says the returning housekeeper.

"Nae reason to get blood on the floor," says Collie. His eyes come to rest on me. "Who are you?"

"They came to ask about a wedding," says the housekeeper.

"We don't do weddings."

"That's what I told them, Mr. Collie. But they're asking on behalf of someone famous."

"Who?"

"They can't tell us."

"Can't or won't?"

He is still looking at me rather than Florence, having decided that I'm the decision maker and Evie isn't worth acknowledging at all.

"They spotted us from a helicopter," says Diana, trying to be helpful.

Behind her, across the estate grounds, the rest of the shooting party is returning, climbing a stile and emerging from the trees, then crossing the lawn towards the main house. The men are dressed in three-quarter-length trousers, flat caps, and tweed shooting jackets. Their twelve-bore shotguns are broken, the barrels pointing to the ground, and birds hang from the belts of loaders and pickers-up.

"Fookin' amateurs," grunts Collie. "The sixth drive and one cunt cannae tell the difference between a bird and a beater."

"Do we need to call the police?" asks the housekeeper.

"Nae. We'll sort this out."

The beaters are standing over the man on the ground, talking in broken English. Collie leaves us and walks towards the group, summoning one of them by name. Together they walk across the garden to a pergola. Collie is a foot taller and twice as wide, but the smaller man is angry and waving his hands around. Eventually, Collie reaches into the inside pocket of his coat and retrieves an envelope, which he hands to the man, who counts the contents, before slipping the envelope into the pocket of his corduroy trousers.

The hunting party has almost reached the house.

"You should leave," says the housekeeper.

"What about the wedding?" asks Florence.

"You'll have to get permission from Lord Buchan."

"Is Lord Buchan here?" I ask.

"Now isn't the time. He's with a group of chums from London. You could leave your details," says the housekeeper.

One of the hunters, a barrel-shaped man with ruddy cheeks, approaches the tree, asking after the beater.

"What a bugger!" he says. "Damn gun misfired. How is he?"

A fellow shooter answers, "He'll be fine, Toby. Don't concern yourself."

I recognize the voice and look more closely. Lord David Buchan takes off his flat cap, revealing his curly hair and bushy eyebrows. He's dressed for the shoot, in olive-green trousers and a matching oilskin jacket.

"I should compensate him," says Toby. "How much would be enough? Two hundred? More?"

"I have it covered," says Lord Buchan. "Go into the house. Get a drink. Calm your nerves."

A butcher's van has pulled through the gates and is following the crushed gravel drive, approaching the house.

"At last, my pâté," says the housekeeper, scurrying to intercept the driver.

Lord Buchan is herding his shooting party into the house. Mr. Collie has finished his business. "You're still here," he says. "No weddings. You should leave."

"I need to use the bathroom," says Evie.

"Find a pub."

"I'm busting."

The old man sighs. "OK, make it quick."

The housekeeper takes Evie inside, as an ambulance steers onto the grass to allow the butcher's van to pass. Lord Buchan is standing on the steps when he notices us. He seems to do a double take at the sight of Florence.

"Who do we have here, Wallis?" he asks.

"They were just leaving," says Collie. "They were looking for a wedding venue."

Buchan doesn't respond. He is staring at me. "Have we met before?"

"No."

"You look familiar. I'm very good with faces."

"I've met your brother," I say.

"Did he send you?"

"No."

"You're not here about a wedding venue, are you?"

"No."

Collie interrupts, fuming. "Ah'll see them out."

Buchan waves him away. "Lock up the guns, Wallis, and make sure my guests are looked after."

The paramedics are treating the wounded beater, who is sitting up on a stretcher. Lord Buchan turns back to me.

"You have two minutes to explain yourself. Then I call the police."

"My name is Cyrus Haven. I'm a forensic psychologist who consults for Notts Police. This is Florence Gatsi, a lawyer who works for Migrant Rescue."

"My brother's pet project," says Buchan. "How is the people-trafficking trade? Enough deaths for you? Enough misery?"

"We don't cause the deaths," says Florence.

"You encourage people to come."

"We make it safer."

"Safer," he says, laughing without closing his eyes. "The safest choice might be to stay at home, or to apply for asylum in the first safe country they enter."

"The 1951 Refugee Convention does not require a person to claim asylum in the first safe country they reach," says Florence.

"The Refugee Convention is no longer fit for purpose. It was written more than seventy years ago, in a different world, during the Cold War. The Soviet Union is no more. Refugees are coming from across the globe. And most of them are economic migrants, not fleeing persecution."

"Next you'll tell me that Britain is full?"

"No. We have the space but not the infrastructure and the services. And the majority of people in this country feel that we're full."

"Because that's what you tell them."

"On the contrary. They see the queues, the surgery waiting lists, the lack of housing, the soaring rents, the congestion . . ." Buchan has an eye for an opening—and here is an opportunity to sermonize. "Do you think it's a good thing, Miss Gatsi, that so many people risk their lives trying to reach Britain in small boats?"

"No."

"And is it a good thing that much of this illegal immigration is run by criminal gangs, who exploit refugees?"

"Of course not, but Migrant Watch is not part of the problem."

"You keep telling yourself that. And while you're congratulating yourself, think about all of those undocumented migrants who are clogging up our courts, delaying proper asylum claims. Most know they have no hope of staying here, but they game the system, making appeal after appeal, working illegally. And when they're finally kicked out, they plan their next working holiday."

"You are demonizing people who are asking for our help."

"Nonsense! I am not against immigration, and I believe Britain should take our fair share of the persecuted and oppressed. What I am against is people taking advantage of our hospitality and our welfare system and our courts. Our nation is a mess and I want to clean it up."

"You're right, it is a mess," says Florence, her features hardening. "But it's not a mess caused by fruit pickers from Romania or Nigerian nurses or Syrian cleaners or Polish nannies or Estonian car washers or Vietnamese manicurists. It's a mess because the financial elite avoid paying their taxes, and failed banks get bailed out by the state, and the richest one percent hold more wealth than seventy percent of the population. Migrants didn't make councils stop building council houses, and they didn't drive down wages or cut funding to the National Health Service or cause inflation at double figures or increase our energy prices, or vote for us to leave the EU. Yet they get blamed because it takes the focus away from the real architects of the mess. People like you."

Buchan blows out his cheeks, impressed rather than annoyed. "Where are you from?" he asks.

"I was born in Zimbabwe."

"Did you come here to study?"

"No. My parents are lawyers. They claimed asylum."

His lips curl into a half smile. "Of course they did."

Florence bristles with indignation. "Our house in Harare was fire-bombed and my parents were arrested because they exposed corruption and vote rigging."

"And we gave them a new home. I hope they appreciate our generosity."

"Why?" she asks, looking ready to kill him. "I'm sick of being told I should be grateful. My parents are both trained lawyers, but they arrived here with nothing. They shared a three-bedroom house with four other families. They worked multiple jobs, double shifts, in dry cleaners and factories and restaurant kitchens. They paid taxes. They obeyed the law. They earned the right to be here and made sure that I would never have to struggle the way they had to. Yet all the time they were told to be grateful and never complain and to bow and scrape to people like you, who treated them as culturally inferior. So pardon me if I don't genuflect and say, 'Thank you, master.'"

Lord Buchan seems unsure whether to argue or applaud.

"You are a very impressive young woman. What does my brother pay you?" he asks.

"That's none of your business."

"Come and work for me. I'll give you five times as much."

"I think I'm the wrong color for you."

The comment lands like a slap.

"Whatever you may think of me, young lady, I am not a racist."

"No, you're a hypocrite."

Almost before Florence utters her next sentence, I want to warn her that she's said enough. But her blood is up, and she has this man in her sights.

"Where are these men from?" she asks, pointing to the beaters who are sitting in the shade, some of them eating sandwiches wrapped in waxed paper, and sipping on bottles of cordial that have come from the kitchen.

"A local employment agency."

"Are they documented?"

"I assume so. That's the law."

"But you don't know for sure?"

"Mr. Collie handles the staffing of the estate."

Again, I try to stop Florence from continuing, but she ignores me. "Are you funding illegal patrols in the North Sea that are deliberately sinking refugee boats?"

"That's enough, Florence," I say. "We have no proof."

"No. I want to hear this," says Buchan. "What makes you think I had anything to do with that tragedy?"

Florence finally keeps quiet.

"Did my brother send you here?" asks Buchan. "Is that what he told you?"

"No," I say. "We're sorry for the intrusion."

Lord Buchan only has eyes for Florence. "I am not a monster, Miss Gatsi, but I will fight to protect my reputation. If you defame or slander me, I will seek recompense, and you *will* pay."

"Just like your other victims."

57

Evie

The housekeeper hurries me up the curving stone steps, through the double doors, and into an entrance hall with a checkerboard pattern on the floor. I gawp at the tapestries on the walls and the polished wooden staircase that rises, back and forth, to the upper levels. A chandelier hangs from the ceiling on a long chain, plunging between the floors like a huge static pendulum.

"The bathroom is along the corridor, third door on the right," she says. "Don't dillydally." She's carrying a package wrapped in butcher's paper. "I have to get this to the kitchen. Show yourself out."

I follow the corridor and find the ladies, which is surprisingly small and poky for such a grand-looking house. I wee and wash my hands and smell the nice soaps and handwash, before using a small white hand towel to dry myself. I wonder if I should hang it up or throw it in the wicker basket.

Leaving the bathroom, I walk back towards the entrance. I glance up at the chandelier and feel a sudden rush of memory that feels like vertigo. The sensation is so powerful that I stumble, bumping a table and knocking over a vase, which I catch before it falls. Heart thumping, I set the vase back on the lace doily and sneak a look up the stairs and then out the front door. I want to get Cyrus, but they won't let him in here. I make a decision and begin climbing, trying to step lightly on the marble, as though expecting it to creak like the stairs at home.

On the first floor there are twin corridors that run in opposite directions. I can see a cleaning trolley to my right and choose the other direction. Most of the doors are closed, but one is open. A bedroom. I see a suitcase on a luggage rack. Polished shoes. A double bed. Clothes hanging in a wardrobe.

Why do I remember this place? Have I been here?

Cyrus once told me that children find it difficult to recall memories chronologically because they don't have enough experience to link events to a particular moment in their life. They lack a mental calendar they can reference. That's why most people can't recall things that happen before they're six or seven years old. I was nine on the voyage. I should remember what happened afterwards. How did I get off the boat? Who looked after me? Where did I stay?

There is another bathroom at the end of the corridor next to a small lounge with oil paintings on the walls—mostly of dogs and birds and fish and people with guns or standing thigh deep in water, wearing waders that make them look like Oompa Loompas.

I come to a smaller staircase that goes up and down. I climb higher, reaching the next floor, where the furnishings are more basic, as though the owner ran out of money when they reached this level. There are fewer rooms and a narrower corridor, and the windows are smaller and seem to be painted shut. The ceiling slopes, matching the roofline, creating a church-like peak where the chain from the chandelier is attached to a thick metal pulley and tied to the far wall. Why would they need to lift it up and down? To change the bulbs or to clean the brass arms?

I don't know what I'm looking for, or where I'm going, but one foot follows the other. Passing the larger staircase and the skylight, I enter the corridor on the far side. I stop outside a door. When I touch the handle, I jerk my hand away as though it's electrified. In that instant, I picture a younger version of myself, lying in a small attic room, gazing up at a window that offers a narrow glimpse of sky. A woman is standing in the doorway. She has a tangle of grey hair and pale green eyes that look at me as though I am trespassing. Everything about her is faded—her hair, her clothes, her skin. She is carrying a tray of food. I try to speak but it hurts, and the only sound I make is a kitten-like squeak. She presses a finger over her lips and makes a shushing sound.

"The doctor said yer vocal cords are damaged. Ye're nae supposed to talk."

"Mama," I croak.

"Are you deaf? Ah said nae talking. Eat yer soup."

I am still holding the door handle. It turns in my hand and reveals a small room, which is exactly as I remember, with a single bed and a table and a high window and a chest of drawers. Even without looking, I know the top drawer is lined with a square of wallpaper cut to fit inside and the bottom one is stiff and has a broken handle. There is also a worn semi-circle in the rug where the door opens and a water stain on the ceiling above the bricked-up fireplace and one of the floorboards has a knothole that is big enough to drop a marble into.

Voices break the spell. Men laughing and talking loudly downstairs in the dining room. Drinks are being poured and food is being served.

Quickly retracing my route, I'm almost at the foyer when I miss a step and grab hold of the banister to stop myself from falling. Another flashback. A room full of books. A fireplace. A painting on the wall of an old man in hunting breeches with tartan wrapped around his chest and draped over his shoulder. He is leaning against a plinth, while two golden retrievers lie at his feet, one of them asleep.

"What are you doing?" barks a voice, breaking the spell. The house-keeper is carrying a tray of food to the dining room. Her features rush to the center of her face. "Have you stolen something? Empty your pockets."

"I'm not a thief," I say.

The tray she's carrying is heavy, making her arms wobble.

"I was looking for a room with books," I say.

"What?"

"Books."

"You have to leave."

"Is it this way?" I point past her.

"No. Get out!"

She's lying. I run along the corridor, stopping at each door. Turning handles. Peering inside. A cloakroom. A lounge with a leather sofa. A games room with a pool table. The housekeeper puts down the tray and yells for help. Men are responding.

Another door. The right one, or the wrong one. I'm in the library, where shelves of books reach to the ceiling. Heavy drapes cover a bay window. I see the painting above the mantelpiece. It's the one I remember, of the old man and his dogs. My knees begin to shake, and the room falls away. I'm a child, standing in the same room. A younger man is standing next to the fireplace. Thin and pale-skinned, he is wearing a three-piece suit.

"Is she ready?" he asks.

"She hasn't spoken, but she understands," answers the woman.

"Maybe she's simple."

"I don't think so."

He shrugs. "Well, he's looking for a daughter, not a dinner companion. Dress her in something nice. He'll be here at six."

58

Cyrus

I'm driving too quickly along the road that follows the natural contours of the land like water running downhill. Trees arch overhead, the canopies almost touching, showing only glimpses of blue and white behind the leaves. Cloud and sky. We emerge from woodland onto a ridge with a wide view of the western horizon. I look for somewhere to pull over. The engine ticks as it cools.

Evie hasn't said a word since we left Glengowrie. She fainted on the floor of the library and regained consciousness as I carried her to the car. Now she's hugging her knees, rocking in place, staring into the distance.

"I'm sorry," she whispers, lifting a hand to wipe her eyes.

"What happened?" asks Florence.

"I remembered."

"What did you remember?"

"The chandelier, the room upstairs, the man in the painting."

"What painting?" I ask.

"It was in the library; he had two dogs. Golden retrievers."

"Are you sure it was the same house?" I ask.

Evie nods.

"How long were you there?"

"I don't know."

"Days? Weeks? Months?"

She shakes her head.

"Tell me why you remember this painting."

"The same man was there in the library, standing beside the fireplace, only he was younger than in the painting. How is that possible?"

I look at Florence. "What do you know about David and Simon's father?"

"Not much. He inherited wealth from his father, who had made a fortune buying and selling property in the poorer parts of Liverpool and Manchester after the Second World War."

"When did he die?"

She takes her phone and types in a search. "Ten years ago."

"That means he was alive when the *Arianna II* caught fire and sank. Is there a photograph?"

She hands over her phone. The image is in black and white, showing a middle-aged man with curly grey hair swept back from his forehead. He's wearing a blazer and a wide seventies tie and is gazing skyward, letting the natural light fall on his face.

"It's in the National Portrait Gallery," says Florence.

I show the image to Evie.

"That's the man in the painting," she says.

"Did he . . . ?" I stop myself.

"No, not him," says Evie. "I met the younger one. He was lighting a fire."

"Have you seen him since?"

"No."

My mobile begins singing. DI Carlson's name lights up the screen.

"Where are you?" he asks but doesn't wait for an answer. "Angus Radford has been granted bail on compassionate grounds to attend his brother's funeral. The surety is half a million pounds. His father lodged the paperwork ten minutes ago. Radford will be free within the hour."

I begin to calculate how long it would take Angus to get here. Seven, maybe eight hours by road from Grimsby. He could fly to Edinburgh, but that would take almost as long with transfers and waiting around.

Carlson is still talking. "Radford's barrister has made a complaint to the Independent Office for Police Conduct, alleging that his client was interviewed without his lawyer being present. You're named."

"It wasn't a formal interview."

"That hasn't stopped them. You're also accused of harassing and intimidating his family."

"That's ridiculous."

"I'm not arguing, Cyrus, I'm telling you. Leave Scotland."

"OK, but I need something from you."

Carlson stifles a complaint, letting me continue.

"Twelve years ago, Angus Radford skippered a trawler that was smuggling migrants into Britain. That boat sank off the Scottish coast. Only one migrant survived. She can identity Radford and the crew."

"This is your friend Evie Cormac."

"Yes. After the boat sank, Evie was taken to an estate that belongs to the Buchan family."

"Hold on, hold on. Are you talking about Lord David Buchan?"

"The estate belonged to his father."

"Christ!" mutters Carlson. "Be careful what you say to me. I'm required to act upon any information that you give me and take it to my superiors. And I'm not sure they're going to want to hear this."

"There's something else. The gamekeeper at the estate is Angus Radford's maternal grandfather, Wallis Collie."

"OK, that's it. Stop talking."

"This has to be investigated," I say.

"OK. But be quiet. Let me think."

"You're scared of Buchan."

Carlson loses his temper. "No, I'm careful and methodical because I'm a professional investigator, not some amateur, poor man's Poirot, who randomly hurls criminal accusations at politicians and public figures. How did you *ever* get a job with the police?"

"You're right," I say to Carlson. "I'm a liability. Thanks for cutting me loose."

I hang up and sit in silence, gazing at the countryside. Florence and Evie have been listening.

"How could they let Radford go?" asks Evie.

"Without Arben the case against him has fallen apart," says Florence.

"But the migrants . . . ?"

"It's not over," I say. "He's on bail, that's all. They'll find new evidence."

In the meantime, we need to leave, but I don't relish the idea of driving eight hours back to Nottingham, and Evie isn't in the right mindset to share the wheel. Florence must be exhausted.

"When was the last time you slept?" I ask her.

"I'm fine."

"No, you need a shower and a decent meal and a comfortable bed."

"Do I smell that bad?"

"I love how you smell."

"Ugh!" grunts Evie.

"Aberdeen is less than an hour away. We could find a nice hotel and rest up," I say.

"With a restaurant," says Evie.

"And a bath," says Florence.

"And a bar," I add.

59

Cyrus

Two hours later, we are gathered around a table, with damp hair, clean clothes, and menus in hand. The motel is four stars, in a leafy area away from the granite heart of Aberdeen. My Fiat is parked several streets away in a multistory car park, alongside Florence's Kawasaki.

"You didn't have to get me my own room," says Florence, who breaks a bread roll. "I would have shared with Evie . . . or with you."

Evie makes a gagging sound and Florence laughs. Her phone is ringing. She wants to ignore it but notices the name.

"Simon Buchan," she whispers. "He's never called me."

She takes the phone outside. A waitress tops up my wineglass. Evie is on lemonade—still vowing to "never drink again."

"How are you?" I ask when we're alone. She's been quieter than usual since we left Glengowrie Lodge.

"I keep picturing myself in that room," she says.

"You're remembering."

She nods. "The housekeeper was the only person who talked to me. She brought me food and emptied my chamber pot and gave me medicine. I wanted to ask her about Agnesa and Mama, but it hurt when I tried to speak. She said my lungs and vocal cords had been damaged by chemicals in the smoke, which is why I had trouble breathing and speaking. She brought me an oxygen tank and showed me how to hold the mask over my mouth and nose and to inhale slowly when I was out of breath."

Florence returns to the table, looking stunned. "Simon knows I'm in Scotland."

"Is that a problem?"

"I left without telling anyone. Not even my housemates."

"Maybe DS Ogilvy called the charity to check up on you."

"I didn't tell Ogilvy where I worked."

There is a moment of silence before Evie pipes up. "Maybe someone is tracking your phone."

"I'm a junior employee. Why bother?" says Florence.

"You told Lord Buchan that you worked for Migrant Watch?" I say. "He must have called his brother."

Florence doesn't look reassured. "Simon said I was making a nuisance of myself and jeopardizing the mission of the charity."

"How?"

"The text messages from a sinking migrant boat are being used as evidence against us. Critics are accusing Migrant Watch of organizing the crossing and being responsible for the tragedy."

"But that's not true," I say.

"I know, but the optics are terrible and the *Daily Mail* is calling for the charity to be struck off or prosecuted."

"What did Simon say?"

"He told me to take some time off."

"He sacked you?"

Her eyes are shining. "I don't know."

"He's an arsehole," says Evie, who has eaten her bread roll and stolen mine.

"No, he's not," says Florence, her voice trembling. "He's a good man."

A waitress arrives with our meals. Evie asks for ketchup with her fries, using an American accent. Florence pushes food around her plate, picking at the edges, no longer hungry.

Evie tells us more about Glengowrie Lodge, and her days spent locked in an attic room. The woman who brought her food was probably Mrs. Collie, the housekeeper.

"Did you see anyone else?" I ask.

"No, but I heard children playing in the garden outside."

"Does David Buchan have a family?" I ask Florence.

"He has two ex-wives and no children."

"Wallis Collie raised eight children at the lodge," I say.

"Who would now be grown up," says Florence.

"I think they were grandkids," says Evie. "The housekeeper called them 'mah weans.'"

After we've eaten, we walk back to our rooms, dropping Evie first. I pause outside Florence's door, unsure of how to say good night. I have slept with this woman, but that feels like a century ago. Florence slips her hand behind my head and pulls me into a gentle kiss.

"Good night," she says, lingering for a moment as her door closes. If this were a romantic comedy, I would raise my hand to knock, but the door would open simultaneously and we'd kiss and wrestle our clothes off and stumble across the room, tumbling into bed. I watched too many movies like that with my mother on wet winter Sunday afternoons, curled up in front of the gas fire. Romantic comedies *have* spoiled me for real life.

Alone in my room, I replay the events of the day, remembering conversations and trying to look for hidden meanings. I know how the *Arianna* avoided detection on the voyage to and from Spain. And I know how Evie escaped the sinking trawler, although Sean Murdoch didn't confirm that he picked her up.

What did he call her? The runt of the litter. That was an odd term. It's normally used to describe the smallest and weakest in a litter of puppies or kittens. Did he know that Evie had a sister?

Unless? Unless?

I have an overwhelming urge to talk to Evie—to take her back onto the trawler and have her relive the last moments with her mother and sister—but I can't plant a seed in her mind that Agnesa might have survived. The idea is crazy. Dangerous. Cruel.

60

Evie

I dream of children playing in the garden and singing.

> *Ring around o' Rosie*
> *A pocket full of posies*
> *Ashes. Ashes.*
> *We all fall down.*

My history teacher, Mr. Poole, told us this nursery rhyme dates back to the Great Plague and that a "rosie" was a stinky rash that developed on sufferers, and that posies were put in pockets to conceal the smell. Once I knew the origins, it stopped being cheerful or playful.

I heard it first in the attic room in the big house. I stood on tiptoes, trying to reach the windowsill to pull myself up and glimpse the children who were singing in the garden. Were they like me? I wondered. Would I be allowed out to play one day when I could talk?

The room had a sagging single bed with brass knobs on the frame, a night table with wormholes, and a single wooden chair with a faded floral pattern on the cushion. By the end of my stay, I knew every cobweb in every corner. I knew when the sun arrived as a thin strip of light on the wall, and how it thickened and descended and crossed the floor.

The housekeeper came three times a day, bringing me food and medicines and emptying my chamber pot. She would straighten my bedclothes and fluff up my pillows and tell me not to speak.

"I know yer don't understand most of what Ah'm saying," she said, "but I'll keep talkin' because you must get lonely up here."

She would point to the tray of food. "Now eat everything. Ye're skinny as a twig."

Later, she asked, "Do you understand me?"

I nodded.

She touched her throat with her hand. "Does it hurt?"

I nodded again.

"Less than before?"

Another nod.

The children were still singing. I looked at the window.

"Sorry about the racket," she said. "Mah weans make more noise than a bagpipe being beaten to death with a broom."

I didn't know what a bagpipe was or why it had to be beaten with a broom. I made a writing gesture, wanting a pencil and paper.

"Cannae do that, pet. The laird won't allow it," she said.

After she'd gone, I pushed the bed closer to the window and lifted myself by bracing my elbows on the sill. I could see the fields and trees and the fringe of mountains that were changing color as the sun went down. But not the garden. It was always below me, out of sight, like the faces of the children.

One morning, the woman brought a dress for me to wear. A dark blue smock and a white blouse. "It's old, but nice enough," she said. "And it should fit because you're still a twig."

She waited for me to get changed and escorted me along the hallway and down the marble stairs. "Keep going," she said, her hand on the small of my back. "Right to the bottom."

At the foot of the stairs, I waited for her directions. We went along a wide corridor to the library. That's when I saw the painting above the fireplace of the old man with his dogs. A figure squatted beside the fire, with a blackened stick in his hand. I thought he was burning books, but the flame was feeding on kindling and cut wood.

He tossed the stick into the fireplace and straightened, brushing his hands together.

"Hello, Adina, welcome."

His hands were pale and hairless, with long tapered fingers. He motioned me to come closer, into the light of the bay window.

"You're not as pretty as she is, but that can't be helped."

I tried to speak but couldn't make my voice work.

He was leaning on the mantelpiece. "Do you know how many children die in the world every year, Adina? Five million. War, poverty, disease, famine, neglect—it's a terrible toll, a waste, but you are safe now."

The woman was still in the room. "Is she ready?" he asked.

"Yes, sir."

"Does she understand English?"

"Aye, but her voice was damaged."

"Is it permanent?"

"The doctors said it could take another month."

"Well, do something with her hair and put some color in her cheeks."

That evening, wearing the same dress, I made my way down the stairs and across the foyer and through the doors. Turning back, I saw what the house looked like from the outside—and the garden where the children sang "Ring o' Rosie."

A car was waiting. The rear door was open. A man sat inside. He was tall, dark-haired, and tanned, dressed in a charcoal-grey suit. A gold ring glinted on his wedding finger. He patted the seat next to him.

"Hello, Adina. You can call me uncle."

Cyrus answers my knock. He's dressed in boxer shorts and tattoos.

"It's five in the morning," he says.

"We have to go back," I say.

"Why?"

"He said I wasn't as pretty as she is."

"As pretty as who?"

"Exactly."

61

Cyrus

It's a simple plan. One question. One answer. We're going to find Sean
Murdoch and ask him if anyone else survived the sinking. If he lies or
tells the truth, Evie will know.

I have left a note for Florence, slipping it under her door, telling her
that we are going back to St. Claire for a one-stop visit and I don't want
her risking her career by tagging along. She's done enough for us.

As we near the Fiat, I study the surrounding streets, peering into the
shadows and doorways, half expecting to see Angus Radford waiting for
us. I know he can't have found us here, not yet, but memories of Arben
keep haunting me.

We drive out of Aberdeen, heading north along the A90. New streaks
of the day are arriving, lines of orange light that run across the sky, illuminating the clouds on the horizon. The roads are quiet at this hour,
but I continuously check the mirrors, looking for vehicles that might be
following.

Next to me, I can feel Evie grow tense as the miles disappear.

"One question. One answer," I say, reassuring her.

Forty minutes later, we enter St. Claire. The Waterfront Inn is closed.
The kitchen door is locked. I knock and wait. Evie is nervously shuffling
from foot to foot, hiding under her hoodie.

Isla Collie opens the door a crack.

"Is Sean here?" I ask.

"You have to leave," she whispers, pleading with her eyes.

"We have to see Sean," says Evie, showing her face.

"Go, please," she whispers.

An unseen voice from inside: "Who is it?"

"The postman," she replies.

"At this hour?" says the voice.

"It's a package."

"Ah don't think so," says the voice. "Invite them in."

It's an order not a request.

Isla opens the door. We step into the darkened bar. Only a few lights are glowing, illuminating the bottles of spirits behind the bar and the chrome of the beer taps. The place looks deserted, until I see a lone figure, nursing a drink in the corner near the jukebox. An open crisp packet is on the table. Smoke curls from a cigarette in an ashtray.

Angus Radford clears his throat. "Company. At last."

62

Evie

I should be frightened, but I feel a strange sense of calm as if the worst has already happened. Perhaps I have been afraid so often and for so long that I've become inoculated to fear, and nothing has the power to make my heart race, or my palms sweat, or my throat close.

Angus Radford kicks a chair across the floor, telling Cyrus to sit. Then he pats the stool next to him and motions to me. I don't move. A sawn-off shotgun is resting across his lap. He drops his right hand to the trigger. I shuffle nearer, fixated on the weapon. I remember what a bullet did to Finn Radford.

When I reach the stool, Angus leans closer and he sniffs my hair. I snap with my teeth. He pulls away. Laughing.

"I didnae recognize yer at first," he says. "What do they call yer now?"

"Evie."

"You were just a scrap of a thing. Your sister was the looker. You missed out."

"Her name was Agnesa," I say angrily.

He laughs again. "I know her fuckin' name."

"What happened to her?"

"She died."

I look for the lie, but it's not there, and my heart breaks along a familiar fault line.

"They all died except you," he says. "I guess that makes you the lucky one."

"No," I whisper.

The scar on his neck catches the light from the wall lamp and looks boil-like and seething, as though a snake is uncoiling beneath his skin, trying to burrow its way out. He turns on his phone. Makes a call. Talks.

"They're here . . . No . . . They found me." Laughter. "They just walked into the bar . . . yeah, both of them . . . made it easy for us . . . Get the boat ready."

He ends the call and picks up his whiskey, taking a sip, looking at me over the rim of the glass. From somewhere nearby comes the abrupt thud of a door slamming and the sound of footsteps receding.

Angus yells, "Isla! Where's my breakfast?"

She doesn't respond. He curses and takes another chip from the torn packet on the table.

"You killed them?" I say, wanting to claw out his eyes, picturing my fingers sinking into his sockets.

"It was an accident."

"You should have opened the hatches."

"We were fighting a fire."

"We were trapped."

"You were already dead."

"Not all of us."

Angus pauses and examines his empty glass. "Doesn't matter anymore."

"I think it does," says Cyrus. "I'd like to hear the story and I think Evie is owed."

"No, if anything, she owed me," he says. "I could have left her to die with the others."

He walks behind the bar and pours himself another drink. Swallowing. "How much do you remember?"

"There was a fire," I say.

"Yeah, well, we got that under control and then *BOOM*!" He opens his cupped hands, indicating an explosion. "It breached the hull. I dragged Cam's body out of the engine room and we tried to revive him, but it was too late. The pumps couldn't cope with the water coming in. By the time we opened the hatches, well, it was a fucking mess down there, nothing but smoke and bodies floating in water. I told Finn to close it up, but he wanted to be sure. He jumped into the hold and began pressing his ear to chests and feeling for pulses. I said it was too late, but he kept looking, with water up to his thighs, in darkness, with me yelling, 'Get the fuck out! We're sinking,' but then he found you. Still breathing.

"'Leave her,' I told him. Finn was holding you in his arms, lifting you up, begging me. The soft prick wasn't going to leave you behind, so I lifted you out. Both my hands were burned, my face, I was in agony, but I saved your skinny arse." His face twists in disgust.

"I told Finn to get out but he stayed down there, checking for more survivors. The stern was underwater. We'd launched the life raft. The coastguard was coming. But he wouldn't fucking listen. What was I supposed to do?"

"Save people," says Cyrus.

"How? The *Arianna* was lost, and we were a hundred miles from shore."

"You had life rafts. Immersion suits."

"Not for everyone. And how was I going to explain someone like *her* to the coastguard?" He points to me. "It was better if none of you survived and the *Arianna* was never found . . ."

"You condemned them to death," says Cyrus.

"They were *already* dead."

"Not me," I say.

Angus grunts dismissively and there is a long silence. Ice cracks and falls in the ice maker.

His phone is ringing. He listens. "Two minutes. We'll be waiting out back."

He rests the shotgun on the bar and bends to retrieve a roll of masking tape.

"You won't get away with this," says Cyrus.

Angus finds this amusing. "They always say that, don't they—on TV cop shows and in the movies? Does that make it a cliché, or a trope?"

"A cliché," says Cyrus.

"That's what education does—helps you come up with the right word at the right time."

"The police know we're here," says Cyrus. "We've told them that you and your brothers were smuggling migrants."

"And what proof do you have? There is no boat and no bodies, and your only witness was a child. And we all know that children make up stories."

He motions to me. "Give me your phone."

"Why?"

"I won't ask again."

I hand it over.

"And yours?" he says to Cyrus. "Now your car keys."

Angus twirls them around his forefinger.

"What are you going to do?" asks Cyrus.

"I'm going to put these phones in your car, and somebody will take it for a drive, proving that you left here, alive and well. Maybe we'll throw the phones off a cliff at some popular suicide spot and leave your car nearby."

"Nobody is going to believe we committed suicide."

"They'll believe whatever makes their lives easier," he says, tossing the spool of masking tape at me. I drop it clumsily. He points at Cyrus. "Tape up his hands. Behind his back. Around his wrists. Do it properly or you'll be doing it again."

I fumble with the spool, trying to find the end of the tape with my thumbnail. Cyrus stands and puts his hands behind his back. I'm close now.

"If you get the chance, run," he whispers.

"No."

More urgently. "Listen to me, Evie. Get away and call Carlson."

"I'm not leaving you."

"No talking!" says Angus, who is pouring Scotch into a hip flask. Spilling some. Cursing. Not cleaning up.

Cyrus is holding his wrists a little apart as I wrap the tape, creating a gap that allows his hands to move. He pushes his wrists together when Radford checks my work.

"Now you," he says, putting down the shotgun and picking up the tape. I contemplate lunging for the gun, but I wouldn't know what to do. Does it have a safety catch, or do I just point and shoot?

The moment has passed. I hold out my hands. He binds them at the front and not the back, adding an extra loop around my waist to keep my hands tightly pressed against my stomach.

"OK, this way," he says, shoving me towards the kitchen. "Don't try to run, or I'll put a bullet through your spine."

We pass through the kitchen and a storeroom before reaching the outer door. A car is waiting—a dark-colored four-wheel drive. The doors are open. Another nudge.

"Where are we going?" asks Cyrus.

"To see a man about a boat."

63

Cyrus

My face is pressed into the nylon floor mat of the car and Angus Radford is resting his feet on the small of my back. Evie is next to him, leaning as far away as possible, braced against the door. Another man is driving. I recognize him. The jeans, the gelled hair, the crooked teeth, the face like a ferret—he's the man who offered to help me change a tire, moments before he clubbed me and bundled me into the boot of the Fiat and abducted Arben Pasha.

I try to slow my breathing and to think rationally, but my mind keeps wanting to review rather than plan. This is my fault. I have put Evie in danger. My arrogance. My carelessness. My mistaken belief that I could fix her if she confronted her past and remembered what had happened to her mother and sister.

Evie has been right all along. She's not broken. I'm the one with the missing pieces. I left a part of myself in the kitchen next to the body of my slain mother, and another piece in the living room, where my father lay dying, and two more upstairs with my dead sisters. That's why I became a psychologist. It's why I visit my brother, Elias, every fortnight in the secure psychiatric hospital. And why I punish myself in my weight room and run like I want to never finish. It is my survivor's guilt—not hers.

The car is moving. "What happened to Arben?" I ask, trying to appear calm.

"We didn't touch him," says the driver. "He fell into a coma."

"You could have saved him."

Angus lifts one foot and rams his boot heel into the back of my head, telling me to shut up.

"Hey!" protests Evie, lunging at him. I try to warn her, but it's too late and he knocks her head against the side window. She cries out in pain. I struggle against the tape around my wrists, wanting to protect her, but the boot heel presses against my neck.

I decide to conserve energy and to concentrate on the journey, feeling my body weight shift through each corner and estimating how far we have traveled from St. Claire. Eventually, the car bumps over a grate and comes to a halt. Radford and the ferret get out. Evie and I are alone.

"Cruden Bay," she whispers. "I saw a sign."

I twist myself around and straighten, until I'm sitting next to her. We are parked on the edge of a small concrete harbor, which is three hundred feet long and half as wide, with low concrete walls and a narrow channel separating it from the sea. The parking area is dotted with boats, which are covered and wheel-clamped. More boats are moored in the still water inside the break wall. The only dwellings I can see are two cottages with pebbledash exteriors overlooking the parking area, and a smaller building with a blue-painted door and matching window frames that could be some sort of harbor office. Closed today.

Angus points out to sea. A sleek-looking boat appears from behind the headland, bouncing over the swells. Within minutes it has reached the inner harbor and pulled up alongside a set of stone steps. I know this boat. It's where I met Willie Radford when he summoned me to St. Claire Bay Marina. The name is painted on the stern: *Watergaw*.

The two men return to the car and drag me out. Evie follows, walking next to me, close enough for our shoulders to touch. I look around, hoping there might be witnesses, but the harbor looks deserted and the cottages are empty.

A figure appears on the gangplank. Willie Radford is wearing a rain slicker and bib and braces. He steps back and sweeps his arm across his chest, welcoming us on board. The boat moves under my weight. Evie stumbles. Willie reaches out to help her, but she knocks his hand away.

"Welcome on board, Dr. Haven," he says. "And you also, lassie."

"Have we met?" she asks.

"Aye. Many years ago."

Willie points us to a bench seat at the stern. Evie sits next to me. My hands are bound behind me and hers in front, tight against her stomach.

Mooring ropes are cast aside and the twin engines engage, churning up the oily water. The cruiser pulls away from the dock and turns towards the harbor entrance. A swan glides past, rising and falling on the ripples.

Angus takes a seat near the ladder, resting the shotgun between his spread knees. His father has the helm, steering us into open water. The ferret has stayed behind to clean up and remove any trace of our visit to the Waterfront Inn.

"What does *Watergaw* mean?" I ask, trying to engage Angus in conversation.

"It's a Scottish word," he says. "You ever seen a broken rainbow—one of those wee patches of color that disappear into clouds and don't have a beginning or an end? That's a watergaw."

Looking back to shore, I can still make out the gorse and the nettles and the stunted trees and the outlines of buildings. Sheep dot the pastures. Farmhouses are the same chalky white.

Angus takes out his hip flask and unscrews the lid, taking two swallows. A gust of wind blows his fringe across his eyes.

"You once proudly told me you were a fisherman," I say. "Fourth generation. And now look at you. Aren't you embarrassed?"

A spark of anger. "You know fuck all about me."

"I talked to Finn. He did a lot of whinging about fishing quotas and illegal catches and bureaucrats in Brussels. What's your excuse?"

"Did he tell you that forty years ago, there were nearly five thousand fishermen working the trawlers in Scotland? Now there are nine hundred. The smaller boats have been forced out. Young people are going off to the cities, leaving behind empty shops and abandoned houses and closed schools."

"You think you're the first industry to have to change? Talk to coal miners, factory workers, garment makers. It's always been the same—you adapt or you die."

"Yeah, well, I decided to adapt."

"By exploiting the vulnerable."

"By offering them a new life. We got 'em jobs and houses. We helped arrange visas. Some of them are married now and have kids at the local schools. We saved our community."

"We've seen the accommodation," I say. "Tents, caravans, pit toilets, bucket showers."

"Short-term solutions," he says, taking another swig from his flask.

"Where was my job, my house, my visa?" asks Evie.

Angus shrugs. "You were too young."

"You sold me."

"We had you adopted."

"Do you know what happened to me?"

"You're alive. Can't have been that bad."

Evie tries to launch herself across the space, but I manage to hook my legs around her, stopping her progress. Angus laughs and calls it "touching."

"What about Arben Pasha's sister and the other woman? Have they been sold or offered a new life?" I ask.

Angus doesn't answer.

"Where are they?"

More silence.

"So, tell me, Angus, when did your philosophy change?"

"What d'yer mean?"

"The people who died off the coast of Cleethorpes. You deliberately rammed their boat. You ran them down. You watched them die."

"They hadn't paid."

"Who were they supposed to pay?"

He doesn't answer.

"Are you the Ferryman?" I ask.

He laughs and shakes his head.

"Is it your father?"

"He's an old man."

"David Buchan?"

"Ye're gettin' warmer."

What does that mean? Someone close to Buchan, in his circle? A right-wing agitator or disrupter. Another thought occurs to me. Someone closer still. David Buchan described his brother, Simon, as the nation's biggest people smuggler. He said it facetiously because Migrant Watch provided weather reports and tidal charts and navigation advice to small boats crossing the Channel. It was labeled as humanitarian work and registered as a charity—but could also be brilliant cover for the Ferryman—a means of making money at both ends of the journey: charging migrants for safe passage and using them as cheap labor when they arrive in Britain.

My mind races, putting together the pieces and making the connections. When we dined together, Simon Buchan asked me about Arben, pumping me for information. He offered to provide him with clothes, accommodation, a phone, an education. He said that he would fund his asylum application. And then he gave me a bullshit narrative about the perils of philanthropy, and I ate it up with a spoon and washed it down with an expensive French pinot noir. I admired him. I wanted to *be* him. And I felt sorry that he had a brother like Lord David Buchan.

I couldn't have been more wrong. At least Lord David spoke up for what he believed. Yes, it was reactionary and xenophobic, but I didn't doubt his sincerity, even if I disagreed with his arguments. And I'd rather deal with an articulate, honest bigot than a fake progressive like Simon Buchan, who creates charities and good causes so he can hide his true nature, profiting from desperate people.

The boat is still motoring eastwards, and the shore has slowly receded to become a dark outline. The sea is all around us now, the hiss and rush of it, the collapse of waves into white water. Even the seagulls have deserted us, blown back towards the land.

Angus takes another slug from his hip flask and gets to his feet. He takes two paces to the stern of the boat and undoes his trousers, pulling out his penis to urinate.

Evie turns her face away.

"Nothing you haven't seen before." He laughs as a stream of urine arcs towards the waves. His shotgun is propped against the bench seat.

In that instant, I charge forward, head down, and ram him in the small of his back before he can step away. He cries out in surprise and fights for balance, but neither of us can defy gravity. We're falling, over the railing, into the churning wake of the *Watergaw*.

The cold hits me like a slap, and I immediately inhale a mouthful of water. My hands are useless, bound behind me, but I kick with my legs to keep my head above the surface, coughing and snatching a breath. I roll beneath the waves again and fight to free my hands, twisting back and forth, feeling the tape cut into my wrists. Exhaustion is slowing me down. My legs are burning and arms aching and panic squeezes my heart. This can't be how it ends?

Thrashing to the surface, gasping for breath, I kick off my shoes and try to rip my hands out of the bindings. My chest spasms and water spurts from my mouth and nose. The *Watergaw* is already a hundred feet away. Angus Radford is closer, yelling for his father, waving his arms. He's not interested in me—he's more worried about saving himself.

His head goes under. He surfaces again, looking distressed. Coughing. Spluttering. Drowning.

64

Evie

One moment Cyrus was here and then he was gone. It happened so quickly that I couldn't react. At the same time, it had an almost dream-like quality, like in one of those action films where everything slows down and the bullets travel at walking pace and people lean out of the way to dodge them. I saw Cyrus moving and I thought, No, he won't, he can't, that's crazy stupid. But he did and now both men are in the water, but only one of them is shouting and waving his arms.

Cyrus disappears beneath the surface. His hands are taped behind his back. He can't stay afloat. Did he expect me to go with him? He knows I can't swim.

An orange life buoy is attached to the railing, secured by clips and a monkey grip. My hands are taped to my waist, but I can move my fingers. I pull it free, but it's heavier than I expect. Unable to throw it, I drop it over the side and the rope uncoils. I glimpse a flash of orange bouncing over the whitewash.

The boat turns suddenly, and I lose my balance. The old man has heard the yelling. The shotgun slides across the deck. I crawl towards it. The old man yells at me to stop, but he doesn't leave the wheel. He's trying not to lose sight of his son.

I have to lie on my stomach to pick up the shotgun, but there's no way I can reach the trigger and aim. Looking down into the galley, I see a dining area with bench seats and a table. Hugging the shotgun against my stomach, I stumble down the steps and try to close the door behind me, but the latch is too high for me to reach.

Putting the shotgun down, I begin opening drawers and cupboards. Angus is still yelling, but less often now. I don't know if Cyrus is alive.

There is a cooktop with a steel cover. On the wall is a magnetized knife rack, but I can't reach it with my hands.

Leaning over the countertop, I use my forehead to butt at the handles until a blade falls onto the electric hob, within reach. Holding the knife in my fingertips, pointed towards me, I move the blade back and forth across the tape.

I've drawn blood, but keep cutting, not feeling the pain. Cyrus is going to drown. He can't swim without hands. Why did he do that? He can't die. Not now. Not ever. He can leave me, but he can't die on me.

I free my right hand and rip the tape from around my waist. Using my teeth and fingers, I loosen the rest of the binding until both hands are free. The boat is slowing. The engine idles.

The old man comes down the steps and goes to the stern. "Swim this way," he yells, lowering steps over the side.

My hands are free. I pick up the shotgun and climb out of the galley. Angus Radford is thirty feet away, floating on his back. Cyrus is holding him around the chest, pulling him towards the ladder with strong strokes. Masking tape trails from one hand as he swims.

As they get nearer, Cyrus helps Angus to climb the ladder, pushing as the old man pulls. Bedraggled and exhausted, Angus collapses onto the deck, rolling onto his side, coughing and spluttering. Water gushes from his mouth and nose and he sucks at the air and coughs again.

I wait for Cyrus to come up the ladder. The old man reaches over the side, offering his hand.

"Leave him," says Radford.

"He saved your life."

"I was fine."

The old man pulls up the ladder. I point the shotgun at Radford's chest. "Save him, or I kill you now."

Angus blinks at me through the seawater dripping from his hair. "Know how to use that?" he asks.

"I'll pull the trigger and find out."

He slowly sits up, leaning against the bench seat.

"No further," I say.

"What's yer name again?" he asks.

"Evie."

"That wasn't always your name."

"Adina."

"Yeah, that's right, I remember now. Yer sister talked about you a lot."
I motion to the old man. "Lower the ladder."

"No," says Angus. "That's a single-barrel, twelve-gauge shotgun. One
shell. One shot. She cannae stop both of us."

"I don't have to stop both of you," I say, raising the gun to my shoulder and pointing it at his chest.

"Yer won't do it," he says, feeling in his pocket for his hip flask and
realizing that it's lost somewhere in the sea.

"Give me tha' gun, lassie," says the old man, stepping nearer.

I swing the barrel towards him and back to his son. My finger twitches
on the trigger.

"Help me!" yells Cyrus.

"Give me the gun, and we'll lower the ladder," says the old man. He's
telling the truth, but they're going to kill us anyway.

Trying to take the tremor out of my voice, I focus on Angus Radford,
hating him with every sinew and fiber of my being. "I know you plan on
killing us today, but I promise you one thing," I say.

"And what's that?"

"You're going to die first."

I pull the trigger and his face dissolves into a bloody pulp that wipes
away his crooked grin and his scarred face and his cruel eyes. For a
moment, he stays where he is, sitting upright, but slowly he topples sideways to the deck, gasping shallowly.

The old man is staring at me in disbelief, his mouth open, a cry
lodged in his throat. Suddenly, he finds his voice, screaming in rage and
charging at me. I duck his arms and use the shotgun as a club, but it
bounces off his shoulder and I lose my grip. It skitters away from me.
He comes again and I scramble away, trying to reach the ladder. The
deck is slick with blood, and I seem to be running on the spot, getting
nowhere.

Hands pull me back from the ladder. Close around my neck.

"That's enough," says a new voice, yelling above the *pock pock* of a
different engine.

A figure is silhouetted on the bow of another boat. Sean Murdoch is holding a rope in his hand, which is attached to an orange ring. Florence is next to him, helping pull Cyrus towards them.

"She killed my boy," groans the old man, as he releases me and cradles Angus, rocking his body back and forth.

Murdoch has no sympathy. "Well, I guess that makes things even."

65

Cyrus

It's strange how quickly anger can disappear and adrenaline can leak away, when the source of it is lying dead in a pool of his own blood. I know the signs of "post-adrenaline blues"—the depression and disappointment and the questioning of choices—but I feel none of that. My only concern is for Evie.

Reunited on Sean Murdoch's boat, I hold her against me, listening to her sobs and smelling her hair and feeling something shred inside me.

"I killed him," she whispered.

"You saved my life."

"All I could think about was Mama and Agnesa and those poor migrants."

"Shhh."

"And then I thought of losing you too. And I couldn't . . . I couldn't . . ."

"I'm fine. We're safe."

Florence is moving about the galley of Murdoch's boat, wrapping us in blankets and brewing cups of tea. Hot and happy with relief, she opens a packet of sugared biscuits and offers them around.

"You shouldn't have left me," she says accusingly.

"I'm sorry. I thought we could—"

"Do this alone?"

"Something like that."

Florence explains how she found my note and rode to the Waterfront Inn. By then Isla Collie had alerted Sean Murdoch about what had happened at the pub and they set out to find us.

"How did he know where to look?" I ask.

"The *Watergaw* has some sort of tracking device that is picked up by satellite."

I smile at the irony of that.

Evie is still leaning against me. She sits up and pushes me in the chest.

"What's wrong?" I ask.

"You saved his life."

"He was drowning."

"He was going to kill us."

"I know."

"That makes no sense."

"Not everything does."

She scowls at me like I'm a complete moron, before dropping her head back on my shoulder.

For the next hour we listen to waves slapping against the hull, throwing salt spray higher and higher over the bow, blurring the air. Cliffs appear on the horizon. Two lighthouses. A harbor. Lead-grey clouds edged in silver are rolling across the sky.

A police launch meets us and provides an escort for the final few miles, directing us to a mooring near the port authority headquarters. The *Watergaw* is now under tow, but Willie Radford has stayed on board, under guard, handcuffed in a cabin, keeping Angus company on his final journey.

There are detectives and ambulance crews waiting on the dock. We are taken in separate unmarked cars to the same police station and kept in different interview rooms for the interrogations. The detectives are from Aberdeen not St. Claire. I don't know where Ogilvy has gone, but I don't see him at the station or hear his name mentioned.

After the first round of interviews, I feel like I've revealed my entire life story. I am taken over every detail of my time in Scotland, my conversations, phone calls, movements, and interactions. Why did I make certain choices? Did I consider the consequences? Who gave me the authority?

Evie endures the same, but has Florence sitting in with her, making sure the detectives give her regular rest breaks and something to eat. Her hands are swabbed for shotgun residue and her clothes are taken away for testing, but they let her change into her own spare clothes because nothing at the station will fit her.

I worry about her mental state and how this will affect her. I have pulled a trigger and killed a man. In the aftermath of that shooting, I relived the moment for months, replaying it in slow motion in my mind, feeling the weight of the pistol in my hand and my finger pulling the trigger, pushing the hammer backwards, compressing a metal spring. I felt the kick of the weapon and saw the twist of his body and the look of surprise on his face. I don't want Evie to have similar nightmares. At the same time, this could help draw a line under what happened to her. Psychologists use terms like "closure" and "resolution" but I don't think it's possible to wrap things up in neat and tidy packages. Life is real and passionate and messy; and closure means something is done, when it's never done and it's never going to be done.

New interrogators arrive. Border Force has sent a team to investigate allegations of human trafficking and illegal immigration. They unpack every detail of Evie's journey to Scotland on board the *Arianna II*. There is talk of searching for the wreck, but the depth of the water and the passing of years makes discovery unlikely and salvage even less so.

After Border Force comes the National Crime Agency. I'm surprised when they send Derek Posniak, my old friend from university, who even dresses like a spook in a trench coat and a small porkpie hat, tilted over his eyes. We talk in a holding cell, rather than an interview suite, without cameras and recording equipment.

"Everything is off-the-record," he says, lowering his voice, as though he doesn't trust anyone with this scant piece of information. The Ferryman is real, I tell him, and give him Simon Buchan's name, outlining the clues that point to his involvement. Maybe it's a condition of employment for spies that they never look surprised or act as if anything they hear is unexpected or out of the ordinary. Derek was like that. He didn't turn a hair. Could he have known already? Maybe nothing is secret in a world that trades in secrets.

"Are you going to investigate him?" I ask.

"Who?"

"Simon Buchan."

"That's above my pay grade."

"But you'll pass on the information."

"I'll make my report to my superiors, who will report to their superiors, and so on and so on."

"You don't sound confident."

"Not my job," he replies, straightening his sleeves after shaking my hand.

"There is a way to link Simon Buchan to this," I say, hesitating, suddenly unsure if I can make the argument. A thought has been loitering at the edge of my consciousness like a truant schoolboy. It involves several notebooks and a hotel register, each with a famous painting on the cover. Florence has a notebook with Monet's *Water Lilies and Japanese Bridge* on the cover. Her friend Natalie Hartley from the anti-slavery charity had an almost identical book, which featured Van Gogh's *Starry Night*. And when Evie and I checked into the Belhaven Inn, Maureen Collie used a guesthouse register with *Girl with a Pearl Earring* on the cover. These were all part of the same series, produced by a stationery provider.

"Follow the paper," I whisper to Derek.

"You mean the money."

"No. The paper."

He raises an eyebrow.

"Most companies and government departments choose a single supplier for their stationery and office supplies—pens, notebooks, paper, ink cartridges, staplers. Economies of scale. Bulk orders save money."

"I still don't understand," says Derek.

"Simon Buchan has a large number of business interests, some for profit, others not-for-profit. I think they all use the same stationery and office products supplier. That supplier can be your link to all of his businesses—the charities, labor hire firms, employment agencies, laundries, nail salons, restaurants, commercial kitchens, hotels, factories, and construction sites. Follow the paper and you'll uncover the network."

Derek finally looks surprised. "You really are an odd fish, Cyrus."

"Why?"

"Other people might *say* they care, but you actually try to make a difference."

"Is that wrong?"

"No, it's laudable and weirdly old-fashioned, but somewhat naive."

"You're a cynic."

"That's part of my employment package."

Derek doffs his hat before departing, leaving behind a sense of melancholia and lost opportunities.

I'm finally allowed to see Evie. We meet in the same lounge where we spent the night after Finn Radford's suicide, eating sandwiches and iced coffee from a local café.

"I miss Poppy," says Evie.

"I miss her too."

She seems to have forgiven me for throwing myself into the North Sea and rescuing Angus Radford. Maybe she's right and I should have let him drown. She wouldn't have had to pull the trigger and face the repercussions.

"Florence says I'm not going to be charged with anything, but I'll have to give evidence at his inquest," says Evie, biting into a sandwich.

"It was self-defense."

"I *wanted* to kill him."

"Try not to mention that to the coroner."

"That's what she said."

She chews and sips her iced coffee. Later, she opens a brown paper bag and finds a chocolate brownie. "There's only one," she says. "Want to share?"

"You break, I choose."

Evie breaks it apart, but immediately nibbles the biggest side. "Guess this one's mine," she says, grinning, with chocolate staining her teeth. I suddenly dare to think that she's going to be OK. She'll get through this. We both will. Mutually assured survival.

"When we get home, you have to do something for me," says Evie. "But you have to promise not to laugh."

"OK."

"And not to look at my scars."

"OK."

She hesitates, embarrassed.

"What is it? You can tell me."

"Can you teach me how to swim?"

66

Evie

Sean Murdoch is standing on the pavement outside the police station, holding a cap in both hands like he's come to ask for a job or a favor. We descend the steps and move from shade into sunlight. He lifts his head, about to speak, when a seagull takes off from the chimney pots above us, squawking like a lonely child.

Murdoch follows it in flight, and then turns back to me. "Awright, lass?"

I nod and step closer to Cyrus.

"I wanted to apologize for being part of this," he says, stumbling over the words. "I didnae mean for people to get hurt."

"Have you been interviewed?" asks Cyrus.

"The police will get around to me," he says. "I'll tell them everything."

"You'll go to prison."

"Most likely, but I should have said something before now."

He looks at me. "You're the girl they found all those years ago in that house in London—the one they called Angel Face."

"How do you know that?" asks Cyrus.

Murdoch scratches his cheek. "Worked it out. Everybody was talking about the little girl they found hiding in the walls. She didnae have a name or a past. Then I saw a photograph and I knew who you were. I always hoped someone would come forward to claim you—an aunt or an uncle; you must have had some family."

I don't answer.

"Why didn't you say anything?" asks Cyrus.

"That would have meant confessing. I had a family and I knew what would happen to anyone who broke ranks."

"You were frightened of Angus Radford."

"I was frightened of the people he worked for."

"And who were they?"

Murdoch drops his gaze to his work boots.

"Is Simon Buchan one of the people you're afraid of?" asks Cyrus.

Murdoch presses his lips together and sighs. "I only met him once—years ago. He had a handshake that made me want to wring my fingers out or to count them."

"Where did you meet him?"

"At Glengowrie Lodge. Angus was delivering some people to him."

"Migrants?"

"Most of 'em. Yeah."

"Men or women?"

"Both. Mr. Buchan was angry about us using the main gate. He told Angus to use the goods entrance next time. That's what we were—deliverymen."

"What about Lord David Buchan?" asks Cyrus.

"Met him once or twice. He didnae spend much time at Glengowrie Lodge before his father died. He bought the place from Simon when the inheritance was divided up."

"Two women are missing from the small boat that sank off Cleethorpes. Do you have any idea where they might be?" asks Cyrus.

"No."

Cyrus looks at me. I shake my head. Up until that moment, Murdoch had been telling the truth, but now he's lied to us.

"I'll ask you again," says Cyrus. "Do you have any idea where the women might be?"

There is a beat of silence. Murdoch clears his throat.

"I don't know for certain. But there's a place outside of Leeds. An old convent. Grade II listed. Victorian. Someone turned it into a boarding-house for farm workers, but then it became some sort of halfway house for migrants. Women mainly."

"What's the address?"

"I never went there."

"Not good enough."

"OK, OK, let me think. It was called St. Mary of the Field or St. Margaret of the Field. That's all I know. I swear. And it was years ago. Might not even exist anymore."

Cyrus looks at me. I nod. It's the truth.

Florence bought Cyrus a new phone. He calls DI Carlson, passing on the information. In the meantime, I'm left with Murdoch, who fidgets and shuffles, still holding the cap in his hands.

"Ah'm not trying to wash my hands of this," he says. "Ah know I've done terrible things, but I want to make amends."

"How?"

"That's why I'm here . . . to explain." He glances behind him to his car, an old Land Rover, patched and repainted to deal with rust. "If you come with me, I can show you everything. I promise you nothing bad is going to happen."

He's telling me the truth. I wait for Cyrus to finish his call. "It's your decision," he says.

I hang back, staring at the open car door. I have lived in darkness for so long that I've grown scared of the light. Cyrus is always telling me that I can change things; that everything I want is on the other side of fear.

The Land Rover smells of wet dog and a Christmas tree air freshener. Murdoch apologizes for the mess, saying he should have cleaned it up first. He doesn't talk as he drives out of St. Claire along the coast road, past factories, car yards, and a new housing estate. A roadside stall is selling eggs, jam, and fresh strawberries, payment by an honor system. Soon we're in the open countryside, where the fields are stitched together in a patchwork of squares. After a few miles we turn off onto a narrow road, leading towards the sea.

A village appears. Oyster-colored dwellings are surrounded by stunted trees and dry-stone walls and small gardens, growing vegetables or flowers. The road twists back and forth, descending to the shoreline, where the shingle beach is partially blanketed by seaweed. There is a pub, a post office, a phone box, and a row of brightly painted cottages, some of them with bed-and-breakfast signs.

Murdoch parks the car at the base of a steep cliff and we walk up a set of wooden stairs weathered by salt and wind. At the top is a small whitewashed cottage with a pitched slate roof surrounded by a neat garden. Below us, a concrete seawall juts into the ocean, protecting a quiet, underused stretch of beach. The North Sea is grey, the sky is blue, and a freighter inches north on the horizon.

Murdoch takes off his boots in the entrance hall. His big toe pokes through a hole in his left sock. We enter a sitting room with a picture window filled with the view.

"Is this your place?" asks Cyrus.

"It's where I grew up. My parents left it to me," says Murdoch.

There are family photographs on the mantelpiece. A child in them. Addie as a toddler. Addie starting school. Addie flying a kite. Playing with a dog. Sailing a dinghy. Riding a carousel horse.

There is a lone photograph lying facedown on a side table. Murdoch turns it over and hands it to me. Everything stops and the room falls away. I'm staring at Agnesa, who is smiling back at me. The light is behind her, creating a golden halo around her head, and strands of her hair have pulled free from a tortoiseshell clip, framing her face.

I study everything about the photograph, her eyes, her nose, her lips, the window behind her. It's only then that I realize the picture was taken in this same room, with light from the same window. How is that possible?

"Where is she?" I whisper.

"She died nine years ago."

"I don't understand."

"A drunk driver ran a red light. Agnesa was in the passenger seat. The car hit us on her side, and threw her onto my lap, crushing her chest, trapping us in the wreckage." His voice chokes. "She died in my arms."

I'm staring at the picture. "But she died on the *Arianna II*."

"That's what I wanted to tell you. She lived."

67

Cyrus

Evie launches herself at Murdoch, pounding his chest with her fists, screaming insults and profanities into his face. She calls him a liar but knows everything he's told her is the truth. He takes the punches without flinching, almost leaning into the blows as though he deserves every one of them.

Growing tired, Evie slumps into an armchair, clutching the photograph of Agnesa to her chest. Murdoch crosses the room awkwardly, skirting Evie, and takes up a position beside a potbellied wood heater, summer cold. He begins talking slowly, pausing occasionally to take an extra breath and find the right words.

"When Angus and Willie Radford came to me with the idea of smuggling people, I could have said no. Nobody put a gun to my head." He glances at Evie as if to apologize for his poor choice of words. "Ah'm not going to make excuses about owing money to the bank or worrying about losing my boat. I knew what I was doin'."

"How many trips?" I ask.

"Five—no, six. Angus had other skippers who helped him. I only agreed to carry the satellite transponder and to fish Dogger Bank— giving them an alibi while they went to Spain or France or Belgium to pick up migrants. On that last voyage, the *Arianna II* went to Spain and returned. We rendezvoused at Dogger Bank and swapped the AIS transponder, before separating for the journey home."

"How were they going to explain having no fish on board?" I ask.

"Angus was going to say the *Arianna*'s ice machine had broken or the nets had been torn. I had a full hold and we could share the catch."

Murdoch closes his eyes and opens them again like a man who's hoping he might have finished his story, but there is more to come.

"Everything had gone to plan until the storm. When a fire broke out in the engine room, Angus called me on the radio. He said Cam was dead and the boat was sinking. We were sixteen miles away. Whatever happened after that, I knew we were all in a load o' trouble.

"Angus had delayed making the Mayday call, because he wanted me to reach the *Arianna* before anyone else. Ah thought we'd be picking up everyone on board and we'd keep them safe until the coastguard and RNLI boats reached us. Even when he radioed, saying they were abandoning ship, I thought he'd found a way to save the migrants. I didnae realize . . ." He swallows the rest of the statement.

"How did Agnesa escape?" asks Evie.

"She was in the wheelhouse. Cam used to sometimes collect her from the hold when he was on watch. I guess he wanted company. The fire alarm sounded. He went to investigate, and the explosion killed him. Angus and Finn dragged his body into the galley. They put out the fire and opened the hatches, but the hold was full of smoke. You know the rest."

Murdoch pushes a ball of spit around his mouth and swallows. "Agnesa was still in the wheelhouse when Finn found you alive. Angus was going to dump both of you overboard if the chopper arrived before the *Neetha Dawn*, but we reached you before then, and took you on board, hiding you in the crew quarters. When the coastguard chopper arrived, they winched Angus and Iain Collie off the deck, and transferred them to the Aberdeen hospital. We didnae tell the coastguard about you."

"But she needed medical attention," says Cyrus.

"Border Force would have investigated. They would have salvaged the *Arianna* and found the bodies. We could'nae take that risk." His eyes are pleading with Evie. "We arrived in St. Claire early the next morning. You were still unconscious. I told Agnesa that we were taking you to hospital. She begged to stay with you. I promised her that you'd be safe. I'm sorry."

Evie doesn't answer. She is still holding the photograph of Agnesa, sitting in the same chair in front of the same window in the same house where the image was taken.

"Why didn't Agnesa come looking for me?" she asks, her voice wavering.

"Ah told her that you died at the hospital. That you never woke up from the coma."

I hear the soft gasping of the sea, but realize the sound comes from Evie.

"I even brought home a ceramic urn, full of ashes, and said they belonged to you," says Murdoch. "That were a terrible thing to do, but you were gone by then."

"Sold off," I say.

"They didn't tell me the details."

With three quick, stiff steps, Evie is on him again, pounding his chest, screaming, "You knew! You knew!"

I pull her away, pinning her arms. She collapses against me, weeping. Murdoch keeps muttering, "Ah'm sorry. Ah'm sorry." His eyes are shining.

I take Evie to the sofa and we sit together. Murdoch leaves the room and returns with a box of tissues, which he offers to Evie. He takes one for himself and blows his nose.

"Is this where you brought Agnesa?" I ask.

"Aye. It was somewhere quiet. None of us knew she was pregnant. Not then."

"You kept her prisoner?"

"For a while, aye, but after a time she stopped trying to escape. I offered to look after her and the wee bairn. I'd never been married—never found any woman who would say yes. Ah'm not stupid. I know she didn't love me the way that I loved her, but Agnesa had nowhere else to go. After a while, I think she grew to like me, or trust me at least."

He addresses Evie. "She never stopped talking about you. It was Adina this and Adina that. And when the baby was born, there wasn't any question about what she was going to be called."

It's only then that I realize what he's saying. The photographs. This house. The girl with the pink hair and ear piercings.

Evie whispers, "Addie?"

He nods.

"Does she know?" I ask.

"I told her last night—the whole story—just like I'm telling you."

Evie looks around, eyes wide, caught between panic and joy and grief. "Is she here?"

"She's waiting to see you."

Murdoch kneels on the floor as though praying for forgiveness.

"After Addie was born, Agnesa got a job at a local primary school, working as a teacher's aide. She had better English than most of the teachers. She was learning how to drive and I promised to buy her a car when she got her full license.

"What Ah'm trying to say is that she made a good life for herself here. And she was happy in her own way. She sewed. She tended the garden. She read books. She wrote diaries. Ah've kept them. They're yours."

Opening a drawer in a dark bureau, he removes a photograph album and several notebooks. Each has a famous painting on the cover: *The Girl with the Flaxen Hair* by Hans Heyerdahl and *Woman with a Parasol* by Monet. I think back to what I told Derek Posniak. Follow the stationery.

I open the album because Evie doesn't look like she has the strength to turn the pages. The ten-by-eight prints are neatly laid out, held in place by photo corners. In one Agnesa is dangling her feet over the side of a dinghy. In the next she's pushing a toddler on a tricycle, then feeding ducks at a pond, then standing in front of the ruins of a castle, dressed in a man's winter coat that is two sizes too big for her.

The past and present are at war in Evie's mind, but her smile and her tears tell me which one is winning the battle. She is looking at her sister and seeing her for the first and last time.

68

Evie

Outside, there is a battle being fought by seagulls who are bickering over who gets the chimney and who gets the valley of the roof. It ends when they launch off in unison and swoop down to the beach.

Cyrus is holding the photo album. I touch each image with my fingertips. Agnesa is older but the same, beautiful but more grown up. I want to be angry at her for not coming to find me, but she thought I was dead.

A new page. More pictures. A birthing suite, and a newborn covered in gunk is being weighed and swaddled in a blanket. Agnesa looks exhausted but happy. Tucked under her chin, the baby has one finger pressed against her cheek, as though deep in thought, contemplating her future. My pose. My dimple.

Murdoch's phone has been on silent, but the screen lights up. He picks it up, reads the message, and puts it down again on the coffee table. Then he walks to the window that overlooks the sea. Two people are waiting at the bottom of the steps to the cottage. Addie is with her aunt, who is holding on to her shoulders, as though trying to stop her from climbing.

Addie waves nervously. I wave back. She's wearing red shorts over a blue one-piece swimming costume. She turns, seeking permission from her aunt. Moments later, she's running, taking the steps two at a time. I open the front and meet her on the path. I think she's going to fly into my arms, but she stops suddenly as though unsure of what happens next.

"I'm named after you," she declares, "but nobody calls me Adina."

"Do you know what it means?" I ask.

She shakes her head, hair swinging.

"Adina is a Hebrew name, meaning delicate."

"I'm not very delicate," she says.

"Neither am I."

"Can I hug you?" she asks.

"Yes."

I expect to flinch when her arms close around me, but it doesn't happen. I relax and hold her and smell her wonderful girlish smell of deodorant and pool chlorine. She steps back. Her legs are thin and tanned and her bare feet milky white. Her face is a prettier version of mine—with a small nose, brown eyes, and a high forehead.

"You're too young to be my auntie," she says, making it sound like a challenge.

"You're too old to be my niece," I reply.

"And we're almost the same size."

"You're going to be taller."

"What are we, then?" she asks.

"We could be friends."

"Or sisters," says Addie. "I've always wanted one of those."

I can't swallow the lump in my throat.

Addie is still talking excitedly. "Sisters keep secrets for each other, so you can't tell anyone about the smoking or the thieving."

"I guess not."

"Or about Flossie and Soot and Ziggy."

"Who?"

"My cats."

"OK."

"And you have to help me convince Dad to let me have a dog."

"I'll try."

Another silence. "Can I show you something?" she asks eagerly, taking my hand and leading me along a small brick path down the side of the cottage and up steps into a terraced area, with a wooden bench seat and a view over the headland and a rock platform exposed by the tide. Addie picks a wilting flower from a rosebush and breaks the petals in her hand. She releases them over my head like snowflakes and laughs.

"This is my favorite place in the whole world," she says.

"Why is that?"

"This is where my mum used to sit every afternoon and read books and watch me play in the garden. I don't remember much about her. I was only three when she died."

"I can tell you about her."

It's then that I notice the small square of polished metal screwed into the uppermost railing of the bench. The bronze plaque reads:

IN LOVING MEMORY OF AGNESA OSMANI,
WHO STOPPED HERE A WHILE AND ENJOYED THE VIEW

I don't realize I'm crying until Addie puts her arms around me and says, "I miss her too."

I'm not sure how I feel. I'm exhausted and disappointed and angry and sad and excited and scared. My sister has come back to me. She has added a drop of condensed color into my black-and-white world, giving definition and shade to things that have been lost in grey.

I finally feel as though I belong here. The contours of the country have become mine. The sun is mine, the grass, the trees, the birds, the bees, the waves, the wind. This is my home and I know what comes next. I'm going to have the biopsy on my brain. And if they say I need an operation, I will. And if they want me to wait and see, I'll wait and see.

I have a reason to fight now. A sister. A niece. A purpose.

69

Cyrus

Evie is still in the garden with Addie, sitting on the bench, half in shade and half in sunshine. I watch from the kitchen window, trying to imagine what it must be like to discover that Agnesa survived the sinking and gave birth and made a new life for herself.

"That used to be her favorite reading spot," says Murdoch. "It's where I scattered her ashes."

"Why are you telling us this now?" I ask.

He looks at his hands. "Because I know what's coming."

"You're going to prison."

"Aye."

"You're hoping Evie might forgive you and plead for leniency on your behalf?"

"No, no, nothing like that. Ah deserve what's coming to me."

"Why, then?"

"Somebody will need to look after Addie when I'm gone. Evie is her only family."

"What does Addie say about that?"

Murdoch glances out the window. "They seem to like each other."

A part of me wants to push back and argue that Evie isn't ready for that sort of responsibility, but I stop myself because this isn't my decision. I'm the only person in the world who believes that Evie is going to be all right, even though she's not there yet. Maybe Addie can help her.

Evie is not the same damaged teenager that I first met at the secure children's home in Nottingham, sitting in a circle with other teenagers, looking completely alone and separate from the others. Back then she was all surliness and sass, her face hidden behind hanging locks of hair, her feet drawn up, as though frightened of touching the floor. Not quite a woman, not quite a girl, yet there was something ageless and change-less about her.

I knew immediately there was something different about Evie. She was mercurial, nihilistic, infuriating, abusive, and self-destructive, yet desperate for love. And while she is not the same person that I met four years ago, she is more than the sum of her parts.

As I watch her in the garden, sitting next to Addie, knee to knee, head to head, laughing like best friends, I realize something else about Evie. She has been like a little sister to me—filling a hole in my life that once belonged to the twins. Life is not colorful without her. Life is not inter-esting without her. Life is not life without her.

I will never stop caring. I will never stop worrying. I will never stop loving her.

70

Three months later

Evie

Cyrus has brought home a Christmas tree that is so fat we can't get it through the front door without breaking any branches. He's carrying the base, while Addie and I have the top end. There is lots of shouting and laughing.

"Lift it higher."

"Tilt it to the right."

"Go back."

"Not that way."

Addie keeps yelling the word "pivot," which she finds hilarious. And when Cyrus gets annoyed, it's even funnier.

"You're both impossible," he says, dropping the tree, which completely blocks the entrance. Addie is now lying on her back on the hallway rug, crying with laughter. Poppy licks her face and they wrestle.

"We could just leave it here," I say, picking pine needles out of my hair.

"We're not having a tree in the doorway," he says.

We take a breather, before trying again, wrangling the tree into the front room, and then debating the merits of the corner versus the bay window. We choose the window and set up the stand, filling the base with water.

"My job here is done," says Cyrus.

"Aren't you going to help us decorate?" asks Addie.

"No. I brought it home. The rest is up to you."

"What about the star on the top?"

"Use the stepladder."

Addie begins going through a box of decorations that we keep in the attic. Some of them are so old and brittle I'm scared to handle them, but

Cyrus has bought some new Christmas lights, as well as a wreath for the front door.

I don't remember decorating a Christmas tree before now. At Langford Hall the staff did it for us and the decorations were approved as "safe," i.e., not a self-harm risk or a possible weapon. In Albania, we celebrated Krishtlindjet, but it was mainly about giving presents and feasting and didn't involve dressing up a tree.

Addie makes this Christmas special. She's been in Nottingham for three days and is here until she goes back to school after the New Year. After that, who knows? Sean Murdoch will go to trial next year, along with six other trawlermen, accused of facilitating illegal immigration. Willie Radford faces further charges of abduction, human trafficking, and offenses under the Modern Slavery Act.

Simon Buchan is the man who spoke to me in the library at Glengowrie Lodge when I was a child recovering from smoke inhalation. He was standing beneath a painting of his father, which is why he looked like a younger version of the same man. Within hours of Angus Radford's death, Simon Buchan vanished and hasn't been seen since. The newspapers have speculated on where he might have gone, naming countries that could be hiding him. Russia and Cuba are likely, along with others that don't have extradition treaties with Britain. In the meantime, the authorities have seized his houses and cars and businesses. I asked Cyrus what happens to the money. He said it goes to the government, but what's the point of that?

Arben's sister, Jeta, and Norsin Samaan, the Syrian girl, who were plucked from the North Sea, were rescued by Border Force when they raided an old convent on the outskirts of Leeds. They had been auctioned off to a criminal gang involved in prostitution and creating illicit porn films. Both are now being supported by the anti-slavery charity run by Florence's friend Natalie. It doesn't have Simon Buchan's money anymore, but other donors have come forward.

Cyrus has met with Jeta. She's still deciding if she wants to stay in the UK or go back to Albania. I know what it's like to be an orphan and to have no *other* in my life. That was my fate, until I met Cyrus. Now I have a second person, Addie, and I understand how love gets doubled rather than divided when a family grows.

Addie knows that she is coming to live with us if Sean is sent to prison.

"Will I have to go to school?" she asked.

"Yep."

"And I guess I can't smoke."

"Nope."

"Or vape?"

"Nope. But you get to hang out with me."

"You can tell when people are lying, can't you?"

"Is that a problem?"

"I imagine it could be."

"You could try to lie less."

She laughed. "Like that's going to happen."

I hold the ladder as Addie reaches up to place the star on the uppermost point of the tree. She is better at decorating the tree than I am. She's done it before and she's more patient. She's also bossy like Agnesa used to be, but in a good way.

Later, I show her my secret hiding place in the attic, which is no longer a secret and seems rather childish now that I tell her about it. She lies next to me on the old rug, belly-down, chin propped, her eyes locked on mine, as I tell her stories about her mother. We wrap Christmas presents for Cyrus and Mitch and Lilah and Sean Murdoch and Addie's aunt Isla, but not for each other, because that would spoil the surprise. I've also bought a gift for Florence—gold and silver hair rings for her dreadlocks. She and Cyrus are still bumping uglies, which makes me happy in a sad sort of way, or sad in a happy sort of way.

Liam has asked me to a New Year's Eve party at a pub in Nottingham. I've tentatively said yes because he's promised that none of his exgirlfriends will be there, and that he won't leave me sitting on my own. That makes me sound ultra-needy and that I want to be his girlfriend, but I'm just a girl he "wants to get to know," he says.

I have added Agnesa's journals and photograph album to my collection of precious things. I read her entries every day, admiring her handwriting—the way she sloped her words to the right and looped her descending letters and let some words trail off lazily, letting readers choose how they end.

Most of her entries are short and factual, but others reveal more

about her inner thoughts and desires, her dreams, her plans . . . I flick
between them, picking random dates.

May 12, Thursday 2011

*I cannot believe that I didn't want children. I hated the idea of
having something growing inside me. It felt like I'd been diagnosed
with a terminal illness, and that my body wasn't mine anymore. I
was scared to death, but that all changed the day Addie was born. I
held her in my arms and knew I would do anything in the world to
keep her safe.*

*Every morning, I wake about an hour before Addie stirs, but
rather than getting a head start on the day, I lie in bed with her and
watch her sleeping.*

*I love her sweet sighs and the rise and fall of her round belly and
the way her lips pucker as though she's suckling in her sleep. And I
love to bury my nose in her soft tuft of hair, breathing in that milky
baby smell.*

Agnesa

September 12, Wednesday 2012

*Addie woke me four times last night, grizzling rather than cry-
ing. I took her into bed with me and helped her settle. It reminded
me of sharing a bed with Adina when we were growing up. They
have the same wavy hair and the same dimple on their right cheek,
and they're both contrary and cheeky and refuse to eat anything
remotely resembling a vegetable in color or texture.*

*I don't believe that people are reborn, or that we come back as a
rabbit or cow. Instead, we each carry a blueprint inside our genes
and we build on what's gone before.*

*My beautiful baby daughter carries some of Mama and Papa and
my sister inside her. She is their legacy. And I will remind Addie
every day of the people who came before her and made her life possible.*

Agnesa

Acknowledgments

The publication of *Storm Child* marks my twentieth year as a crime writer and my eighteenth novel. I can't believe how quickly that time has passed and how many words that represents.

Perhaps even more surprising is how the act of writing still excites me and come to the blank page with the same enthusiasm and trepidation and self-doubt that has always been a blessing and a curse.

As always, I have people to thank. I was helped many people along the way, particularly in Scotland. Any factual mistakes are mine, as the use of artistic licence when the truth stood in the way of pace and story. As my great mentor Stephen King always says, "The story comes first."

I'd like to thank the Marine Accident Investigation Branch, the Royal National Lifeboat Institution, HM Coastguard UK, Michael and Francis Clark of Nor-Sea Food Ltd, as well as all the many trawlermen, harbormasters, and local experts who patiently answered my questions and made my time in Scotland so enjoyable.

As always, I am indebted, as always, to my wonderful agents, Mark Lucas, Richard Pine, and Nicki Kennedy, and to my editors, Rebecca Saunders, Tilda Keys, and Colin Harrison. Working in the background are wonderful publishing teams at Little Brown Book Group UK, Hachette Australia, the Scribner in the US, as well as my many foreign publishers far and wide, most notably Goldmann in Germany.

Finally, I make special mention to James and Megan O'Leary, who generously bid at a charity auction and bought a character name in this novel. The money went towards the Northern Beaches Women's Shelter, a safe haven that allows homeless women to rebuild their lives. James and Megan didn't buy the name for themselves, but for their friend Meredith Bennett, who has no idea that she's being immortalized on these pages.

And before I forget—and I never forget—I thank my beautiful, long-suffering, endlessly supportive wife and mother to my children. Every time I threaten to retire, she threatens to leave me. Clearly, more books are coming.

About the Author

Michael Robotham is a former investigative journalist whose bestselling psychological thrillers have been translated into twenty-five languages. He has twice won the UK's prestigious Gold Dagger award for best crime novel and twice received a Ned Kelly Award for Australia's best crime novel. His recent novels include *When She Was Good*, winner of the UK's Ian Fleming Steel Dagger award for best thriller; *The Secrets She Keeps*; *Good Girl, Bad Girl*; *Lying Beside You*; *When You Are Mine*; and *The White Crow*. After living and writing all over the world, Robotham settled his family in Sydney, Australia.

Turn the page for a sneak peek at
the latest book from Michael Robotham,

THE
WHITE
CROW

Available from Scribner in July 2025

1

In a real dark night of the soul it is always three o'clock in the morning. F. Scott Fitzgerald wrote that line almost sixty years before I was born but it's true enough today. London is not asleep at this hour. Merely resting her eyes and humming impatiently, waiting for the sun to rise. She is like an aging toothless beast, chewing through years that she struggles to swallow.

I'm behind the wheel of a police car, driving along Prince Charles Road toward Hampstead in North London. The headlights sweep across the wet asphalt, reflecting from the polished surfaces of parked cars whose hoods are beaded with raindrops. Beside me, Police Constable Rowan Cooper has a mobile phone tucked against his ear, taking down food orders.

We are on a breakfast run to a Jewish bakery in East Finchley that serves the best salt-beef bagels in London outside of Brick Lane. Our colleagues at Kentish Town police station are hungry or bored or both, although "boredom" is not a word that is ever used. A quiet night is a good night. Good nights are rare.

"What do you want?" asks Coop.

"Smoked salmon and cream cheese."

"You're such a girl."

"I'm a pescatarian."

"Is that like being an Anglican?"

"No, but I *am* going straight to Heaven."

Coop is one of the few people who call me Philomena rather than Phil. My mother is another one. She insists upon it. She rang up my station sergeant on my first day at Kentish Town and told him that I should be addressed as "PC Philomena McCarthy." The sergeant thought it was a windup and I was teased for weeks.

Coop is fresh out of training college, but with the self-confidence of someone much more experienced. Maybe it's a male thing. When I graduated from Hendon and became a trainee, I was desperate to fit in rather than stand out, which is a female thing. That was four years ago and I'm more comfortable in the uniform now, but still wary of drawing attention. With a family like mine, it's best to keep a low profile.

This is my last shift on a six-day roster that began with two early starts, followed by two afternoons and now two nights before a four-day break. Tomorrow, by which I mean today, I have a family event—a christening at a church in Greenwich—when I'm going to be a godmother to my cousin Rosie's first baby.

After that, Henry is spiriting me away for a romantic weekend in Paris, which is supposed to be a secret, but I found a printed receipt for Eurostar tickets in his jacket pocket when I was looking for cash to pay our cleaner. I also saw clues on his Facebook feed—Airbnb apartments in the Latin Quarter. There are no secrets from Siri.

It will be our first trip abroad since our honeymoon—an extremely wet ten days in the Maldives, when a tropical storm called Bethany broke rainfall records. We spent the entire time in bed, bingeing Netflix and having sex, in between shoving towels against the balcony doors and dodging drips in the restaurant.

Sex is also high on the agenda this weekend, I suspect, because we've both been so busy of late, and Henry wants to sell me on the idea of starting a family. The seduction will be nice—the champagne, caviar, and a view of the Seine—but I'm not going to change my mind. Not yet.

We've only been married a year and I'm quite happy to keep practicing. It's not as though my biological clock is ticking loudly in my ears. I'm twenty-nine. Henry is thirty-one, and we have a mortgage that needs two incomes to manage. Don't get me started on the alimony payments to his ex-wife, who treats Henry like her personal ATM.

When it comes to babies, my answer is "not yet," but I do have a rough timetable in mind. Thirty-four for the first, another at thirty-six. One girl. One boy. If only I could order them on Uber Eats with a side of garlic bread.

For now I'm enjoying my career. I transferred from Southwark to Camden eight months ago, and nobody at Kentish Town police station has mentioned my family connections—although a few of them will know. Some children have to live up to parental expectations. I have to escape mine.

My father is Edward McCarthy and my uncles are the McCarthy brothers, who the tabloids refer to as "colorful local identities" or "excons" but never "gangsters" because my father has a barrister on speed dial.

I have never understood why people use the term "organized crime." They never talk about "organized nursing" or "organized teaching" or "organized accountancy." Why do criminals get this added descriptor? Maybe because most crimes are chaotic and impulsive and stupid, which is why the perpetrators get caught. Not Edward McCarthy. Accusations and insinuations slide off him like he's John Gotti, the Teflon Don. Nothing ever sticks.

"With extra mustard," says Coop, relaying the last of the order. "We'll be there in fifteen."

Satisfied, he puts his phone away and drums his hands on the dashboard. Eating is like a competitive sport for Coop, a reality that's beginning to show around his midriff, although he keeps telling me he's training for the London Marathon.

At this hour, the roads are mostly deserted, except for garbage trucks and street-sweeping vehicles and the occasional black cab, which come in all colors these days. The rain has stopped and misty yellow halos glow around the streetlights, which reflect from puddles on the road.

We're on Haverstock Hill, not far from Belsize Park station, when a cyclist hurtles out of a side street, running a red light. I see a flash of yellow and hit the brakes. Wheels lock. Rubber squeals. The cyclist swerves and turns his head at the last moment, his eyes full of fear. The car nudges his back wheel. The bike wobbles, but the cyclist stays upright and carries on riding down Haverstock Hill, pumping on the pedals, his Lycra-covered arse swaying.

"Fuck!" says Coop, bracing his hands against the dashboard. His notebook and phone have fallen into the footwell.

"Maniac," I say, sucking in a breath.

"You want to go after him?"

We both consider the question, while thinking the same thing. Paperwork. If we catch up with the cyclist, we'll spend the rest of the night writing reports, preparing statements, and filing formal charges. After twelve hours of work and half a day at court, we'll watch him act like a choirboy in front of the magistrates, who will give him a rap over the knuckles and tell him to be more careful next time.

"I think we scared him," I say.

"Shat himself," says Coop.

The police car is idling in the middle of the intersection. I look in the mirrors before moving off.

"Did you see that?" I ask, turning my head.

"What?"

"On the road. Behind us. A child."

"You saw a kid?"

"Yeah."

He follows my gaze. The road is empty.

"Are you sure?"

"Yeah."

I pull over and park on the corner, before walking back to the intersection. Coop jogs to catch up.

"When you say a kid, how old?"

"Young. A boy, I think."

"Where was he?"

"Standing on the corner."

We've reached the place. Most of the houses are set back from the road with railing fences or brick walls or neatly trimmed hedges surrounding small front gardens. We look up and down Haverstock Hill.

"Maybe it was a dog," says Coop.

"No."

Our shoulder radios crackle and buzz in unison.

"*All cars. All cars. Emergency attendance. Major incident in progress. Hatton Garden. Please proceed to Holborn Circus and establish a perimeter.*"

Coop on the radio: "Kilo Quebec Three Zero, responding. Twelve minutes away. Over."

"You go," I say.

"We should stick together."

"I'm not leaving a child out here."

I talk into my radio. "Kilo Quebec Three Zero. This is PC McCarthy. I've spotted a child dressed in pajamas. I'm searching on foot."

"What is your location?"

"Haverstock Hill at England's Lane."

"Do you have a description?"

"A little boy wearing flannel pajamas."

"Approximate age?"

"Hard to say. I only got a glimpse."

"Do you need assistance?"

"I'll let you know."

"Understood. Control out."

Returning to the patrol car, I collect a flashlight and a thermal blanket before watching Coop drive away. My radio is broadcasting comms chatter about the Hatton Garden callout. Some sort of robbery. So much for a quiet night.

Back in England's Lane, I walk slowly along the footpath, searching under cars and peering over hedges. The roots of trees have pushed up under the paving stones, making it uneven in places. Redbrick mansion blocks line both sides of the road, broken by the occasional free-standing house or semidetached. Most are probably heritage listed. Expensive. Darkened. Asleep.

Coming to a partly open gate, I step inside and hear a rustling sound in the undergrowth, among the soggy leaves. It could be a cat or a fox. London is full of foxes, who have become experts at urban living, raiding rubbish bins and breeding in the parks and heathland.

Sweeping my flashlight back and forth, I crouch and look under the hedge. The beam of light picks up a pale white foot. A shin. An ankle. Five muddy toes. Pajama bottoms.

"Hello," I say.

The foot disappears.

I sit on the damp grass, feeling it soak through my trousers. The garden smells of compost and grass clippings.

"My name is Phil. Do you have a name?"

Silence.

"Let me guess. Perhaps you're Peter like Peter Rabbit, or Stuart like Stuart Little. Are you a rabbit or a mouse?"

A small voice says, "No."

"You sound like a mouse. Mice make me jump. I'm always scared they're going to run up my trouser leg. You wouldn't do that, would you?"

"No."

"I think I need some proof that you're not a mouse. Maybe you could show me your fingers. Mice don't have fingers."

There is a pause and a rustle of leaves. A small hand appears from under the bushes.

"Mmm," I say. "Maybe mice do have fingers. They definitely don't have toes. Do you have toes?"

After another pause, two legs appear from under the hedge.

"I guess you're not a mouse. But what else could you be?"

"I'm a little girl."

"No. That's not possible. Little girls don't live in hedges. Little girls should be tucked up in bed." I slide a little closer. "I'll have to start again and guess your name. You sound like a Jasmine, or an Ariel, or an Elsa. Definitely a princess?"

"I don't want to be a princess."

"I see. Then maybe your name is Ninty Minty or Cutie Patootie?"

"I'm Daisy," says the voice.

"That's a pretty name. Like the flower. I love daisies. What are you doing out so late?"

"I couldn't wake Mummy."

"Oh, I see."

"And I'm not allowed to talk to strangers."

"That's very good advice, but I'm not a stranger. I'm a police officer. And I want to take you home."

Again, I wait, but nothing moves inside the hedge.

"I tell you what I'm going to do, Daisy. I'm going to lie down and have a sleep. I'd rather it be somewhere warm and dry, but I can't leave you out here."

Unfurling the silver foil blanket, I lay it on the grass and curl up.

After a while, the leaves begin to move. I partially open my eyes and watch a small face appear. Daisy crawls out of the hedge and kneels next to me, gently shaking my shoulder. She has a pageboy haircut and a smudge of mud on her cheek.

"I need to do a wee," she says.

"OK, well, let's get you home."

Daisy shakes her head. She is squeezing her thighs together, holding it in.

"You could go just here," I suggest.

"In the garden?"

"I was always weeing in the garden when I was your age."

Daisy looks at me dubiously.

"You have to be careful not to splash your feet," I say. "Pull down your pajama pants and squat down. I'll hold your arms so you don't fall over."

Daisy does as she's told. Her little bottom is sticking out toward the hedge.

"Nothing is coming," she says.

"Think of running water."

"Why?"

"It helps."

I begin singing a nursery rhyme from my childhood. "Rain is falling down. Rain is falling down. Pitter patter, pitter patter, rain is falling down."

Soon I hear the telltale splash of urine on the grass.

"What am I going to wipe with?" asks Daisy.

"With a tissue," I say, pulling one from my pocket.

She tugs up her pajamas and I wrap her in the foil blanket.

"When you said that you couldn't wake Mummy, was she in bed?"

"No."

"Where was she?"

"In the kitchen."

My heart sinks. "Where do you live?"

She points into the darkness.

"Can you show me?"

Daisy takes my hand and leads me onto the pavement, limping slightly. Her hand is freezing.

"How old are you?" I ask.

"Nearly six."

"What's your last name?"

"Kemp-Lowe."

"Is that two names or one?"

"It's my name."

We turn into Antrim Road, walking past redbrick mansion blocks and Victorian town houses, most of them converted into flats.

Daisy stops outside a large private house. The painted iron gate is open and stone paving leads to a door framed by wisteria.

"Is this your house?"

She nods.

"How did you get out?"

Daisy points to the front door, as though it should be obvious.

"Does one of these cars belong to Mummy or Daddy?" I ask.

She looks up and down the road and indicates a silver Mercedes, top of the range. Clearly, her family has money. I punch my call button. "Kilo Quebec Three Zero to control."

"Control, receiving."

"I've found the child. Her name is Daisy Kemp-Lowe. Aged five. She says she couldn't wake her mother. I'm outside the house now. Can you run a plate for me?"

"Control received."

"Silver Mercedes. Hotel Victor Six Three Golf Mike Charlie."

We wait, sitting on the front steps. I wrap the foil blanket more closely around Daisy, before noticing blood on the sleeve of her pajamas.

My radio squawks. *"Control to Kilo Quebec Three Zero. That vehicle is registered to a Russell Kemp-Lowe. Seventy-five Antrim Road."*

"Received."

I look at Daisy. "Let's get you back to bed."